What Readers A

TEXAS RO

"Very good story with great characters and plot. A good lesson in following the path that you were meant to follow. I look forward to reading more of the Miller's Creek series." ~Amazon Reviewer

"Uplifting book, easy to read, engaging. Cathy Bryant is an excellent author. Her love and faith in God is evident in every word she writes." ~Amazon Reviewer

A PATH LESS TRAVELED

"I 'stumbled' across this book for free in the e-book section. I know I 'found' it for a reason. If anyone is looking for the path to God, this is a very important book." ~Amazon Reviewer

"How often we miss God's perfect plan by following our own. Well written and so refreshing to read a great novel showing God's amazing grace and faithfulness." ~Amazon Reviewer

THE WAY OF GRACE

"The Way Of Grace is a beautiful story of showing mercy and grace as Christ did. A few unexpected turns and keeps you wanting to read on. I Love this series of novels. Can't wait for the next one." ~Amazon Reviewer

"Cathy has done it again! Her books just keep getting better. With an air of mystery, this book grabs and holds the reader's attention from the start. Rather than just a

'predictable' book, the story takes some unexpected twists and turns. It's not just a 'happily ever after' book; instead, the reader encounters a story of danger, courage, life-changing choices, love, and the amazing grace of God." ~Amazon Reviewer

PILGRIMAGE OF PROMISE

"Though I have not read the earlier books in the series it did not take away at all from the story, which was engaging, humorous at times, and impeccably well done. Bryant has some really great talent and knowledge, something that is very obvious in her writing and characters. It was really hard to quit reading!" ~Amazon Reviewer

"For me, Pilgrimage of Promise was Karen Kingsbury meets Nicholas Sparks." ~Amazon Reviewer

A BRIDGE UNBROKEN

"I am new to this series but A Bridge Unbroken grabbed me, pulled me in, and kept me hostage until I had finished. Cathy Bryant is so very good at taking her readers and immersing them into the story in such a way that you are emotionally involved. In a way it reminded me of L.M. Montgomery's ability to the same thing." ~Amazon Reviewer

"This book is another home run for Cathy Bryant! She has a shown a knack for writing books with a balance of romance, mystery, suspense and Christianity all in one book, or actually, into a series of books. There were times I was sitting on the edge of my seat in anticipation. I

loved how I thought I had it figured out only to realize ~ not so much!" ~Amazon Reviewer

THE FRAGRANCE OF CRUSHED VIOLETS

"I urge you, if you need to let go of something, no matter how big or small, take the time to read this book. Even if you think you are a forgiving person, like I thought I was, take the time to read this book. You won't regret it." ~Amazon Reviewer

"This was a very heart-felt book about forgiveness. It's about forgiving what is inexcusable. This caused me to pray and forgive decades-old grudges." ~Amazon Reviewer

MILLER'S CREEK COLLECTION

"I have read all three books twice and would read them again. They each have a good story, easy to follow, well written. The characters are "real" people that I can identify with. I would recommend these books to anyone who loves a good story. I think what I like best is that they are written without any offensive language." ~Amazon Reviewer

"I love, love, love all of these books. They are well written, with characters that you will fall in love with. I laughed and cried throughout these books. You won't be able to put them down." ~Amazon Reviewer

MILLER'S CREEK FORGIVENESS COLLECTION

"This is a wonderful book combination. The first book, A Bridge Unbroken, is a suspense and romance novel that had me hooked from the first pages. It is a story with lots of twists and turns that definitely kept me reading

Crossroads

a Miller's Creek novel

Book Six

CATHY BRYANT

WordVessel Press

Books by Cathy Bryant

MILLER'S CREEK NOVELS

Texas Roads

A Path Less Traveled

The Way of Grace

Pilgrimage of Promise

A Bridge Unbroken

Crossroads

OTHER FICTION

Pieces On Earth

LIFESWORD NON-FICTION

The Fragrance of Crushed Violets

Believe & Know

New Beginnings

The Power of Godly Influence

Life Lessons From My Garden

Crossroads

WV **Published by WordVessel Press**
Santa Fe, New Mexico

ISBN-13: 978-1-941699-05-8

To my beautiful grandchildren.
You are my legacy to the world. My heart's prayer is that you will come to know the One who made you and who loves you first and best. My heart's cry is that our family circle will be unbroken both here and beyond.
Nana loves you always and forever.

Go stand at the crossroads and look around.
Ask for directions to the old road, the tried-and-true road.
Discover the right route for your souls.
~Jeremiah 6:16 (MSG)

Special Thanks

Words never seem adequate when it comes to expressing my gratitude to so many who help out in various ways in bringing a new book to completion.

I want to begin with a very special thank you to a special friend. Sherlee Grinstead has served as a beta reader on most of the Miller's Creek novels. In addition, she lifts me up to the Father on a regular basis, helps in the promotional efforts of spreading book news as one of the Miller's Creek Main Street Team, and encourages me when I'm feeling low. I couldn't ask for a better friend, Sherlee, and I take great comfort in knowing that if I never get the privilege of meeting you during our earthly lifetimes, I will one day hug your neck in heaven.

Next I want to say thank you to my wonderful husband. He supports and encourages my calling as a writer, puts up with my long and irregular hours, helps as a promoter for the books, and never objects to my requests for a shoulder rub after hours behind the computer. I love you, sweet man. I thank the Lord that He saw fit to give you to me, and I look forward to the next chapter.

Another person that needs a hearty 'thank you' is my mom. Our weekly phone chats are such a blessing to me. She never fails to make me laugh, and I always feel better afterwards. As a reader who devours Christian books on a regular basis, her advice in regard to my stories is invaluable. So much of who I am is because of who she is. Love you, Mom!

To reader friends, beta readers, reviewers and Main Street Team members, may God richly bless you for the encouragement and help you are to me. I pray that the stories in some small way are a return blessing to you. Thank you for all your help.

Special thanks to Debbie King for allowing me to use her gorgeous photograph for the cover of this book.

And to my heavenly Father, the Shepherd of my soul, I praise and thank You for loving me at my worst, guiding me on this journey, and making a way for all to come to You through Your Son Jesus, the Christ. Thank You for changing me from glory to glory and for continuing to finish the work You began in my life so many years ago. May all I say and write and do advance Your Kingdom and bring You glory. May this story help us all in being ready to give a defense for the hope that only comes from You.

One

Out of pure reflex, Mara stiffened her right leg and stomped the brake pedal to the floor, tires a-screech against the asphalt as the undeniable odor of burning rubber reached her nose. She gritted her teeth, her breath in rapid spurts, and yanked the steering wheel hard to the right. Her clenched jaw relaxed just enough to spout words that had conglomerated in her sour-tasting mouth. "Please don't let me run over this stupid animal."

Just who did she think she was talking to? She shrugged. No one. Nothing. Thin air. Her salty lips had simply taken on a life of their own without permission. The new-to-her Cadillac Escalade finally bounced to a halt, and her body echoed the move.

Once her brain stopped sloshing around in her skull, Mara jerked her head to the left to see the armadillo--almost the exact color of the pavement--waddle nonchalantly through the bar ditch and under a barbed-wire fence. The squatty body animal disappeared behind the thick growth of mesquite, cedar, live oak, and clumps of prickly pear cactus.

She brought a trembling hand to her throat and willed her shallow breaths and racing heart to a slower pace. Yet another thing to adjust to in the small back-roads country town of Miller's Creek.

Critters.

She sniffed at the still form of a black and white pile of fur in the road next to her. The rancid smell of squished skunk--who hadn't fared as well as the armadillo--stung Mara's nostrils, bringing tears to her eyes and wrinkles to the bridge of her nose.

Yeah, she'd experienced rural Texas before, but it had been years, her childhood a murky fog that took up residence in the distant recesses of her mind. Had she blocked out painful memories by imprisoning that part of her life behind lock and key?

Her gaze flitted to the dashboard clock, and set her into instant motion. "Oh no. Please no." This couldn't be happening. Not on a day when she actually had a prospective customer to help pay her bills and feed her family. She quickly released the brake and pressed the accelerator, the horses beneath the hood rapidly roaring to life and charging down the road.

Now she'd never make her four o'clock appointment with Carter Callahan. Of course it wasn't as though he'd given her ample time to find him a house. He'd called right before lunch and said he needed a house, and then promptly ended the call with some mumbled excuse about being on duty and without giving any details as to what kind of property he wanted. Fearful that as a policeman on duty he had more important matters to deal with, she'd opted not to call back. Instead she'd spent her afternoon viewing possible properties to show him.

Mara quelled her anxious thoughts with a sip of warm and non-fizzy Diet Coke, the flat and tepid liquid leaving the after-taste of artificial sweetener on her tongue. She made a face and clunked the can into the console drink holder. Was this her third one today, or her fourth? She inched the accelerator closer to the floor.

At five minutes after four, she pulled up outside the building she'd leased from Otis Thacker, more proof of the number one rule in real estate. Location, location, location. Nestled between recently-renovated turn-of-the-century buildings on the picturesque town square, and boasting creamy-white Austin stone, cinnamon-colored cedar posts, and rustic tin roof, the place screamed central Texas. The perfect store front for her new business, one that needed to turn a profit. And soon.

The unlocked seat belt slipped from her fingers and clanked against the door as she scooped up her purse and manila file folders. She climbed from the SUV, glanced down the thick slab of elevated sidewalk, and slammed the door.

No sign of Carter Callahan.

Had he come and left already? More than a little disgruntled at the missed appointment and chance at a potential sale, she trudged to the door. At some point, she'd just have to bite the bullet and hire a receptionist for times like these, but with money so tight, it was hard to justify the expense.

Mara moved across the large open space dotted with office furniture she'd purchased at a hotel sale, and into her office, where she plunked the folders atop the granite-looking counter top behind her desk. Next she slung her suit-case-sized purse--an ironic microcosm of her hectic life--onto the desk, contents spilling from inside. She snatched up her eBay iPhone, and fingers ablaze, punched in Carter's number, scrawled on a nearby pink sticky-note.

The electronic beeps from her phone bounced off walls and oak floors.

"Police department."

A disgusted sigh whooshed from her lungs. Not exactly who she'd hoped for. "Ernie? Is that you?"

"Yep. Mara?"

"Yeah, it's me. Sorry to bother you. I'm trying to reach Carter Callahan. Is he there by any chance?"

"Nope. Just left. Said he had a couple of errands to run."

Hope ignited in her chest. Good. Hopefully he hadn't forgotten her. But how much longer would she have to wait? "Did he happen to say what errands?"

"Something about paying the electric bill and stopping by the post office to mail a package."

Her spirits instantly deflated. Okay, so maybe he had forgotten her. "If you happen to see him would you have him call me at the office?"

"Okey-dokey." Ernie drawled out the words, Texas-style, right before the line went dead.

Mara eyed the clock. How could he be so inconsiderate of her time? Yeah, she'd been late too, but she'd dropped other things to get there as soon as possible. As the second hand of the clock ticked off the ever-fleeting time, she ticked off her to-do list for the rest of the day. Pick up Ashton from the daycare by five. Cram down a few bites of leftover goulash before the Miller's Creek Talent Show rehearsal. Follow up on a few leads and hopefully line up showings for the next day. The rehearsal should be over by seven or seven-thirty, which would give them ample time for outdoor play, Kindergarten homework, and Ashton's nightly bath before story time and bed. Then...

Her thoughts strayed to yet another evening by herself, and unexpected loneliness landed like a lead blanket. A solitary sigh escaped. She'd known being a single parent would be difficult. Had known moving to a new place to start a business would be challenging. But one thing she hadn't taken into consideration was the mind-numbing isolation of interminable nights.

Mara gave her head a gentle shake, careful not to dislodge the rock hard hair-sprayed bun she'd crafted early that morning to keep her naturally curly hair in check.

Snap out of it, Mara.

Life in Miller's Creek was certainly better than living with the man who no longer loved her. She rubbed the bridge of her nose. No use dwelling on it. Giving in to the Black Abyss would be counter-productive and foolish. She had to find a way to distract herself from the depression that threatened to swallow her alive.

From outside her office the front door bell buzzed, announcing a visitor. Carter hopefully?

Mara stood, wiped sweaty palms against her polyester skirt, pasted on her most brilliant business smile, and moved to the main office, her high heels clicking against the wooden floors. She extended a hand toward the larger-than-life man silhouetted against the backdrop of front plate-glass windows. "Hi, Carter. I'm Mara Hedwig. So nice to finally meet you in person."

He engulfed her hand with both his bear paws, an equally large grin splayed on his scruffy-but-handsome face. "Hey, Mara. Sorry I'm late. Blame it on my crazy life."

His crazy life? He had no idea what crazy was until he'd experienced just a fraction of the *la vida loca* she lived. She bit back a retort. "Well, we'd best get a move on it if we're going to get to these houses I've lined up for us to see. Let me get my things." She clicked back to her office, sipped a quick drink of her fourth Diet Coke, and grabbed the folder with Carter's name scribbled on it, along with her purse and keys.

A few minutes later they stood outside on the sidewalk in the humid-hot dog days of a sizzling Texas summer as Mara locked up the building and moved toward the driver's side of the Escalade. "We'll go in my car."

Carter released a low whistle as he folded his over-sized frame into the leather passenger seat. "Business must be good."

Not exactly. But definitely the impression she wanted to make, and the reason she'd purchased this way-too-expensive gas-guzzler. According to the latest real estate how-to book she'd read, potential clients were drawn to perceived success.

Rather than responding to his comment, Mara smiled politely, clicked her seat belt into position, and cranked the engine to a gentle purr. Two minutes later they pulled up outside the first place, a tiny frame house within easy walking distance of the town square and Miller's Creek police department. She glanced at her expensive-looking knock-off wristwatch as she parked. If she could get him in and out of here in five to ten minutes, she might just be able to keep her five o'clock deadline. "Here's our first listing. A one-bedroom, one-bath, detached home with a carport."

Carter's dark eyebrows met in the middle. Not a positive sign. "Don't think this one will be big enough for me and my daughter."

"Daughter?" Mara's frozen smile melted from within, her stomach churning up bitter acid in response. "Sorry. You didn't really give me a chance in our phone conversation to find out what you were looking for. I assumed you wanted a place for just you."

He shook his head. "No. My teenage daughter Chloe lives with me now. The apartment complex we're in isn't ideal, and we're beyond over-crowded." His gaze focused somewhere down the street. "Didn't know one teen-age girl came with so much paraphernalia."

"Oh." Mara pursed her lips, her brain clicking through options like a line of people at a Six Flags turnstile. "Well, if this one's too small, we won't even bother with it." At least that would save some time. She opened his client folder and whisked through a few papers, quickly spotting the information she sought. "The next house I lined up is a two-bedroom, two-bath, probably more suited to what you're looking for."

Carter grinned to reveal even white teeth that practically sparkled against his tanned skin. He scratched his chin whiskers. "Sounds more like it. Definitely don't enjoy sharing a bathroom with a teen-aged female. Don't get a whole lot of mirror time anymore."

Mara laughed as she pulled away from the curb. Like he needed mirror time. "Just so you know, I'm pretty sure the teenage girl doesn't like sharing a bathroom anymore than you do."

His charming smile and deep chuckle set off a strange twist in her stomach.

Okay, back to business. Now would be a great time to ask a few questions. "Other than the two beds and two baths, is there anything else you're looking for?"

"Not really. All comes down to space and budget."

Mara released a semi-silent sigh of relief as she turned a corner. Good. He'd brought up the money issue first. "How much are you wanting to spend?"

"I'd like to keep it close to what I'm paying for the apartment. Seven hundred a month."

Quick calculations erupted in her head. Thirty year mortgage, twenty percent down. He'd be able to afford over a hundred thousand with no problem. A smile flickered inside and worked its way to her face. Which meant that after splitting realtor's fees with the listing agent she could plop at least three grand in her almost-depleted bank account. "I'm sure we can find you something very nice for that amount."

Carter's eyes widened. "Really?" His tone held shocked surprise.

"Really." Mara pulled up in front of house two and grimaced inwardly. Ugh. The old bungalow had definitely seen better days and was well under what he could afford. But this wasn't a good way to impress a new client. Oh well, at least she could see what he liked and disliked about the place, info that would make further research all the easier.

They stepped from the vehicle at the same time and made their way down the narrow and crumbling sidewalk to a small stoop of a porch. Mara retrieved the key from the lock box with fumbling fingers, painfully aware that Carter used the time to scan the declining neighborhood. Rats!

Yet another minus to add to his list of negatives about the place.

He stepped up beside her. "Well-established neighborhood. I like that. We don't get too many calls from this part of town. I like that even better. Mostly older folks around here."

Mara swung the front door open, filing his comments within compartments in her brain to add to her files later that night. "So you'd rather have friends for your daughter in the neighborhood?"

Carter's face took on an indiscernible look. "Not really, but I guess it depends on the friends." His tone held a trace of sarcasm.

Her eyebrows climbed despite her attempt to keep them down. Over-protective dad? Poor Chloe. Mara held one hand toward the tiny living space. "This, of course, would be your main living area, and it leads to an eat-in kitchen."

Carter sauntered across the stained and tattered carpet to the kitchen, his eyes roving over every square inch. "More outdated than what we're used to, but it'll do."

This time Mara locked her eyebrows in down position and forced her lips into a placid smile. Hello. Could he not see how horrible this kitchen was? No telling how many layers of grease coated the mustard-gold stove or what kind of creepy-crawlies lurked in darkened crevices. Not to mention the musty smell. Yeah, time to move on. "The bedrooms are this way." She took off down the hallway, then flattened herself against the wall to allow his brawny build to pass by. "The first doorway on the left is the second bedroom, and across the hall is a bath." If you could call the postage-stamp-sized bath a room.

He poked his head around the door frame of the pink-tiled bathroom and grimaced. "It's a bit tight for me. And pink's definitely not my color." His gaze roved to the low shower head. "I'd have to chop myself off at the knees to fit under that thing."

"This isn't the master bath. Maybe it's more your size."

He scratched his head. "Maybe, but I'll probably give Chloe the master. Trust me, she'll need it for all her stuff."

Mara traipsed to the master bedroom with the en suite bath. It wasn't much bigger than the first.

Though Carter didn't speak, she could tell by the turn of his lips that it wasn't to his taste. "How big is the back yard?"

"Fairly large, actually." She moved to a window and peered out the dust-covered blinds, then stepped aside for him to look. "It would give you plenty of space for entertaining."

One side of his upper lip curled. "Yuck. Yard work. And just so you know, I'm not much into entertaining. Just need enough space for the dogs."

She should've seen that one coming. He was definitely the dog type, which meant he definitely wasn't her type. Not that she was on the market anyway. "So you'd rather have a small yard?"

"Definitely. Don't mind yard work, but my free time is next to nil."

She nodded. "I totally understand." Understatement of the millennium. "Are you interested in this one at all?"

"Maybe. How much?"

"Well under budget at fifty-five."

A puzzled expression clouded his face. "Fifty-five?"

"Yes. Fifty-five thousand. Is that a problem? I'm sure you're pre-qualified for more than that." She hesitated. "Aren't you?"

His chuckle broke lose along with a sheepish grin. "Uh, I'm looking for a place to rent. Not to buy."

Steam built in her ears and threatened to explode out the top of her head. Well. He could've at least asked if there were rentals available when he called. All this time she'd assumed he was looking to buy. And she'd make next to nothing on finding him a rent house. Her smile slipped, but she ducked her head and headed to the front door without comment.

Once she'd turned off the lights and secured the house, Mara hurried to the SUV with Carter right behind. She inched the speedometer needle a hair above the speed limit as they made their way to the final house for the day. What was the best way to broach this subject of rental houses? She cleared her throat and assumed her best business voice. "You should know that the next house I have lined up is also for sale. Sorry about the miscommunication, but my business revolves around sales. Since you didn't mention rent houses, I assumed you wanted to purchase a home."

"You don't do rentals?"

She sent an apologetic smile. "Not at this point. And quite honestly, I think you might have trouble locating a rent house in a place the size of Miller's Creek. Most people only rent when they become desperate and can't sell their house." She peered in the rear view mirror as she slowed to a stop at an intersection.

A heavy sigh sounded from the other side of the car. "Problem is, I don't wanna buy. Chloe graduates next May, so I'll more than likely move to a bigger place where there's better pay. Need the extra income to send her to college."

Mara pulled the SUV onto the shoulder of the road and braked to a stop, then turned to look at him squarely. Might as well end this now so she could get on with the next portion of her day's crazy agenda. "So you don't want to see the next house?" She sent a quick glance to the dashboard clock. Hopefully he'd take the hint. Already she was late in picking Ashton up from the daycare.

"You need to be somewhere?" One dark eyebrow cocked upward, reminding her of the furry caterpillars that had already made their appearance in the trees outside her front door.

"Not if you're interested in buying this house." Sometimes bluntness was the only thing that got through to this kind of guy. She bit back the urge to tell him how he'd wasted her time. Time she wanted--and needed--to spend with her daughter.

He considered her words. "I have an idea. Let's swing through the Dairy Queen drive-thru so I can pick up a burger. I missed lunch, and my stomach thinks my throat's been cut. Then we'll hop on over to that other house. Maybe I just need to bite the bullet and buy a house."

His first words had generated an automated response of 'you've-got-to-be-kidding-me' in her brain. Had he not followed them with the hint of a possible purchase, she'd be dropping him off and pronto. She gulped deep breaths of air to squelch her growing frustration at his devil-may-care attitude. Okay, she could do this. After all, she was a mom, right? She'd grab some chicken nuggets for Ashton at the DQ to save time. Not the healthiest meal, but on their tight time frame it would have to work. Another plan hatched in her mind, and a triumphant grin landed on her lips. And the daycare was on the way to the next house, so she might as well pick Ashton up on the way.

Ten minutes later, the SUV now flooded with the smell of fast food--Mara pulled back onto the highway as Carter noisily dug around in the bulging white paper sack. He pulled out a small white box with red lettering and sat it on the console between them. "Here's your chicken nuggets."

"Oh, they're not for me. They're for my daughter. Her day care is on the way to the next house, so I'm going to pick her up. Do you mind?"

"Not at all." He spoke the words through swollen cheeks, much like a squirrel during nut season, his voice muffled by the wad of burger in his mouth. As they pulled up outside the daycare, Carter stuffed in the last morsel of his double-patty burger with bacon and cheese and licked his fingers with a slurping sound.

Mara ignored his caveman manners, put the vehicle in park, and killed the engine.

Carter lifted his gaze. "Hey, this is Mama Beth's daycare."

"Yes, it is."

"Mind if I go in with you?"

A wild chase of panic and frustration erupted inside. Would they ever get through this house showing? "Sure. Why not?" A dead-pan tone crept into her voice as she exited the Escalade and hurried to the front door to punch in her security code. A second later they entered the sprawling ranch house which had been converted to a daycare, each room set up for various activities especially geared to preschool-aged children.

Dani Miller rounded the corner of the hallway, a baby on her right hip. "Hi, Mara." Then she looked past her to Carter. "Well, what are you doing here, big guy?" She eased around Mara to give him a sideways hug.

Carter laughed, a rich melodious sound that echoed through the space. "Mara's showing me some houses, but wanted to stop and pick up her daughter. So I thought I'd come in and say hi."

A strange calculating twinkle developed behind Dani's big blue eyes. "Ah, I see. Y'all follow me. The kids are outside."

A minute later they stood in the fenced-in play yard beside Mama Beth, who looked out over the handful of children yet to be picked up. Ashton leaned against the elderly woman's right side.

Mara knelt in front of her daughter and enveloped her in a hug. "Guess what I have waiting for you in the car?"

Ashton smiled a tiny smile, the fatigue of the day resting in her eyes. "What?"

"Chicken nuggets from Dairy Queen."

Instead of being happy about the uncommon treat of fast food chicken nuggets, her daughter pointed to Carter. "Who's that?"

Mara latched on to her daughter's finger and pulled downward, then rose to her feet. "Don't point, sweetie. It's impolite. I'm showing Mr. Callahan some properties."

Mama Beth made eye contact. "Can I speak with you just a moment before you go?"

Did these people not realize her stretched-to-the-max schedule? "Certainly. Go get your things together, Ashton. I'll be inside in a second."

"I'll help." Carter winked at Ashton and elicited a contagious giggle from the little girl. The two headed inside where Dani still cared for the bed babies.

Concern hovered in Mama Beth's blue eyes as she laced her fingers in front of her. "I don't mean to make you worry, Mara, but I'm a little concerned about Ashton."

Mara's heart stopped momentarily, then resumed beating at a quicker pace. "Why?"

"She's just been so tired when she gets off the school bus. Today she curled up in a corner and went to sleep, even with the other children playing and making noise."

Mara kept a straight face. "Kindergarten's a big change for her. I'm sure that's all it is."

"Well, you'd be the one to know." The woman didn't sound convinced. "I just wanted to make you aware."

"Thank you." Mara laid a hand on Mama Beth's arm. "I appreciate you looking after her so well. I'll definitely keep an eye on her."

This seemed to satisfy the older woman, so Mara said her good-byes and hurried inside.

Carter and Ashton stood near the front door, unaware of her approach. With her typical child-like curiosity and grown-up demeanor, Ashton cocked her head to one side and looked up at Carter. "Are you going to be my new daddy?"

"Ashton!" Mortified, Mara hurried down the hallway to her daughter's side, grabbed the heavy backpack from her arms, and took hold of her hand. "Sweetie, let's not ask people that question, okay?"

"Why not?"

Mara stepped outside to the vehicle, then opened the back door for Ashton to crawl in. "Because it's not polite or relevant." Once her daughter was securely buckled in, Mara slid into the front seat, unnervingly aware of Carter's amused gaze latched onto her every move. Without giving him the satisfaction of acknowledging his amusement, she handed the box of chicken nuggets to the back seat, started the car, and backed out of the parking lot.

The car grew more quiet and awkward with each passing moment. And even worse, it was becoming all-too-apparent that she was hopelessly lost. On today, of all days. Had she missed a turn?

"Where is this place anyway?" Carter whispered the words, almost as though afraid of igniting her already-short and frazzled fuse.

Mara yanked the steering wheel sharply to the right, careened the car off into the grass at an intersection in the middle of nowhere, threw the gear shift into park, and reached for her county map. How could she have been so stupid not to get the location firmly fixed in her mind before bringing a client? "I think we're on the right road. And why are you whispering anyway?" The words belted out of her mouth as she slid her right index finger across the map to locate the road she needed.

"Ashton's asleep." His voice still in whisper mode, he jerked his head and left thumb toward the back seat.

She pulled down the rear view mirror. Sure enough, Ashton's head lolled to one side, eyes closed, the unopened box of chicken nuggets clutched in her hands.

Alarms rang in Mara's head and heart, but she quickly pounded them into submissive silence. Nothing to be overly-concerned about at this point. She sent a weak smile Carter's way. "Must've had a busy day at school. Probably just missed her nap." Without waiting for his response, she turned her attention back to the map.

"What road are you looking for? Maybe I can help."

Mara checked the folder for the address. "Um...County Road 2142."

A cheeky grin appeared on his face. "Other side of town." He pointed to the map. "We should've turned left instead of right."

Ugh. Fifteen minutes in the wrong direction? Mara semi-folded the map and tossed it to the floorboard. "Sorry. I'm still learning these back roads." She adjusted the rearview mirror to check for traffic, put the car in gear, and whipped around to drive the other direction, still battling panic at the sight of her sleeping daughter's paler-than-normal face.

"No prob. Maps can be confusing." Carter's sincere tone calmed her frayed nerves.

Twenty quiet minutes later, they drove onto a dirt driveway of a small rock house. A quick glance in the mirror confirmed what Mara expected.

Ashton was still asleep.

Now what should she do? "Um, I can let you in the front door to look at the place while I stay outside with her."

A frown pulled his dark brows together. "Why don't you just let me carry her? I don't mind."

Mara nodded her okay and moved to the back door to release Ashton's seat belt. Carter leaned in from the other side, his broad shoulders filling the doorway. He easily lifted her little girl from the seat. Ashton stirred momentarily, then rested her head on Carter's thick shoulders, her strawberry blond waves bright against his dark shirt.

Mara swallowed back a sudden onslaught of emotions and hurried up the front porch. Thankfully the lock box cooperated, and in a minute's time they entered the house, soft snores sounding from Ashton. The living room, though large, smelled of dust from months of disuse. Mara wrinkled her nose. "A little smelly."

"Just needs to be aired out." Carter's dark eyes scanned the space as he carefully cradled her daughter in his arms. "Really hadn't thought about a house in the country, but I like the space. And the peace and quiet."

"If your daughter drives, it would mean extra gas money each month." She clasped her hands in front of the electric blue business skirt she'd donned early that morning. The one she couldn't wait to exchange for a pair of sweat pants.

He nodded. "Good point. But let's go ahead and check out the rest of the house while we're here."

"Of course." Mara hurried him through the rest of the house, discreetly checking her watch as they entered the last bedroom. "You could use this for guests or a home office."

"You need to be somewhere?"

Man, nothing escaped this guy. He must have eyes in the back of his head. "We have an event this evening, but business comes first." She injected a happy sing-song to her words.

Carter's jaw clenched and pulsed. "Uh, no. Your family comes first."

"I know that, but this is more important than what we have scheduled for this evening." Sort of.

Without another word, and with disapproval oozing from his face, Carter strode from the room and down the hallway toward the front door, the old floors squeaking beneath his weight.

Questions rolled in her mind, but Mara followed and quickly locked up the house as she glanced over her shoulder toward the SUV.

With a soft tenderness Mara hadn't expected from this over-sized, always-aware mixture of handsome jock and caveman, Carter gently set Ashton into the seat and secured her seat belt.

Unwanted feelings unleashed inside, wreaking havoc with her stretched-out nerves. In many ways, Carter was exactly the kind of man Mara would've wished as a daddy to her little girl. Not that it mattered. Life had proved that road a dead-end.

The trip back into Miller's Creek was even more quiet than the trip out, this time with the added burden of Carter's obvious disapproval sucking the oxygen from the vehicle. Anxiety-ridden thoughts pelted Mara's brain, not just about Ashton, but about Carter Callahan. Had she somehow offended him?

Two

Carter popped a piece of Dentyne in his mouth, stepped up onto the sidewalk outside Mara Hedwig Realty, and watched her quickly-disappearing Cadillac Escalade speed down the street. What was this all-important appointment she and Ashton had for the evening? Probably a date with some business dude from somewhere in the area.

A pit formed in his stomach at the thought of the pretty woman seeing someone. He raked a hand over his head. Mara wore no wedding ring and made no mention of a Mr. Hedwig. Plus, Ashton's statement about a new daddy only confirmed his suspicions that she was indeed a single mom. A single mom that very much wanted him to buy a house. But why would he buy a house in Miller's Creek when he yearned for a more exciting job with a bigger and more active police force?

He dug the keys to his Harley out of his blue jeans left-front pocket, straddled the motorcycle, cranked up the engine, and used his feet to back the bike onto the road. Before winter hit he needed to sell this ride--no matter how much he loved it--and get a car for him and Chloe. Yet another sacrifice required now that Chloe was his sole responsibility. For the time being, his daughter enjoyed riding behind him on the way to school. But once icy January weather arrived, she might not like it so much.

He came to a stop at an intersection red light on the town square and waited for it to change to green. Even at this hour, downtown Miller's Creek buzzed with people, some just now leaving work, others hoping to grab a few last-minute shopping deals before the stores closed. Carter glanced at his watch. Might as well head on over to the High School Auditorium to watch Chloe practice for the upcoming talent show. Though her dreams of singing professionally scared the living daylights out of him, he at least needed to encourage and support her in whatever way he could.

"Hey, Callahan!" The words came from the street corner where Matt Tyler stood with both hands cupping his mouth. "When you gonna ditch that boy toy and get a real man's ride?"

Carter laughed. "Can it, Tyler. You don't even know what a real man's ride is." He shouted the words to be heard over the Harley's engine.

The light changed. Motor sputtering as he inched forward, he waved goodbye to Matt and urged the Harley on toward the school, his thoughts once more on Chloe. Being the primary parent of a rather temperamental teenage daughter had proved more challenging than his military tours in Iraq and Afghanistan. He wanted to trust her, really he did. But there were signs that she was just as mule-headed as he'd been at that age. To make matters worse, she had her mother's raw beauty and petite frame, which had all the boys her age going ga-ga.

Lord, help me get through to her. Show me how to discuss all this uncomfortable stuff with her without setting her off.

A few minutes later, Carter sauntered through the double steel doors leading into the auditorium. Good timing. Chloe was already up on stage. His forehead wrinkled as he did a double take. But dressed in what?

Even from the back of the darkened space, he could tell her outfit was more than a little revealing. The tiny sparkly t-shirt she wore only covered half of her midriff and left very little to the imagination. Paired with way-too-tight jeans, Carter was sorely tempted to rush up on stage and drag her behind the curtain for a drill down.

Instead he inhaled a deep breath and released it through his nose. A confrontation would only make matters worse. Better to wait for a later time to address the subject of proper public attire.

A sudden flurry of movement down front distracted him, and his gaze followed the commotion.

"Excuse me. I don't mean to be rude, but according to the schedule you sent, it should be my daughter's turn to rehearse her song." The distinctive authority-laden voice belonged to Mara Hedwig. She clutched a piece of paper in one hand as evidence and Ashton's hand in the other.

"Yes, we're running a bit behind." Bella Masterson, the new High School choir director, smiled politely, but her tone held a barely-controlled edge of frustration. "Chloe will be through shortly, and then Ashton can have her turn."

"Mommy, I don't want to." The little girl's words held a whine.

With a close-lipped smile to Bella, Mara turned and escorted Ashton up the center aisle, then stopped just a few feet away in the semi-darkness and leaned over near her daughter's face. "Ashton, this is something you wanted to do. Remember?"

"Not anymore."

Mara released a heavy sigh. "We talked about this at length. You said you wanted to do it. I've been around the world and back to get you here. You will go up there and sing your song. You know that once we start something, we do not quit. Do you understand me?" Her voice raised in pitch and volume with each syllable.

It was all Carter could do to glue his boots to the ground. Poor little Ashton. Obviously she was tired and not feeling well. Who would've guessed the beautiful and well-polished Mara to be an over-controlling stage mom whose business mattered more than her little girl? He brought a fist to his mouth and cleared his throat to let them know they weren't alone.

Mara's carefully coiffed head snapped upward, her eyes squinting through the darkness. "Carter, is that you?"

"Hey, long time no see." He intentionally kept a friendly lilt to his voice.

She raised her upper body into an upright position, her long legs and high heels bringing her height to almost match his, a broad grin glowing on her elegant features. "If I'd known you were headed this direction, I could've given you a ride." She nudged Ashton forward to where he stood. "What brings you here?"

Carter glanced down at Ashton, whose gaze was focused on Chloe on stage. "That's...uh...my daughter up there." The words stuck in his mouth like peanut butter, thanks to Chloe's outlandish dress. He turned his attention to the precocious little girl at his side. "Ashton, I see you finally woke up from your nap."

She faced him, sans smile, her eyes large and doleful.

A one-sided smirk landed on Mara's face. "Sorry. She's a bit cranky when she wakes up."

"Me too." He playfully punched Ashton's arm.

A giggle parted her lips into a shy smile, and she stepped behind her mother to hide.

How could he get through to Mara that this time with her daughter was precious, and not to waste it in pursuit of a career? And why hadn't someone said the same thing to him when Chloe was that age?

Chloe's song ended. She and Bella exchanged a few words, then his daughter headed down the stairs on the left side of the stage and disappeared into the darkened back section of the other side. But from that darkness came the voices of several adolescent boys.

Mara sent a knowing look. "Um, it appears your daughter has friends here."

He glanced toward where Chloe stood with no telling who. In the dark. His forehead creased. "So it seems." Now what?

"I'm not trying to tell you what to do, but you might want to go nip that in the bud." Mara smiled as she spoke, but her eyes were wide, and a hint of anxiety laced her voice.

"Ashton?" Bella called out from the front.

"I guess we'd better be going." Mara herded a very reluctant and whimpering Ashton down the aisle toward the front, wiggling her fingers in the air at him in farewell. "Good luck."

"Thanks." Carter waved back, then immediately focused his attention on the very dark corner on the opposite side. His lips clenched as he tugged at the waist band of his blue jeans. Time to break up...whatever it was.

He rapidly closed the distance between him and his daughter, praying for wisdom with each stride. Best to keep things light and upbeat.

As he neared, the tell-tale smell of cigarette smoke assaulted his nostrils. Several scrawny high school boys with saggy pants came into view in the semi-darkness, one with both arms around his scantily-dressed daughter, his head bent low over her shoulder.

Fury unleashed inside, more powerful than anything he'd ever experienced during his time in the military, and his fists clenched in response. "Hey, Chloe, ready to grab a bite to eat?" The words came out with a military bark.

The boy's arms, once wrapped around Chloe, now fell to his side. At the same time, his eyes and gaping mouth widened, and he took a step backward. The guys around him shuffled to one side, but their juvenile snickers sounded along with a few whispers.

"Dad!" Chloe's face held both astonishment and anger. "What are you doing here? I told you'd I'd be home around nine." She crossed her arms and jutted one hip out to the side while giving her dark curls a toss. Her lipstick-coated lips were pooched out and pinched tight to let him know exactly how she felt about his unexpected presence.

Yeah. Nine. When this little shindig was almost over at seven? Just what did she have planned for those two extra hours? He swallowed hard, pretty sure he didn't really want to know the answer to that question. "Just came to hear my talented daughter sing."

"Well, you heard me. Now can you just leave?" A petulant pout took up residence below her spark-shooting eyes.

With practiced concentration, he kept his facial expression calm and cool, though he was pretty sure matching sparks shot from his eyes as well. "Actually, I'd like a word with you. Then I'll be taking you home." His tone held gruffness in spite of his attempt to diffuse the situation.

"Could I speak with all the parents please?" Bella made the call from down front.

Carter latched onto Chloe's elbow and pulled her in front of him.

She cast one longing look over her left shoulder as they marched down the aisle to where Bella and a growing number of parents stood. "Call me later, Ben, okay?"

"Next week's rehearsal will be at the same time," explained Bella. "Then I need all the kids here a week from this Saturday at five for a quick run-through. The talent show will begin at six-thirty sharp." Once she spouted out the instructions, Bella turned to talk to one of the parents who'd commanded her attention.

Carter faced Chloe, doing all he could to get his point across without sounding too harsh. "Mind telling me why you're dressed like that?"

"What's wrong with how I'm dressed?" Chloe hands were fisted, her arms ramrod straight. Obviously she wasn't worried about making a scene based on the way she screeched out the words.

To his great relief, Mara stepped forward, hand outstretched toward Chloe, Ashton still in tow. "You must be Chloe. I heard you sing earlier. You're very talented."

Chloe at least had the good manners to shake her hand. "Thanks."

Mara sent him an understanding smile, then dropped Ashton's hand and began to dig around in her overly-large handbag. She pulled out a neatly-folded sweater and held it toward Chloe. "Here. This might keep your dad from killing you in public."

At first Chloe just glared at the sweater Mara offered, but then reluctantly uncrossed her arms, took the proffered piece of clothing, and put it on, her teen-aged sulky face still very much in place. "Thanks."

Carter smiled at Mara, appreciation coursing through him at how well she'd diffused the tense situation. Behind him Chloe huffed. He glanced over his shoulder as she slouched into a nearby seat, arms crossed once more.

Ashton took the seat next to Chloe, adoration shining from her big blue eyes. "You sing really, really pretty."

A tentative smile appeared on Chloe's face. Good. Carter turned his attention back to Mara as conversation ensued between the two girls. "Thanks for coming to my rescue."

"You're most welcome. I figured if I had the opportunity to rescue one of my own kind, I should at least give it a try." Her broad grin was back, and her words held more than a tinge of humor.

"How'd you know I was single?"

Mara shrugged. "You mentioned that you're looking for a house for you and your daughter."

"Ah." Carter could only nod, fairly certain that the goofy grin had appeared on his face, the one that always developed when he had no idea what to say to a very attractive woman.

Mara leaned in closer with a conspiratorial air, her perfume wafting to his nose. "Is Chloe's mom still in the picture?" Her voice was a hushed whisper.

"She lives in Morganville. What about Ashton's dad?"

Now a pained expression darkened her light brown eyes, and the broad grin faded. "Dallas. We don't hear from him much. Especially now that he has a new wife and child."

His chest tightened. What kind of guy could leave such an adorable little girl and beautiful wife? "So sorry."

Her neck stiffened and her chin raised. "Don't be. It's for the best." She held out a hand, urging her daughter to latch hold. "C'mon, Ash. Time to get you home."

His brain whizzed into overdrive. "Hey, I've got a good idea. Why don't we have a picnic at the park tomorrow evening?"

Ashton perked up and began tugging on her mother's suit jacket. "Can we, Mommy? Please?"

Mara dug around in her purse again, this time retrieving a planner which she rapidly flipped through. "Let me check my schedule right quick."

A chuckle fell from his mouth before he could stop it. "You have to schedule a picnic? Don't you ever do anything without consulting your calendar?"

"Rarely." Her tone dry, Mara ran an index finger down one page of her planner. "Do you even know what an appointment calendar is?"

A chortle sounded behind him. "Dad? A calendar?" Chloe's laughter continued, verging on hysteria, as she wrapped both arms around her waist, her head toward the ceiling. Great. With Chloe's wild hyena act Mara would probably see him as some sort of buffoon.

Mara glanced up, a teasing smile on her lips. "As it turns out, you're my last client tomorrow. So provided you show up on time, we just might be able to do a picnic at the park."

Ashton jumped up and down. "Yay!"

Something warm and gooey trickled through him, like thick hot chocolate on a cold day. "Good. I have another great idea. Why don't y'all join us afterwards at the church for Wednesday night Bible study and prayer?"

Instantly Mara's face clouded, and she tucked her planner back inside her bag, avoiding anymore eye contact. "Well, we'd best be going. Come on, Ash."

"But what about the park picnic, Mommy?"

"Yeah, what about that?" Carter called out the words as Mara rounded the corner of one section of the auditorium, headed for the back door as quickly as her high heels would allow.

"We'll discuss it tomorrow at our appointment." Mara hollered back as she grabbed hold of Ashton's hand and hurried out the double doors.

Carter's mouth fell open as the door slammed behind mother and daughter. The brush off?

Chloe appeared beside him. "Way to scare her off, Dad." Hands in both pockets of Mara's sweater, his daughter traipsed up the aisle toward the exit.

Carter followed, his thoughts in a swirl. What was it about the mention of church that so quickly changed Mara from friendly and fun to cold and distant?

Three

The elderly couple sitting across the desk from Mara late Friday afternoon were unbelievably cute. They had to be at least in their seventies, but still they held hands as though in their teens, and their eyes literally sparkled with love. What she wouldn't give for that sort of lasting relationship. But she wasn't about to kiss any more frogs in a search of a non-existent Prince Charming. She had neither the time, energy, nor the inclination.

"As I was saying before my beautiful bride tried to cut me short," Mr. Williams sent a teasing wink to his wife and squeezed her hand with a tender smile, "I think we need to ask a higher price for the house. What do you think, Mara?"

Mara finished a sip of Diet Coke and sat the silver can on her desk. "Well, I'd say that depends on what your objective is. If your goal is to get top dollar, then yes, ask a higher price."

The door buzzer sounded, and heavy footsteps fell across the floor. A second later, Carter's thick frame appeared in the doorway. "Oh. Sorry. Didn't realize you had clients with you." He smiled and raised a hand of greeting toward the Williams. "Hi, Zeke. Hi, Shirley."

The couple returned his greeting and carried on a brief conversation with him as Mara's gaze flitted to the clock above her office door. "You're a bit early."

His eyebrows raised perceptibly, but to his credit, he didn't reply.

Mara continued. "We'll be through shortly."

"Okay. I'll wait out here."

"Thank you." She turned her focus back to the couple. "On the other hand, if your goal is to move on with your lives, and money isn't an issue, I'd recommend listing low to attract buyers."

Shirley Williams faced her husband, loaded for bear. "Exactly my point, Darling. We don't need the money. We've been dreaming of moving closer to the kids for years, and in case you hadn't noticed, we're not getting any younger." Her tone held both a plea and censure.

Zeke paused to consider her words, then shook his head. "I think we should be patient. Who knows? One of us could get really sick. Then we might need that extra money."

The two stared at each other for a long minute, unspoken communication issuing forth from the both of them. Finally Zeke Williams turned back to Mara with a beleaguered look. "Obviously this is something we need to discuss at home. Can we get back to you later?"

Mara nodded and stood, suddenly anxious to get on to her next client appointment and the inevitable conversation she'd rehearsed in her brain all day. She held out a hand to Mr. Williams. "Of course. Just give me a call when you've reached a decision." After shaking his hand, she also reached toward his wife.

"Thank you, dear." The elderly woman patted her hand. "We appreciate you."

"My pleasure." Mara walked the couple to the outer door of the building and said her goodbyes. Once it closed behind them, she inhaled a deep breath, released it, and then turned to face Carter. "Thanks for waiting."

"No problemo. Ready to look at more houses?"

"Sure. Let me get my things."

Soon they were on their way to the first listing she'd lined up. She breathed deep to calm her restless nerves. The scent of his cologne wrapped around her head in a way that, oddly enough, brought a modicum of comfort. "Just so you know this next house isn't a rental. In fact, I wasn't able to come up with any rentals today. But I'll keep trying."

He nodded, but his immediate frown clued her in to the fact that he wasn't happy about the news.

Time to change the subject, but too soon for the church conversation, and she still had no clue how to address her suspicions about Chloe. In the end she opted for a safer stream of talk. "So what do you do in your free time? You know, when you're not rounding up bad guys or terrifying adolescent boys with your Big Bad Dad impersonation?"

The frown immediately morphed into a good-natured grin, and a chuckle sounded from deep in his chest. "That's about all I have time for anymore. But I really enjoy lots of things--hiking, fishing, hunting, rappelling, parachut--"

"You jump from airplanes?" A shudder that ran down her spine. "Makes me nauseous just thinking about it."

"That's cause you're the type who always wants to be in control."

Well. It obviously didn't take the mental capacity of a rocket scientist to figure *that* out. But just why was she so internally bothered by the fact that he'd already pegged her control issues? "Granted."

"You'd love it if you gave it a try."

"Well I guess we'll never know, will we?" She maneuvered the Caddy into a driveway. "Here's the first house."

The house tour took all of five minutes. Carter quietly assessed the place, and in short order declared that it wouldn't work for them.

Back on the road again, this time for a house on the edge of town, Mara thought through his previous list of activities. Though she'd never admit it out loud, that spontaneity and grab-the-bulls-by-the-horns kind of life somehow appealed to her, though the idea of parachuting filled her with unspeakable dread.

"So what do you do in *your* free time?" Carter turned his full attention on her.

"Ha! No such thing. At least your daughter is older and can do things on her own."

"I don't believe you. Bet you have Ashton fed, bathed, and in bed by ten o'clock every night."

"Nine."

His laughter erupted again. "Just proved my point. Now what do you do in the time after she's in bed?"

"Work and read."

Carter yawned.

A woeful smirk landed on her face. "Thanks for the commentary on my dull life."

"Dull life, huh? I'll have to see what I can do about that. Life's short. Might as well make it an adventure."

His words about infusing her life with excitement sounded more like a threat than a promise, and for some reason, she couldn't think of one thing to say in response. But threat or promise, it hinted at something blissfully other than her regimented schedule. They arrived at the second house on the list a minute later. "This house is two-bed, two-bath." She made a move to open the driver's side door, but stopped short with one glance at Carter's wrinkled nose. "Something wrong?"

"Don't really like this neighborhood. Sorry."

Mara re-clicked her seat belt, started the engine, and pulled away from the curb. "No problem." Except there was a problem. She was quickly running out of time to bring up the whole church issue and her concerns for Chloe. Only one house left in queue. At least this one was out in the country, near the lake. Now to somehow muster her courage.

He leaned one elbow on the console, his eyes focused on her in an unnerving sort of way. "Anyone ever tell you that you have pretty eyes?"

"Well, that's random." Her mind scoured every possible resource for a way to segue *that* remark into the much-needed conversation about church, but not one thing came to mind. "Anyone ever tell you that you don't have a filter?"

He feigned a hurt look for a moment, then broke into his all-too-engaging grin. "Just believe in calling it like I see it."

"But how you see things is your opinion. And as highly as *you* regard them, not everyone else is equally as fascinated."

He clutched his chest as though she'd stabbed him, making a mockery of her truthful, though snarky, words.

A traitorous guffaw lurched from her mouth at his antics, and there was no stopping her clothes-hanger grin. She couldn't even come back with an intelligent retort.

Instead, she just leaned her head against a fist, her elbow at rest on the door, wishing with everything inside her that she wasn't so drawn to his larger-than-life personality.

Carter relished the silence between them on this peaceful drive toward the lake near where his folks lived. The drive was spectacularly beautiful with rolling hills and tranquil tree-dotted countryside, just the kind of place he'd like to live. But how could he merge his preference of country living with the need for more excitement in his job?

In spite of the serene surroundings, his thoughts once more turned to Chloe. How in the world could he protect her from making the same mistakes he'd made? Obviously her so-called 'friends' couldn't be trusted, the girlfriends he'd thought had been Chloe's escort to last night's rehearsal. Somehow he had to find a way to keep her busy from the time she got out of school until he got home from work.

He pressed his lips into a flat line and peered out the passenger side window. Ernie had been kind enough to let him take all day shifts once Chloe had come to live with him full-time, but the day shift didn't end until five, or even six on days when his boss didn't come in early to relieve him.

"Something bothering you?" Kindness cloaked Mara's question as her well-manicured fingers gripped the steering wheel.

"Yeah, actually there is. I'm struggling with how to handle Chloe. She gets out of school a little before four and is basically unsupervised until I get off work."

"You're right, that's an issue. Sounds to me like she needs an after-school job."

The clouds of his problem with Chloe instantly parted, revealing glorious light. "Awesome idea. Know anyone that's hiring?"

Mara shook her head, but immediately started working her lips, as though in deep thought.

A plan hatched in his mind. "I have a great idea."

Mara smiled. "I'm starting to think those are your favorite words. What is this so-called great idea of yours?"

"Chloe could work for you. Answer phones. Do filing, cleaning, whatever you needed her to do."

Now the silence between them escalated to deafening levels, and Mara troubled her lips once more. At last she huffed out a resigned sigh. "I suppose I could at least interview her for a job, but no promises. I don't handle teenage girl drama very well. It's all I can do to handle Ashton's occasional bouts."

A ton of questions danced through Carter's mind. But how did he ask them without sounding nosy, especially when she'd already accused him of not having a filter? Finally, he could hold back no longer. "If you don't mind me asking, what happened between you and Ashton's father?"

At first she kept her gaze focused on the road, then glanced his way. "The short story is that we were going through a difficult time. A time Ashton and I both needed him more than ever. But he handled hard times by having an affair."

Her words seared a hole right through his stomach, and he struggled to keep his hands from fisting in auto-response.

She peered over at him once more. "What about you? How did a guy like you end up in Miller's Creek with a teenaged daughter in tow?"

Every muscle in his body stiffened. But Mara had been open with him. Time to reciprocate. "I'm former military, and my folks live nearby. Only made sense for me to land in the area."

"And why doesn't Chloe live with her mother?"

Carter shrugged, reliving painful memories, doing all he could to get the words out and hopefully protect his heart from further collateral damage. "When I got back from my second tour in Afghanistan, Chloe's mom told me she wanted out of the marriage. Said she was tired of being a military widow. Two months later, she and Chloe showed up on my doorstep with all of Chloe's belongings." He hesitated and slid suddenly sweaty palms down his thighs. "Guess after all the years she took care of Chloe on her own, it was my turn." His brain whizzed through possible ways to lead into his belief that Mara needed to focus more on Ashton than her career, but the jumbled words in his head wouldn't cooperate and settle into cohesive thoughts.

A grim look settled on Mara's face, her lips flat and pinched. And surprisingly, her eyes glistened with unshed tears. "That's hard." The words barely came out, and when they did were charged with thick emotion. "But that's life, isn't it?" This time heavy cynicism coated her statement.

His intuition went on full alert. "So that's why you're opposed to church."

A snort-like laugh sounded. "You mean religion."

"No, I mean a faith-based relationship with God. There's a huge difference."

"Well, since you brought it up, we might as well get this little conversation out of the way." Mara didn't look at him, and her voice had taken on a hardened edge. "Just so you know, I was raised in the church. My father was a preacher who uprooted us every few months before the people of the church ran him out of town on a rail. I've had to fight tooth and nail to get where I am today. Life for me has been far from a fairy-tale. Now I'm on my own with a five-year-old, and the last thing I need is someone trying to shove his beliefs down my throat." She finished the monologue with her left elbow on the car door and leaned her head against her fist, her lips turned down at the corners.

The air inside the car went from balmy to icicle-sharp in a heartbeat. How was he supposed to answer? Obviously she'd grown up in the faith, but the enemy had dealt her faith a fatal blow. Or maybe even several. "Sounds like a pretty pessimistic outlook on life to me."

"Yeah, well, what you call pessimism I call realism." She steered the Caddy into the weedy front yard of their next house, threw the gearshift into park, and killed the engine.

Carter kept his gaze and attention focused on Mara's hardened features, all the while praying for wisdom. "You may think you're being realistic, Mara. But I think you're an idealist who's had her dreams crushed one too many times."

"There you go with those opinions again." Now she glared at him, open hostility oozing from every pore of her face.

"Ease up. I'm not trying to start some kind of theological debate."

She lowered her head. "Sure could've fooled me."

"Trust me. I hate an intellectual-type debate of any kind because I stink at it." Embarrassing memories from high school debate class flooded his mind, but Carter pushed them away and scrounged for words to distill the charged air. "I think we just need to change the subject."

"I thought you'd never ask." Mara yanked on her door handle and scooted from the car. The door slammed behind her.

Suddenly world-weary and sure of very little, Carter climbed from his side of the SUV and focused for the first time on the dilapidated house in front of them.

"I guess I should've come to see this one before I brought you out here."

Mara's quietly-spoken words were an understatement if he'd ever heard one. Though the surrounding countryside was nothing short of spectacular, the house she'd chosen to show him looked more like a shipwreck.

The perfect analogy for Mara's shipwrecked faith.

Four

An explosion rocked the night, followed by the rapid gunfire of automatic weapons. Carter rolled from bed, smoke clogging his nostrils, throat, and lungs, the sounds of pain and terror on every side.

The Taliban.

Sirens, their cry piercing, joined the cacophony.

Heart beating wildly, Carter fell face-first to the floor and peered around the darkened space interspersed with tell-tale flashes of light. John, his best friend, sat in one corner of the room, trying to drag himself to a sitting position as blood seeped from a gaping abdomen wound.

"John!"

"Carter, that you?" Even his tone held breathless evidence of the struggle towards life and away from death.

"Stay down! I'm coming after you!" Carter slithered along the floor like a snake, using his elbows and upper body strength to pull himself along. Then just before he reached his buddy, a second explosion shook the ground. Out of instinct coupled with military training, Carter quickly ducked his head and covered it with his hands.

After the dust and fallout debris settled around him, Carter raised his gaze. "NOoooo!!!!" Along with the corner of the room, John was gone.

Now the scene took on a frantic edge. Without warning, Carter was whisked outside to broad daylight and the white-hot heat of the Iraqi desert. A veiled woman and her young child took cover in a nearby doorway. In what seemed like slow motion, he turned and waved both arms, yelling at them to move inside. Street terrorists, like dark shadows, flitted from doorway to doorway to take out anyone who stood in their way. But it was too late. The earth trembled and knocked him to his knees, and a cloud of dust filled the air, immediately coating his tongue and making its way to his lungs. Bits of rock and human bone pinned him to the ground.

Carter whimpered and bolted upright on the sofa bed, covered in sweat, trembling, and gasping for air.

Just the same old dream, but with a new layer of intensity.

He inhaled deeply and released a breath in the dark room. It had been a long time since the dream had affected him this way. So long that he thought he'd passed the worst part of PTSD. But somehow, this time it felt different. More personal.

Carter clutched his knees to his chest and lowered his head until his pulse slowed and his stomach settled. Several minutes elapsed before he felt well enough to lean back against the sofa to check the clock. Six a.m. At least he'd almost finished a full night's sleep. Good thing, since there was no going back to sleep after that kind of nightmare.

He inched to the side of the sofa bed, sat there a moment to let the room quit spinning, and then stumbled to the bathroom to shower off the marathon-like sweat.

Later that morning, after he'd dropped Chloe off at school, he slouched in his chair across the dining room table from Matt and Gracie Tyler in their beautiful home.

The couple were both counselors. Gracie the attorney-type, and Matt the kind Carter sorely needed at the moment to understand why the dream had come back, but with a twist.

"And you say the scene with the woman and child had never been in your dreams before?" A huge frown rutted Matt's forehead.

"Never." Carter sipped his coffee and met Matt's gaze. "And the weird thing is, I never even experienced anything like that when I was in Iraq or Afghanistan."

Matt ran a hand across his mouth. "Hmmm. Anything going on in your life right now that's out of the ordinary?"

A light clicked on in Carter's brain. Mara and Ashton? "Is it possible for something from my life now to get confused with the past? At least in my dreams?"

Matt leaned back and rested one protective arm on the back of Gracie's chair. "Of course. Our fears today can get easily mixed up in past traumas."

Carter fixed his gaze on the table, his brain sorting through Matt's comment in relation to last night's dream.

Matt raised his cup to his lips and took a sip, then released an airy and satisfied 'ahh.' "Which begs for me to ask the next question.

"What's that?" Not that he was completely certain he wanted to know the answer.

A compassionate-eyed gleam appeared. "What are you afraid of, buddy?"

The coffee contents in Carter's stomach blazed into flame. He let out a disgruntled snort and raised a hand to scratch his head. "There's someone I know who doesn't believe in God. I want to help her and her daughter, but I don't know how."

"What do you mean by help her?" Gracie gently probed, the attorney side of her coming to the forefront.

"I don't want to see her separated from God, and I want her to come back to the faith."

Matt and Gracie exchanged a glance. Then his friend leaned forward, his elbows and forearms at rest on the table. "*Back* to the faith? She was a believer?"

"I think so. She grew up in a Christian home. Her dad was a preacher."

"And why has she turned her back on Christianity?"

Why indeed? "Not sure, but she mentioned something about her dad moving them around a lot, and her husband cheating on her."

Matt grimaced, and Gracie's soft dark eyes filled with tears. "Someone we know?"

Carter nodded, but with slight hesitation. "Mara Hedwig. She's been showing me some houses. I have to get Chloe out of those apartments." And away from the misguided boys that constantly flocked to their door. His brain spun out of control, back and forth between Chloe's problems and his concern for Mara and Ashton. "The thing is, I don't know how to get through to Mara. She's so smart and knowledgeable and well-spoken. Makes me feel like a dunce. She's also rigid and uptight."

"I don't see her that way at all." Gracie spouted the words quickly, like a school teacher correcting a wayward student. "I think she's just very cautious, afraid of saying or doing the wrong thing. That's a hard way to live."

He nodded his head in agreement. "I can see that about her. She really wants to succeed at her business, and appearance is everything to her since she's new in town and looking to make a good impression."

Across the table, Matt chuckled. "That's more than a casual observation there, bucko. You been thinking about her a lot?"

Heat rushed to the tip of Carter's head. "A little." The truth smacked him across the face. He rested one elbow on the table and dropped his head to an open palm. Oh, man. Since when had he developed feelings for someone he barely knew, and a non-believer at that?

"How's Chloe adjusting?" Gracie asked the question out of the blue while slipping on the suit jacket that had hung on the back of her chair.

Carter straightened and sent an appreciative smile for the save. "Okay, I guess. She still fights me about going to church. Says I'm trying to cram my beliefs down her throat." Hadn't Mara basically said the same thing? "She goes to all the youth events, but she's not happy about it."

Concern clouded both their faces, then a second later, Gracie rose to her feet. "Well, I hate to eat and run and miss all the fun, but I've got a trial in Morganville."

Matt stood and kissed his wife, enveloping her in a hug. "Have a great day, hon."

She smiled and patted his cheek. "You, too. Try to behave while I'm gone, will ya? See you tonight."

Carter lowered his gaze as the couple shared another kiss. Matt took his seat as Gracie made her way across the kitchen floor to the back door. Must be nice to have that kind of relationship with someone. Would he ever find it? He glanced at Matt as the back door clicked into closed position. "You're one lucky guy, dude."

"Don't I know it?" beamed Matt. "Nothing I wouldn't do for that woman. You didn't live here when I moved to Miller's Creek to see if Gracie and I could pick back up where we left off, but I fretted and worried over her long before she belonged to me. She was on the verge of making some really bad mistakes, and I felt completely powerless to stop her."

Powerless. The perfect word to explain how he felt about Mara. "I feel the exact same way."

"With Chloe or Mara?"

"Both."

"Don't fall for that. God lives in you. Can't get anymore powerful than that." A broad grin landed on Matt's face, and his sand-colored eyes glowed with faith.

"I know in my heart that you're right, but what can I really do to help them?"

"Pray. Keep the doors of communication open."

Carter's ego took a fatal blow and deflated inside. "That's the part that scares me most."

"What? Communicating?"

He nodded. "I want to say the right things the first time around. I might not get a second chance with either one of them."

Matt rose and sauntered to the bookshelves that lined one wall of the open concept living area. He yanked out a few books and carted them back. They thudded to the table. "These might help."

"Books?" He had to be kidding. A cynical laugh sounded from Carter's mouth. "Look. I know you're a bookish kinda guy, but I'm not. That's why I went the military route rather than college."

"So if Mara or Chloe have questions about God's existence or want to know why a good God allows suffering, you're already prepared to answer those questions?"

He froze. No way. An exasperated breath flew from his lungs, and he fell back against the chair. "I think this is exactly why I'm so afraid of all this. I have an uncanny knack for sending Chloe into a rage without even trying. And Mara's so smart, I don't stand a ch--"

"So you're giving up on them?" Matt's expression had changed from its normal friendliness to one that held a challenge.

"I didn't say that."

"Sure sounded like it to me."

Carter stared at the ceiling, a silent prayer winging its way from his heart. *God, I'm not good at this sort of stuff. I don't know how to verbally communicate well.* He turned his attention back to Matt's stern face. "Maybe you could talk to them."

Matt slowly shook his head from side to side, his lips cemented in a firm line. "Nice try, but I'm not the one God's placed in their lives. You are." He leaned across the table, his expression full of encouragement. "You can do this, Carter. Somehow you've bought the lie that you're no good at books and communicating, but God must think otherwise or He wouldn't have placed you in this situation."

Carter's chin dropped to his chest, his shoulders sagging.

Matt clamped a hand on his outstretched arm. "Buddy, I could talk to both of them 'til I'm blue in the face, and it wouldn't make a dent 'cause there's no connection. But you've been given this opportunity to make a difference. Not a doubt in my mind that with God's help you can do this."

As usual, his friend was dead-on, but still his faith wobbled on shaky knees. "Pray for me?"

Matt's broad grin returned. "You know it."

"Looks like I got some homework." Carter slid the stack of books toward his side of the table.

His friend laughed. "Yeah, well. It'll give you something to do at that fast-paced job of yours."

Carter snickered at Matt's good-natured tease. But if the truth be known, deep inside him, all his brawn and might had melted into a pool of slimy Jell-o.

Mara hurriedly punched in the security code at the daycare late Friday afternoon. The last-minute appointment with the Williams couple had once more thrown her behind, leaving very little time to pick up Ashton and get back to the office for Chloe's job interview. The whole situation reeked of disaster, especially if her suspicions about Chloe were correct.

She rushed down the eerily quiet hallway toward the large open room at the back where kids normally played as they waited for their parents. But it was Friday, and like most Texas towns, the week had ended mid-afternoon in preparation for the football game.

Ashton, Mama Beth, and Dani, her baby girl on one hip, placed toys on the shelf, and turned as she entered. Mara sent an apologetic grimace. "Sorry I'm late again."

"Mommy!" Ashton walked toward her, arms outstretched, and hugged her around the thighs.

Mara placed a hand on her daughter's soft hair.

Ashton looked up, her face pallid, and her lips strangely gray.

"You feel okay, sweetie?" Thick cotton coated Mara's mouth as she brushed back Ashton's damp bangs to feel her forehead.

A little smile moved to Ashton's face. "Yeah. I've just had a really hard day." The words were laced with adult drama. She buried her head against Mara's legs as Mama Beth and Dani joined them.

Mara smiled at them. Hopefully they'd understand her tardiness. "Sorry again about being late. I forget how small towns in Texas close up middle of the afternoon for Friday night football."

Dani laughed. "I had a hard time adjusting to that, too." Her smile faded, and a small furrow developed between her vivid blue eyes. "Could I talk to you a minute while Mama helps Ashton get her things together?"

"Sure."

Dani stepped aside to let the older woman and Ashton pass, then waited until the others exited the room.

Mara's heart thumped against her rib cage. But she pasted her 'everything's-great' smile into place for whatever was about to come.

"I'm worried about Ashton." Sincerity shone from the petite woman's face. "I haven't said anything because I figured it was just taking her awhile to adjust to school."

Panicked thoughts stampeded through Mara's brain, and she struggled to keep the smile in place. "She's been very tired after school, and it's been a long week for both of us."

Dani frowned and nodded, her gaze on her own baby girl, who now gnawed two fingers, drool on both her hand and face. "Ashton slept most of the afternoon."

Mara's heart did a queer little flop, then pounded once more. "This afternoon?"

"Yeah. She got off the bus, refused her snack, laid down, and went straight to sleep. She only woke up a few minutes ago. How she slept through all the other kids playing I'll never know."

Clanging bells rang in Mara's ears. This couldn't be happening. Not again. Now there was no keeping the smile in place. She ducked her head and headed to the front, calling back over her shoulder in what she hoped was a normal voice. "Thanks, Dani. I'll keep an eye on her this weekend and make sure she gets plenty of rest."

Mama Beth and Ashton waited at the front door, chatting away like best friends. Ashton looked Mara's way. "Mommy, can I go to a place called Sunday School with Mama Beth? She's the teacher, and she said I was welcome to attend." Her voice held excitement, in spite of the dark circles ringing her eyes.

Please not this on top of everything else. "Well, I hope you thanked her for inviting you. We'll talk about it later this evening, okay?" She infused kindness into her voice in spite of the instantaneous resentment that bubbled inside.

An angelic smile covered Ashton's face as she turned back to the older lady. "Thank you very much for inviting me."

"You're welcome, sweetheart."

Mara took hold of Ashton's hand and opened the door to the dusky evening, then waved goodbye and moved to the car. A few minutes later they arrived at the office in downtown Miller's Creek to find Chloe and Carter waiting. Words of apology rang from Mara's lips as she jumped from the car. "Sorry. We're running behin--"

"Again?" Carter's face revealed mock disapproval.

Mara laughed as she helped Ashton unbuckle, then hurried her up onto the sidewalk.

"No worries." Carter's easy grin reassured her, but as he glanced down at Ashton, his smile faded, and a tiny frown appeared between his soft dark eyes. He patted Ashton's shoulder. "How's my girl today?"

"I'm very well, thank you."

Carter raised his gaze, a smirk on his lips. "Five, going on twenty-five?"

Mara unlocked the front door. "You nailed it. Chloe, how are you today?"

Less sulky than the night of rehearsal, the pretty teen-ager was dressed in blue and white cheerleader garb, and the slight scent of vanilla perfume floated from her. "Great. A little nervous. I've never interviewed for a job before."

A big grin broke out on Mara's face as she opened the door. "I promise not to bite." She faced Carter. "Why don't you and Ashton sit out here and work a puzzle or something while I visit with Chloe in my office?"

With a half-skip in her step, Ashton latched hold of Carter's hand and tugged him toward the large cabinet that held her toys. "Oh, goody. Mr. Carter, do you like to work puzzles?"

"I sure do." He sent a wink toward Mara and Chloe.

"Cinderella or Barbie?" Ashton held a puzzle box in each hand and launched into a monologue about the pros and cons of each, then inserted her personal preference.

Mara leaned toward Chloe with a giggle. "Just a word of warning. He might be a little grouchy after this."

Chloe smiled and waved a dismissing hand. "Don't worry. It'll be good for him."

The two entered the office. Mara motioned to a chair and shut the door. "Have a seat. Want something to drink?"

"No thanks." Chloe sat in one of the faux-leather chairs and peered around the office. "This room is so pretty."

"Thank you." Mara reached for the questions she'd jotted on a yellow legal pad earlier that day and took a seat. "Have you ever had an after-school job?"

The teenager gave her curls a shake. "No. Mom and I spent that time doing fun stuff like shopping or going to the movies and stuff."

A sudden wash of sympathy gnawed holes in Mara's heart. She averted her gaze as a bad taste landed on her tongue. Based on what little Carter had mentioned, Chloe must feel somewhat abandoned by her mom. And at her age without another female in the house. A double blow.

"But I've done some babysitting, so if you ever need anyone to watch Ashton, I'd be happy to. As long as it's not on a Friday night."

"I'll keep that in mind. Now about the job. Do you think you could watch over the office without me here, answer the phone, take messages, do a bit of filing and paperwork?"

Chloe nodded. "Sure. Doesn't sound hard."

"I might need you to do a bit of cleaning and straightening, too. Would that be a problem?"

"No."

For just a brief minute, a glimpse of Carter's optimistic outlook on life shone through in his daughter. Mara scrambled for words to address the next topic, one that would definitely not come easy. "Chloe, I need to ask you a personal question. I'm not trying to pry, but I need to know the answer before I let you have this job."

The girl's cheerful smile dissipated, and she shifted uncomfortably in her seat.

Would she lie or tell the truth? Mara cleared her throat. "Chloe, are you bulimic?"

Her face paled, and her eyes grew large. Then the pouty teenager face appeared. "No." Her voice held disdain.

Mara rose to her feet. "This interview is over. Sorry."

Chloe sat up ramrod straight. "Okay. Yeah I am. How'd you know?" The words came out half-whispered.

Mara summoned a reserve of strength she wasn't sure she possessed, and once more took her seat. "Because I used to be bulimic, too."

"You?" Her mouth gaped open. "But you seem so...so together."

Oh, if only she knew the truth. "Sometimes, but for a while, I felt so bad about myself that I made myself throw up. I convinced myself I was fat and that being skinny would make me feel better."

"But you're not fat. I'm the one who's fat."

Mara shook her head. "No you're not. You're a beautiful young lady who doesn't need to lose one ounce."

"I haven't vomited in a couple of weeks." Shame and regret tinged her words and face.

Oh, this would be so hard, but she had no choice. "I need you to look me in the eyes so I know you hear and understand me."

The teenager met her gaze, her chin slightly lowered.

"I'll give you this job on one condition. If I ever even suspect that you're making yourself throw up, I will fire you. Do you understand?"

Chloe nodded. "Yes, ma'am." She lowered her gaze to her twitching hands. "Are you gonna tell my dad?"

Mara's mind went into a tailspin. She didn't want to keep anything from Carter, especially as it concerned his daughter. But a big tough military guy like him probably wouldn't handle it well. "Not unless you give me a reason to."

Relief flooded Chloe's features. "I won't. I promise."

"Good. I'm going to hold you to that." Mara stood to use her gangly height to her advantage, her eyes constantly on Chloe. "I'm not trying to spoil your fun, Chloe. I'm making this requirement because I care. I don't want you to ruin your health."

"I know."

They shared a smile, a sort of covenant in their newly-founded relationship. Mara hurried around the desk and hugged the teenager's neck. "Welcome aboard. You start Monday afternoon. I'll pick you up from school. If I'm running late, you wait. Okay?" Now to find a way to include Chloe's salary in an already tight budget.

Chloe's eyes sparkled. "Okay. Thank you, Mara."

"You're welcome."

Both Carter and Ashton glanced up from the far corner of the room when the door opened.

Mara raised fingers to her mouth to stifle a laugh, but without success. Thankfully Chloe's laughter joined her own.

In their absence, Ashton had crowned Carter with a rhinestone-studded tiara and wrapped a bright pink boa around his neck. But the funniest addition was the matching fuchsia lip stick that rimmed his mouth.

He broke into a cheeky grin and swiped at the lipstick with one big paw, smearing it across his face. "What are you two laughing about? Haven't y'all ever seen a muscle-bound fairy princess before?" He made muscle man arms, then removed the boa and tiara as Chloe bounded across the room.

"Daddy, I got the job. Mara's going to pick me up from school and bring me here to work every afternoon." She wrapped both arms around his waist and leaned her head against his chest.

"Congratulations, sweetheart." His arms still around his daughter, he looked up at Mara with an appreciative smile.

Chloe then proceeded to plop down beside Ashton. The two girls chatted away as Carter made his way to where Mara stood in the doorway. "I owe you big time."

"No big deal."

"It's a very big deal." He followed her gaze to the two girls. "They act like sisters, don't they?"

"How would you know?"

"Uh, I have three."

His dry tone elicited a giggle from her throat. "You? Three sisters?"

"Yep, and two brothers." He glanced back at the girls, and his smile inched into a frown. "Is Ashton okay?"

All-too familiar fears descended, but she pushed them away. "What do you mean?"

"She looks a little pale to me."

Thankfully the conversation ended there. A conversation she wasn't prepared to have. Chloe once more sprang across the office, every ounce the cheerleader, while Ashton walked, very ladylike, behind her. Chloe's eyes held a plea. "Mara, could you and Ashton have a picnic in the park with us before the game? I promise to make Dad behave."

A smile she had no chance of stopping popped onto Mara's face. "Well, under those conditions, how can I possibly refuse?"

Five

"Oh, I can't eat another bite." Mara scooted the Styrofoam plate across the picnic table away from her, the aroma of fried chicken still tantalizing her nose, and chewed the last bit of juicy morsel. Truthfully, she'd gorged herself to encourage Chloe to eat more. The plan had worked. Now to get this picnic ended so she could get Ashton home to rest.

"I'm full, too." The teenager stood and carried her plate to a nearby trash can.

"Careful, Chloe. You'll pack on the pounds if you keep eating that way." Carter's voice teased, but the words darkened his daughter's face.

Mara shifted on the wooden bench. How could she warn him without breaking her promise to Chloe?

The teenager caught Ashton's attention. "Hey squirt, you need to hurry up so we can have time on the swings before I leave."

Ashton, who'd been rather listless, perked up instantly. "Mommy, may I be excused?"

Mara peered at the still-full plate. "How about one more bite of chicken and one more bite of mashed potatoes first?"

"Do I have to?" Her voice held the whine that had been all too-familiar here of late.

Though tempted to let it slide just this once, Mara stuck to her guns. "Yes, you have to. It won't take you two seconds. Snip snap, and you'll be done." She added their favorite Z-snap in the air.

Ashton giggled, gobbled a bite of potatoes, and followed it with a bite from her chicken leg. She stood, picked up her plate, and slid off of the bench, then headed toward the trash can with Chloe on her heels.

Beside her, Carter chuckled. "Snip snap? Really?"

"It worked, didn't it? Don't knock it 'til you've tried it."

"Didn't know you had such, uh, sophisticated moves." He tore off a chunk of chicken with his fingers and brought it to his mouth, grinning at her the whole time.

Mara dug a piece of crushed ice from her Diet Coke and chunked it at him.

It landed on his cheek, slid downward, and disappeared behind his shirt collar. He didn't even flinch, but sent a mock glare. "You really wanna play that game? 'Cause I'm pretty sure I'd win."

She quickly held both hands at shoulder height. "No, no, no. I'm good."

Carter stood and stretched. "Don't remember the last time I enjoyed a meal so much. Even if it was just a bucket of chicken and the fixings from Granny's."

"I enjoyed it, too." The girls' laughter sounded from the swings. "And from the sound of it, I'd say they're having fun, too." The creek gurgled in the distance and a soft evening breeze rustled the mesquite branches near creek's edge. They swayed like grass-skirted hula girls, motioning with long green fingers, urging her toward the creek.

"How 'bout a walk to work off the fried chicken?"

She glanced to where the girls played. Whatever had ailed Ashton earlier obviously no longer bothered her. In fact, it had been a long time since she'd sounded so happy. This would be the perfect time to address the religion issue. "Sounds good to me."

After they'd cleared the table, Mara and Carter made their way toward the relaxing song of the creek.

"Ashton enjoying school?"

"Loves it." Mara plucked a piece of tall brown grass and twirled it between her fingers. "The schedule seems a little grueling, at least for kindergarten kids. She comes home exhausted and whiny everyday. If it weren't for the weekends, I'd be tempted to throw in the towel."

"I hear that. Chloe's schedule keeps me hopping, too." Carter worked his way down the creek bank to a more level surface right beside the water. He turned and offered a hand.

Mara gripped his fingers, made it down the embankment in spite of her high heels, and fell into step beside him. These shoes weren't exactly the proper footwear for this kind of outing. "Hang on a sec."

She balanced on one foot, crossed her leg over one knee, and removed the first high heel and knee-high stocking, then repeated the process for the other foot. Tucking the stockings into her shoes, she took off walking.

Carter caught up to her with one step. "Doesn't that hurt your feet?"

"Nope. The first thing I do when I get home is kick off my shoes. I go barefoot just about everywhere except the office."

He cocked his head to one side. "Interesting."

"And you find me removing my shoes interesting, why?"

Carter laughed. "'Cause your public and private personas don't match up."

Hmm. He'd pegged her well, considering all he had to go on was her socks and shoes. Time to change the subject before he figured her out completely and decided she wasn't worth his time. "How about Chloe? Is she doing okay in school?"

"Pretty good. It helps that she made the cheerleading squad. Wish her grades were better, and that she'd stay away from the boys, but other than that, I can't complain."

A sudden bout of guilt stabbed at Mara. But a promise was a promise. Besides, she'd keep a close eye on Chloe and make sure she kept her end of the bargain.

"You planning on staying in Miller's Creek?" Carter asked the question, head down, hands stuffed in his pockets.

"That's the plan. I don't want Ashton moved around constantly like I was. I want a stable environment and roots for her, and I'll do whatever I have to do to make that happen." She kept her focus straight ahead in spite of Carter's hole-burning gaze.

"So I was right. There is more to you than meets the eye." His voice held respect she hadn't heard directed her way. Ever. "You're prim and proper and business-like. Very polite and eager to please, but there's a toughness to you I hadn't seen until now."

A blush worked its way up her neck and landed on her cheeks, bringing her clothes-hanger grin with it. "It's the Mama gene."

He nodded, but didn't respond. They walked in silence a few minutes longer, then Carter broke in. "You promise not to get mad and give me a tongue-lashing if I ask you a question?"

She shot a warning look. "I'm not quite sure how to answer that. I'll *try* not to get upset."

Carter frowned. "I know you mentioned your dad being a preacher and everything, and that you moved a lot when you were a kid. And I can't imagine how hurt you must've been when your husband cheated on you. But why are you so mad at God?"

Boiling inside, Mara halted and rested a hand on one hip, Chloe-style.

Carter faced her and held up one finger. "You're not trying very hard."

"Look, let's not beat around the bush. I'm a single mom. I don't have the time or energy for games."

"Fine by me. Don't much believe in anything but complete honesty anyway." His face held complete sincerity.

Mara resumed her walk. "I believed in God at one time, but with all the bad around me, I saw no evidence that he cared. So I choose to no longer believe the convenient lie that there's a benevolent being."

"I don't see it that way."

"Well, pray tell, please enlighten me."

"Evil isn't God's doing. We live in enemy-occupied territory. The biggest battle of all time between forces of good and evil happening all around us."

"An interesting perspective, especially coming from a military man, but one without proof."

His face darkened, and he shoved his hands deeper into his pockets. "Guess it all depends on how you look at it."

"Guess so. While we're on the subject, I'd appreciate it if you wouldn't try to proselytize my daughter. I don't want her caught up in the myth of a doting grandfather-figure in the sky. I'd much rather her know the truth now than face hurt and disappointment down the road."

"Not trying to proselytize your daughter or you. Just trying to understand." His lips closed quickly, like he wanted to say more, but changed his mind at the last second.

"Then why do you and Mama Beth keep trying to get us to go to church?"

His shoulder muscles inched toward his ears. "That's just how things are done in small towns. You meet a new friend, and you make them feel welcome by inviting them to church."

Though his words held a certain amount of truth, she didn't buy all of it. "So you're saying your only motivation is friendship?"

The creek, soft breeze, and his big feet thudding against the rocky ground were the only sounds.

Case closed. His silence answered her question and proved her point.

"Actually, I care about you and Ashton. I don't know why, but I do. Maybe it's because I see you with the same single parent struggles I have. I couldn't make it without God's help."

A lemon-sized lump landed in her throat, making it impossible to swallow. How long had it been since someone had actually verbalized their care for her and her daughter? She came to a stop.

Carter halted and gazed back at her, his eyes so full of sorrow Mara could barely breathe. "Thank you for caring. It means more than you know."

They resumed their walk. And again, Carter brought an end to the silence. "Can I ask another question?"

"With the same stipulations, I presume?"

He grinned. "Of course. I try to make you mad, and you try not to get mad." They both laughed, then Carter sobered. "This might sound a little odd, but do you let Ashton believe in Santa Claus, the tooth fairy, and the Easter Bunny?"

"Yeah. What's your point?"

He slid his bottom lip between his teeth.

"Okay, what am I missing? Why'd you ask that question?" The words pelted out with a frustrated snip.

His expression grew deadly serious. "I just have a hard time understanding why you let her believe in myths, but not in God."

How was it that this muscle-bound military man was able to gun down every one of her objections. Mara refused him eye contact and kept walking.

"Don't be mad. I just want to understand."

She couldn't answer. Instead her mind whizzed with multiple thoughts and questions. Was it possible that she'd transferred her anger and pain to God? Was he real? If so, then why had he allowed heartbreak after heartbreak in her life? Was it really because a force of evil tried to keep her on his side?

Her thoughts flew to Carter's previous comment about her not being a realist, but an idealist who'd had her dreams crushed one too many times. The truth of his words settled around her like a harem of hornets. How had he uncovered that aspect of her personality so astutely, one of which she'd been completely unaware? Maybe he should know all Ashton had endured in her short life. Maybe then he wouldn't be so quick to tout God's goodness.

A scream sounded from the playground above them. "Daddy!!" Chloe's voice held sheer panic.

Her heart cradled in her throat, Mara raced up the embankment. As she crested the small rise, she spotted Chloe on her knees. And on the ground next to her, Ashton's crumpled body.

"Will you come find me as soon as you know something?" Chloe leaned against Carter as he sat on the Harley in the dirt parking lot behind the already noisy football stadium. Salty tears streaked her cheeks, and she chewed her bottom lip as she struggled to keep further tears at bay.

"You know I will. I'm headed to the hospital now. Sure you're gonna be okay?"

Chloe nodded. "Love you, Dad."

"Love you, too, baby girl."

She hugged him, then walked toward the field, her head and shoulders bowed down as though carrying the weight of the world.

Regret pierced Carter's heart and flooded his mind with brief snippets of time past. When had the little girl with long curly pigtails grown up? If only he could go back and do things differently. But life just didn't work that way.

He cranked up the bike. The motor rumbled beneath him as he drove from the bumpy dirt parking lot and on toward the hospital. Since he'd first laid eyes on Ashton earlier that afternoon, her appearance had him concerned, but then she seemed more like herself. And Mara did what he suspected she always did.

Carried on as if everything were fine.

Carter brought the Harley to a stop at the highway intersection. Was this the family crisis Mara had referred to when mentioning her husband's affair? Had Ashton been sick before? Was her illness back? And why in the world hadn't Mara said something? If given the chance, a few questions were in order. Questions she wouldn't like.

A fist of emotions pounded him in the chest--concern mixed with apprehension and more than a little anger. Within a few minutes he steered the bike into the parking lot of Miller's Creek General Hospital, parked, and entered the emergency room. A strong antiseptic smell greeted him as he removed his aviator sunglasses. Behind the counter, his buddy Chance was embedded in deep conversation with Dr. Green. He looked up as Carter approached. "Hey, buddy."

"Hey. Looking for Mara Hedwig and her daugh--"

"--back here. I'll take you."

Carter's first glimpse of the scene almost knocked him to his knees. Ashton, more frail-looking than ever, lay in the bed, her eyes barely open. Mara sat on the edge of the bed stroking her face and talking to her softly, but stood when he and Chance entered.

Chance donned his professional persona. "And how's Miss Ashton doing? Can I bring you some ice chips or water?"

Ashton didn't speak, but raised droopy eyelids toward her mother.

Mara offered her calm business face, as if the whole scenario were no big deal. "That would be wonderful. Thank you, Chance."

"I'll be back in a minute." The door clicked shut behind him.

Carter honed in on Mara. "You doing okay?"

"Of course." The mask she wore was obviously one she was accustomed to wearing. One that made him question if he knew her at all.

An image of her terrified face at the park flashed to the front of his mind. He released a small breath between pursed lips. Mara still very much cared for her daughter, but had gone to a familiar place to self-protect. A technique he knew all too well. She was a soldier like him, just fighting a different sort of battle. "Sometimes I think God must've chipped you out of the Rock of Gibraltar."

Her chin tilted upward, but other than that slightest of movements, she remained stoic. "That's a little harsh, don't you think?"

"Didn't mean to sound harsh. I meant it as a compliment."

"Do you treat everyone this way, or am I the only recipient of your goodness?" Her voice held icy coolness.

To respond would only promote further animosity, so Carter moved to the opposite side of the bed and took Ashton's hand. "Hey, Princess, how you feel?"

"I'm okay," Ashton whispered.

He came close to making a comment about her being cut from the same fabric as her Mama, but thought better of it.

Mara must've had the same thought because she glared at him as though daring him to say one word.

Why all this hostility? And why was it directed at him? He sifted through possible answers as Chance entered the room, a colorful cup in one hand, and rolled the bed table over to Ashton. "Here you go. Ice chips are served."

The little girl attempted a smile that didn't quite reach her eyes.

"Thank you." Mara, her professional mask firmly in place, spooned ice chips in Ashton's mouth as a knock sounded at the door.

"Come in." Mara's raised voice still remained remarkably calm.

The door opened, but Dr. Green didn't fully enter, his gaze on Mara. "Mrs. Hedwig, could I speak with you a moment?" His eyes cut to Carter.

Carter's pulse hammered in his ears. She probably wouldn't go for it, but he wanted to be near in case she needed him. Wanted to hear what the doc had to say, so she wouldn't hide it from him. He stepped forward as she made her way around the corner of the bed.

Mara looked at him questioningly, the cold hostility still evident.

"Can I come, too?"

"If you must." She stepped past him and out into the hallway.

Carter followed. A look of discomfort resided in Dr. Green's features. This wasn't gonna be good news. And judging by the steely sheen in Mara's eyes, she knew it, too.

"It's back, isn't it?" She asked the question so matter-of-factly. So emotionless.

"Afraid so. Her blood work wasn't good. The white blood cell count was very low. I suggest you call your oncologist as soon as possible."

She lowered her head for just a moment, her lips pressed together. Then she inhaled deeply, squared her shoulders, and smiled. Smiled! "Thanks, Dr. Green. Are we through here?"

"Yes. But please let us know if she takes a turn for the worse between now and when you see your oncologist."

She nodded, the tight smile still in place.

White-hot anger he hadn't felt since his military days flooded his entire system. Anger that Ashton had to go through this. Anger that Mara hadn't told him. Anger that she handled it all like some sort of Superwoman robot. Fists clenched, his nostrils flared with the acrid odor of smoke, and it took every ounce of willpower inside him to keep from punching a hole in the wall. With slow, deep breaths, he brought his anger under control. *Stop it, Carter, so you can help Mara get Ashton home.*

Back in the room, Carter did all he could to help Mara, who--now totally uncommunicative--teetered on the verge of panic and tears. In the end, he simply lifted Ashton from the bed and carried her out to the Escalade, Mara behind him with her purse and Ashton's things. Once he had the little girl safely fastened in her seat, he kissed her cheek. "I'll bring you a big surprise tomorrow, okay?"

She nodded weakly.

His heart plummeted to his stomach, rousing up nausea and an acidic taste on his tongue. He closed the car door, put his hands on his hips, and sucked in a deep breath of the night air to gain control of his emotions.

Mara's doe-like eyes were awash with fear and sorrow. "Thanks for all your help."

Carter nodded, then closed his eyes and silently prayed for wisdom. Though fearful of her response, it had to be said. He moved closer and took her hand. "Mara, please let God and His church help you through this."

The wall went up, her glare icy. "If there is a God, which I'm certain there is not, I do know this. You're not him." The knife-like words held surprising calm. "As for the church, it's been my experience that people act one way in public and totally different in private with all sorts of strings attached." Her lips tightened, and she punched an index finger into his chest, for the first time showing at least some sort of emotion. "There is no free ride."

His mouth fell open, and he could only stare back at her. Finally he found his voice. "I don't know what happened to make you so opposed to the church, Mara, but you couldn't be more wrong. You basically just called us a bunch of hypocrites, and you don't even know us."

"I don't recall using that word, but yeah, it fits."

Carter challenged her with his eyes. "That's the pot calling the kettle black. You act like you're something you're not when you're out in the community trying to drum up business."

The words must have struck their target, because the mask slipped for a moment before she skillfully set it back in place. "That's different. It's work."

He shook his head as a nerve in his jaw began to pulse. "Not different at all. You have no right to judge us by your past, especially since you haven't stepped one foot inside this church."

For a brief minute the wall gave signs of collapsing, but then suddenly, without another word, she climbed in the Escalade and tore out of the parking lot, leaving him to stare up the cloudy night sky with one terrified thought nibbling away at his brain. Had he gone too far?

Six

With a glance in the driver's side mirror, Carter flipped on his blinker and eased into the right lane of downtown Dallas city traffic, his mind still hashing out the same old stuff. Okay, so he sometimes came across as trying to play God. Wasn't that what Mara had insinuated that night in the parking lot when he'd last seen her? Did she still feel the same way? Is that how Chloe saw him, too?

Lord, help me out here. I just want these two to come to know You. Help me know when I'm being too pushy. The prayer did nothing to relieve the pressure that compelled him onward into the battle fray with Mara.

Across the front seat in the used Ford Taurus, Chloe's eyes were glued to her new iPhone. "Okay, Dad. The next exit is the one we need. Harry Hines Boulevard."

"Here it is." Carter exited onto the busy road, the buzzing pulse of the city already whizzing through his veins. How cool it would it be to live and work in the big city, with all the hustle and bustle. Anything to replace the mind-numbing boredom of the Miller's Creek police department.

Chloe wrinkled her nose at the line of cars in front of them. "Man, how do people put up with all this traffic?" She glanced over at him. "It'll be a few blocks, but our next turn will be left onto Medical District Drive. The children's hospital will be on our right."

Carter detected the thin wire of tension in her voice. "You okay, Chlo?"

"Yeah. Just a little nervous about seeing Ashton. What if she looks really bad? I don't wanna make it worse for her, you know? And I'm afraid my facial expression will give me away."

A sad smile tugged the corners of his mouth. Though he'd never have wished this scenario on Mara or Ashton, it had triggered a compassion in his daughter he hadn't witnessed before. He laid a hand on her shoulder and squeezed. "You'll do fine, babe. Ashton will be ecstatic to see you."

Hopefully Mara would be, too. *Lord, let it be true.*

His pulse quickened and his breathing grew shallow, a reaction not lost on him. How was it that just the thought of her had this effect? Not unlike a high school boy in the presence of a girl he really wanted to like him in return. And no matter how much he'd prayed through things since Mara and Ashton had been in Dallas, the strong and overwhelming emotions still careened through him like an out-of-control driver on the interstate. If only she were a believer and cared for him the way he already cared for her.

Chloe pointed up ahead. "There's our turn."

Within a few minutes they'd squeezed into a spot at a parking garage across from the hospital and traversed the enclosed bridge walkway across the road. Not long afterward, a nurse in Minnie Mouse scrubs escorted them down a hushed and sterile-smelling hallway to Ashton's room, where she lay, pale and sleeping.

Mara, seated on the right side of the bed, startled to an upright position when the door opened, her mouth agape. She stood, smoothing her clothes, then moved toward Chloe and gave her a hug. "Thank y'all for coming."

Carter swallowed the lump in his throat. Though she whispered to keep from waking Ashton, coarse emotion flowed beneath the words.

She faced him, as though unsure of what to do or what to say, a mixture of uncertainty and sorrow in her fatigue-lined eyes.

He closed the gap and engulfed her in an embrace. "Sorry y'all are going through this." Carter stepped back, battling emotion that threatened to swallow him whole. "You doing okay?"

"As well as can be expected."

In other words, about to fall apart.

Ashton stirred. "Mommy?"

Mara was at her side in a heartbeat, one hand on her daughter's forehead. "I'm here, baby."

"I'm thirsty."

In one fluid movement, Mara reached for a nearby pitcher, poured water and ice into a plastic cup, and then helped Ashton to a sitting position. "You have company."

A tiny smile appeared on Ashton's pale face. Once she finished the water, she handed the glass back to Mara, and her thirsty eyes drank in the sight of him and Chloe. "I knew you'd come see me."

Chloe bounced to the bed in typical cheerleader style, a stuffed elephant she'd bought under one arm, and plopped down on the bed. "Of course we did, squirt. You didn't think I'd let you have all the fun, did you?"

Ashton's smile morphed into a full-blown grin. She took the plush pink elephant Chloe offered and hugged it to her chest. "Thanks for the elephant." She sent a shy smile his direction.

Carter moved to the bed, tousled her already-mussed hair, and pressed a kiss onto her forehead. "How you doing, tiger?"

"Okay, I guess. Just ready for this all to be over."

How could he respond to that comment? Not knowing what to say, he lifted his gaze to Mara's. "We have more things out in the car. The church..." His words trailed off, fearful of her response to the gifts from his church friends.

Instead she swallowed hard, her lips taut, her eyes brimming with tears. "If Chloe doesn't mind keeping an eye on Ashton, I can help bring them up."

Relief smoothed out the jagged edges of his trepidation.

"Guess what, Chloe. Mom bought the movie *Frozen*. Wanna watch it with me?"

His daughter reached around the IV tubes to tickle Ashton playfully. "Of course, you silly goose. But you're gonna have to make room for me in that bed. It's not fair for you to have the most comfy seat in the house all to yourself."

Ashton laughed and scooted over, while Mara stepped to the DVD/television combo unit and started the movie.

A few seconds later Carter waited in the hallway while Mara shut the door behind her. She didn't even glance at him, but headed toward the elevator, her gaze lowered to the floor. Tension escalated, drawing his neck muscles into tight knots as he followed. Once at the elevator, still strangely quiet, she punched the down button. How in the world was he supposed to start a conversation with her when she obviously wanted nothing to do with him?

The elevator dinged and the doors slid open. They stepped on, and Mara pushed the floor number that would take them across the enclosed walkway to the parking garage. Only when the doors closed behind them did she look at him, regret and apology in her light brown eyes. "I'm so sorry for the way I treated you that night in the hospital parking l--"

"It's okay."

She shook her head vehemently, her eyes gathering tears. "No, it's not okay. I don't even have a good excuse. I guess I was just overwhelmed and angry, and I took it out on you." She lifted both hands to swat at tears that had escaped down her cheeks. "Thank you for coming in spite of my temperamental outburst."

"We had no choice, Mara. Chloe and I missed both of you. I felt like we were supposed to come." He stopped short of mentioning God's direction.

The elevator dinged again, and the doors slid open to welcome a middle-aged couple and an old man. Mara once more withdrew into her shell, her only sound an occasional sniff. When they finally exited the elevator and began their walk across the enclosed bridge, she opened up again. "So is this gift from the church your doing?"

"No. At church last Sunday, I mentioned that Ashton was in the hospital so people would know to pray. When they heard Chloe and I were coming to visit this weekend, they organized a group to take up a collection and dropped it off at the apartment last night." Carter stopped behind the Taurus and dug for his keys.

"You bought a new car." Mara spoke the words absently, as though her heart and mind were elsewhere.

"Just new to us. I sold the Harley."

"But your motorcycle..." Now she peered up at him, a knowing look on her face. "You loved it, didn't you?"

He nodded. "But I love my daughter more."

She released a small sigh. "What we won't do for our kids." She swung her arms back and forth for a moment and gazed around the darkened garage. "Anyway, let's get that box up to the room."

A snort sounded from Carter's nose as he unlocked the trunk. "Don't you mean boxes?"

Mara's mouth fell open. She stepped forward and stared into the loaded back-end of his car. "All this is for us?"

"And more. Chloe helped me take out all the canned goods. Didn't much think you'd have a use for them here. I'll drop them off once you return to Miller's Creek."

Both palms landed on her shocked face. "I don't know what to say."

He bit back the desire to tell her that not every church operated the same way as the ones she'd grown up in. Instead, he lifted the lightest box from the back of the car and handed it to her. Next he stacked a few wrapped gifts on top of that, picked up the heaviest box and two more gifts, and then slammed the trunk. "We'll have to make a second trip to get the stuff out of the back seat."

"You're kidding. There's more?"

"Oh yeah. Lots more."

All the way back to the room, Mara chewed her lower lip, her eyes dark and distant. But once they swung open the door to Ashton's room, she morphed into her happy and excited mom impersonation. "Surprise! Ash, just look at all this stuff, and there's more in the car. It's like Christmas!"

"All that's for me?"

Carter winked at the little girl. "Most of it, but I think some of it might be for you *and* your mom."

Mara glanced at him quizzically, then stepped to the bed where she set down the box and gifts. She picked up the remote and paused the DVD. "Let's take a look at all these goodies, and then you can finish your movie."

Dolls, toys, clothes, coloring books, and games were pulled from the boxes. For Mara, there was a soft blanket, paperbacks, and a box of her favorite chocolates he'd managed to sneak into the pile. A dazed expression that cried out 'overwhelm' landed on Mara's face. "I don't know what to say to all this except thank you. Please tell your friends how much we appreciate it."

"They're your friends, too, Mara." He spoke the words quietly, praying she took the comment in the right way. He needn't have worried.

For the first time that day, Mara smiled that over-sized grin that melted his heart every time.

"Uh, I...I mean, if you want to--uh--Chloe could, I mean, well..." Apparently her over-sized grin in combination with a melted heart also caused stuttering.

Mara raised both eyebrows, an amused smirk on her lips. "I don't bite. Spit it out."

That was all the impetus he needed to overcome the stutter. "Sure could've fooled me. I still have the teeth marks to prove it."

Her eyes rolled upward with a slight shake of her head. "Okay, well except for that one time. Now would you get back to what you were trying to say."

Carter inhaled, grinned broadly, and spurted out his comment. "I have a great idea."

Loud guffaws sounded from her mouth, and her eyes twinkled. "Nothing surprising there. You're the king of great ideas. Now what is it?"

"Why don't we order take-out pizza for the girls?"

"And--?" She crossed her arms, an indecipherable smile on her face.

"Chloe could stay here and watch Ashton so you could get away from here for a while before we have to go back."

Mara turned toward the girls, their gazes once more glued to the TV. "Well, I guess there's no point in asking them if it's okay."

A half hour later--after a detailed lecture to both Ashton and Chloe--Mara sat beside him in the Taurus, her head at rest against the back of the seat, her eyes closed, a small smile at play on her lips.

He took a mental snapshot for the long weeks of separation most likely ahead, put the gear shift in reverse, and backed out of the parking space.

"So where are you taking me?"

"How does a spa day sound?"

She opened just her left eye. "Heavenly, but you don't strike me as the spa day type."

Carter chuckled. He'd never met a woman who could make him laugh the way she did. "Not talking about me, goofy. I can always wander the streets while you're relaxing."

Mara opened both eyes and pulled herself to an upright position as tiny frown lines appeared between her eyes. "You'd do that?"

"Yeah. Why do you ask?"

She shook her puzzled face from side to side, but said nothing.

Carter pointed down the street. "We passed this little shop on the way in. Looks like they might do the girl spa thing. Wanna check it out?"

"Sure."

A few minutes later, after insuring that Mara was all taken care of, Carter exited the old building into the crowded sidewalks, grateful Dani had suggested the place along with a few folded dollars. He'd added her donation to the rest of the money the Miller's Creek folks had doled out. But would Mara accept it? He shoved the thought aside for the time being and hurried to where he'd parked. There should be just enough time for him to make a quick trip to the other end of Harry Hines before time to pick up Mara.

Though the trip to the Dallas police station took longer than expected, at least it gave him the opportunity to make a face-to-face connection and pick up the documentation needed. Should he get so lucky as to land a position--and if Mara and Ashton ended up staying in Dallas for a while--he and Chloe could be close by.

Carter hurried inside and quickly located the correct office. A woman dressed in police blues smiled at him from behind the counter. "Can I help you, sir?"

"Yeah, I'm here to pick up information about becoming a police officer here in Dallas."

She reached toward vertical file trays on her left and whisked out several papers as her eyes assessed him. "Any experience?"

"Yes ma'am, I currently work for the Miller's Creek police department."

The woman frowned. "Miller's Creek? Isn't that the little historic town everyone in Dallas likes to go to on the weekends? Where is it anyway?"

Way to go, Carter. Good way to make yourself look like a backwoods hick. "Southwest of here. I also have military experience."

"How many years?"

"Twelve."

She slid the packet of papers across the counter toward him. "Sounds like you might be just the kind of guy the chief is looking for. All the info is in the packet."

"Thanks." His heart was much lighter as he made his way back to Mara. With the time he had left, he played games on his phone in the waiting area of the spa.

When a refreshed and rejuvenated Mara appeared a half hour later, her toothy grin stretched from one ear to the other, and her face gleamed.

His breath went AWOL for a brief minute. Never had he seen a woman with such natural beauty. He rose to his feet and pocketed his phone as she approached. "Well, look who's happy."

Without warning, she just about strangled him with a bear hug, her head against his chest. "Thank you so much, Carter. I really needed this." When she pulled away, there were tears shining in her eyes. She used her long fingers to wipe away the moisture on her face. "Where are these tears coming from?"

He leaned forward, his face a few inches from hers. "They're called tear ducts." He followed the remark with a cheeky grin.

"Ha." Sarcasm dripped from the one syllable, but her happy smile stayed in place. "Thank you, Captain Obvious."

"Ready for the next part of your adventure?"

Her eyes widened. "There's more?"

"Mama Beth gave me strict orders to treat you to a nice meal outside the hospital. And nobody in Miller's Creek goes against Mama Beth and lives to tell about it."

"Hospital." The previous relaxation of her posture disappeared, and she swatted at her jacket pockets in search of her cell phone. "I need to call the hospital to make sure Ashton's okay."

Carter punched speed dial for Chloe on his own phone. Once the ring sounded, he handed the phone to Mara.

"Chloe, this is Mara. Y'all okay?"

Even from a few steps away, Carter could make out Chloe's animated and cheerful voice.

Mara's hearty laughter broke out at something his daughter said, drawing the attention of several stodgy-looking women who waited for their spa treatments. Her face glowed with happiness in spite of the disgruntled glares.

Carter's heart did an odd somersault in his chest. How good to see her smile, to hear joy in her voice.

"We're going to grab a bite to eat, and then we'll be back. You're sure y'all are okay?" Mara paused to listen, the beautiful smile still plastered across her face. "Try not to have too much fun without me. Bye, sweetie."

His heart still wasn't functioning well. Something about the rapport between Mara and Chloe just made his whole insides feel like mush.

Mara handed him the phone. "All is well, so I think I'll take you up on that offer of any kind of food that doesn't come from a hospital."

Carter grinned and offered his elbow. "What's your dining pleasure, my lady?"

She latched on with both hands. "I've been really hungry for crab legs. Do you like seafood?"

"Love it. Hold on a sec." He took a step back to the receptionist. "Excuse me. Can you give us directions to a nearby seafood restaurant?"

A half hour later Carter sat across a white linen-topped table from Mara, the tantalizing smells of seafood setting off a growl in his stomach. He took a long swig of sweet tea. Hopefully that would take care of his grumbling tummy until their food arrived. He sat down the sweat-covered glass, the ice a-clink against the sides. Now was as good a time as any to ask the question that had been on his heart and mind all day. "If you don't want to talk about this, just say so, but how's Ashton really doing? She still looks pale."

"I don't mind talking about it at all. She's doing better than expected on the new chemo. Dr. Watts said she probably wouldn't even lose her hair this time." She paused to sip her diet Coke. "She's had very little nausea, and each day she's a little stronger. If she keeps improving, the doctor said we might get to go home soon and take her treatments there."

"I'll pray for that to happen." As soon as the words slipped out, he wished them back. This avoidance of anything remotely religious was more difficult than walking on eggshells. Faith was such a huge part of him that it came out as readily as 'hello.' "I'm sorry, I--"

"No, it's okay." Mara patted his forearm, and then quickly moved her hand away. "I mean, I'm still not ready to jump on the whole religion bandwagon and church thing, but I'm grateful to everyone. Very generous."

"Oh, that reminds me." Carter reached into the right hip pocket of his jeans and removed his wallet. "This comes with all the packages." He withdrew the big wad of bills and held it toward her.

She stared at the money for a long while, then shifted her gaze to his. "You're kidding."

"Does it look like I'm kidding? This isn't Monopoly money." He gave the wad a shake. "Here, take it. It's yours."

Reluctantly she took the money. "I don't know if I should accept this, except..."

"Except what?"

Hesitation darkened her eyes. "Except I really need it to pay bills. With me being away from the office all week and unable to work and everything." Her gaze fell, and she rolled her lips between her teeth.

Carter took her hand in his own, the money still clutched in her fingers. "Don't be embarrassed, Mara. Just accept it as God's way of taking care of you through His people."

Confusion washed across her face. "But why would God take care of me if I don't believe in him?"

"Because He loves you."

"But why? Especially when I'm against him?"

"Your doubts and questions don't diminish who He is. He is love."

Their gazes locked for a long minute, her hand still in his, and then at last she spoke. "I'm trying to be more open-minded about the possibility of God, but I'm also still angry. Why would he let Ashton's leukemia come back?"

"I'm glad you're trying, but..." He couldn't say it. He just couldn't. If he did, she might not ever speak to him again. And that was a chance he just couldn't take.

At that moment the server arrived with a large tray full of food. Perfect timing. The waiter sat huge platters of aromatic crab legs in front of both of them. Carter's mouth watered as he silently prayed his thanks for the food, then cracked open the first crab leg and dipped the steaming salmon-colored meat into a ramekin of clarified butter. He raised the fork to his lips only to find Mara glaring at him from the opposite side of the table.

"You were saying?" Her enigmatic expression hid any clue of what lay behind those intelligent eyes of hers.

A knot formed in his too-tight chest, and he set the crab-laden fork on the edge of his plate. Finishing his earlier statement might prove detrimental to his health and well-being. He sucked in a big breath. "Mara, please don't. I don't want hard feelings between us. Let's just drop it and enjoy our lunch."

"I'm a big girl. Go ahead and say what you started to say."

The mouth-watering meal before him suddenly lost all appeal. Okay. If she wanted to push the issue, so be it. "How can you be mad at someone who doesn't exist?"

Seven

Good question, but one Mara had no idea how to answer. Rather than explode like last time, she picked up the chrome crab crackers and used her unexplainable and pent-up feelings to rip into the crab legs.

"Mara, please." Carter's voice pleaded softly from across the table.

She didn't dare look at him for fear of losing control of her emotions again. What was it about him that made her so weepy-eyed? "Let's just enjoy this meal, okay? It's not that I don't want to discuss it, but I don't want to spew acid like I did that night in the parking lot." Thankfully her voice didn't reveal the tremble inside.

He didn't respond, but a minute later, when she garnered the courage to look up, he sat, head lowered, picking at his food.

Guilt rained down on her. He'd done so much for her and Ashton, but the topic just wasn't one she could discuss calmly at the moment. Maybe changing the subject would help. "So how are things at the Miller's Creek Police Department?"

Still he didn't look up. "Boring as always."

"That's a good thing, right?" Mara stuck a forkful of steaming crab meat in her mouth and closed her eyes at the delicious taste. How long had it been since she'd allowed herself something so decadent?

"In one way, I guess." Carter took a meager bite of baked potato, but still didn't raise his gaze, his dark eyebrows creased into a thunderstorm-like frown. "I'm just the kind of person--"

"--who needs more action?" Yeah, she could see that about him. His military career had provided him all the excitement he needed to thrive. Something he'd never find in Miller's Creek. The thought troubled her. Was he thinking about leaving?

As if reading her thoughts, Carter finally glanced up. "While you were enjoying your spa treatment, I picked up a job application from the Dallas police department."

Mara lowered her gaze quickly, afraid of giving off signals and thoughts she needed to keep hidden, especially from him. "That's nice." A minute later, she sneaked another peek at Carter, but again he sat with his eyes averted as he rearranged the food on his plate, the creases on his forehead even deeper than before.

For the rest of the meal, Mara concentrated on her food, forcefully refusing thoughts of her still-unvoiced objections to his earlier question about God's existence. But try as she might, she could not rid herself of anxious thoughts centered around the possibility that Carter and Chloe might not be a part of their lives for much longer. Just how was she supposed to make it without them?

Only later, when they were in the car and headed back to the hospital, did she allow her thoughts to return to his question about her anger toward God. She had to do something to bring Carter out from under the dark cloud that hovered over his face. "Look, about your question about God." The words sounded both abrupt and explosive in the awkward silence.

"I don't have a question about God."

"Okay, then my anger toward God."

He glanced across the seat at her, but didn't smile or speak.

"I can't deny there's something or someone bigger than us that made the world."

"At least that's a start in the right direction."

She shook her head. "Don't take what I say as religious belief, Carter, or you'll be sorely disappointed. Even if there is a higher being, I don't believe he cares about us as individuals."

Carter's shoulders squared and his face darkened as though preparing for battle. "I beg to differ. God can't get any more personal than loving you so much that He took on human form to rescue you. He certainly can't get more personal than indwelling the lives of believers. If He's not personal to you, it's not His doing, it's yours. If you wanna get warm, you stand next to the fire. If you wanna get wet, you jump in the water. That's just the way it works."

She released a cynical laugh. "Your comment assumes the Bible is true. I believe it's just a bunch of religious rhetoric written by men."

Now his mouth fell open as he faced her momentarily. "Hang on a sec. The Bible's the most scrutinized book in all of history. It was written over thousands of years by hundreds of people who all bore witness to a personal encounter with God. People have tried to destroy it, but it's still here. The prophecies inside it--against astronomical odds--have come true with amazing accuracy. Archaeological evidence supports it. So don't tell me the Bible's not true."

Mara turned her head to look out the window, grasping for any semblance of rational thought in her head to rebut his monologue on the accuracy of the Bible. "Sorry, but I still don't buy that God cares about me."

"How can you say that after what you've received today at the hands of His people?"

She slumped lower in the seat, for the first time noticing how nice his cologne smelled. How could she explain this in a way that would make sense? "I'm grateful for everything, Carter, but to me it came from really kind-hearted people, not God."

His hands tightened on the steering wheel and his lips tightened on his face. He peered into the driver's side mirror, punched the accelerator, and swerved into the left lane of traffic.

"Don't be mad at me, Carter. If God really cared, then where was he when Ashton had to ingest that chemical poison the first time? Not only that, how could he let her go through it a second time? Why would he subject a four-year-old to something that made her vomit all day and lose her eyelashes?" The words grew more vehement and took on a life of their own as angry tears flooded her eyes and blurred her vision.

Bitterness burned a hole in her chest and erupted from her mouth in guttural sobs. "Where was he when my marriage fell apart? Where was he when I endured a painful and lonely childhood?" Her shoulders shook as more cries racked her body.

Even through the tears, she saw Carter face her, his jaw clenched and pulsing. But it was his soft brown eyes--oh, his eyes--which held an unspoken sorrow that reached across the seat and enveloped her in a soft blanket of comfort.

Carter made the turn into the parking garage, grabbed his ticket, and took the first available parking space near a window. He put the car in park, then scooted across the seat and pulled her into his arms, which only served to make her cry harder. When at last her tears subsided, Carter reached into the floorboard of the back seat and handed her a box of tissues. "God was there, Mara. You just couldn't see past the hurt you were facing. He's the one who carried you through it, and made you strong enough to endure it." He paused, obviously collecting his thoughts. "He's like the wind. You can't see it, but you know it's there."

Her heart beat faster at the possibility and hope behind his words. Had God been there, helping her through? No, she wasn't going to cave. "There's evidence for the wind, because you feel it and see the objects it blows. A personal God may be true for you, but not for me." She blew her nose.

"That's like saying gravity is real for one but not another."

Touché. Challenge rose in her chest and leaked out in her tone. "I thought you didn't like theoretical debates."

A heavy sigh escaped, sagging his shoulders. "That's the problem, Mara. You're assuming God is merely a theory. I don't see Him that way at all. He's real to me. Every bit as real as you are."

Her lips tightened. "Which brings me back to square one of why He allows what He allows." Yet another traitorous tear slid down her cheek, and she quickly brushed it away, only to have her eyes flood with more. Another one escaped. And another.

But before she could swipe them away, Carter raised a thumb and gently swabbed at her cheeks, his other arm still encircling her shoulders protectively. "All I can say is what I know to be true, Mara. God isn't behind the evil in our world. Satan is. Like it or not, we live in the middle of spiritual civil war. The good news is that only one of the forces in the battle has absolute power." He rested his forehead against hers for a moment, then pulled back.

"Well, I'd like that absolute power to answer a few questions." She shrugged away from his arms and plastered herself to the car door, her arms crossed, a soggy Kleenex balled up in her fist. "If he's the personal God you claim him to be, then surely he'd allow me to state my objections to the way he runs things."

"Careful, Mara. Don't forget who He is." His dark eyes smoldered. "I wouldn't start a fight with God. To say that He's wrong and you're right is like saying steam is higher than the water it's made of. When you argue against God, you're setting yourself against the One who gives you the ability to argue at all. Not a wise move, if you ask me." He released a heavy sigh in the semi-darkness of the parking garage. "Trust me, I find it just as hard as you do to make sense of God's delay. But I have to believe He's waiting so more people will turn back to Him. So you'll turn back to Him."

His words sharpened themselves on her bones, and set off a spark that sent angry flames searing through her veins. Mara fought against another onslaught of tears. "Spare me the religious platitudes, will you? Do you think you're telling me something new? I grew up on those lies, remember?"

"They're not religious platitudes or lies." Now the fury rattling her bones to the marrow sounded in his voice as well. "Look, I'm sorry for all that's happened to you to turn you against God, but He's not the One to blame. Satan is attacking you at your greatest vulnerability, and you're blaming it on God."

Greatest vulnerability? Her gaze flitted to his face.

Carter's eyes met hers, and he studied her with an unnerving intensity, one that somehow also brought great comfort. His expression softened, his eyes gleaming with compassion. "Oh, Mara, can't you see? The enemy knows Ashton is your last shred of hope. Satan wants for you what he wants for everyone else in the world. He wants you to hate and disavow the God who made you and loves you." His expression took on heartrending sorrow. "And you're letting him have his way."

The thought sliced through her. Could it be true? Her forehead tightened to the point of pain, and she raised trembling fingertips to ease the tension.

"God can use all this for good if you'll let Him."

The words exploded like a grenade in her brain, sending jagged-edged shrapnel throughout her body. Enough already. If God was the sort of tyrannical dictator who made bad things happen to little girls, even if it was to bring about supposed good, then she wanted nothing to do with him. The familiar coldness settled over her, bringing with it an icy calmness. She wiggled free from Carter's embrace and turned her head away, looking at nothing in particular. "If there really is a God, then he'll have to prove it by sparing my daughter's life." Her voice sounded as though miles away, and each word landed like nails in a coffin.

Relief flooded over Mara when Carter and Chloe at last headed out the hospital room door an hour later. But one look at Ashton's sad face quickly let her know that her daughter didn't feel the same way.

Tears welled in Ashton's blue eyes, and she began to softly cry. "I just wish they could stay."

"I know, sweetie, but they have to get back to Miller's Creek." Mara moistened her lips. Hopefully the next ploy would make Ashton feel better. She donned her best smile and infused her words with a teasing excitement. "I thought we'd give your father a call."

Instead of the eagerness Mara expected, horrified dread landed on her daughter's pale face.

"We don't have to call him, Ash. I just thought you might like to talk to him." Besides it was only fair that he shoulder his part of parenting his sick child, especially since he lived nearby. All throughout the long, lonely week she'd considered making the call, but something about the way her time with Carter had ended now spurred her on to carry through.

"No, it's okay. I know he's really busy. Especially with a new family."

The forlorn words ripped through even the calloused flesh of Mara's heart. Rather than give in to threatening tears, Mara shoved them deep and rifled through her purse until she found the business card with Jim's phone number. She also grabbed her cell phone, quickly dialed the number, and waited for someone to answer. Her pulse quickened with each ring. Was she emotionally ready to handle whatever might come her way?

"Hello?" The new wife's voice answered.

Mara inhaled deeply. "Hi, Shelley. This is Mara. Is Jim there?"

Silence filtered through from the other end. Finally Shelley spoke, hesitation in her voice. "Actually, he isn't. Uh, can I--take a message?"

Visions of Jim standing nearby, feeding his new wife words, sent waves of hurt and spite careening through her body. "Yes, please. Tell him that his other daughter is sick again. We're at the Children's Hospital." Hands and voice quaking, Mara punched the 'End Call' tab on her phone, then quickly moved to look out the window. Hopefully Ashton hadn't picked up on her rage.

"Don't be mad, Mommy. It's okay."

Mara couldn't respond without turning into a weepy mess in front of her daughter. Instead she crossed her arms and continued to stare out the window at the streetlights of downtown Dallas. Down below her, normal people lived normal lives. They shopped and met friends for dinner, then went back home. Would her normal ever come? Finally, she gained enough control to put her happy Mommy-smile neatly back in its place. "How 'bout a game of Old Maid?" Fitting.

"Sure."

Later that evening, after Ashton had fallen asleep, Mara picked up her cell phone and stepped out into the hallway to keep from disturbing her daughter. One more phone call to make. One she'd put off as long as she could. She pushed the speed dial number she rarely used, then leaned against the wall, one arm encircling her waist.

"Reverend Arnold's residence." Her mother's voice had lost none of its passivity.

"Hi Mama, it's Mara."

"Good to hear from you, honey. It's been a while since you called."

Same old standard conversation. Never mind that it was just as easy for her mother to call her, something she'd never done in all the years since Mara had moved away. Fresh tears sprang to her eyes.

"Mara? You still there?"

Mara leaned her head back, focused on the suspended ceiling grid, trying to find her voice. "Yeah, I'm here."

"Is something wrong?"

"Who is that?" Her father's gruff voice sounded in the background, followed by the muffled voice of her mother.

"Mara, this is your father speaking."

Out of habit, her spine automatically straightened. "Hi, Daddy."

"What's wrong?" After all these years, he still had the bulldog edge to his tone, probably from decades of calling down hell-fire and damnation from his pulpit.

"What makes you think something's wrong?"

"Because you never call unless something's wrong or you need something."

Bitter bile burned her throat, and Mara swallowed against it. He'd never been one to mince words, no matter how tactless or hurtful. Though she knew he waited for some sort of apology, she refused to give him the satisfaction. Nor would she lose her temper, no matter how badly she wanted to ream him out and hang up. "I thought you and Mama might want to know that Ashton's back in the hospital."

The line grew quiet. Finally, he spoke. "Well, I'm very sorry to hear that. We won't be able to come over tomorrow, with it being a Sunday and all."

"I know."

"But we might could come one day next week."

Not what she wanted at all. "That's not necessary. There's a good chance the doctor will let her go home soon. Arrangements have been made for her to take treatments there."

"Well, that's good. Give her our love, and keep us posted."

The tears returned. She bit her lip to hold them at bay long enough to choke out a few words. "Will do. Bye."

She slid her back down the wall to a sitting position and allowed her emotions free rein. No 'I love you.' No 'How are you holding up?' Nothing that indicated love or concern for her. Only the familiar coldness of a hard-hearted man who loved only himself.

From the driver's side of the car, Carter could hear Chloe's even breathing. She'd been sound asleep before they'd even left Dallas. Her day with Ashton, while enjoyable, had literally worn her out.

A tender smile curved his lips upward. His daughter was definitely a cheerleader. Not just for the Miller's Creek Mustang football team, but for a little girl with leukemia who needed a champion in her corner.

As was usually the case whenever he thought of Ashton, thoughts of Mara were never far behind. His mouth fell open to release a sigh. That woman could go from zero to sixty faster than his old Harley ever dreamed. One minute she seemed to be doing well, even initiating conversations on subjects she'd made taboo for him. But in the next millisecond, her anger escalated--not the molten lava kind of anger--but the kind that dripped icicles.

Oh, God, help me know how to help her.

The large green sign for their exit loomed ahead of him in the headlights, so Carter flipped on the right blinker and eased off onto the access road that led home. What he wouldn't give to have Mara and Ashton back in Miller's Creek where he could keep an eye on them. Their being so far away in Dallas was sucking the life right out of him. His rampant thoughts were immediately brought to a standstill by one over-arching question.

How much more could Mara and Ashton endure?

God, I feel so powerless.

The one-sentence prayer was immediately followed by the thought that he wasn't powerless at all. He might not have enough personal strength and control to change the situation, but he knew the One who did.

For the rest of the trip through the dark and deserted countryside, dotted here and there with the lights from various homesteads, Carter focused his attention on interceding before the mercy seat for a precious little girl and her beautiful-but-confused mother.

If only she could make the merry-go-round of life quit spinning long enough to hop off for just a few seconds to get her bearings. Late Monday afternoon, Mara leaned her weight against the shelf that intersected the back wall of her office and brought both hands to her face. She'd experienced fatigue before, and plenty of it. But never had it affected her like this. Never had she wondered if she'd have enough energy to take another step. Or another breath for that matter. And they'd only been home from their stint at the Dallas Children's Hospital for a week.

"Mommy?"

Ashton's voice brought Mara to an upright position, and she hurried to where her daughter lay in the corner of the room on the soft blanket Carter had brought. She squatted low and laid a hand on the side of her daughter's face, careful to keep her happy Mommy-smile in place. "What is it, pumpkin?"

Her daughter managed a weak smile. "Are Carter and Chloe here yet?"

The happy-Mommy smile slipped a bit, no matter how hard she tried to keep it in place. Ashton had become far too attached to the father and daughter duo. And with the differences of opinion between her and Carter, the whole situation reeked of potential disaster. "Not yet, but it's still a little early."

"Will you wake me up when they get here?" With concentrated effort, Ashton turned onto one side, away from Mara, and snuggled her head into the pillow.

A bitter taste landed in her mouth, and the Mommy-smile disappeared completely. "Sure." Mara lingered a moment to watch Ashton sleep. A sickly sweet and fruity smell rose to her nose, immediately casting her to the past. The same smell Ashton had the first time she'd gone through chemo.

Mara rose to a standing position, stepped to her office chair, and fell into it, staring darkly across the room, her thoughts once more on Carter and his unrelenting push toward God. What was she going to do about him?

She leaned her forehead into one palm. Had there ever been a day in the brief time they'd known each other where she didn't leave the conversation feeling like the Wicked Witch from the West? While what Carter offered sounded so appealing, she knew better. She'd been indoctrinated into the Christian life as far back as her earliest memories. Had learned all the Sunday School answers. Had read her Bible and prayed. But what good had it accomplished?

She gave her head a shake. No. It made absolutely no sense to travel that road again. Especially now that Ashton was well enough to be back in Miller's Creek.

A queasy feeling landed in her stomach, and Mara turned to her messy desk to take a quick sip of Diet Coke. So much to do, and so little desire to do it. It was as though Ashton's leukemia, her ex-husband's and parents' lack of concern, and thoughts of Carter had completely robbed her of every ounce of energy or motivation. And she needed both to make a living and pay the mounting stack of bills.

Mara straightened her posture and rolled her chair closer to the desk with a quick glance at the clock. Carter and Chloe wouldn't be here for at least another half hour. Plenty of time to get things shuffled into order. Then Chloe could watch the office and Ashton while Mara showed Carter the rent house she'd scrounged up earlier that day.

When the front door squeaked open several minutes later, Mara leaned back in her chair with a sense of accomplishment in her semi-organized desk. And just in the nick of time.

Carter's broad frame appeared in the doorway, along with that easy smile of his. "Hey, lady."

Ashton raised to a sitting position, rubbing her eyes, and garnering Carter's attention. Immediate tenderness softened his features, and he strode to her, knelt, and pulled her into a hug. "How's my favorite munchkin?"

A smiling Chloe appeared in the doorway. "I thought I was your favorite munchkin." She put both hands on her hips and added a hurt whine to her words. Carter and Ashton laughed while Chloe half-walked, half-skipped to where Ashton sat and knelt to the floor beside her. She put one arm around Ashton's frail shoulders. "Well, I guess if I'm going to lose my favorite munchkin status, I'd rather lose it to you than anyone else." She tweaked Ashton's nose.

A weary sigh escaped Mara as she stood. All this Norman Rockwell stuff was wearing painfully thin. She looked at Carter, who watched her with narrowed eyes, like some sort of large cat considering potential prey. "You ready to see the rent house I found?"

His eyebrows crinkled into a frown as he studied her. "Sure." He turned to Chloe. "You gonna be okay here by yourself?"

The teenager's face took on a pained look as only an embarrassed teenager could. "Of course." Chloe looked to Mara. "Anything you need me to do? Papers to file or anything like that?"

"Nope. Just take care of my munchkin." She added a little extra emphasis to the word *my*. Hopefully, Carter would get the point.

Instead it was Chloe's eyebrows that shot up, and her mouth rounded to a tight O.

Mara grimaced. Okay, time to put the Wicked Witch act to rest, at least for the time being.

A few minutes later she and Carter exited the Escalade outside the three-bedroom, two-bath rent house she'd happened on earlier that day. Mara had dropped by earlier that afternoon to familiarize herself with the layout. And she'd known almost immediately--with that same exact feeling she got right before she made a sale. This house was perfect for Carter and Chloe.

Carter folded his large arms into a Mr. Clean pose and examined the ranch-style house.

"Well, what do you think?" She gauged his expression for subtle clues.

He nodded his approval. "So far, so good. Nice yard, but not too big. Roof looks to be in good condition. No maintenance exterior. Great neighborhood. What's not to love?"

Mara started toward the front door. "Shall we take a look at the inside?"

"Lead the way." Carter followed and let out a low whistle as he entered. "Wow, this is great."

A small entryway opened up into a spacious living room with a fireplace. Mara checked her notes. "The laminate floors were installed last month." She tapped the toe of her high heel on the dark flooring. "This isn't the cheap stuff either. These floors will take a beating without showing a mark."

"That's good, because between my dogs and Chloe's cats, they'll definitely get a beating." Carter's gaze lifted to the beams that spanned the cathedral ceiling and then wandered to the far side of the room with an open kitchen, breakfast bar island, and dining space. "Really liking this floor plan."

"It does have a good flow." Mara pointed to a hallway which led out of the dining room. "Down that hallway are two bedrooms and a bath." Next she pointed to their right. "And this leads to the master bedroom and en suite."

"How much they asking?"

"Seven hundred a month."

"We'll take it." Everything about him--from his tone to the light in his eyes and his steady stance--exuded confidence.

"Don't you want to see the rest of the house?"

"Of course, but I still want it. You need to call someone to let them know? You know, before it gets snatched up by someone else?"

A fickle smile popped onto Mara's face. "Sounds like that's exactly what you want me to do. You check out the rest of the house while I give the owners a call."

A few minutes later, she traipsed to the backyard where Carter stood, hands in pockets. He peered around the shaded and well-landscaped backyard, but turned as she approached. "Never in a million years did I think we'd find a place this nice in Miller's Creek. You did a good job."

"Wish I could take credit, but it was sheer luck that I took a different route to work and saw the 'For Rent' sign." Mara yanked her head away, doing all she could not to get caught up in those soulful eyes of his. What had she been thinking? Living this close to him could be treacherous. She shoved the negative thought away, and instead focused on how nice it would be to have Chloe nearby.

"I don't believe in luck. God has a reason for everything."

The firmly-spoken words forced her attention to his just-as-firm face, but she opted not to respond.

Carter eyed her a moment longer, and then his shoulders sagged. "What did the owners say?"

"The house is yours. You can move in whenever you'd like."

He brought a hand up to scratch his stubbled chin. "When is Ashton's next treatment?"

"Wednesday afternoon." Why did he want to know?

"I have Thursday off this week. Guess I could start moving stuff in then. I know Chloe's supposed to work for you that afternoon, but do you think--"

"She can have Thursday off, but I'll need her Friday afternoon, if that's okay."

He nodded. "Think Ash will feel up to having dinner with us in the new digs on Friday evening? We might have to eat off boxes and out of paper sacks, but we'd love to have you both over."

Mara shrugged. "Who knows how she'll feel? But I do know she'll want to be with you and Chloe any chance she gets." Okay, why had those words slipped out of her mouth?

A slap-happy grin appeared. "I'll take that as a yes. By the way, we feel the same about her."

Only Ashton?

He must've sensed her discomfort, because he placed one of his bulky arms around her shoulders. "I hope you know that you're both special to us."

Mara managed a nod, but steady drips of bitterness came close to leaking through the thin veneer of her plastered-on business persona. She pulled away, headed for the door, head to the ground. "Okay, well, I need to get back to the office."

The events of the next two days fluctuated between dragging by or hair-on-fire mode for Mara, with no sign of Carter. Apparently he'd taken her not-so subtle hint to heart. She'd picked Chloe up from school each afternoon to work in the office and dropped her off at the apartment with nary a sign of him. So by the time Wednesday afternoon rolled around with the first scheduled treatment for Ashton, Mara couldn't have been more surprised when Carter strode through the door.

Though in a recliner that allowed her to watch cartoons on television, Ashton brightened immediately and clicked off the TV with the remote.

Carter sent a wary smile to Mara, but turned his full attention to Ashton. He pointed to the IV bag of chemicals that dangled nearby and shot poison into her body via a port. "With a smile that sweet, you must have sugar water in that bag."

Her daughter laughed infectiously, and a Benedict Arnold smile tugged at Mara's lips.

He stepped to the opposite side of the recliner and gingerly sat his tall frame on one arm of the chair. "You feeling okay?"

Ashton nodded, but didn't answer. A pretty sure sign that the chemo was already affecting her stomach.

Carter gave a side-nod of his head in Mara's direction. "And are you keeping your Mom in line?"

Surprisingly, her daughter rolled her eyes and shook her head and shoulders from side to side. "She won't do a thing I say."

This time it was Carter whose contagious laugh brought a smile. "Would you like the Miller's Creek police to have a word with her?"

A broad grin stretched across Ashton's face, and she giggled. "That would be perfectly delightful."

Carter chuckled as he cast a glance at Mara. "How long has she been talking like she was twenty-five?"

"Since when has she not?"

Ashton cleared her throat in a very ladylike fashion, turning both Carter's and Mara's attention her way. "Anyway, I would definitely like it if you would have a talk with her."

Carter gave a mock salute. "Yes, ma'am." He leaned close to Ashton, his voice a stage whisper. "But if you don't mind, I'll wait until I'm sure she's not armed and dangerous."

Ashton's eyes widened knowingly, her lips prim and proper, and she sent a rather precocious and snooty look at Mara. "That's certainly advisable."

After a round of laughter from all of them, Carter stood. "Well, munchkin, I've gotta be going since it's my day to pick up Chloe. Speaking of school, when do you start back?"

Mara rose to her feet and smoothed her wool skirt, intentionally focusing her gaze on Ashton. "The school district has a special teacher for homebound students. I've arranged for Ashton to begin meeting with her next week."

Carter shifted his weight from foot to foot. "Mara, could I speak with you a minute?"

Clanging bells and shrill whistles went off in her head. What was this all about? She forced her breathing to a slower pace and faced her daughter. "Will you be okay while I see Carter out?"

Ashton's eyes narrowed perceptively and her duck-lips quirked to one side, the kind of look she always assumed when something had just occurred to her. Then she giggled, grinned, and nodded.

Mara shook a warning finger back and forth. "I don't know what you're up to, young lady, but something tells me it's not good. What just popped into that head of yours?"

"Nothing." Ashton sang the words with a happy, yet secretive, grin. "And I'll be just fine, thank you. Take all the time you need."

Carter kissed Ashton on the cheek and tousled her hair. "Take it easy, kiddo."

"Okay."

As they exited the room, Mara cast one more curious glance at her daughter, but Ashton had already laid her head back and closed her eyes as though praying, her Cheshire-cat grin still in place.

"What was that all about?" A bemused frown clouded Carter's face as Mara clicked the door shut behind her.

She crossed her arms and gave a non-committal shrug, careful to keep her face a blank. "Who knows? But I'm pretty sure she's hatching a plan."

"Plan? What kind of plan?"

"I haven't the foggiest, but knowing her, she'll let me know when she's ready."

"She seems to be feeling better."

Mara nodded and lowered her gaze to the cream-colored tile floors. "Yeah, everyday seems to bring her closer to her normal self." She lifted her gaze, a feigned expression of disinterest pasted in place. "Thanks for coming, Carter. You brought a bright spot to her otherwise cloudy day, and I appreciate it. Now what was it you wanted to discuss?"

His eyes softened, but not so much that he couldn't pin her down with that penetrating gaze of his. "She wasn't my only reason for dropping by. Is there anything you need? Anything I can get for you or do for you?" Sincere concern and kindness poured from him.

Her forehead wrinkled. Why was he being so nice? Was she not sending the right body language, or was he just that inept at reading it? "Not that I can think of."

"You look a little confused."

"Just trying to figure out why you're being so nice to me." She kept her words calm and even.

He didn't respond, but based on the tilt of his head and deep breaths, it was only with great effort that he held in his comments. Which probably meant that the words confined to his mouth dealt with his faith in God. Carter lowered his head a minute, then looked back up at her, his eyes bearing testimony of profound hurt. "Guess I'd better be going. Still on for this weekend if Ashton feels up to it?"

Something deep inside lurched, as though the world had shifted at his intention to leave, but she kept her tone light. "Sure. Thanks again."

He studied her face for a long unnerving minute--until she thought she'd burst from his honest perusal--then latched onto her fingertips, leaned in close, and tenderly kissed her forehead before striding down the hallway and out of view.

Her head spinning for real now, Mara frowned and brought tentative fingers up to the spot still warm from his kiss. How long had it been since anyone had expressed any sort of affection for her? The question lingered and teased as Ashton finished up her treatment and they traveled back home to a hopefully uneventful night. Long after her daughter was asleep, Mara sat in the darkened living room, her thoughts on all that had transpired.

Maybe there was something to the Christian faith she'd refused to see based on the bad experiences of her childhood and young adulthood. Did Carter's kindness--in direct opposition to her determined attempt to keep distance between them--give evidence that maybe there was something to this faith of his? Was it possible that God really cared about people? That He engineered certain times and places and events for humans so that their paths and lives could intersect with those who could help?

She closed her eyes and leaned her head back against the plush sofa, weary of questions for which she had no answers. How could she connect with the loving God Carter believed in--one whose existence she'd denied? And would she look like a total hypocrite if she even tried?

Nine

Late Friday afternoon, Carter opened the oven door in the new house and sniffed appreciatively, the fragrant aroma of slow-cooked barbecued brisket wafting to his nose. The sinfully delicious smell watered his mouth in anticipation. Hopefully Chloe, Mara, and Ashton would like it as well. The front door slammed and brought a frown to his face. Chloe? He glanced at the clock. What was she doing home so early?

His daughter rounded the corner of the entryway and stomped over to where he stood, her cheeks flushed, her breathing heavy, and her eyes filled with tears.

"I thought you were working this afternoon." He forced his tone to low and even. Maybe that would help Chloe calm down.

"I was supposed to, but Mara--" Her face crumpled as a horrific sob tore from her throat.

His chest pounded. He grabbed Chloe by both shoulders and pulled her close. A myriad of possible options assaulted his mind, none of which were good. Were Mara and Ashton okay? "But she what?"

No answer came other than his daughter's continued sobs.

He stroked her wiry curls, praying for wisdom. Praying that all was well with Mara and Ashton. "C'mon, Sweetheart. I know it's hard, but tell me what happened."

Chloe pulled back and used her fists to swipe angrily at the tears that coursed down her red cheeks. "That witch fired me, after all I've done for her and Ashton. I was so mad, I ran all the way home."

Carter's hands dropped to his side, and his mouth dropped open. "Fired you? What for?"

She shook her head. "I don't know. I guess she had a bad day. You know how she can get sometimes."

He certainly did. Had been on the receiving end of her harsh tongue on more than one occasion. She'd been acting aloof and distant since that night at the hospital. Was firing Chloe just another attempt to push him away? Using his daughter as a pawn to deliver a personal blow? Carter strode to the dining room and yanked his leather jacket from the back of a chair. Well, whatever her motive, there was no way was he was gonna let her get away with this uncalled-for situation with Chloe.

"Where are you going?" Chloe's eyes were wide and round, and her sniffles and sobs had completely stopped.

"To give that woman a dose of her own medicine."

She ran to him, her once-flushed cheeks now pale. "No, Daddy. It's okay. Please don't."

"No, it's not okay. I've let it go on long enough." His lips flat-lined as he strode to the front door. He turned back and pointed at Chloe. "You stay here. I'll be back."

Her mouth hinged open, but no words came. The only sound was the slam of the door behind him.

In less than five minutes he pulled up outside Hedwig Realty. The buzzer went off as he opened the door, and Mara appeared in the doorway to her office. A big smile broke out on her face. "Hi. I thought that might be you."

How dare she look so happy? "Yeah. I'll bet."

Her smile faded. "You're mad."

"Am not."

Both eyebrows arched. "Well then, you need to inform your face. 'Cause you sure look mad to me."

"Just where do you get off firing my daughter?" The words erupted out of him.

Mara crossed her arms, flames flickering in her brown eyes. "And just where do you get off stomping into my place of business without giving me a chance to explain?"

The atmospheric pressure in the room plummeted, the air thick and heavy. He stared her down for another minute or two, but she didn't back down or relax her stance. Finally, it was him who conceded defeat. This little face-off wasn't going to solve anything. "Okay. Let's sit down and talk about this without the attitudes."

"I will if you will." She pivoted on the toe of one high heel, marched back into her office, and around to the other side of the desk.

Carter followed, sucking in great gulps of air to quell his ire. He took a seat across the desk from her and looked around the room. "Where's Ashton?"

"Mama Beth offered to watch her so I could get some work done."

Then for a long, awkward moment neither of them spoke, but just glared at one another, both with taut lips and wary eyes.

Carter cleared his throat. "Guess I'll start. Why'd you fire Chloe?"

She didn't answer, but swallowed hard, averted her gaze, and blinked rapidly. She finally looked up at him, her lips twisted in an odd pose. "This isn't going to be easy to hear, so please don't get mad at me."

In spite of the flurry of questions that assaulted his mind, he managed a nod.

Mara swallowed again and leveled her gaze at him. "Chloe is bulimic."

He snorted in disbelief, his head already bobbing from side to side. Chloe bulimic? Not a chance. Just an attempt on Mara's part to pass the buck.

"Hear me out before you go into denial." She paused and waited for his affirmative response.

Well, it wouldn't hurt to at least hear what she had to say before he lambasted her for jumping to conclusions. "Go on."

"The day I interviewed her I suspected as much."

He lurched forward in his chair, eyeballs bulging. "Then why in the world didn't you say something?"

She raised both palms chest-high. "I'm getting there. Give me a chance."

Carter slumped against the back of the chair and blew hard through puffed-out cheeks to release the air that had built up in his chest.

"Anyway, as I was saying, the day of her interview I warned her that if she didn't stop, she'd not only lose her job, but that I'd tell you. Today I came in the back door after a client appointment and found her two-fingering it in the bathroom."

Carter's lungs screamed for oxygen, suddenly incapable of drawing a breath or allowing one to escape, as all the air in the room went MIA. His stomach belched fiery acid into his esophagus. He brought a hand to his abs and swallowed against the horrid taste in his mouth.

"I'm sorry, Carter."

His gaze met Mara's. The sorrow in her brown eyes left no doubt in his mind that she told the truth. "What should I do?"

"Nothing yet, other than love on her, but I'm hoping this little incident will teach her a lesson."

He shook his head, deflated in every ounce of his being. "Uh, Chloe doesn't learn lessons so easily. She's a lot like I was at that age."

"What? Hard-headed?" Mara's lips curved into a wry grin. "Surely not you." Sardonic humor coated her words.

Carter attempted a smile, but fell short of the goal. He leaned forward, elbows on knees, and brought both hands to his face with a groan. "I have absolutely no idea how to handle this." If Chloe had kept this hidden from him, what else might she be hiding?

"I have an idea." Through spread fingers he watched Mara rest her crossed arms on the desk.

"Isn't that my line?"

She laughed. "Most of the time, but not in this case. First of all, I think after you talk to her about this, you need to make her life more structured."

"Just because overly-regimented works for you, doesn't mean it'll work for me."

"Oh, puh-lease. I'm not talking about locking her in her room until she's twenty-one."

Hmm. Not a bad idea, actually.

"Kids need a structured environment so they feel safe."

"Huh?" That might make sense in her world, but not in his.

"Think about it. If Chloe knows there are boundaries--and consequences for crossing those boundaries--her world will have structure. Whether you believe it or not, knowing the limits brings security. At the very least give her a curfew and a few wardrobe regulations."

The words sunk in deep. Mara, for all her faults, had just proved herself in the parenting department. "Such as?"

"No skin-tight jeans or shirts that reveal her midriff. That kind of outfit sends the wrong signals to guys her age."

Agreed. A talk he'd been meaning to have with her anyway. But how? Just the thought made him queasy. He leaned back and dropped his chin to his chest with yet another sigh. And then there was the problem of taking her shopping. The only thing worse would be the dreaded female doctor check-up.

"What's wrong now?"

He lifted his head, hoping Mara could hear and see the plea in his voice and eyes. "Would you take her shopping for more modest clothes? I'll give you the money."

"What?"

"Please. She won't go shopping with me anymore. It's always those girl questions that guys hate."

A laugh burst from Mara's mouth, her eyes a-twinkle. "What questions? Oh, let me guess. Questions like, does this dress make my backside look big?" Her raucous laughter returned. She leaned her head against the back of her chair, her hands crossed over her abdomen.

The horror he felt inside settled on his face. "Yeah. And worse."

Mara's laughter stopped abruptly. She rocked back and forth in her chair, her grinning face cocked to one side, then picked up a pencil and twirled it between her long elegant fingers, obviously deep in thought. Finally she dropped the pencil to the desk with a soft thud and leaned forward. "It's a deal, but only if you let me have her all day tomorrow for a little experiment."

"Experiment?"

"Yep, I want to hire her back, but she's going to have to earn it."

Would her plan--whatever it was--work with Chloe? Reluctantly, he nodded. "Deal." He wearily rose to his feet, suddenly feeling like he'd aged ten years in the past half hour. "You and Ash still coming for dinner?"

"Do you think it's wise, under the circumstances?"

He thought through possible scenarios, then nodded. "Actually, I think it might be good for Chloe to see that you and I are on the same page."

That huge grin of hers creased her face. "Ah, send in the back-up troops, so to speak?"

Carter grinned with her. "Yeah." He exited her office, but turned before he opened the outer door.

Mara leaned against the office door frame, her arms and legs crossed, and an oh-so-attractive smile on her lips. "See you at five-thirty."

At five-thirty on the dot, Mara--with a very excited Ashton clutching her hand--rang the doorbell at the new Callahan house.

"Coming!" Carter's deep voice boomed from inside, and a second later the door opened. He bent low and scooped Ashton up into his arms, twirling her through the air until she shrieked with laughter. "There's my girl!" He hugged Ashton's neck and winked at Mara over her shoulder.

Mara sent a sheepish smile as she entered, a luscious aroma emanating from the kitchen. "I forgot to ask if I needed to bring anything."

"Nope. It's all under control."

"Who's here?" Chloe, damp ringlets framing her face, moved up beside her dad, bringing with her the scent of strawberry shampoo. On seeing Mara, her smile faded. She instantly turned her attention to Ashton, who still clung to Carter's neck in a death grip. "Hi, Ash. What're you doing here?"

"We're having dinner with you guys, don't ya know?"

Chloe's smile was brief. She faced her father. "You should've reminded me, Dad." Her tone held recrimination. "The game starts at 7:30, and I'm supposed to be there at least an hour-and-a-half early."

Carter shook his head. "Actually, I called Heather's mom. She told me that cheerleaders don't have to be there until a half hour before."

Chloe paled. "Oh." Her lips worked like she felt the need to say more, but couldn't find words.

"And we'll have a chat later about the lying." Carter caught Mara's eye as if to ask, 'How's that for setting the boundaries?' and ushered them all into the living room, where he released Ashton to a standing position.

"You've gotten a lot accomplished." Mouth agape, Mara peered around the space. Not a box in sight, all the furniture in place, and even pictures on the wall. "Chloe, I'm sure your dad is grateful for all the help."

Carter's bushy eyebrows climbed his forehead. "Excuse me?"

"I didn't help." Chloe voice held a testy edge. "I had practice and homework on the other days, and was too upset by what happened this afternoon to do anything." She punctuated the catty comment with a flip of her curls and retreating back, then fell to the sectional sofa and picked up a magazine.

"Chloe, I need to speak with you in private. Right now." Carter barked the words, his tone laced with impatience.

"Oh, all right." The pouty teenager stood and stomped from the room, Carter hot on her heels.

"Ooh, I'll bet Chloe's in big trouble." Ashton peered up at Mara with the clear blue eyes she'd inherited from her father. "Why is she acting all huffy?"

"I think she's had a bad day."

"Well, that's a no-brainer."

Mara smiled, but gave Ashton an easy slap on her rump and raised a warning finger. "Watch the tone, sister."

Chloe and Carter re-entered the room just as she spoke the words.

Carter nudged Chloe with his elbow. "See? You're not the only person in the world who gets reprimanded for their behavior. Now what do you have to say?"

"Sorry for the way I acted." The words were somewhat reluctant, but at least she'd lost the attitude.

Carter clapped his hands together in front of his chest. "Okay, everyone. All the food's ready and on the island.

Let's fix our plates." He stepped aside with one hand held out toward the kitchen. "Ladies first."

"Thank you." Mara followed her nose to the delicious smells. "Wow. You did all this yourself?" On the island sat containers of barbecued brisket, potato salad, baked beans, and homemade hot rolls. Off to one side stood a double-decker chocolate cake.

He bobbed his head. "Yeah. I know I kind of went overboard, but it's the first time in a long time that I've had a kitchen big enough to cook in. Didn't know how much I missed cooking 'til I started all this last night."

Mara tried not to be too impressed, but it was hard not to be. "Well, it looks and smells wonderful." A man who could cook. What wasn't to love about that?

A few minutes later, they all took their seats in the dining room. "I'll ask the blessing." Carter reached for her hand and started a chain reaction around the table until a complete circle was formed. "Dear Lord, thank You for this food and for the ones You've provided to share it with us. Bless it to nourish and strengthen our bodies so we might better serve You. In Jesus' name we pray, Amen."

Just as they released hands, a cat wandered from beneath the table and rubbed against Mara's leg, mewing out a request for a scrap of food. "Ay-yi-yi-yi-yi." An involuntary shiver scuttled down Mara's spine. She scurried her legs away from the cat and waved her hands. "Shoo, kitty."

"Kitty?" Ashton's face lit like a sunbeam. She jumped from her chair, crawled under the table, and pulled the cat into her lap. "Hey, pretty baby." Her mothering voice brought smiles to the other three.

Amusement hovered in Carter's dark eyes. "You're afraid of cats?"

"Just haven't been around them much." It didn't help matters that as a child one of the neighborhood boys had mentioned how they crawl into bed with you at night and suck the air from your lungs. Mara opted not to share that information to avoid passing on her fear to Ashton. She scooted her chair away from the table. "C'mon, Ash, lets go wash your hands. You know you have to be careful about germs." She grabbed her daughter beneath the arms and hoisted her into the air, legs dangling, and hurried to the kitchen faucet.

A ginormous dog, almost as tall as she was, scratched at the back sliding-glass door. Chloe hopped to her feet and slid open the door, mischievous triumph sprawled across her features. The Buick-sized dog bounded into the dining room with a smaller yapping dog right behind. Both came straight for Mara as though delighted at the opportunity for fresh meat. Mara backed into the corner of the cabinets, heart pounding, and tried to keep a smile plastered on her face. She gripped Ashton tightly and lifted one high-heeled foot to keep the dogs at bay. Hopefully this wouldn't end like some sort of bad shark movie. "Uh...would you mind calling your dogs off before they eat me?" Her voice squeaked out in a Minnie Mouse pitch.

Carter grinned wickedly. "Ah, they might lick you to death, but they don't enjoy tough meat. Say hello to Mutt, our Great Dane, and Jeff, our mutt."

Ashton squirmed in her arms. "Mommy, let me down. I want to play with the dogs."

"Absolutely not. It's dinner time."

Between the two of them, Carter and Chloe rid the room of pets while Mara scrubbed Ashton's hands with an over-abundance of dish soap. Within a few minutes, they were all back to filling their plates and stuffing their faces.

Mara released a relieved sigh and sank her teeth into a hot roll that practically melted in her mouth. Oh man, she could fill up on these alone. "Carter, these rolls are delicious. I'd love the recipe."

"Happy to oblige. The secret ingredient is butter. Lots and lots of butter."

She stopped chewing and pulled the roll away from her mouth. Butter? If she wasn't careful, her weight would climb even more. Mara laid the roll on the side of her plate and stuck her fork in a piece of brisket so tender no knife was needed. One taste sent her over the top, and she closed her eyes to relish the moment. "The brisket's good, too. How do you get the meat so tender? Mine always comes out of the oven looking and tasting like shoe leather."

"Low and slow."

Mara frowned.

"Low heat for a long time."

"Oh." The table grew quiet as everyone focused on the food on their plates. Was it an appropriate time to address tomorrow's plan with Chloe? On second thought, why ruin the good meal with a side order of indigestion? It could wait until after dinner.

A few minutes later, Ashton put a decisive end to the silence. "Mommy, can I have a kitten?"

Mara clanked her silverware onto her empty plate. "Sweetie, pets take time, and you know how busy our schedule is."

"You mean how busy *your* schedule is." Ashton's voice held overly-dramatic inflection, and she rolled her eyes to add effect.

"I happen to think a pet would be good for Ashton."

Mara shot daggers at Carter.

A lazy grin appeared on his handsome face as he raised a forkful of creamy potato salad to his mouth. "It could stay at your office. Might keep Ash from being so lonely."

Lonely? Was Ashton lonely? The thought troubled her.

Ashton perked up. "Yeah, and it could catch that mouse you keep seeing."

Carter's eyebrows popped up and back down. "Problem solved." He forked a big wad of meat in his mouth, his face triumphant.

Two could play this game. "Chloe, I guess your dad told you that you and I have plans for tomorrow."

"Plans? What plans?" Chloe's face turned a vivid purple, and she turned a belligerent expression Carter's way. "I already have something to do tomorrow. Heather invited me over for the day and for a sleep-over."

Carter shot Mara a look that said, 'Gee thanks,' then focused his attention on Chloe. "You're going back to work for Mara tomorrow, and there will be no more of what we talked about earlier this afternoon. Right?"

Chloe didn't answer, but her stormy face said it all.

Mara caught her attention. "We start at seven in the morning."

The teenager's mouth fell open and the storm cloud grew darker. "On a Saturday? On the morning after a football game?" Her voice rose in volume with each word.

"And you'll probably want to wear some grungies for what I have planned. If you do a good job, I might consider giving you your job back."

A frown crossed Carter's face, but he said nothing and continued to chew his food.

"And what about me?" Ashton asked the question with pooched-out lips.

Carter pinched her cheek. "How about the two of us hanging out tomorrow? I could take my favorite munchkin on a date." He shot Ashton a wink that elicited a giggle.

Now it was Mara's turn to frown. This hadn't been discussed. Of course, neither had she given him the details of how hard she planned to work Chloe tomorrow. Would he know how to take care of a little girl who was very sick and needed to be watched over constantly? "I don't know..."

"I promise to take good care of her, Mama Bear."

"And if I get sick, he can always bring me to you." Ashton's face held an excitement not expressed in a very, very long time.

Carter nodded. "Yeah. What she said."

"It appears you two are switching daughters tomorrow." Neither Chloe's face nor her tone held one smidgen of excitement, while Ashton was about to bounce out of her chair from sheer joy.

"Sounds like a plan to me." Mara regretted the words as soon as they popped out of her mouth. Ashton squealed, bounced from her seat, and landed in Carter's lap, her arms wrapped around his neck.

"Yay. I can't wait." Chloe's dread expressed itself in a lackluster tone as she picked at her rearranged, but uneaten, plate of food.

Hmm. Maybe an extra portion of potato salad and two or three more rolls wasn't such a bad idea after all. Mara picked up her plate and over-loaded it with a second helping of everything, and a triple portion of rolls. And next on the menu? An extra-large slab of chocolate cake.

Ten

Dressed in an old t-shirt, raggedy pair of blue jeans, and the tennis shoes reserved for yard work, Mara hustled a barely-awake Ashton up the sidewalk to Carter's new house early the next morning. What had she been thinking when she'd told Chloe seven a.m.? There was just so much to do in a short amount of time. That's why she'd opted to start early. Today would be a bigger test for Chloe than the teenager realized, but hopefully the plan would work.

She and Ashton came to a halt outside the front door. Mara had just raised her finger to punch the doorbell, when the door opened and Chloe appeared, dressed and ready to go.

Surprisingly, Chloe sent Mara an apologetic smile, then stooped to lift Ashton--blankie, stuffed animal, and all--into her arms. "Hey, squirt."

Ashton yawned in response.

"My thoughts exactly. Y'all come on in."

Mara followed Chloe into the house.

Carter leaned against the kitchen counter, face unshaven, sipping from an over-sized cup of steaming coffee that wafted its aroma all over the space. "Morning."

Her heart leapt to her throat, but she swallowed it back into position. "Good morning."

"Wanna cup?"

"No thanks. I'll grab some at the office. Chloe and I need to get to it." Mara side-stepped over to where Chloe still held Ashton. "You be good for Carter, okay?" She glanced up at him. "You have my cell phone number, right? Just call if you--"

"We'll be fine, Mara, but if she doesn't feel well, I'll give you a call."

A tight smile landed on her lips. She must've sounded as nervous and frantic on the outside as she felt on the inside. "What do you have planned?"

"There's a small zoo in Morganville. I thought we'd start there, and then picnic at the park." He cocked his head to one side, with eyes squinted. "You do trust me, don't you?"

Trust? That was something she'd been in short supply of for some time, but, yeah, if there was anyone who had proved himself trustworthy, it was Carter. She nodded.

A wry smile lifted one corner of his mouth. "Yeah, right."

Mara turned to Chloe, whose face held calm resignation. "Ready to hit it?"

"Ready as I'll ever be." The words held just a hint of dryness.

A few minutes later, Chloe and Mara arrived at the office. Downtown Miller's Creek had not yet begun its buzz, though there wasn't one parking spot in front of Granny's Kitchen, thanks to the group of men who called themselves the old geezers. Once inside the office, Mara laid her things down and faced Chloe. "Today we're going to clean this place from top to bottom." She pointed to cobwebs on the light fixtures and ceilings. "Our first goal is to demolish those cobwebs. I'll grab a ladder while you get the duster."

As the morning wore on, Chloe and Mara worked hard and side-by-side. Sometimes they talked, at other times not, but a comfortable camaraderie existed between them in spite of the disagreement from yesterday. In addition to ridding the place of dust and cobwebs, they washed the plate glass windows inside and out, cleaned out file cabinets, shredded old documents, scrubbed the bathroom and kitchen area, and steam-cleaned the carpeted areas of the office. At around noon, Mara checked her watch and gazed over at a very tired Chloe. "Ready for some lunch?"

Chloe didn't speak, but simply nodded, the hair around her forehead dampened by sweat and her cheeks ruddy.

"Good. Me too." She grinned at Chloe. "You've done a great job this morning, so the least I can do is treat you to a good lunch. Let's shake this place."

Rather than eat in Miller's Creek, Mara drove to Morganville for phase two of her plan. Once inside Montana's Steakhouse, Mara slid into one of the faux leather booth seats across from Chloe and inhaled deeply of the sumptuous aroma of mesquite-grilled steaks. Time for some fun and relaxation. Only one less-than-savory task remained, and that was to broach the subject of what had happened yesterday.

After they placed their order, Chloe peered around the soothing interior space of the restaurant. "I always wanted to come here, but Mom said it was too expensive."

"It is a little pricey, but you deserve it after all the work you've done."

A smile broke out on her pretty face. "Thanks. I actually enjoyed it more than I expected. The office looks good, and I like how we decorated my desk area."

"I enjoyed it, too. To be quite honest, I was afraid the time this morning would be a little, um..." How should she word it?

"Tense?"

A laugh fell from Mara's mouth. "To say the least."

Chloe's laugh joined her own. "Dad threatened to ground me for two weeks if I didn't act right."

"Ahh, that explains it. And here I thought you'd come to your senses since yesterday." Mara took a sip of the Diet Coke the waitperson sat in front of her, her eyes glued to Chloe's face.

Chloe frowned, her gaze averted for a moment, before she looked back up at Mara. "I did a lot of thinking last night. I really blew it yesterday, and I acted like a spoiled brat last night. I'm really sorry."

A sense of pride and accomplishment coursed through Mara. The plan had worked. "It takes a strong and mature person to admit when they've messed up. Good for you."

Chloe nervously fingered a sweaty glass of Dr. Pepper. "Are you gonna let me have my job back?"

"That depends entirely on you."

"I promise to stop, if that helps."

A sudden rush of compassion flooded her heart. It was so hard to be a teenager. So confusing to know how to act and to be. So difficult to discover yourself as a person. Mara reached across the table and rested a hand on Chloe's arm. "As hard as it might be to believe, I know how hard it is, Chloe. I've been where you are now."

"Your parents weren't divorced."

"No, they weren't. But in my case, that didn't make things any easier." Would the situation have been any better without her dad in the picture?

"How old were you when you started--you know?"

"Making myself throw up?"

Chloe nodded, her eyes especially large in her heart-shaped face.

"Fourteen. My family moved a lot. And by a lot, I mean every six to nine months. I just wanted to fit in, and I thought if I could make myself skinny, I might be more popular." She hesitated. "When did you start?"

"Right after Mom dumped me on Dad's doorstep. I just felt like no one loved me or wanted me."

Mara's throat constricted. "Oh, Sweetheart, that's not true. I don't know your mom, but Carter loves you very much."

"I know that now, even if he does get on my last nerve sometimes. But whenever I feel stressed, the temptation is always there. I know it sounds strange, but somehow throwing up makes me feel better."

"Like you have some control?" How well she remembered that feeling.

"Yeah." A frown covered her face. "But there's also some sort of self-loathing going on at the same time, and I want to inflict pain on my parents for making me hurt."

Mara blinked against the sudden sting of tears. Their food arrived, so the conversation broke off as they doctored their baked potatoes and ate.

Chloe looked up from her plate appreciatively. "Thank you for bringing me here. The food's delicious."

"Well, I must confess it was somewhat of a selfish decision, but I'm glad you're enjoying it." Mara chewed a bite of steak as she pondered how to say what needed to be said. Once she swallowed the juicy morsel and chased it with a swig of Diet Coke, she spoke. "I want you to come back to work, Chloe, but please promise to talk to me, especially if you're feeling tempted to throw up. I'd like to help if I can."

Tears welled in the young woman's hazel eyes. "Thanks."

Definitely time to change the subject. Within a few minutes, she had the old bubbly Chloe back and engaged in animated talk about the latest fashions. After dessert, Mara drove to the mall to initiate the final phase of the plan.

As they parked, Chloe peered over at her, question marks in her eyes, her face encircled by brown ringlets. "What are we doing here?"

"Well, your dad gave me a wad of cash to spend on new clothes for you."

The teenager's mouth rounded in surprise. Then just as suddenly, her lips stretched into a smile, and she laughed. "Dad hates to shop."

"Most men do, you know. Shall we hit the mall?"

"You bet, but first let me straighten up a bit." She reached into the back seat for her backpack with one hand, while simultaneously pulling down the sun visor for the lighted mirror. Within a few minutes, she had hair fixed and makeup refreshed, like the true teenage girl she was.

The rest of the afternoon was spent shopping for several cute, but modest, outfits for Chloe, followed by a haircut, facial, manicure, and pedicure. Only as they drove up in front of the new house later that day and Mara put the car in park, did a made-over Chloe--in attitude and appearance--reach across and embrace Mara in a huge hug.

"Thank you so much, Mara. I haven't had that much fun in a long time."

Nor had she. "We'll have to do it more often."

Chloe reached for the door handle, a happy sparkle in her eyes. "I'm game if you are."

"How about...?"

Chloe looked back at Mara, and in unison they said: "Christmas shopping!" The two laughed and climbed from the vehicle, in female chat mode about the bargains they'd snagged that day.

Mara helped carry in the multiple packages, determined to get Ashton and make her exit as quickly as possible.

Carter met them at the door with a finger to his lips. "Shh. Ashton's asleep."

Chloe turned to Mara when they reached the couch where Ashton lay sleeping. "Just set those packages there. I'll come get them after I dump this load. Thanks again." Without another word, she scurried off down the hallway and disappeared into her bedroom.

Mara kept her voice to a whisper as she addressed Carter. "How'd Ashton do?"

"Fine, but I could tell at lunch that she was sleepy, so I brought her home. We watched some old Disney movies until she fell asleep, and she's been asleep ever since."

Mara pushed aside her concern at the long nap. It wasn't all that uncommon during chemo. "Thank you,

Carter." She gently lifted her daughter into her arms. Ashton barely stirred.

"How'd the day with Chloe go?"

"Wonderful. Ask her. I'm sure she'll give you all the gory details."

Carter moved to open the door, and followed her to the Escalade.

Mara snapped Ashton's seat belt securely into place and then hopped into the front seat. "Thanks again, Carter. Talk to you later." She started the engine and pulled away, eager to immerse herself in work to keep from thinking about the handsome policeman and his beautiful daughter. Since when had Chloe come to mean so much more than just a teen-aged after-school employee?

Carter stared down the street after Mara's vehicle, mentally kicking himself for not getting the words out quick enough. It would've helped if Mara hadn't snatched up the sleeping Ashton and bolted out the door, almost as if she suspected an invitation to church was imminent. Would it kill her to at least make an appearance to thank everyone for the generous gifts they'd sent?

He scratched his still-furry face and ambled to the front door, feeling more than a little lethargic. The boring afternoon with Ashton asleep had left him with nothing to do but veg in front of the TV. He'd much rather have been out doing some rock-climbing or something action-oriented.

The front door slammed behind him. "Chloe?"

Her head and shoulders peeked through her bedroom door down the hallway. "Yeah?"

Carter faced her, hands on hips. Should he just out and ask her how the day went, or should he find a back door into the conversation? He raised a hand to smooth down his hair and let it continue down the back of his neck. And why was it so dad-blamed hard to initiate a conversation with temperamental females? "Uh..."

Chloe scooted down the hallway and hugged him around the waist. She leaned her head back, a semi-smile on her face. "Thanks for the new clothes."

He grinned, relieved for the open door into the conversation. "You're welcome. Guess you had a good day?"

His daughter moved away and pounced onto the couch, her head lolled back against the cushion. "It was exhausting. You wouldn't believe all the stuff Mara had me do this morning. Dusting--including the ceiling--washing the windows inside and out, rearranging furniture, steam-cleaning the carpet--"

The world flashed red, and Carter didn't wait to hear more. He stormed out the front door in full stride toward Mara's house. How dare she treat his daughter like her personal slave? He'd just rounded the corner, Mara's house in view--and Mara gently lifting Ashton from the backseat of the Escalade--when Chloe called out behind him.

"Dad!"

He turned and motioned her forward, but kept walking, fearful of losing the chance to talk to Mara.

His daughter's employer turned around, Ashton in her arms, and closed the door with her backside. The look on her face held...

What? Trepidation? Guilt? Good. She deserved both for the way she'd treated Chloe. In five steps--anger mounting with each one--he stood toe-to-toe with her.

Her face went white. "What? Is something wrong?"

He kept his voice low to avoid waking Ashton. "Just where do you get off treating my daughter like your personal slave?"

"What?" Now her face held confusion, and sparks shot from her brown eyes.

Chloe arrived beside him, her face flushed and out of breath. "Dad, stop it. You misunderstood."

The words thudded against his eardrums, but didn't register. Instead, his gaze remained riveted on Mara. "You could've at least checked with me before you made her clean your place. Just who do you think you are?" His temper ratcheted up a notch, right along with his shoulders.

Chloe stepped between them, placed her palms on his chest, and pushed. "Dad, stop it!"

He took a step back, for the first time fully realizing that Chloe stood in front of him. "Why should I?"

"You didn't let me finish what I was saying. Yes, I worked hard this morning, but so did Mara. Everything I did, she did. Then she took me out for a wonderful lunch, clothes shopping, a hair cut, pedicure, and manicure. It was the most fun I'd had in a really long time."

Carter's eyes darted back and forth between his daughter's sincere expression and Mara's angry one.

Ashton roused, rubbed bleary eyes with both fists, and looked around at all of them. She smiled and leaned toward Chloe with hands outstretched.

The pretty teenager took Ashton in her arms, then peered at Carter. "Don't go all military on me 'til you get the full story, will ya?" She strode toward the front porch and perched on the steps, Ashton in her lap. The two started an animated conversation, complete with laughter and smiles.

Carter moved his gaze from the picturesque scene on the front porch to Mara, who now stood with arms crossed and an enigmatic expression. He cleared his throat. "It--uh, appears I owe you an apology."

Mara leaned in, a hand cupping one ear. "Excuse me, I don't think I heard you correctly."

Carter lowered his head as a chuckle escaped. "Yeah, you heard me. When Chloe told me what all you'd made her do, I thought..."

Her expression softened. "You thought I'd been an insufferable tyrant."

He released a half cough into his right fist. "Slave driver, too."

A smirk appeared. "Thanks for your glowing opinion." Without warning she punched his upper arm. Hard.

"Ow!"

"Oh, please, spare me." Mara shook out her hand, fingers spread wide. "Ouch! That probably hurt my hand more than those rock-hard muscles of yours."

A laugh rumbled from his chest as his gaze returned to the front porch. "Why don't you let them in the house, so we can go for a walk, and I can give you my real opinion?"

"I can hardly wait." The droll words fell from her lips, but even as she spoke, she moved toward the house sorting through her keys.

A few minutes later, she joined him on the curb and held out an opened tin box. "Altoid?"

"Is that some sort of hint?"

"It's a suggestion." The expression on her face relayed impatience. "If you don't want me smelling your bad breath, don't get in my face."

He laughed, grabbed a mint, and tossed it in his mouth, the zingy and icy hot taste quickly cutting through his recent bout of cotton mouth.

The sun was setting on the horizon as they headed off together at a leisurely pace, and the locusts began their nightly song. A faint whiff of burning leaves added to the fall scene as they walked along in silence. Finally, Mara initiated the conversation.

"I love this time of evening. It's so peaceful and serene. Like a perfect ending to a perfect day."

"So you had a good time?"

"No."

His brows hitched. "No?"

"I had a great time." She sent a teasing smile. "While Chloe isn't without her share of problems, she really is a lot of fun to be around. I needed the fun day as much as she did. We both enjoyed it. Even the working part."

"I'm glad." He paused, searching for words. "Sorry about over-reacting back there."

"Apology accepted."

"Did you, um, get a chance to talk to her about, you know?"

She eyed him like he'd grown horns. "Bulimia? Yes, but please don't be one of those parents that can't even put words to the problem. Call it what it is, and do it in front of Chloe. Don't treat it like an unpardonable sin. That only makes the situation worse."

Carter nodded, head down, as they strolled the neighborhood. He shoved his hands deeper into his jean pockets. Where had she gained such parenting wisdom?

She sighed beside him. "Sorry if I came across a little harsh, but it really is so important that you keep the lines of communication open between the two of you."

"I'm trying."

"I know you are."

He lifted his gaze to hers, surprised to see the depth of understanding and compassion that flooded her eyes.

"It must be hard to be the single dad of a teenage girl."

"It is. Especially since I was on TDY during most of her childhood. It's like being thrown into a box with a strange creature you barely know, who has emotional outbursts you don't understand, and mood swings that rival the Tasmanian Devil."

Mara stopped and doubled over, clutching her stomach as her raucous laughter echoed off the nearby houses. Finally she brought her out-of-control laughter to a chuckle and then a snicker, an apologetic gleam in her eyes as she bit her lip to keep from laughing more. "Sorry I laughed so hard, but that cracked me up." She paused to wipe laugh tears from her eyes and resumed the walk. "Don't take any of it personally, Carter. She's just trying to figure out who she is and how she fits into life on this messed-up planet."

He mulled over the statement. Her explanation made perfect sense. "Can't believe I'm saying this, but thank you for working Chloe hard this morning."

"You're welcome. Sometimes hard work gets our minds back on track."

"Agreed." He pursed his lips. Would she be upset if he brought God into the conversation? More than likely. But it had to be said. "It reminds me that sometimes God allows us to go through hard times to get us back on track."

The conversation ended abruptly, and the only sounds were their footsteps on the pavement and the crescendoing song of the locusts.

He sent a sideways glance Mara's way. Had he overstepped his bounds for the second time in less than half an hour?

"You know, I'd never really thought of things in that light before, but it makes sense." Her words rang out, not with hostility, but sincerity and--dared he hope--acceptance?

A light breeze could have pushed over his six-four, hundred-and-eighty-pound frame.

"Do you think that's why Ashton's leukemia came back?" She didn't raise her head or turn his way.

"I wouldn't go that far, Mara. But I do believe God loves you so much that He'll do whatever it takes to get your attention."

They walked in silence for a few more steps. Mara raised her head, but kept her eyes pinned straight ahead, her long brown hair tousled by the wind. "Food for thought that I'll chew on later tonight." She smiled at him, a drop-dead gorgeous grin that sent fireworks ricocheting around his heart. "Did I mention how much I enjoyed my time with your daughter today?"

He caught her contagious smile, and it landed on his lips. "I'm glad. Fun agrees with you. You should do it more often."

To his surprise, a pink tinge flushed her cheeks. She turned her gaze away again. "I intend to. Chloe and I've already talked about doing our Christmas shopping together later this year."

"What about me?" The words slipped out softly, before he could stop them.

Her head whipped his way. "What about you?"

"Would you have some fun with me sometime? I could use some of that myself."

Understanding softened her eyes. "I can see that. Boring job. Temperamental teenage daughter you have trouble understanding. Being a single parent."

He released his pent-up breath like a balloon losing its air. "It's so much harder than I thought it would be."

"Yeah, it is." Mara fixed her penetrating gaze on him. "I think it would be good for the two of us to plan a fun day. Platonically speaking, of course."

"Of course. And I just happen to know where we can find you some free baby-sitting. How about next Saturday?" His heart thudded in his chest. Was this really happening?

"Sounds good to me. What's on the slate?"

"That's for me to know and you to find out."

Mara's eyebrows raised perceptibly, and she lifted one finger. "May I just remind you that I do not jump out of airplanes."

Laughter sounded from deep in his chest. "I'll keep that in mind. Why don't we head back to the house and let me treat us all to burgers?"

She didn't answer with words, but her full-blossomed smile appeared.

One that left him weak in the knees. Would his next question make her smile disappear?

Before he could squeeze out the words, Mara blurted out: "Would you and Chloe mind picking us up for church in the morning? I'd like to personally express our thanks to everyone for their help."

Eleven

Jumbled thoughts battled in Mara's brain and took her pulse on a wild gallop as she and Ashton followed Carter and Chloe up the steps to the massive double doors of Miller's Creek Community Church. What had she done? And why this unexpected panic attack at the last minute? The red-brick building with enormous white pillars and beautiful stained glass was picture-perfect from the outside and most likely just as gorgeous on the inside. But churches weren't made of bricks and windows and stained glass. They were composed of people. People who could sometimes be mean-spirited and hateful. At least that had been her experience.

"You okay?" Carter's question of concern pulled her from her troubled thoughts.

She sent a trembling grin, one hand to her queasy stomach. "Yeah, just a few nerves."

He reached over and patted her on the shoulder, a comforting smile on his lips and assurance in his eyes. "No need to worry. I'm here."

Yes, he was. That thought alone was enough to bring her breath and pulse rate closer to normal. Mara squared her shoulders, bolstered by his encouragement. She was here for two reasons only. First was to thank these people for their generosity. The second reason was more selfish. She had to see for herself if this church leaned toward her father's brand of religion or toward the loving relationship with God Carter believed with every pore of his being. That was all there was to it. Nothing more.

Within a minute, they stood inside the church foyer. Steve Miller, the mayor and head honcho of Miller's Creek, dressed in his typical garb of western shirt, jeans, and boots, greeted them immediately. "Hey, Mara. Carter. Girls. Good to see you here."

Steve offered his hand, and Mara shook it. "Thanks."

He bent low to speak to Ashton. "Dani is always talking about what a sweet and smart girl you are."

"Thank you very much. Miss Dani's a good teacher. And so is Mama Beth." Ashton offered her hand like a miniature grown-up.

Steve laughed, gave her hand a shake, then straightened his tall, lanky frame. "Y'all follow me, and I'll find you a seat."

Everything blurred, and an involuntary shudder trickled down her backbone as they entered the sanctuary and moved down the crowded aisles where people talked and mingled. Scenes from her childhood flashed before her eyes, and she could almost picture her father on the preacher's pew in front of the choir loft, his stern gaze warning her to be on her best manners. She breathed in deeply and sent a polite smile to Steve as she took a seat between Carter on her right and Ashton and Chloe on her left.

Carter rested an arm on the pew behind her and leaned close. "Your face is whiter than a sheet. Sure you're okay?" He whispered the words, then leaned back to study her.

"Trying to be. This just brings back lots of memories." She paused to catch her breath which suddenly seemed in short supply. "And not good ones."

His eyebrows met in the middle of his forehead, and his soft dark eyes searched hers. "Sorry. Anything I can do?"

"Just stick close. Please."

Once more he sent a reassuring smile. "You know it. Just remember these are normal, everyday people. People you come into contact with all the time out in the community."

She nodded and focused her attention up front where the music minister and the choir entered. The minister moved to a guitar and slid the strap over his head, then stepped to a microphone. "Good morning."

The congregation settled in their places and shouted out their greetings in return.

Instantly, Mara was transfixed. This was nothing like what she remembered. She gazed around the room. Only Otis Thacker boasted a dark suit and sour-grape expression. The rest seemed genuinely happy to be here.

The music started, and immediately people in the congregation began to sway and clap with the slow beat. Words popped up on a screen behind the choir loft and on either side of the baptistry. Within a few seconds, beautiful music filled the air and sounded from all around her.

Ashton tugged on her left hand, her smile wide and bright.

That one act gave Mara the courage to catch her breath, raise her gaze, and do her best to join Carter's booming baritone voice. But soon she stopped. Not only because of her lousy singing voice, but because the lyrics had taken on a life of their own in her heart. Words about how God was peace, joy, and life, and how death had lost its sting, dripped hope into the darkened recesses of her soul. Then, in what seemed like a triumphant shout, the music climaxed, and the congregation sang about running to the arms of God. They lifted hands above their heads and raised their faces to the ceiling in gratitude and praise.

Mara sneaked a peek at Carter. His face glowed from an inner light, and that same confidence she'd witnessed on previous occasions radiated from him. His confidence didn't rest in himself, like so many cocky and arrogant men in her past life, but rested in something, or rather Someone, bigger than all of them.

The song ended. Matt and Gracie Tyler stepped from the choir loft, picked up mics, and moved to stand on either side of the music leader as instruments sounded. Their voices blended in beautiful harmony as they sang about God's faithfulness, His angel armies, and no need to fear. Again Mara stood spellbound.

As the song came to a close, Carter peered over at her, and his expression softened. He reached up a thumb to gently flick tears from her cheeks. Had she been crying? When had that happened? And why?

A man she could only presume was the pastor moved behind the pulpit, a joyous smile on his face. "What a glorious way to start off our worship."

Hearty amens from men and women alike sounded throughout the space.

"Before we pray today, I understand we have a very special guest."

Mara's heart fluttered. Oh, please, don't let him call me to the front. Shadows of the forced testimony times from her childhood crept in, once more bringing darkness.

"Ashton, would you mind coming to the front so everyone can see who we've been praying for?"

A self-important grin appeared on her daughter's face as she stood and stepped past her and Carter to the aisle.

Now Mara's pulse pounded like a bass drum in her head. Her baby girl was headed to the front. Of a church. Her breaths came in short, shallow spurts, and her mouth went dry.

Carter gave her a reassuring side hug.

Mara breathed deep, forcing the panic attack away.

The church broke into uproarious applause as the pastor handed her daughter a microphone. "Ashton, we're so glad you're doing better."

"Thank you."

"We want you and your mom to know that we've been praying for you and will continue to do so."

For some reason unbeknownst to her, Mara rose to her feet. Instantly Carter, and then Chloe, stood as well, following her lead. Mara moved out into the aisle, Carter's heavy footsteps sounding behind her as the congregation applauded some more.

Matt grinned broadly at her from the stage and handed her a microphone.

Mara faced the congregation, Carter and Chloe still close beside. What she wouldn't give for a Diet Coke to rid herself of the nasty white glue coating the roof of her mouth. With trembling hands she brought the mic to her mouth. "Ashton and I'd like to express our gratitude for your prayers and generosity. We really appreciate it."

The smiling congregation rose to their feet, applauding once more.

The pastor smiled at her, nothing about him one whit like her father. "Our pleasure, Mara. Please consider this place your home and these folks your family."

Home? Family? The smile that had previously held in place now slipped, and she handed the mic back to Matt. "Thank you." She mouthed the words, grabbed hold of Ashton's hand, and moved down the steps and back to her seat.

In the minutes to come, Mara comprehended very little, her thoughts replaying the uncomfortable scene that had just unfolded. Carter continued to sing, but also cast anxious glances her way. Only when the pastor returned to the pulpit was she able to gain control over her wayward thoughts.

The short balding man opened his Bible and smiled at the crowd. "If you'll notice in your bulletin, our passage today is found in Luke 15:11-32. This is familiar to most of us, the parable Jesus told about the prodigal son." He went on to put in everyday language--so simple even Ashton could understand--that a prodigal was someone who had wandered away from God.

The pastor read the passage, then turned once more to the congregation. "First, let's look at the son, the one who wanders away, who travels to a far country, and misspends his inheritance. Notice that the passage doesn't give his reasons for leaving. But based on what he does next, we can only assume he was motivated by greed and selfishness."

"Next, notice the consequences of his choice. Famine, poverty, hunger. Not exactly what he'd expected. But finally he came to his senses and considered returning to his father's house as a slave. What would we call this new attitude of his?"

At first the church was silent, then Andy Tyler called out: "Humility."

The pastor smiled. "Not something that comes easy to us. And in our culture, humility isn't often touted as a virtue. Returning to his father meant humbling himself to admit that the path he'd chosen hadn't been the right one. The religious word for this humble return and admission is called repentance."

Mara let the words sink in deep. How many times had she heard her father, face bright red and angry, pound the pulpit and yell the word "Repent!" Somehow the new definition in her head didn't jive with her father's version.

"Now let's take a closer look at the father in the story. Notice that he's standing, not sitting, not off doing other things. And not only is he standing, but he's looking, not at his to-do list, not at the work of his estate. He's looking in the direction of his son's departure." He pointed down the aisle as if someone had just walked in the back door. "And that's when he sees him."

Mara swallowed against the sudden lump in her throat.

"He doesn't say, 'I think I'll teach that boy a lesson and make him come begging to me for all the hurt he's caused.' Instead, he sprints toward his son, heart as light as his feet. And before the prodigal goes down on his knees to beg for a job, the father embraces him with strong sturdy arms and a heart of love." The pastor's voice cracked with emotion.

Tears pooled in Mara's eyes. Oh, how she longed for that kind of love from her father.

The man on the platform bowed his head and procured a hanky from his pocket, dabbing his eyes before he once more looked up. "Most of us realize the symbolism of this passage."

Symbolism? Mara lowered her gaze to the Bible on Carter's knees and re-scanned the verses.

"The son is you and I. Even those of us who profess Jesus as Savior and Lord can easily be swayed by the pull of lesser things--money, greed, selfishness, pride, our own way--rather than the way of obedience to the Father." He paused between each item of his list, as though allowing time for personal thought. "But hopefully, we all reach a place of realizing our debt, our poverty, our hunger. I pray that we realize our sad state in a far country apart from the Father." His volume increased, but not in red-faced anger. Instead his expression had taken on a profound sorrow that clawed at her heart.

He smiled kindly. "I hope we humbly decide to return to Him."

Her pulse quickened once more. Had her life become the far country he spoke of? In an instant she knew it to be true. But still questions remained in her heart and head. Questions she needed to sort through, preferably with someone like Carter.

The pastor moved behind the pulpit and closed his Bible. "We won't be having an altar call this morning, but I want you all to know my door is always open. Not only that, but the people of this church who work with and around you in this community are also available for your questions."

Mara's eyes opened wide. How had he known about her questions?

"But most importantly, know this." He held up one finger. "If you've wandered from God, if you're living in a far country apart from Him, if life is pressing down so hard you feel like you'll burst from the pressure, turn back to the Father. He's not a distant and disinterested God. He's not so busy doing something else that He doesn't know everything about you. " He paused, his eyes scanning the crowd. "He's waiting. And He's specifically waiting for you to return. He won't slap handcuffs on you and make you a slave. Instead He'll meet you halfway with a glorious hug. He'll give you a robe of white in exchange for your tattered rags. Then He'll throw the biggest 'welcome home' party you've ever seen."

Why? Why would He do that for somebody that had turned their back on Him?

"And He'll do it all because He loves you. Let's pray."

Her heart ached with an intensity she hadn't seen coming from a brief church service. Mara heard none of the prayer, so focused was she upon the story and its implications on her life.

Once the prayer ended, Carter laid a soft hand on her shoulder and pulled her to his side gently. "You okay?"

All she could do was nod. Then suddenly, they were surrounded by a throng of people, telling her how happy they were that she'd come to church, relaying stories of how God had worked miracles of healing in their lives, offering hugs and prayers, encouragement and love. Though the combined scents of various perfumes and colognes melded together in a way that made her head swim, she did all she could to return the kindness of these people and relay her gratitude.

Finally the throng thinned, and Mama Beth stepped forward to give her a hug. "Oh, Mara, words can't express how glad I am to see you and Ashton here." Mama Beth released her hold and leaned down to hug Ashton, then stood and returned her gaze to Mara and Carter. "I'm having lunch at my house with all the gang and then some. We'd love to have you join us."

Ashton jumped up and down, her blond curls bouncing. "Oh, goodie. Can we please go, Mommy?"

Mara smiled at her daughter, then looked to Carter. "Depends on if Carter and Chloe have other plans."

Carter grinned. "Nope."

She faced Mama Beth with a happy smile. "It appears you can add four more to your guest list."

Carter escaped to Mama Beth's peaceful front porch with its rocking chairs and porch swing while Mara joined the ladies in the kitchen to set up for lunch. He breathed deeply of the fragrant fall day, still warm, but with just enough of a cool nip to actually make it seem like fall.

The air refreshed him and chased away the remnants of cobwebs from the painful morning at Mara's side in church. He'd seen and felt it all, her expressive face and eyes a dead giveaway to the battle that raged within. But he'd also experienced her raw courage, even if a bit wobbly, as she'd moved to the front to sincerely thank the people of Miller's Creek for their help.

How could that woman be both an open book and an intriguing enigma at the same time?

The front screen door squeaked. Matt and Chance exited the house and moved toward him.

Matt grinned. "I thought we might find you out here." He nodded his head to the house. "Too much commotion in there for you?"

Carter shook his head. "Nope. Just feeling a little overwhelmed. Thought fresh air might help."

Matt studied him, and a knowing look took up residence in his eyes. "Uh oh."

"Yeah, I see it too." Chance also eyed him as though he'd just made an important diagnosis. "You're in love, brother."

Carter gave his head a shake. "No. I care about her, but I refuse to fall in love with a non-believer."

"Don't sell God short." Matt spoke the words softly, but with confidence.

Chance nodded. "Dakota and I are living proof God can work miracles. Keep your chin up."

The door squeaked again as Steve and Andy joined them on the porch.

Andy laughed. "Are we a bunch of wimps or what? Like they always say, 'if you can't stand the heat, stay out of the kitchen.'"

They all chuckled.

As usual, Steve was the first to sober, always the one a few steps ahead. "Carter, does Mara need anything?"

He raised both arms and shoulders. "I've asked the same question, but she won't answer. I do know that she really needed the money we gave her last time."

Steve frowned and lowered his head, lost in thought.

"This isn't exactly the best time of year for selling real estate." Matt intoned the words as he leaned against the porch railing and crossed his arms.

Steve nodded his agreement. "My thoughts exactly."

"And insurance won't cover all her medical expenses." Chance, the medical expert in the crowd, offered his two-cents' worth.

Within the house, the bustle of feet sounded and made its way to the front door. Mama Beth appeared in the doorway and swung open the squeaky screen door. "Shame on you all for retreating while the women do all the work. Lunch is ready, no thanks to you."

They all lined up like the little tin soldiers they became with General Mama Beth in charge. As they filed past, Andy was the only one with the guts to kiss her on the cheek. "Don't be mad at us. We knew it was all in your more-than-capable hands." He sent a dimpled grin to add emphasis to his words.

Her face stayed stern for only a second before her lips twisted into a smile, and she let out her familiar cackle. "Charmers, the whole lot of you." She bustled off toward the new addition at the back of her turn-of-the-century farmhouse. "Don't know why we put up with any of you. Guess 'cause we love you."

Once in the new space, a room almost as big as the rest of the house, Carter waded through the delicious smells of Mama Beth's renowned cooking and up beside Mara, who stood demurely in the blue-green suit that complimented her reddish-brown hair and light brown eyes.

As Mama Beth herded the kids to long folding tables on the other side of the room, Mara leaned close and whispered. "Isn't this room gorgeous?"

He stared up at the lofty cathedral ceilings with white-painted framework exposed and then let his gaze drift to the over-sized stone fire-place at the far end. Beautiful light cascaded into the space from the bank of windows on both sides. "Yep." But none of it could compare to her beauty.

His lips immediately pressed together in consternation. This had to stop. And now. Somehow he had to find a way to protect his heart--and Chloe's--should Mara refuse to return to the One who made her and loved her more than he ever could.

Twelve

The words from Monday's call with Dr. Watts still rang in Mara's ears. "It's nothing to be concerned about at this point, but there's no evidence that the chemo we have Ashton on is working."

How could she not be concerned? And after bumping Ashton's treatments from once to twice a week on a new chemo, Ashton had grown progressively weaker and more sick than ever before. So weak and sick they'd canceled their sessions with the homebound teacher. To make matters worse, her baby girl's silky strawberry blond curls weren't falling out by clumps, but by handfuls.

Mara propped her head on her palms Friday afternoon, elbows rested on her desk, as she stared at the bleak figures in her checkbook, then peered over to where Ashton lay sleeping on a pallet in the corner. The quickly-escalating medical bills had eaten into her savings. It didn't help matters that November through February were the worst months for real estate. Just how was she supposed to meet their expenses with very little savings and no income?

She swatted at angry tears and leaned back in her chair. It was just like God to deal her Monday's blow the day after she'd decided to go to church. Why had she even bothered?

A sleepy yawn escaped. Maybe staying up until two a.m. hadn't been such a wise decision, but her research into potential treatments somehow helped her cope. If the current medication didn't work, she'd already pinpointed a new experimental treatment, one she'd pass on to the oncologist in their next weekly phone call.

The front door buzzer sounded, so she rose to a standing position and hurried to the office door to prevent whoever it was from waking Ashton.

Carter and Chloe moved toward her, Chloe with smiles, Carter with a sort of edgy wariness she'd not seen in him until the past Sunday after lunch at Mama Beth's house. Almost as if he was no longer interested in a friendship with her. Like he needed distance.

Mara raised a finger to her lips and whispered. "Ashton's asleep. She had a pretty rough night."

Now both their faces registered concern.

Fiery compassion smoldered in Carter's dark eyes. "The new medicine's making her sick?"

"Yeah."

A slight whimper sounded from Chloe as she moved to her desk and plopped down in the chair.

"Sorry. I didn't mean to upset her." Mara lowered her gaze and draped gangly arms about her waist.

"No worries. Just proves how much she loves Ashton."

"Thanks for picking up Chloe and bringing her here. It's hard for me to cart Ashton around when she feels so bad. Especially since..." She let the words dwindle away. Talking about Ashton's hair wasn't going to help matters.

"Since what?"

An ache landed in her throat. It was such a vain thing to be worried about. Finally she squeaked out the words. "Her hair."

Chloe's head snapped around in their direction. "She's losing her hair?" A horrified expression covered her pretty features, her eyes big and round.

For some unknown reason, Mara half-smiled. Spoken like the woman-child she was. "I know there are more important things, but yesterday I found her crying in front of the bathroom mirror." Without warning, a half-cry fell from her mouth.

Carter immediately pulled her to him, his head leaned against hers. "I'm so sorry, Mara."

"Mommy?" Ashton's voice sounded from behind them. "What's wrong?"

Mara instantly bolted to attention, fingers rapidly dispensing tears from her face. She turned to Ashton, who leaned against the office door, and cranked up her happy-Mommy-smile. "Well, it's about time you woke up, sleepyhead!" She hurried over and lifted her baby girl into her arms, the sickly-sweet smell of death still clinging to her. "I was just telling Carter and Chloe how tired I was. Nothing for you to worry about." She tweaked her daughter's button nose.

Ashton didn't seemed convinced. Instead she wriggled free, ran to Chloe, and snuggled into her lap.

Chloe stroked her balding head and whispered something in her ear that made the little girl giggle.

Carter sent a sad smile, then laid a hand on Mara's shoulder. "You look tired."

"I am. I've stayed up late every night this week looking for treatment options."

"Find anything?"

"Yeah." A sneeze sneaked out her nose.

"Bless you!" All three of the others chimed in chorus, then Carter spoke. "You need to take care of yourself, Mara."

"I'll be all right."

"We still on for tomorrow?" Carter asked the question, but without his normal enthusiasm. Was he looking for a way out?

"I don't know." Mara glanced to where Chloe and Ashton sat, both of them staring back at her. "It's been a rough week, and I'm just not sure I should leave h--"

"Mommy, you promised Chloe could keep me tomorrow. You always tell me to keep my promises."

"Yeah, but..."

Carter squeezed her shoulder. "She's right, and you know it. Chloe has a cell phone. We can check in as often as you'd like." Still the smile didn't reach his eyes like it had before. And fatigue lined his face.

"Yeah, and you don't want me mad at you again, either." Chloe tilted her chin defiantly.

Mara laughed in spite of everything. "Okay, okay. I know when I'm outnumbered."

Saturday dawned bright and beautiful, a cool nip in the air, but without gusty winds or being uncomfortably cold. Carter and Chloe arrived mid-morning. Chloe clutched a bulging bag and made a beeline to where Ashton lay on the couch. "Hey, squirt, look what I brought."

"What?" Ashton weakly pushed herself to a sitting position, her eyes focused on the bag.

"We're gonna play dress up!" Chloe reached in and removed a tiara, some fairy wings, a basket of make-up, and a long blond wig.

"Mommy says I'm too young for real make-up."

"Well, today's special." Mara sent the teenager a grateful nod. How thoughtful of Chloe to try to make Ashton feel beautiful.

Carter eyed Mara from head to toe. "You're dressed exactly right for what I have planned."

She peered down at her old sweater, blue jeans, and tennis shoes. "And just what do you have planned?"

"Like I said before. That's for me to know and you to find out."

"No jumping out of airplanes, right?" Mara couldn't help the wary tone.

He held up two fingers in a peace sign. "Scout's honor."

Mara smirked. "Well, you just proved you weren't a Boy Scout. It's three fingers, not two." She moved to the couch to get her jacket and bottle of water, then dropped a kiss on Ashton's head. "You guys have fun, and don't hesitate to call if you need us."

The bored teenager look instantly appeared on Chloe's face. "Dad's already given me the drill-down."

"Oh." Mara grinned, suddenly anxious to flee from illness and the threat of death. Immediate guilt pricked her heart at the desire for escape. "Well, I guess you have it all under control then."

"Definitely. Now will you two get out of here so the fun can commence?"

Mara shrugged on her jacket. "Okay. Your not-so-subtle hint has been received." She strode to the front door, Carter right behind, an amused gleam in his eyes that matched her own.

"Caddy or Taurus?" Mara jangled her keys as he closed the door behind him and checked the lock.

"Definitely Caddy. Just need to get a few things out of the back of the car."

Carter opened his car trunk and removed harnesses, ropes, and a small cooler, then placed them in the back of the Escalade.

"Um, what is all that?"

He shrugged and sent a feisty grin.

Mara sighed. "I know, I know. That's for you to know and me to find out." Severely questioning the decision to give him control of her life, she climbed into the passenger side of the car.

Fifteen minutes later they pulled onto a dirt road that led to the rodeo grounds. He came to a stop in the empty parking lot, and studied her face. "Don't worry, Mara. I promise to take care of you."

Okay, that was a loaded statement. "Who's worried?"

He chuckled. "You are. Judging by the expression on your face, I'd say your nerves are stretched to a ten out of ten." Carter opened the door and lowered his long legs to the ground, quickly traversing the distance to her side of the car. He swung open her door and bowed, one hand across his waist, the other extended. "My lady, if you'd be so kind as to escort me on my journey, I'd be eternally grateful."

She climbed out with a snicker. "Whatever."

He gathered the ropes and harnesses and slung them over one shoulder, then headed toward a well-worn path that led uphill.

Mara followed. After several minutes of climbing, her lungs pleading for oxygen, they arrived at the top of a rocky bluff that overlooked the rodeo grounds and Miller's Creek. Fall had painted the area in rust and gold, and the country town of Miller's Creek glowed like a sparkling gem beside the snaking creek. A lovely place to raise her little girl. She shook off ensuing and desperate thoughts and focused her attention on the scene below. "Wow, this is beautiful. How'd you find this place?"

"By talking to the locals." Carter dropped the ropes atop a large boulder and handed her a harness. "Here. Put this on." He also tossed a pair of leather gloves her way. "And these."

She took the mess of nylon straps and buckles and watched while he stepped into his own harness. Following visual cues, she managed to put it on the same as his, then pulled on the gloves. "I did mention that I'm not jumping out of an airplane, right?"

"More than once." Carter stepped close to make sure her buckles were securely fastened, then picked up one rope and, in a flurry of movement, secured it to the thick trunk of a live oak tree and checked it by pulling against it with the full force of his weight.

Her mouth went dry. "No jumping out of airplanes."

He shook his head with a laugh. "Do you see an airplane?"

A relieved smile settled on her lips. "No."

"Okay, then. Besides, who needs an airplane?"

The smile faded, and Mara turned her head, eyeing him with a sideways gaze. She cleared her throat. "Let me be a little less specific. No jumping. Period."

"Aww, c'mon. You're taking all the fun out of it." Carter secured a second rope to another large oak and tested it the same way. "We're not jumping out of an airplane." He sent an evil grin. "We're jumping off this cliff."

Mara carefully stepped to the edge and peered down. Big mistake. The scene below blurred as her head swam and pulse quickened. "Uh, no. You go right ahead. I'll meet you at the bottom, going down the way I came up."

"You're the one who said you needed a little fun in your life. Seems to me that this might just be a good way to accomplish that goal."

She moistened her lips. "I did say that, didn't I?"

Carter fastened his steady gaze on her. "Look, why don't we sit down and talk for a bit until you've had a chance to calm your nerves? I promise you'll be safe. I'm right here with you, and I've done this thousands of times."

"Thousands?"

"If not millions." He moved to a nearby boulder, sat, and patted the rock. "Come have a seat, and let's talk."

She obliged.

"Talk to me about you."

"Me?"

"Yep. How is Mara?"

She sent a mock glare. "Why are we talking about me in third person?"

"Because Carter enjoys talking about Mara in third person. Now quit stalling. How are you?"

Mara considered his question. How was she? One word pretty much summed it up. "Mara's angry."

"At?"

"God." There she'd done it. Said what was on her heart, though in spite of his upcoming lecture.

"Understandable."

Her eyebrows leaped upward. "Really?"

"Yeah, really. I've been doing a lot of thinking since our conversation in Dallas. If I were in your shoes I'd for sure be asking questions. In fact, I've already asked several."

Ask God questions? Was that allowed?

"Trust me. God's big enough to handle your anger, your doubts, and your questions." He stood and moved to the smaller of the two trees and ran the rope through a few places in his harness. Next he motioned her over and did the same for her, then checked every connection a second time. "I still believe we can't make demands of Him, but have you tried asking those questions in prayer?"

No. She'd pretty much just slammed the door in God's face, especially since Monday's bad news. She shook her head from side to side.

"Maybe you should." He backed to the edge of the bluff and casually leaned his weight off the side.

Her air supply suddenly cut short, Mara gasped and grimaced.

"It's okay, Mara. I'm connected and secure." He sent a gaze loaded with intention. "And so are you."

Thoughts spun in her head. Were they talking prayer or jumping off a cliff?

"Come stand beside me."

She gulped, inhaled a deep breath, and released it slowly as she moved to the edge of the steep drop-off.

"See how I have my right hand underneath and behind me?"

Mara nodded.

"You do the same, and put your left hand on the rope in front of you."

Though fear and doubt viciously attacked, she followed his instructions.

"Good. Now back up slowly to the edge of the rock and lean back."

The backing up was no problem, but lean her weight off the side of a cliff? "Um, I know this might be your idea of fun, but not so much for me." A tremor in her voice confirmed the truth of her comment.

"You can do it. Sometimes life requires trust in something that doesn't make much sense."

Yeah. Okay. Now she was certain he wasn't referring to rappelling.

"C'mon. You can do it." His words, his eyes, his expression, everything about him exuded the trusting confidence she so envied.

"Your confidence is annoying. You prance about like you're not afraid of anything." Her words held a snappish edge.

Even behind his aviator glasses, she felt his glare. "Let's get two things straight. First of all, any confidence I have is not in myself, but God. And I have never, nor will I ever, prance."

She laughed, but still she couldn't force her shaky legs to trust the rope with her weight. After all, she had a daughter to think about. If anything happened...

"You see how all this is supporting my weight, Mara?"

Mara nodded.

"Who weighs more, you or me?"

"My guess would be you, but what are you getting at?"

"If mine will hold me, yours will hold you. Do it."

She gulped in a great swallow of air, squeezed her eyes shut, and pretended she was simply taking a seat in her office chair.

When she finally pried her eyelids apart, Carter's face beamed at her. "I knew you could do it."

Ocean waves roared in her ears. Without shifting anything but her eyes, she glanced on either side of her body, the rope stretched taut in front of her. "I did it."

"Yep. Wasn't that difficult, now was it?"

She relaxed her tense shoulders. "Not as hard as I expected."

His eyes softened. "Neither is talking to God."

"Are you just gonna leave me dangling off the side of this hill while you spout religious stuff?"

Now his expression registered profound hurt.

"I'm sorry, Carter."

He didn't reply, but clenched his jaw as though once more holding a multitude of words hostage behind his teeth.

Mara thought through all he'd done for her, how he and Chloe had tirelessly helped with Ashton, how he took care of her and expressed compassion when no one else did. "I'll try."

His head jerked toward her, questions in his eyes. "What'd you say?"

"I said I'll try."

"You mean it, or are you just saying it because you feel guilty?"

"I don't say things I don't mean."

A slight smile turned up the corners of his lips. "You're right. You don't. That's one of the things I love about you."

Love? Did he really just use the 'L' word? Of course, he was just using it in the same context as someone who loved pizza or ice cream. Right?

"Don't read anything into it, Mara. It was just a statement."

Heat clawed its way up her neck and into her cheeks. How did he read her mind like that?

"You're an easy read, and I'm trained."

Oh. His military training definitely deserved more careful scrutiny. "Remind me *after* you get me down to bring this subject up again, will you? But for right now, I really want to know what to do next."

His chin lifted as a non-verbal challenge, a position reinforced by the guarded look in his eyes. "Okay, but only if we also spend some time talking about--"

"Okay, okay!"

His laughter echoed off the side of the hill. "You're going to use your feet to push yourself away. But don't push too hard. You'll use them again each time you come close to the rock. Sort of like tippy-toe bouncing down the face of the bluff." He demonstrated by pushing off. At the same time he allowed the rope to slide through his gloved grip. "See how I did that?"

"Yeah."

"Your turn." Carter left absolutely no wiggle room in his comment.

Put your big girl britches on, Mara, and get yourself down this mountain. With a deep breath, she pushed away from the rock and let the rope slide between her gloves. A giggle followed by her typical raucous laugh sounded as she repeated the process, bouncing down the bluff.

"Wait for me." Carter's laughter joined her own.

"No way. I'm having too much fun."

They reached the bottom in no time, Mara breathless with excitement and from laughing so hard.

Carter landed beside her. "I knew you'd love it."

"Let's do it again."

After an additional three trips up and down the hill, Carter released himself from the rope and faced her. "I'm done for now. How 'bout some lunch?"

"Okay."

A few minutes later, he procured the cooler and grabbed hold of her hand as he pulled her through a mass of live oaks and cedars toward the cheerful babble of running water.

They came to a stop beside a crystal clear stream, algae-covered rocks visible at the bottom. Mara pulled free from his grip, stooped, and dipped her fingers in the water. "Is this part of Miller's Creek?"

"Yep. Meanders all throughout this area."

The pungent scent of cedar and mustiness of the damp earth swirled together into one heady perfume. She rose to her feet. "Another beautiful spot. Thank you for bringing me."

Carter smiled a smile that leaked through her skin and into her heart.

A tingle zipped through her insides and landed in her toes.

"My pleasure." He sat on a grassy patch of ground, opened the cooler, and removed chilled shrimp and cocktail sauce, along with a plastic container of some sort of dip and cocktail crackers. "Ever had crab dip?" He dipped a cracker into the creamy mixture, and handed it up to her.

She stuck the whole cracker in her mouth, relishing the texture and taste. "Oh my, that's delicious. You made it?"

He nodded. "Not too hard. Basically crab meat, cream cheese, and a few spices. "

Mara swigged a drink from her water bottle, then plopped to the ground beside him. "You don't play fair, you know."

"Just what does that mean?"

"You've learned my weakness for seafood." She dipped one of the chilled shrimp in the cocktail sauce and popped it in her mouth. "Is this how you interrogated prisoners of war?"

"Not hardly." His tone held an indefinable quality, and he ducked his head, which made reading him impossible.

Her thoughts turned to his years in the military as she munched on shrimp and crackers with crab dip. "It must've been difficult."

"What?"

"To be in the military. Based on your need for excitement--as evidenced by your penchant for extreme sports--I'm guessing you were very good at what you did."

Carter dropped his head again, but not before she glimpsed sheer pain flash across his handsome features.

A whirl of emotions unleashed inside, winding their way to her heart, and stabbing multiple times. Why had she been so selfish? All this time, her thoughts had been focused on herself and her miserable plight. Never, in all the time she'd known him, had she ever considered his own hurts and sorrows. "Wanna talk about it?"

He jutted out his lips and shook his head from side to side, his arms resting around bent knees. "Not particularly."

"I owe you an apology, Carter. I've been such a jerk, thinking only of myself. I never stopped to consider that you had your own set of problems."

"No apology necessary." He stared down the creek bed, silent.

"Do I know how to kill a party or what?" Mara picked up an acorn and tossed it at him, immediately wishing she hadn't. Such a junior high thing to do.

With a sudden flick of his wrist, he caught it and let it drop to the ground.

More of his military training at play. "Did you...?" No. She couldn't ask him.

"Did I what?" He peered at her with sullen face and glazed eyes. "Kill people?" An abnormal iciness edged his tone. "Yeah. It was part of my job. Still is, if need be."

A sudden dose of reality slapped her face. This man beside her--though she'd mostly witnessed his compassionate and fun-loving side--had a willingness to put his life on the line for others no matter the cost. A rare breed of man indeed.

He stood and began putting things away.

Mara joined in, inwardly berating herself. Why had she put him in the position of remembering things he'd rather forget? She longed to speak, but feared making the situation worse. Within a few minutes, they finished cleaning up their impromptu picnic and made their way back to the Caddy.

The trip home was suffocatingly silent. Once Carter parked the car, Mara hurried to the house, anxious to see if Ashton was okay. A touching sight greeted her as she opened the front door. Both layered in way too much make-up, Chloe and Ashton lay on the couch, heads together, sound asleep.

Chloe stirred as she moved closer. "Oh, you're back earlier than I expected."

Yeah. Much earlier than she wanted. "Sorry to wake you. Did Ashton do okay?"

"Um-hmm. She threw up about eleven, but I made her chicken noodle soup. That seemed to settle her stomach."

Carter stepped forward, his face dark and enigmatic. "Ready to go, Chlo?"

His daughter frowned. "I guess so. Let me get my stuff."

Two minutes later, they were out the door. As they drove away Mara realized she'd neglected to say thank you for the most fun she'd ever had. Her heart ached for Carter at the unsavory work he'd done in service to his country. That must surely serve as a wound that never fully healed. She tiptoed closer to Ashton's still form, and an ache for her daughter joined the ache for Carter.

Then a sudden realization hit, as though winging its way directly from heaven. She'd done something today that she never thought she would. She'd dangled from a rope, allowing herself the freedom to trust.

Trust had been a long-time stranger. And being able to experience it had tasted so good.

Surely if she could put her faith in a piece of rope tied to a tree trunk, she could voice a prayer to God on behalf of Carter and Chloe and Ashton.

Dear God, I haven't tried this in a very, very long time, and I'm sure I'm a little rusty at it. But please bear with me and forgive me if I mess it up...

Thirteen

"Well, look who's all decked out." Carter's daughter stared at him through narrowed eyes as he entered the living room--most likely calculating the motive behind his sports coat. She sniffed. "Is that cologne I smell?"

"Maybe." As nonchalantly as possible, he sauntered to the kitchen for yet another glass of water. What was wrong with him? All day his mouth had puckered as though he'd been eating unripe persimmons.

As he gulped down his fifth glass in less than an hour, his thoughts turned to Mara and the upcoming dinner at her house tonight. A frown knotted his eyebrows, and his lips pinched. Truthfully, her invitation was to blame for his dry mouth, change in dress, and cologne. And it bothered him. What happened to his resolve to keep distance between them? *Lord, give me strength to obey You and Your Word. Protect my heart.*

As though echoing his thoughts, Chloe called out from the living room. "You aren't nervous about going over to eat dinner with Mara and Ashton are you?"

He froze. How was he supposed to answer? Through puffed out cheeks he released a long stream of air, then faced her. Might as well be honest. Like him, his eagle-eyed daughter missed nothing. "Just a little."

"Why? That's so not like you."

She was right. What was it about the lanky woman with the often-sharp tongue, a grin bigger than Texas, and a raucous belly laugh that never failed to bring a smile to his face? "I dunno."

A Grinch-like grin slowly spread from ear to ear on Chloe's face. "I think you like her." She sang the words as she swayed her upper body from side to side.

Heat spread beneath the collar of the only button-down shirt he owned. Like her? That was an understatement of the strongest kind. And it ate him alive because Mara wasn't a believer. At least not yet. *Lord, help her realize who You are.*

He took another sip of water. Mara and Ashton had at least been to church a few times now, including Sunday and Wednesday nights, but had yet to make any sort of profession of faith. Hadn't he tried to keep his heart in check? But something about her drew him in with a force he'd never experienced. And the worst part? He had no idea what to do about it. *Lord, help.*

"I'm sorry, Dad." Chloe stood and moved to where he stood in the kitchen. "I didn't mean to embarrass you."

He shrugged and welcomed her hug.

She leaned her head back to peer up at him, her long kinky hair cascading down her back. "You look really nice, and you smell great, too." A light appeared in Chloe's eyes as a bulb inside her clicked on. "And if it's any consolation, I think Mara likes you back."

His arms fell to his side as she pulled away and went to gather her things. A battle ensued inside him. On one hand, the news that Mara might reciprocate his feelings couldn't be good until they shared the same beliefs. On the other hand, Chloe's words sent adrenaline rushing through him unlike any extreme sport or dangerous situation ever could. Also not a good thing.

"Dad!"

He jerked his head toward Chloe, who stood at the front door, exasperation sparking in her eyes. "Huh? You say something?"

"Duh. I've asked three times if you were ready to go. Snap out of it." She waltzed out the front door.

Snap out of it indeed. But how could he when one part of him longed to put his best foot forward and another part wanted to run the opposite direction?

Less than a half hour later, the foursome sat round the table in Mara's stylish dining room, like the real family he wished they could be. Chloe and Ashton chatted non-stop, making it difficult to get a word in edgewise. Mara obviously enjoyed their camaraderie, adding witty comments, followed by uproarious laughter from all three. Did he really want to be outnumbered by females? Maybe he should be more careful about what he prayed for.

Carter chewed a bite of the tasty pot roast, though Mara's classic elegance made it hard to even keep his mouth closed. Usually she dressed in jeans or sweatpants at home, her youthful face devoid of makeup. But tonight she wore pants that flared at the bottom and made her look even taller. Her shimmery dark green blouse picked up the green specks in her light brown eyes. And her perfume must've been bottled in heaven. Yep. He'd been a goner from the moment he'd laid eyes on her.

Chloe once more landed a swift kick to his shin beneath the table, with a look that screamed 'Snap out of it!'

But the harder he tried to think of something to say, the more fear froze the words in his throat.

"Is the food okay, Carter?" Mara peered across the table, tiny vertical waves between her eyes. She made a face. "Does it taste bad?"

"No, no, not at all. It's delicious." He pictured an oversized Army boot in his mind and began the process of mentally kicking himself in the backside.

She didn't seem convinced.

"Seriously. It's really good. Especially the roast. Very tender." What a blubbering idiot. Why couldn't he speak in complete sentences? His efforts to convince her the food was good--which it was--sounded more unconvincing and insincere with each word he uttered.

The doorbell rang. Mara frowned and stood. "I wonder who that is."

Ashton, now completely bald from the chemo, ran to the door. "Daddy!" She shrieked and hopped into the arms of the yuppie man standing there. Dressed in an expensive sweater, khaki dress pants, and all-leather Berluti loafers, he looked as though he'd stepped from a New York runway.

The man hugged Ashton to him and swung her around, her legs flying askew. "Oh, Ash, I've missed you so much!"

Mara glided to the door, her tall elegant looks the perfect match for Mr. GQ.

Carter exchanged a brief glance with Chloe then focused on Mara. Her smile had completely faded, replaced by a nervous twitch of her lips and fidgeting hands.

Mara's ex set Ashton down and looked toward the dining room. "Sorry. Didn't mean to interrupt your dinner. We were just passing through, and I wanted to stop and see Ashton." He paused, his gaze focused on Mara for an unnecessary amount of time. "Hi, Mara."

"Hi, Jim. Please come in."

Yuppie Jim stepped to one side and ushered in a petite brunette holding a toddler. "You remember Shelley. And this," he latched on to the toddler's hand and shook it up and down as he smiled and cooed in a Daddy voice, "is Miss Ella."

Though her ex's words obviously knifed through her, a kind expression landed on Mara's face, and she stepped forward like the classy lady she was, her hand outstretched to the other woman. "Nice to see you again, Shelley. Ella's an absolute doll." Her grin widened as the baby smiled up at her. She motioned Carter and Chloe into the foyer of the living room. "This is Carter and Chloe Callahan. And this is Jim and Shelley Hedwig and their daughter Ella."

A strained look passed over Jim's features as the two men shook hands. Carter squeezed the man's hand with more pressure, then intuitively stepped closer to Mara. Good. Jim definitely saw him as competition. Let him think whatever. It served him right for how he'd hurt Mara and Ashton.

Though she put on a good face, Mara's fidgety hands revealed her discomfort. "If y'all haven't eaten yet, you're more than welcome to join us. We have plenty."

Jim looked at his wife. "We haven't eaten. Honey, you mind if we join them for a quick bite so I can spend more time with Ashton?"

Though her facial expression said otherwise, her lips said: "Sure."

Mara quickly rounded up two folding chairs which they added around the table. Though previously positioned at the opposite end, now Mara squeezed her chair between Carter and Chloe, as though it brought comfort to have them on either side.

Carter laid a hand on her arm and sent a reassuring smile.

Overwhelming gratitude flowed from her eyes, and she smiled before turning her attention to their unexpected guests. "So are you three on your way somewhere or coming back from somewhere?"

Jim swallowed his food. "Headed to San Antonio to visit Shelley's family for Thanksgiving. I took off early today so we could take a detour through Miller's Creek to see Ashton. What were you thinking when you moved her to this dried-up little town?"

Mara forked a piece of roasted potato in her mouth.

"I talked to your Dad last week on the phone." Jim's cultured voice held insinuation.

Now Mara stiffened and sat up ramrod straight.

"He's the one who told me Ashton was sick again." Jim took a bite and chewed, his gaze challenging Mara.

Ashton's smile disappeared, and she visibly tensed, as though sensing what was about to come.

The man lowered his head to his plate as he knifed through another portion of the roast, then raised his gaze and his fork. "Don't you think you could've called me to let me know?"

This guy was a creep of the worst sort. The kind who delivered subtle below-the-belt blows. Carter brought his right fist to his mouth and cleared his throat, then casually draped his right arm over Mara's chair as a sign of support.

She turned a steely gaze toward her ex-husband. "Actually I did call. Shelley must have forgotten to tell you." Her voice remained calm and steady as she peered at the other women, who refused eye contact. She faced her ex-husband again. "And if you would call Ashton more than once a year, you'd know how she's doing."

Big crocodile tears pooled in Ashton's blue eyes. In a fraction of a second, she dropped her fork to her plate with a clang. Her chair tipped and crashed to the floor as she took off down the hallway toward her bedroom, Chloe right on her heels, and Mara not far behind.

Shelley, who'd barely spoken all evening, glared at her husband with more than a tinge of animosity. "I think it's time to leave." She stood, little Ella in her arms. "I'll be out in the car." Without a word to Carter, her footsteps padded across the floor and the door slammed shut.

Jim finished his food at a leisurely pace, then stood, his gaze locking horns with Carter's. "Guess you and your daughter are shacking up with Mara and Ashton, huh?"

"Not hardly."

The man peered around the well-decorated home. "Well, maybe you should. Mara appears to be doing okay for herself. But she always was one to land on her feet. In spite of her issues."

The barbed words stuck in Carter's flesh and sent electricity bolting throughout him. He clamped his jaw and stood, easily towering over the weasel. His hands fisted into tight balls that itched to lay Yuppie Man out cold.

Mara entered and hurried over to where they stood, then latched on to Carter's arm and faced down her ex-husband. "Ashton will be out shortly to tell you goodbye."

True to her word, Ashton and Chloe appeared a second or two later.

Jim knelt in front of his daughter. "Daddy's sorry he made you cry, sweetheart. I didn't mean to."

"It's okay. Thank you for coming to see me." Ashton spoke the words robotically.

With a brief hug, whispered good-bye, and promise to call, Jim stood and left the house without further incident.

Once the door closed, a palpable moment of relief flowed between all four of them. Mara turned to Carter. "I'm so sorry this happened. Thanks for your support. It means more than you know."

"I'm just glad we were here so you didn't have to face it alone."

Ashton moved up beside Mara, wrapped fragile arms around her mama's leg, and leaned against her. "Mommy, can I take my bath and go to bed? I feel perfectly horrible."

Mara dropped to one knee, a hand on her daughter's forehead. "Sure, sweetie. Sorry you don't feel well."

"Can Chloe give me my bath and read me my story?"

"If it's okay with Chloe."

Chloe rose to the occasion in a way that impressed Carter. "Of course. C'mon, squirt. I think you need extra bubbles tonight. What do you think?"

A weary smile appeared on Ashton's face. "I think you need to come over every night so I can get extra bubbles." The two moved down the hallway. "Mom can be a little chintzy when it comes to bubble bath."

Carter laughed and turned to Mara. "Chintzy? Where'd she learn that word?"

She made a 'W' with both arms, her head cocked slightly to the left, then dropped her hands to her side. "Who knows? That child was born talking like a dictionary." Mara hobbled over to the sofa. "Sorry. I gotta take a load off. These shoes are killing me." She slipped off the heels as Carter took a seat beside her.

"Then why wear them? Not like you need the extra inches."

Mara looked at him like he was one fry short of a Happy Meal and held up one shoe with the other hand in a Vanna White pose. "Because this is awesomeness in shoe form. A work of art. The *piece de resistance*."

"Whatever. Stick your feet up here."

"What?"

"You heard me. Give me your smelly, stinky feet."

"My feet do not stink." She feigned a haughty stare, then smiled and landed her feet on the couch.

He took hold of one foot and began to massage it.

She laid her head back on the other end of the sofa and closed her eyes. "I'll give you to the end of eternity to stop."

"Eternity doesn't end."

"Exactly." She hugged a couch pillow to her abdomen and peered over at him with a frank gaze. "Thanks again for standing up for me."

"No prob. Sorry your ex-husband is such a jerk. Has he always been so--"

"--passive-aggressive? Yeah, pretty much."

Carter gave his head a shake. Way too many of that breed of snake in the world. "Makes you wonder why Shelley married him."

"I'm sure he wooed her the way he wooed me. The only difference being that he wasn't married when he wooed me."

Realization dawned, and he stopped rubbing her foot. "You mean, she's the one he had an affair with?"

"Yep, while Ashton was in the hospital fighting for her life the first time."

Raw anger bubbled inside as he massaged her foot once more.

"Ow! Not so hard." She raised to a sitting position. "Don't take it out on my foot."

"Sorry." He inhaled deeply to quell the heat of anger that rose in him like lava in a volcano. "But I'm especially sorry for what he did to you."

"I try not to think about it, honestly. It makes the slide into the Black Abyss all that more appealing."

"Black Abyss?"

"You know, depression. Surely you've visited the Black Abyss some yourself?"

He nodded as his thoughts returned to his time in Iraq and Afghanistan, followed by the news that Jessica no longer wanted him in the picture. "Yeah. If it hadn't been for my faith and family I don't think I could've crawled outta that hole." Her family. Why hadn't he ever thought to ask her more about her family. She obviously had issues with her dad, but what about her mom? "How about your family? Did they help you after your divorce?"

"Ha!" Scorn seared her tone. "Hardly. You forget my father is a preacher and my mother his house *frau*. No. I think his words to me were somewhere along the lines of 'You made this bed, now sleep in it.'"

Her sarcasm-laced words landed in his gut and sent a sour taste spiraling to his mouth. Poor Mara. No wonder she had trouble trusting. And those trust issues had affected her view of God. "I'm so sorry." He released one foot and picked up the other.

"Don't be. I survived."

"Yeah, but your faith didn't."

Her gaze met his. "It's getting there."

He stopped massaging her foot. "Really?"

"Really. That night after our rappelling adventure when you encouraged me to pray, I started talking to God. I specifically prayed that He'd help Dr. Watts accept the possibility of an experimental treatment I found."

"And?"

Her face broke into a glorious grin. "She called today to tell me that if this current medicine doesn't work, that's the next thing we'll try." Excitement colored every word, and animation poured from her face.

Tears stung his eyes, but he quickly blinked them away. *Thank You, God.* "See? I told you." The words croaked from his throat.

"Are you coming down with a cold?"

He shook his head, still trying to make it past the wad of emotion that engorged his neck. "Nah."

A knowing smile appeared, but she didn't comment. Their gazes locked for a long minute, volumes of communication flowing between them without the necessity of words.

Chloe entered the room and headed to where her backpack rested in the floor by the front door. She hoisted it to her shoulder and faced them. "Ashton fell asleep before I got through five pages of the book. Want me to clean up after dinner?"

Mara waved long dismissive fingers. "Heavens, no. I'll take care of it later. Do whatever you need to do. And if you want to watch TV, we'll move out of your way."

"Wish I could, but calculus is eating my lunch. I'm gonna try to make it through at least five of the homework problems due after Thanksgiving."

Mara grinned. "Have fun with that."

"Loads." Chloe's tone flat-lined. She followed her one-syllable answer with a heavy sigh and stoically moved to the dining room table, her loaded backpack in tow.

Mara sat up and pulled her feet away, as though suddenly self-conscious.

Something about the move brought new respect for her in Carter's heart. "What are you and Ash doing for Thanksgiving?"

"We'll probably just hang out here and watch the Macy's Thanksgiving Day parade. Then after lunch we'll watch old Christmas movies. That's our usual agenda."

"Sounds pretty boring. Why don't you join us at my folks' house?"

"That's very kind of you, but really, we enjoy our rut." Her typical sarcasm sounded in her words.

"Sorry. Didn't mean to diss your normal festivities."

"Besides, I wouldn't want to horn in on y'all's Thanksgiving. You have a big family, right?"

"First of all, you wouldn't be horning in. There'll be so many there, two more won't make a dent. And yes, I have a big family."

"The infamous Callahan clan." Chloe spouted the comment with her head still lowered to the open book in front of her.

Mara's eyebrows notched upward. "Infamous?"

Chloe looked at her and nodded. "Oh yeah."

Mara's resulting belly laugh brought a smile to Carter's face. He shrugged. "So we like to have fun. What's wrong with that?"

"Nothing." Chloe scribbled something onto a sheet of notebook paper. "It's your definition of fun that's questionable."

Now Mara guffawed.

Chloe shared a knowing look with Mara. "They torment cats."

"No, we don't. That story gets more distorted every time it comes up. We weren't tormenting it. We were trying to get it down from the tree."

"Well, based on the sounds the cat was making, I'd say it was in torment."

More laughter fell from Mara's lips as she clutched the couch pillow to her stomach and doubled over.

Carter clamped his mouth shut and shook his head. No use in trying to set the record straight with two females in the room.

Mara's laughter subsided. "So how many brothers and sisters did you say you have?"

"Six of us all together. Three boys and three girls."

"Well, at least there are females in there to bring some normalcy to the group."

Now Carter and Chloe shared a laugh.

"I wouldn't characterize any of my aunts as normal," chimed in Chloe. "And they certainly don't have a calming effect on the crew when they're all together. Chaos. Sheer chaos."

Carter donned a goofy grin. "So are you up for some sheer chaos on Thanksgiving?"

Mara giggled. "Well, after hearing Chloe's rousing description, I don't think I can pass it up. Sounds entertaining."

Warmth spread across his chest and moved up to his face. Maybe there was hope for them after all. Especially if she turned back to God, and it sounded like she was already making great strides in that direction.

A disgruntled groan sounded from the dining room, and Chloe lowered her cheek to one fist. "Speaking of chaos. Either one of you two know anything about calculus?"

Carter jumped in to quickly lay Chloe's hope to rest. "Don't look at me."

Mara rose to her bare feet, launched the couch pillow at his head, and ambled to the dining room. "Let me see."

She pulled up a chair beside Chloe and patiently demonstrated and explained how to work the problem.

His heartbeat quickened at the sight of the two of them, side by side, heads bent forward as they worked on Chloe's math homework together. Carter released a quick 'whew' and lowered his elbows to his knees. *Lord, I could sure use Your help right now. I feel like I'm drowning.*

But there was an even bigger problem. He didn't want to be rescued.

Fourteen

"Wow, Carter, you didn't tell us Mara was knock-dead gorgeous." The words boomed forth from some guy that looked so much like Carter, Mara could only assume he was one of the infamous Callahan brothers. Another look-alike also stood uncomfortably close, like 'in-her-personal-space' close. In spite of her determination to stay calm and cool, heat rushed from her chest onto her neck and up to the tips of her ears.

"Cut it out, Caleb." Carter took another look at her flushed cheeks, his eyes an open apology. Before he could say or do anything else, the two hulky he-men descended on him like syrup on pancakes, and the yet-unnamed one locked Carter's neck in the crook of his elbow and scrubbed his head with his knuckles. "Ow! Knock it off!"

To Mara's right, a pretty dark-haired woman, with an apron lashed around her waist and three kids in tow, stepped forward, wiping her hands on her apron. "Sorry about the Neanderthals, Mara. I'm Callie, Carter's oldest sister, and these are my three kids, David, Darcy, and Danny." Callie knelt to speak directly to Ashton, who had a death grip on Mara's hand. "And you must be Ashton. Darcy's so excited to have a girl close to her own age to play with." In a second's time, the dark-headed Darcy had latched onto Ashton and pulled her over to a table full of puzzles, books, and games.

Mara smiled at Callie and offered her hand. "Nice to meet you." The guys continued their rough-housing. "Are they always so--?

"--boisterous?" finished Callie. "Wish I could give the answer you'd probably like to hear, but unfortunately, yes. Come on in the kitchen and I'll introduce you to the more sane members of the family."

Her heart beating out a rhythm to rival any percussionist, Mara followed. The same question that had plagued her all week churned in her mind. What if they didn't like her?

A stunning kitchen like one from a home magazine unfolded before Mara. A long bay of windows overlooked the lake, with a bank of cabinets and granite countertops below. In the middle of the room sat an over-sized island painted barn red.

A middle-aged woman with a round, glowing face approached, both arms outstretched. She engulfed Mara in an unexpected hug, then stepped back, her hands still on Mara's shoulders. "Mara, we're so glad you could join us for Thanksgiving. Make yourself at home here." Then, in a move that made Mara almost jump out of her skin, Mrs. Callahan yelled into the family room. "Boys, quiet it down in there! You're making such a ruckus, I can barely hear myself think!" Carter's mom turned back to Mara with an apologetic smile. "You can call me Jo."

"Nice to meet you, Jo. Thanks for having us."

An older version of Carter and his brothers stepped forward next, his dark eyes warm and soft just like his son's. "I'm Cliff, Mara. Sorry about all the mayhem in the other room. They don't get to see each other as often as they'd like, so when they're all together...well, it's like a box full of rambunctious puppies."

Mara grinned from ear to ear at his description. "Thanks for allowing Ashton and me to spend Thanksgiving with your family."

Two other women--a little younger than her, but older than Chloe--joined the throng.

The tallest one spoke first. "I'm Cara."

"And I'm Cassidy," added the other.

Mara shook both their hands. "All these C names. Hope I can keep them straight."

Callie let out a little snort. "Well, let me add another one to the mix. My husband Carl is parked in front of the television. All the C names convinced me to move on to the letter D when it came time to name my kids."

A sudden load of overwhelm crashed down on Mara, and she struggled to maintain her composure. Where was Carter anyway? Was this what she could expect for the rest of the day?

As if reading her mind, he strode into the kitchen, his hair irreparably mussed.

A grin snapped onto Mara's face, and she chuckled.

"What's so funny?"

Her gaze travelled up his head.

Carter used both hands to smooth his hair down, but to no avail. Then he was swarmed by his other family members as they all hugged his neck and kissed his cheeks. When the crowd dissipated, not only did he have mussed hair, but a lipstick display on his face.

Mara laughed and rubbed both his cheeks with her thumbs. "Didn't anyone ever tell you not to mix your reds, pinks, and oranges?"

He chuckled. "I'll file that useful tidbit in my make-up folder." His eyes focused on her as she finished the job, the scrutiny causing her heart to pound at a rapid rate. "You doing okay?"

She leaned in and kept her voice low. "Am now, but a few seconds ago I was overwhelmed and ready to hitchhike back to Miller's Creek."

Carter's cheeky grin popped on his face. "You'll love them once you get to know them."

"I'm sure I will, but on first meeting, a little bit goes a long way. You should've warned me about those brothers of yours."

At that moment, Chloe wandered into the room, Carter's two brothers right behind. "Mara, these two asked me to officially introduce you to them." Her arms were crossed and her face sullen. She held a hand out to one. "This is Uncle Caleb." Her voice devoid of all emotion, she pointed to the other side. "And this is Uncle Cade."

Caleb stepped forward with a wink at Carter. He grabbed Mara's fingers, then gallantly bowed low and plopped a kiss on the back of her hand. "My lady, so nice to meet you." He leaned forward, his voice conspiratorially low. "I'll give you my cell number later. You know, just in case things don't work out with the lesser brother."

Her eyebrows morphed into question marks, but she couldn't contain her hideous laugh. "Thank you, kind sir, I'll keep that in mind."

Cade butted his brother out of the way, and pulled her into a dance dip. "Like to dance?"

"Er..." She sent Carter a pleading look.

To her relief, Carter pulled her up and spun her around until she landed in the crook of his arm. "Sorry guys, but from here on out, there will be a hands-off policy when it comes to Mara."

"Killjoy." The word pelted from Cade's mouth.

"Yeah, what he said." Caleb winked at Mara. "Actually, we're glad you're here."

"Thanks." Mara's focus shifted to Chloe who leaned against the kitchen counter, her face the picture of dejection. "You okay, Chloe?"

"No. I'm mad at dad for not letting me invite Bryce." Chloe stomped from the room.

"Bryce?" Mara sent a questioning look to Carter.

"Her boyfriend *this* week."

Mara's lips rounded to an 'o'. After she made sure Chloe was out of earshot, Mara turned back to Carter. "Bad start to the day, huh?"

"Yeah. And to make matters worse, her mom was supposed to pick her up later, but called last night to cancel."

Anger spiraled through Mara. How could the woman break Chloe's heart like that? "Maybe Chloe and I can hit the Black Friday sales first thing in the morning."

Horror spread across Carter's handsome face.

"What?" Had she already committed some sort of *faux pas*?

"You're one of those crazy people that stands in line at 2 a.m. waiting for the store to open so you can get trampled."

Her belly laugh broke loose again. "Well, maybe not at 2 a.m., but yeah. What's wrong with that?"

Carter had no time to answer, because Jo, using both hands like a traffic cop, started shooing people toward the large open room with the large dining table. "Time for turkey dinner!"

The noisy crew gathered round the extra long wood table completely covered with food and dinnerware. Mara's mouth watered at the delicious aromas of turkey, dressing, and homemade rolls.

Cliff stood at the far end, his penetrating gaze finally bringing an end to the mayhem. "Let's bless this food." He bowed his head, and everyone followed suit. "Dear Lord, all our blessings come from You, and we are grateful. For the blessing of this food, we thank You. Thank You for those who prepared it. May it nourish us so we might be better servants for You. Thank You for the blessing of family. How grateful we are to be together again this year, safe and sound. May we never take it for granted. And thank You especially for our special guests. May their time with us be blessed with laughter and fond memories. In the precious name of Jesus we pray, Amen."

As they all moved to take a seat, the three brothers piled their hands atop each other, and like a football squad, shouted out a cheer. "Good bread, good meat, good gravy, let's eat!" They raised their hands in the air for effect.

Callie stepped up beside her with a sigh. "Some things never change. I can see and hear them doing that when they're in their eighties, and most likely doing wheelchair races at the old folks' home."

Mara laughed and took a seat in the chair Carter held out for her. Ashton and Chloe claimed the seats on her right. Lunch proved to be as entertaining as Mara expected. She devoured her plate of turkey and homemade dressing, then reached for a sliver of both pecan and pumpkin pie, completely caught up in the camaraderie. Then Ashton's pale face caught her attention. "You feel okay, sweetie?"

Her daughter delivered a convincing smile. "Definitely." She took a bite of the buttery mashed potatoes and looked back up at Mara. "Darcy's really nice. She goes to school in Morganville, but her teacher's an old hag."

Mara pressed her lips together to keep from laughing out loud and simultaneously breathed a sigh of relief. The chemo finally seemed to be working for Ashton. Maybe all the prayers had finally paid off.

After lunch, the guys sauntered as one mass unit to the living room to watch the Cowboys' game. Mara followed the women back into the kitchen.

Jo sighed, placed both hands on her ample hips, and scanned the cluttered counters. "It never ceases to amaze me how it takes days to cook the food and just a few minutes for them to inhale it." She glanced over at Mara. "Be glad you have a girl. All boys do is eat, make messes, and--"

An unruly cheer sounded from the living room.

The older woman gave her head a shake. "--watch football."

Mara helped with the cleanup, her mind flashing a thousand questions. Time for some answers. That had to better than this nerve-wracking lack of conversation. "So how would y'all describe Carter?"

"Easy question," blurted out Cassidy. "As the youngest in the family, Carter's always been my defender and protector. In fact, I think that's his role in our family."

The other two sisters nodded in agreement.

"I'll second that." Jo's eyes held a reminiscent look. "When he was just five years old, I had to pull him out of scuffle with a boy three years older."

"What were they fighting over?" Mara's tone revealed fascination, her impression of Carter confirmed in the testimonies of his family.

"The boy had called Cara a bad name, and Carter would have none of it. That's one example of many I could give." Jo paused, and her lips worked back and forth for a moment. "Since we're asking questions, mind if we ask you a few?"

Mara barely had time to shake her head before the inquisition started. "Where's Ashton's dad?"

"How long have you been divorced?"

"What line of work are you in?"

"How did you meet Carter?"

Man, nothing like getting grilled while Carter enjoyed his football game. She did her best to answer the onslaught of questions. Then Jo delivered the clincher, the one question Mara had hoped to avoid. "Are you a believer?"

Mara gulped and frantically plowed through her brain in search of the right words. "Uh, well, I used to be...that is, I'm considering a move back in that direction. Well, I guess the best answer is to say I'm still on the fence when it comes to God."

Palpable tension squeezed every ounce of oxygen from the kitchen. The room grew deadly silent, the only sound running water and dishes clanking together as they were rinsed and placed in the dishwasher.

Well, her honest answer had tanked, based on their response.

At just that moment, Carter peered around the corner. "Y'all sure got quiet all of a sudden. We making too much noise?"

Jo shook her head. "Nah. I think we're all just ready for a nap. Most of us have been up since before dawn."

Carter glanced around at the lowered heads of the female members of his family, and his questioning gaze landed on Mara. He stepped closer. "Wanna go for a walk?"

"And make you miss your football game? Not necessary. Besides, I should probably finish helping with the cleanup."

Callie sent a smile from her position at the sink. "You two go ahead. We've got this."

"Oh. Okay. Well, if you're sure."

The funeral dirge that began playing the minute she'd answered the faith question continued to drone in her ears as Mara wiped her hands and fled the kitchen. She didn't even stop to grab her coat, but told Ashton she was headed out for a walk and hurried out the front door, gulping in great gobs of air and battling tears.

Carter joined her a minute later and handed her coat over. "Thought you might need this. It's always a bit nippy out here this time of year."

Mara put it on, avoiding his gaze.

Carter shoved both hands in his pants pockets as they strolled toward a forested area. "You okay?"

"Let's just say your family's a lot different than mine. For one thing, there's so many of you and you seem so close."

"We are."

"I didn't have that growing up."

They walked in silence for a while, then Carter spoke. "For what it's worth, I think everyone really likes you."

A cynical laugh escaped. "I'm not convinced. But except for getting grilled by your sisters and mom, I guess I'll live."

He winced. "Sorry about that. Is it safe for me to ask how it went?"

Mara crossed her arms and headed down to the rocky shoreline in full stride. Had she completely blown it?

Carter quickly fell into step beside her. "Slow down a bit, will ya? When I asked you to go on a walk, I meant a leisurely stroll, not a race."

"Sorry." She slowed her pace, still avoiding eye contact.

"You gonna answer my question? How did it go?"

"Fine. Right up to when I told them I was still on the fence when it came to God."

He released a descending whistle.

"It got so quiet in that room, you'd think I dropped an atomic bomb. Though I'm fairly certain they're back there chatting it up now."

"Don't even go there, Mara. One thing my mom and sisters are not are gossips." He latched on to her upper arm and swung her around to face him. "Sorry that was uncomfortable to you, but faith in God is important in my family. I can't help that, and I won't apologize for it."

"Thank you for stating the obvious." She resumed her walk. Why did all this meeting a family-thing have to be so hard? And why shouldn't she be allowed to have doubts about God and faith? It didn't mean she was a bad person.

Carter didn't reply, but continued to amble along beside her.

Mara raised her gaze to the rust- and gold-colored hues of the beautiful scenery, nature coercing her to relax. After several deep breaths of the fresh-smelling air, she managed to release the last vestiges of her angst. "I'm really sorry, Carter. I hope I didn't make things difficult for you with your family."

"Not at all. But if they got quiet, it wasn't because they were angry or judgmental." His words were as soft as his tender smile.

"What was it then?"

"Concern for both of us. My first marriage was to an unbeliever, and that didn't turn out so well."

So Chloe's mom didn't believe either? That sure made Chloe's reluctance easier to understand.

Carter latched onto her fingers and came to a stop, his eyes expressive. "That's why I can't afford to fall in love with another unbeliever."

A tumult of emotions unleashed all at once. Fear he would one day abandon his patience and leave her and Ashton alone. And more than a little anger. This reeked of emotional blackmail. Mara studied Carter's face. One look at the sincerity in his eyes disproved her diagnosis. She lowered her head, shoulders sagging. There was no way she was ready to call it quits, but professing something she still questioned was deception and a route she refused to follow.

Her mouth opened to beg him for more patience, but was cut short as a shout sounded from behind them. "Carter!"

"Over here, Caleb!"

Footsteps thudded ever closer, until Caleb's broad body appeared around the bend, his face awash with fear. "Ashton just fainted!"

Fifteen

A macabre hush and antiseptic odor saturated every surface of Ashton's hospital room as Carter waited for her and Mara to return from yet another round of testing. He rubbed a hand down his face, wishing for a little shut-eye, but at the same time realizing sleep wouldn't come no matter how tired he was.

Ever since Caleb's announcement, Carter's emotions, adrenaline, and need to help however he could had all been in overdrive. Dealing with Ashton's illness very much reminded him of active military duty--high tension, very little sleep, and always trying to stay one step ahead of the enemy.

Steps and the sound of gurney wheels whispered in the hallway. Then the door opened, and an orderly entered, pushing the gurney that held Ashton, Mara right behind.

His insides melted and spewed acid all at the same time. Even in the dim light of the room, it was easy to see the tell-tale signs. Mara's puffy eyes and red cheeks were all the evidence he needed. She'd been crying. And hard.

The orderly gently deposited Ashton, listless and whimpering, back in her bed. As he exited, a nurse entered and added medicine to the IV with a syringe.

Once the nurse left, Mara perched on the edge of the bed and stroked Ashton's bald head with shaky hands.

Ashton, who hadn't opened her eyes the entire time, quickly drifted off to sleep, soft snoring sounds issuing forth from pale lips.

Mara stood, toed off her loafers, and padded to the window in sock feet. Her arms were crossed at the waist, and her hands moved up and down the sleeves of her turtleneck as though to chase away the chill of death.

With a groan in his heart that he refused utterance, Carter moved up behind her and placed hands on her shoulders.

She twisted away and inched closer to the window.

"Don't shut me out, Mara. Let me help."

Still she said nothing, the tears brimming in her eyes lit by the streetlights below.

He lowered his head and released a heavy sigh that caved in his chest. How could he get through to her? Should he just wait until she was ready to talk? Immediately, the answer came. No. Unless he forced the issue, she'd never open up and release the torment behind her eyes. *Lord, help me out here.*

Carter squared his shoulders, stepped directly in front of Mara, and tilted her chin upward. Bile rose in his throat and his stomach roiled--to the point that he wanted to flee--at the raw pain in her eyes. But he couldn't. This was a tour of duty unparalleled by any other. His jaw clenched. Somehow he had to find the strength to walk headlong into her suffering. Into the battle of eternal life and death.

He attempted to convey with his eyes what his heart longed to say. What words couldn't say.

Tears flowed down her cheeks, unstoppable.

"I'm so sorry." He raised a hand to her face to whisk away tears.

"No child should ever have to undergo what my daughter just went through." Her voice was a hoarse and emotive whisper. "Why?"

Carter frowned. "Why what?"

"Why does your God cause little girls to endure spinal taps and bone marrow aspirations and biopsies?"

His heart ached at her words. She'd been making such great strides toward God, and now this spiritual regression, both frustrating and yet understandable. "I don't know. But I do know He has His reasons and a perfect plan for all of us. Even in this, I trust Him."

"I've made baby steps toward Him, and as His way of saying 'thanks' my daughter's leukemia gets worse?"

There was no anger in her face or tone, just a heartfelt desire to understand. How was he supposed to answer something he couldn't understand himself. *Lord, I can't do this. I need You.* One thought landed in his brain. Baby steps. "Remember when Ashton first started walking?"

Mara frowned, but a slight smile curved her lips, and she nodded.

"For her those baby steps were huge, but you knew it was just a drop in the bucket compared to what she'd be able to do in the future. It's the same way with God. Your steps toward Him may seem big to You, but He knows what you can do and what lies ahead of you."

She released a heavy sigh, her face awash with weariness. "So you're saying to trust Him?"

He nodded gently, his eyes exploring hers.

"I thought Christianity was supposed to make your life easier, not harder." An edge of resentment crept into her tone.

Carter shook his head. "Sorry if I gave you that impression. Christ doesn't come into our lives to improve us, but to change us completely. There's nothing easy about that."

The expression on her face showed she didn't follow.

"Think about it this way. If you saw a sign on an apartment building that said 'Under New Management,' but walked inside and saw no changes, what would you think?"

"That the new management wasn't very effective."

He smiled and cupped her face with one hand. "Exactly. When we allow Him access, at first He just does a few minor repairs."

"Like leaky faucets?" She swiped at her wet cheeks.

"Yeah, and stains on the carpet. But you're okay with it because you kind of expected it."

Her eyes closed and she gave her head a gentle shake. "Why do I get the feeling that the next word out of your mouth is 'but?'"

He released a calming breath. "But then He starts to tear down a few walls. It hurts, and you don't like it. You question what He's doing and why."

Mara's face froze. "So you're saying Ashton's illness is because God is working on me?"

"Not necessarily, but never discount what's happening in your life at any given moment. Even if it's horrible, like this, God allows it, and He can use it."

Mara curled her bottom lip under, her eyes distant.

Should he continue? Yeah. Who knew when he'd get this opportunity again? And this was much too important to let the moment slip by. "Those life makeovers don't often make sense at the time they're happening, but later you'll look back on it and see His hand at work. You'll see that He was able to take a run-down wreck of a house and turn it into an exquisite mansion."

Without warning, her face crumpled and she sank to the floor with a keening wail, as though her legs refused to support her weight any longer.

With a groan that barely expressed his heartbreak and tears coursing down Carter's face, he fell to the floor and took her in his arms. He rocked back and forth while he wept, prayed, and did all he knew to soothe her brokenness.

They remained in the same position until their sobs subsided, then Mara pulled back just far enough to search his eyes. She brought a hand to his face, exploring his tear-stained cheek with her fingertips. Then, in a moment so swift it surely had wings, she raised her lips to his.

The door banged open and flooded the area where they sat with sudden and blinding light.

Mara raised one hand to shield her eyes and jumped to her feet.

Carter slowly raised to a standing position and squinted to make out the shape of the person silhouetted in the doorway, suddenly aware of a tension so thick it crushed against his ribcage.

"Hi Daddy." The whispered words fell from Mara's lips like a death toll.

Mara's stomach lurched as she stood. She lifted a hand to her abdomen to quell the nausea and overwhelming dread. Why hadn't they told her they were coming when she'd called them earlier? *Stay calm, Mara. You can do this. You've played the part of the peacemaker on more than one occasion.*

Like an automaton she moved toward her father, ignoring his angry glare. How many years had it been since she'd last seen him? He looked exactly the same as she remembered, still in his preacher suit while Mama wore a homemade dress that stretched down to mid-calf. Mara hugged him lightly, but he shrugged it off, as though contact with her made him unclean. She faced her mother and repeated the process. Thankfully Mama clung to her neck. "Thank you both for coming."

A virulent spew of religious rhetoric erupted from her father's mouth. Mama withdrew from Mara's embrace and shuffled to Daddy's side, head lowered. How like her to side with him, even when he was dead wrong. But she couldn't really blame Mama, considering the indoctrination she'd endured for most of her life.

Carter stepped forward and extended a hand toward her father. Daddy ignored the proffered handshake, his bulging eyes reminiscent of the times he'd pounded the pulpit and preached hell-fire and damnation.

He turned his bug-eyed focus her direction. "You and your loose morals."

From her right, Carter inhaled sharply.

She held up a flattened palm toward Carter. Hopefully he'd receive the message and keep his mouth shut. Past experience had proved that a faulty step in the wrong direction.

Her father strode to Ashton's bedside and stared down at his sleeping grand-daughter. "The sins of the father. Or in this case, the mother. May God Almighty have mercy on your soul."

A jolt of electricity sizzled in her brain. Was Ashton's illness because of her sin? What mistake had she made that brought this on?

Carter took two steps forward, his hands fisted at his side. "You have no right to speak to her that way. She's the best mother I've--"

Her father's curt laugh cut him short. "Based on the scene I walked in on just a few minutes ago? Hardly." Her father's Louisiana drawl dripped acid.

How, she didn't know, but from some place deep inside she drew upon an unseen reserve. She laid a hand on Carter's muscled arm to keep him from advancing, and then smooth and calm as a glassy lake, interrupted her father's tirade. "I was just about to get something to drink from the vending machines. May I get you something, Daddy?"

He didn't answer, but continued to glare, his jowls clamped like a bulldog.

"Mama, would you like something to drink?" Mama cast a sideways glance at Daddy, her head shaking out a slight 'no.'

Carter stepped back to her side and took hold of her hand. At first, like frightened butterflies, her fingers struggled to free themselves, but he maintained his grip and captured her attention with light-filled eyes that bolstered her courage and brought sudden calm. "I'll go with you." He led her out the door.

Mara travelled only a few steps in the hallway before she collapsed once more in his embrace, sobbing. No words came, held at bay by a deep-rooted hurt of lost childhood and the wrath of her father. Finally she brought her tears under control.

"You gonna be okay?" Carter's dark eyes held deep compassion and sorrow and offered the kind of place in which she could easily get lost. It would be so easy to become dependent upon his strength and comfort. So easy to escape in the kiss they'd shared before her parent's arrived.

She wiped tears and sniffed. "As soon as I have some caffeine. Come on."

Once in the vending machine room, she inserted the money Carter pulled from his wallet and pounded the Diet Coke button with her fist. The can rumbled to its destination. Mara popped the top and took a swig of the ice-cold and fizzy drink, already better. She snagged a tissue from a nearby box and blew her nose, then looked up at Carter. "Time to face the enemy again."

His lips flattened, but he nodded. Once more, he laced fingers through hers and led her back to the room.

Mama and Daddy knelt besides Ashton's bed, her father's words billowing forth in holy intonement. "Lord God, Thou knowest the sins of my daughter. Thou knowest and Thou executest righteous judgment. But Lord, if it be Thy will, let Thy righteous indignation fall on her rather than this innocent child. Amen."

Her brain buzzed as chill bumps broke out on her arms, and her mouth fell open. What had she done that was so wrong that God would pronounce judgment on her daughter? Confusion ricocheted in her thoughts to the point that she barely felt Carter's hand tighten around hers.

At just that moment, the door opened behind her. Mara turned.

Dr. Watts, Ashton's oncologist, waited respectfully for her parents to rise to their feet, then turned a sorrowful gaze to Mara.

Her throat closed down, and she dug her fingernails into Carter's fleshy palm. This wasn't good news.

"I have the test results. Do you want to talk outside?"

Mara shook her head from side to side. "No. Just say what you need to say." The words sounded as though miles away.

"I'm sorry to have to tell you that the results of the bone marrow test and spinal tap weren't good."

The air pressure in the room plummeted, and Mara's lungs battled for oxygen. She swallowed, trying to rid herself of the hot knot that made breathing impossible. "What does that mean?"

The oncologist glanced down at her shifting feet for a moment, then turned her gaze back to Mara. "Unless we find a bone marrow donor, Ashton won't survive."

Her knees buckled beneath her, but Carter wrapped a strong arm around her waist and pulled her to his side. She clung to him with all the strength she could muster, oddly focused on the scent of his cologne. The room spun and took on a surreal quality. Was this really happening, or was she in a dream?

Dr. Watts laid a hand on her arm, her blurred eyes full of blurred compassion behind the lenses of her blurred glasses, and then stepped from the room.

The doctor's exit added fuel to her father's fire, as his scathing tongue lit into her once more. "You're an unfit mother." He nodded to Ashton's bed. "God is punishing you for your sin. Jim told me about your live-in boyfriend and his daughter." Now his eyes sent the flames of hell-fire Carter's way.

Mara longed to speak words in both their defense, but her tongue still wouldn't cooperate.

Carter, still supporting her with one arm, came to the rescue, his voice cold and hard, but under strict military control. "I've laid men out for lesser offenses, but out of respect for Mara, I'll let you walk free. We'd like for you to leave. Now." Every muscle in his body stood at attention, as though on duty.

"My pleasure." Her father released the scornful words as he strode to the door. Mama followed with her timid ten steps behind. But Daddy turned in the open doorway, an accusatory finger extended Mara's way. "Your daughter will die because of your sins."

The words punched holes in her shambled faith.

As soon as the door slammed shut, Carter stepped in front and cupped her face with both hands, the bright-white light in his eyes shooting into hers. "Do not believe what he said, Mara. That is not who God is. Do you hear me? Don't believe those horrid lies!"

A dark numbness slithered through every muscle in her body. If only she could feel something to make sure this was real. She closed her eyes and handed control to the numbing emptiness. Her body instantly relaxed as though taken over from an outside force. Mara gently slipped from Carter's grasp. "Thanks for your support and friendship. I really appreciate it." She forced her gaze away from the promise and hope in his soft eyes. "But it's best if you leave, too."

"What? But why?" He grabbed both her arms and stepped in front, scrambling for eye contact.

She sidestepped to Ashton's bedside. "I apologize for allowing this to go as long as it has, but I don't see how a relationship between an atheist and God-worshipper could ever work." How did her words come out so tranquil and serene?

"Mara, I'm not like him." Carter's voice took on a panicked edge as he raked a hand across his head, his face contorted. "I'm not like your father. And neither is God."

The words echoed with a hollow thud against the walls of her heart. For a sliver of time, she allowed his words access, but then gave her head a shake to dislodge the thought. It didn't matter anyway. Not with Ashton's death sentence.

She moistened her lips and busied herself with straightening the bed linens. Better to shoot this rabbit once and for all. For Carter's sake. She faced him and peered at a spot over his right shoulder. "Maybe. Maybe not. But right now, I just want to spend my daughter's last days with her. Without you."

His mouth flew open in objection, but he stopped short of speech. Instead he nodded, then strode to the door. Carter peered back at her one last time. "Okay, if that's what you want. But if you need anything, don't hesitate to call."

Mara didn't answer or acknowledge his presence. It was best if she sent the clearest message possible.

A click sounded, and then retreating footsteps as every carefully-built dam inside her cracked open all at once.

Sixteen

Carter steered the police car into a deserted road-side park on the west side of Miller's Creek early on a December Saturday morning and parked. He yawned and widened his eyes to shake off the sleepiness that weighted his eyelids. How long had it been since he'd pulled an all-night shift? Not that it mattered. He'd asked for extra duty after returning from that fateful night in the Dallas Children's Hospital, where Mara and Ashton still waited for a bone marrow donor, in hopes it would keep his thoughts off the pretty realtor, her heart-breaking situation, and the overwhelming loss that followed him everywhere.

He killed the motor, then leaned forward and crossed his arms over the steering wheel, his eyes glued to the empty road. While the extra hours were good for bringing in extra money, they hadn't accomplished his primary goal. Instead long lonely nights and boring days had only provided more time to think about her, two thoughts in particular rotating in his brain. No wonder Mara had such a struggle with God when her view of Him was skewed by her earthly father. And the second, just how was he supposed to get through to her in light of it?

An engine roared on the road behind him. He started the car and turned to see a black Suburban with dark-tinted windows whiz past. More speeding ticket revenue for Miller's Creek.

Adrenaline pumped through his system, immediately removing the fatigue. He floored the accelerator in pursuit, and the car tires screeched against the pavement. Carter flipped on his lights and siren, but to no avail. Instead the SUV increased speed. Carter followed suit, bounding down the road at 100 miles per hour.

His brain exploded with all sorts of scenarios. This was obviously someone with something to hide. Drugs? Weapons? If he followed the book, it meant calling Ernie after he'd worked until 2 a.m. last night. Besides, by the time his boss got dressed and made it this far out of town, this guy would be long gone. Same for the Sheriff's Department. And the next town in this direction wasn't for another sixty miles.

Without warning, the SUV braked hard and swerved as a deer bounded across the road in the foggy morning. Carter released the gas pedal to maintain control. The black Suburban in front of him slid sideways and then backwards. For the first time, Carter caught a glimpse of the driver. Hispanic male, a black bandana draped across his lower face, and a pistol raised beside his right shoulder.

Carter slumped lower in the seat, but for no reason. The Suburban hit the ditch and careened to one side, then crashed onto its top, rocking back and forth a moment before it stilled. The police car jerked to a stop a few feet away. Carter jumped from the car and shielded himself with the door as he raised his pistol with both hands. "Freeze!"

No movement or sounds came from the overturned vehicle, so he eased around the back of his car and cautiously approached the Suburban. Out of nowhere the driver's side door swung open and the suspect crawled to the ground, pistol still in hand.

Carter pulled the trigger, the sound quickly deadening in the thick fog.

The man screamed, released the gun, and clutched his now-bleeding hand, whimpering.

In a moment's time, Carter sat on top of him, the man's hands pulled behind his back, and the handcuffs secured. Feeling better and more alive than he had in weeks, he yanked the guy to his feet. His dislodged bandana still hung around his neck and sported a skull, a sure sign of Mexican drug cartel.

He half-pulled, half-pushed the suspect to the police car as he read him his rights, shoved him in the back seat behind the cage, then stepped to the front seat to grab the radio receiver. He punched the button. Yeah, Ernie's at-home scanner would go off, rousing him after only a few hours' sleep, but he had no choice. "This is Carter, requesting back-up at PD. Suspect apprehended. Headed to town. Will need medical."

Carter rapidly secured the upside-down Suburban, loaded to the brim with both automatic rifles and plastic-wrapped bundles--probably cocaine--then headed toward the police department. Thirty minutes later, Carter pulled up in front of the painted concrete-block building. Ernie waited by the front door, hands on hips, with an ambulance nearby.

Carter grinned as he stepped from the vehicle. "Got us a big prize this morning, Ernie. My guess is drug cartel out of Mexico."

Ernie didn't speak, but moved to the back of the car with Carter as he pulled the suspect from the seat. Within a few minutes, they had the guy in his cell, hand bandaged. Then Ernie headed to the front door, but turned before he exited. "Stay in the building until your shift is up. Meanwhile, I'll contact the higher-ups and have the vehicle towed and impounded." Without another word, he strode out the door.

A sudden sour taste developed in Carter's mouth, and a frown tightened his forehead. Had it been his imagination, or was Ernie miffed? Yeah, he hadn't followed correct procedure, but there hadn't really been time for any other course of action. He shrugged off the vague feelings and moved to the desk. His boss was more than likely just cranky from a shortened night's rest.

Carter glanced at the wall clock. He should have just enough time to call a few folks to finish setting up his plans for the rest of the day and then change into sweats and tennis shoes for the 5K run later that morning. Hopefully his plan would not only bring Mara and Ashton funding, but also the much-needed donor.

A few minutes after ten a.m., Carter crawled from his Ford into the already-bustling downtown Miller's Creek, a happy spring to his step. Shimmery tinsel-covered decorations decked each light post, memorial Christmas trees filled the town square, and window fronts were all done up, compliments of Trish Tyler.

What better time than the weekend of the Miller's Creek Holly Days Festival to help bring awareness to childhood leukemia and the need for bone marrow donors? A grin spread across his face as he peered across Main Street to the town square, Christmas carols ringing from a nearby speaker. Already the vehicle for the testing, blood work, and sign-up was in place and ready to go. And the old-time wagon from Miller Ranch, which served as the broadcast station for the day's events, was also pulled into its place in front of City Hall.

Carter waited for cars to pass, then trekked across Main Street to touch base with Chance and Dakota, already positioned in the booth where folks could donate money or goods to Mara and Ashton.

Chance glanced up as Carter approached the booth. "Hey, Carter."

Carter took hold of his offered hand and slapped him gently on the shoulder. "Hey." Carter smiled at Dakota. "Hi, Red. How're things going?"

The green-eyed farm girl, who seemed more than content to keep a distance from others, shrugged. "Could be better, but it's still early."

Chance nodded. "Yeah. About ready to find me a bullhorn and start needling folks into adding money to the hat. Maybe we should've done a dunking booth instead."

"Would have, but it's a little chilly for that kind of fundraiser." Carter stared up at the darkening sky, gray clouds passing quickly in the stiff cool winds. "Just praying that cold front holds off until after the light parade tonight."

"Hey, Carter!" Andy Tyler shouted at him from the back of the wagon, hands cupped to his face.

"What?"

Andy didn't reply, but instead motioned him over with long sweeps of his arm.

"See you guys later. It appears I'm being summoned." Carter gave a quick goodbye wave and hurried across the street.

Andy squatted as Carter neared the wagon. "Hey, buddy. You ready to make your first announcement?"

"Me? I thought you guys would do all that." Public speaker he was not.

"People will respond better to you since you're closer to the story. Need time to think through what you're gonna say?"

Carter checked his watch. The Holly Days 5K was scheduled to start in fifteen minutes, an event he and Chloe had organized, and one in which he wanted to participate with his daughter. He released a sigh and peered up at Andy's ocean-green eyes with a shake of his head. "Nah. If I'm gonna make a fool of myself in public, might as well get it out of the way."

Andy flashed his pearly whites as he held a hand out to Carter and helped him into the wagon.

Carter stepped to the microphone. He pulled it from the stand and moved forward. The speakers down front squealed, and people immediately stopped what they were doing and covered their ears. Well, that was one way to get their attention.

Andy latched onto Carter's elbow and pulled him back a couple of steps. Thankfully the painful squealing stopped.

With a deep breath, Carter smiled and raised the mic to his mouth. "Welcome to the annual Miller's Creek Holly Days festival. Everyone having a good time?"

A few cheers sounded as a crowd gathered in front of the wagon, all eyes on him.

A dense sweat broke out on his neck in spite of the cool weather. "So glad y'all are here to enjoy our quaint little town and get some Christmas shopping done, but I'd like to call your attention to another need. One of the little girls who lives here in Miller's Creek is very sick and needs your help." The crowd immediately quieted as they honed in on his words.

"You'll see flyers with Ashton's picture in every store and booth. She has Stage-4 leukemia, and without a bone marrow transplant she won't make it."

Carter forced down the wad of emotion in his throat and moistened his dry mouth. "Please consider making a donation to her and her mom. You can give at any store or the booth on the northwest corner of the square. A portion of the proceeds from all of today's events will also be given to them."

The crowd grew restless, and a few wandered away for more shopping. Now for the most important part of what he had to say. He held up a hand. "Wait, folks, please listen to one more thing. I promise to make it quick. More than anything, Ashton needs a bone marrow donor. If you're not already on the national registry, please take a moment to find out more." Carter pointed across the street. "The vehicle directly across the street from me is equipped to take care of everything. So in this season of gifts and giving, please consider giving the gift that might just save a life. Thank you."

He repositioned the mic in the stand then turned toward Andy. Steve Miller had also joined them on the wagon. Both shook his hand as he turned.

A kind smile lit Andy's eyes. "That's exactly why you needed to make that speech instead of me."

"Agreed." While Steve's face held admiration, it also held a tinge of something else. Something Carter couldn't quite put his finger on.

Carter moved to the back of the makeshift stage. "Well, I better head on over to the Elementary School. The 5K kicks off in a few minutes." He said his goodbyes, jumped from the wagon bed, and then jogged to the corner and three blocks down to the elementary school.

Chloe stood at the flag pole, a number already penned to her shirt, and another card in her hands. "There you are. What took so long?"

"Sorry. Got commandeered to give a short speech on Ashton's behalf."

His daughter's eyebrows shot up. "You?"

He nodded while she penned the number on his t-shirt.

"How'd that go over? Like a lead balloon?" The sarcasm in her voice revealed her less-than-high opinion of his speaking ability.

"Better than expected, thank you. You ready to get this shindig underway?"

Forty-five minutes later, he and Chloe crossed the finish line side by side, both sweating profusely and gasping for air. He shuffled to one side and bent low, hands on knees, then forced himself to an upright position before his legs cramped up. But he'd only taken two steps, when Otis Thacker stepped in front of him, a dour expression on his face. "Hey, Otis." Carter spoke the greeting with a friendly tone, hoping to diffuse whatever had put a bee in Otis' bonnet.

"Hmph!" Otis glared up at him. "Don't remember the city council giving approval for all these events of yours."

Approval? Carter scratched his head. "Didn't know I needed it."

"It's in the by-laws I helped draft several years ago. Any city-wide events must be approved by the city council."

Well, what could he do about it now? He shrugged. "Sorry, Otis, but it's a little late now."

The old man's eyes narrowed. "I'll have to ask you to cancel any other events not directly sponsored by the Chamber of Commerce and the festival."

Sparks shot out the top of Carter's head as his jaw unhinged. Absolutely not! He breathed in deeply to satisfy his lungs. "No can do, Otis. A little girl's life hangs in the balance. I'm not cancelling anything."

Without another word he strode past Otis and over to where Chloe stood, hands on top of her head.

She frowned. "What's wrong with you?"

He shook his head. "Nothing I can't handle. Ready for our daddy-daughter lunch?"

Chloe made a face and peered up at him apologetically. "Sorry, Dad. I already told Heather I'd meet her at Granny's."

Disappointment forced a semi-audible sigh from his lungs. "No prob."

"Are you sure?"

Heather hollered from down the street. "Hey, Chloe., c'mon! I'm starved!" His daughter's best friend waved a hand. "Hi, Mr. C!"

Carter waved back, then peered down at Chloe. "Yeah, I'm sure. Catch you later."

"Thanks, Daddy." She smiled, gave him a quick hug, then ran toward her friend.

He looked on as the two linked elbows and strolled toward the town square, their laughter floating back behind them. So much for the daddy-daughter lunch date he'd hoped for. Just one more sign that his time with Chloe was growing short. Carter released the tension in his shoulders and ambled down the street. Oh well, he'd just grab a burger from one of the vendors and chase it with warm, sugar-sprinkled funnel cake and an extra-large Dr. Pepper.

As the day progressed, the crowds dwindled, the worst turnout for the Holly Daze Festival since its inception. The weather worsened, at first pelting light rain. Then, if that weren't bad enough, mid-afternoon the precipitation turned to freezing rain.

Carter's spirits sank as by mid-afternoon everyone hurriedly put things away. He latched on to Steve Miller as he passed by. "Hey, Steve. What's going on?"

Sorrow darkened his friend's eyes. "We're closing up shop because of the weather advisory. This storm is only gonna get worse. Already the electrical lines and bridges are coated with ice."

Hope plummeted further. "I understand."

The town's mayor patted his shoulder, then hurried off, so Carter headed to the donor van to help them pack up. He sidled up next to Brett, the man he'd worked in conjunction with to coordinate the drive. "How'd it go today?"

The man pressed his lips together momentarily. "Not good. Less than twenty-five, counting you. But I guess it's better than nothing."

Carter had no words. Heart heavy, he helped load folding tables, then waved off the crew before making his way to the donation booth. A rumble of thunder announced his arrival, and the icy rain grew even heavier.

Dakota took off in a trot across the street toward the old farm truck she drove, while Chance pulled the brim of his cap down and handed Carter a thin envelope. "Here are the donations."

Carter looked at his friend expectantly, afraid to even ask.

Chance sent a gentle smile. "Don't be upset. Just turned out to be a bad day for anything outdoors." His friend finished his statement with a chuckle. "And to answer the questions in your eyes, a little over a hundred bucks. See you around." He took off across the street to join his wife.

Carter's stomach sank to his toes as the funnel cake inside turned to lead. A hundred bucks? What good could so little do? He leaned his head back to take in the dark skies. Well, at least Otis got his wish for cancelled events. But what about his wish for a healthy whole little girl and a spiritually-well Mara?

Seventeen

Mara double-checked her calculations, the results no different than the first time. She glared at the numbers in her in-the-red checkbook for a minute longer, then sighed, rose to her feet, and tiptoed to the corner where Ashton lay sleeping. Mara, her heart heavy and numb, knelt beside her daughter and watched her sleep. In the big scheme of things, money meant nothing. Unless a bone marrow donor was found soon Ashton had less than six months to live. After trying a different treatment, the doctor had made the decision last week to let her come home. Their first hospice visit was scheduled for tomorrow.

The front door buzzer roused Mara from her hover, and she glanced up at the clock. That would be Chloe. She wearily pushed her body to a standing position and traipsed to the office door.

Chloe didn't look up, but made her way to her desk, sniffling.

Mara frowned. Did Chloe have a cold? If so, she had to go home immediately. Ashton's body was already weak enough. She scrutinized Chloe a little more closely. No, her eyes were swollen and red-rimmed. "Something wrong?"

The teenager's shoulders heaved and her head lowered as deep sobs shook her petite frame.

Mara hurried over and pulled her into a hug, the soft scent of her strawberry shampoo rising from her silky ringlets. "What is it, sweetie?"

At first there were only sobs, but finally Chloe squeaked out a few words around her tears and sniffles. "Bryce broke up with me. And he already has another girlfriend."

Mara's heart broke. No matter your age, betrayal stung, a fact she knew all too well. "Oh, sweetheart, I'm so sorry." She rolled the desk chair up behind Chloe. "Sit here. I just happen to have a good remedy for heartbreak. It's gotten me through more than one round." She hurried to the coffee pot full of hot water that she kept at the ready, especially during the cool months. A couple of minutes later, she returned to the desk with two steaming cups of hot chocolate, one of which she handed to Chloe. "Here, this will help."

Although her pretty face still bore evidence of tears, at least for the moment they had stopped. She smiled sadly and took the cup. "Thanks." The teenager released a puff of air across the hot chocolate, then slurped it between her lips. She leaned her curly head back against the chair, eyes closed, and swallowed. Then she inhaled deeply and opened her eyes as she exhaled. "Hot chocolate does help." She hesitated briefly, as though gathering her thoughts and words. "Did you cry when you and Dad broke up?"

Mara rested her weight on the corner of Chloe's desk. Yes, she'd cried, and cried like there would be no tomorrow. "Well, we weren't exactly dating, so we couldn't break up."

"But you did things together."

"Yes." What was she getting at?

"And you were over at our house a lot, and we were over at yours."

"True."

"Ever since you've been back, I hardly see you and Ashton unless it's here at your office." She paused long enough to take another sip of cocoa, but tears pooled in her eyes. "I miss the way it used to be."

"I do, too." The truthful-but-traitorous words escaped, clogged with emotion. "But it's for the best." Thoughts that had plagued her since that night three weeks ago returned with fresh force. What if Carter was right about God? What if she was wrong? Would God punish her by taking Ashton away?

"Why did you break up, I mean, stop seeing each other?"

Mara sat her cup on the desk and pretended to scan the stack of mail Chloe brought in. "We just don't see eye-to-eye on some things."

"Things like God?"

Mara released an exasperated sigh, dropped the wad of bills, and nodded uncomfortably. On one hand, she desperately wanted to help Chloe through this rough time, but could she handle all these questions that ripped at her emotions with unsheathed talons?

"I didn't like it when Dad made me go to youth group when I first moved in with him, but now I look forward to it."

Well, that was news. What had brought about the huge turnaround? "Why?"

Chloe shrugged. "I guess because it brings comfort. I'm starting to think Dad's beliefs about God and the Bible might be true."

Mara's shoulder muscles immediately snapped to attention. "What makes you think so?"

"Well, I pray, and I feel like I'm not alone. Like there's Someone there with me."

Impatient anger gained momentum within her very soul. Would there ever come a time when she didn't have to defend her position when it came to God? Time to bring an ax to the root of this tree. "And do you get everything you pray for?" A hard edge laced Mara's tone, as thoughts of Ashton's condition dripped acid into her belly.

"No, but if I did, wouldn't that somehow diminish Him as God of the universe?"

Good point. When had this woman-child grown so wise?

"I mean, if He gave me everything I wanted, that would just make Him like a magic genie, or Santa Claus, instead of the One in control."

Enough of this. Mara rose to her feet, eager to put the conversation behind her. "Speaking of Santa, I'd better get back to work or I won't be able to afford Christmas gifts. You okay now?"

Chloe nodded, but her eyes narrowed, as if she sensed Mara's motives for escape.

Mara took refuge in her office, closed the door quietly behind her, and rested her weight against it. Christmas. How could she possibly pay for Ashton's last Christmas with creditors mercilessly hounding her? She moved noiselessly to the desk chair and once more picked up the dreaded checkbook. But even her financial woes couldn't keep unwelcomed thoughts from her head.

She rubbed at the headache building in her temples as Carter's comment about God not being like her earthly father played over and over again in her mind. There was truth to the statement, and that alone brought cause for concern. Painful memories of her father and the churches he'd pastored had indeed influenced her decision about God and the people that confessed faith in him. How could it not?

Enough. Mara released a heavy breath. She simply couldn't deal with all that right now. There were enough worries on her plate without adding the God questions. She attacked the stack of creditor letters and bills. Ten minutes later she slumped back in her chair, her eyes glazed. There was only one logical step to take next.

Mara leafed through the pages of the phone book until she found the number she needed. She punched in the number on her cell phone and attempted to steady her nerves while the phone rang on the other end.

"Tyler Law Firm. How may I help you?"

It took her a moment to find her voice. "This is Mara Hedwig. Does Andy handle personal bankruptcy?"

"Yes, he does."

"Then I need an appointment. I don't know if I'm to that point yet, but I figure it wouldn't hurt to ask a few questions."

Once the arrangements were made, Mara hung up and waited for calm resignation to follow. It didn't. Instead the darkness clouded around her, the kind that begged for a listening ear and shoulder to cry on. But she had no one.

The only one who'd played that role in her life she'd sent away.

She laid her head and arms on the desk, as tears leaked from her eyes. Bankruptcy meant losing the house and possibly some of her other belongings. Another thought immediately catapulted into her brain. In a town the size of Miller's Creek, everyone would know, bringing with it the potential that no one would ever again trust her with their business.

Later that night, Mara finished up Ashton's sponge bath, inwardly bemoaning the fact that her daughter no longer had the energy to bathe herself, but doing all she could to don a cheerful face for her sick child. She held tears at bay as she tucked Ashton into bed, then hurried to answer her buzzing cell phone. "Hello?"

"Hey, Mara. Andy Tyler here."

"Hi, Andy."

"Listen, would it be okay if Trish and I come over for a few minutes?"

What on earth for? Surely this wasn't about bankruptcy. "I guess so. I just put Ashton to bed, so now would be an okay time."

"Be there in about fifteen minutes."

The doorbell sounded several minutes later, and Mara opened the door.

Andy grinned at her with his typical good-old-boy grin. His wife, Trish, on the other hand, smiled close-lipped, deep sorrow in her dark brown eyes. She wrapped long arms around Mara's neck. "Thanks for agreeing to let us come over."

"Sure. Come on in."

Mara held the door while they entered. Rather than his typical business suit, Andy wore jeans, a sweat shirt, and sneakers. Trish was similarly dressed. Mara motioned them to the living room. "Please have a seat."

The couple took a seat on the couch while Mara moved to the large overstuffed chair nearby. Andy spoke as she curled her legs beneath her in the chair. "I noticed you called earlier today to make an appointment. Something about personal bankruptcy?"

Her insides instantly in shreds, Mara nodded.

Andy's ocean-water eyes took on a compassionate gleam. "Mara, there are lots of folks in this town who'd be happy to help you out."

"People in the church?" The words popped out unexpectedly, and with a bit of a snarl.

A frown knit his forehead beneath his short curls. "Well, yeah, but what does that have to do with anything?"

An icy drizzle settled over Mara's heart, and dripped into her words. "It's been my experience that some gifts come with strings attached and with a bigger price tag than I'm willing to pay."

Andy's face reddened, but a slow breath returned it to almost normal. "Sorry that's been your experience. Just trying to help here, and I think I can say the same for the others."

Immediate remorse rained down on her, and she flushed. "I'm so sorry. Sometimes my pride gets the best of me. Honestly, I'm grateful for whatever help I can get, but I don't want to be a drain on anyone."

A gentle smile returned to Andy's handsome face. "No apology needed." His cell phone rang, and he quickly removed it from the holster at his waist, his eyes scanning the screen. "Sorry, but I need to take this call. Excuse me." He sauntered to the front door, the phone to his ear. "This is Andy." The door clicked shut behind him.

Mara faced Trish. "You've got yourself a good man."

"The best." Trish's dark brown eyes turned to melted chocolate. "I hope you take this in the way it's intended, but I understand the pride thing. I went through something similar when Bo and I were on our own."

Mara cocked her head to one side. On their own? When was that? "I didn't realize you were a single mom at one time. I assumed Bo was Andy's son."

"No, my first husband was killed in a freak horse accident. Bo was about Ashton's age and saw the whole thing."

An unrestrainable grimace worked its way across Mara's face.

Trish brought fingertips to her eyes to brush away tears. "Sorry, I still get emotional when I think of how much Bo suffered while I was trying to support us both. Undoubtedly, the hardest time of my life."

Moisture slipped down Mara's cheek.

In a flash, Trish moved over to where Mara sat, bent down, and hugged her. "I've been where you are." Her tone held a quiver. "I know how hard it is. But don't let your pride shove people away when they want to help." She pulled back, knelt in front of Mara, and took her hands in her own. "Your little girl needs you, so please, let us help in whatever way we can. Don't try to do this on your own."

Mara couldn't speak, her throat swollen with an unusual mixture of pain and gratitude and humility.

The front door opened, and Andy strode into the living room as Trish moved back to the couch. "Sorry about the interruption." He plopped to the sofa beside his wife, patted her knee, then turned his attention back to Mara. "You okay with me speaking to some folks about helping out?"

"Yes. Thank you." The words barely croaked out.

For the next few minutes, conversation turned to lesser matters. Then Andy and Trish administered hugs and words of encouragement, then left.

No sooner had she shut the door behind them than her phone buzzed. She read the screen, then raised her gaze to the ceiling beams. Should she answer? Trish's comment about pride flitted to the forefront of her brain. Mara pushed the green button and moved the phone to her face. "Hi, Carter."

"Hi. Um, don't mean to bother you. Just wanted to see how you and Ashton were doing."

"We're okay." Her wavering voice sent a conflicting message.

"Sounds to me like you're having a rough go of it." His tone held no condemnation or censure. Instead the words were compassionate and gentle.

She wanted to speak, but couldn't unless tears were allowed as well.

"I won't take any more of your time. Please call if you need anything." A brief moment of silence sounded on the other end. "Praying for you. Good night."

Unstoppable tears flowed, with accompanying sobs, as Mara pulled the phone from her mouth. She grabbed a box of Kleenex and moved to the couch. Then someone settled in beside her.

Ashton.

Mara pulled her daughter into her lap and clung to her. Rarely did she let Ashton see this side of her, but tonight she had no choice. Finally, her tears spent, she leaned back and smiled sheepishly. "Sorry about that, honey. Mommy has just had a rough day." She yanked a tissue from the box, dabbed her face, and then blew her nose.

"It's okay to cry. That's what you always tell me. Right?"

Mara nodded and blinked against more tears. "Um-hmm."

"Then why do you hardly ever do it?"

Though her eyes flooded once more, Mara somehow managed to maintain control. Oh, she cried plenty, especially here recently, but always behind closed doors. "It would just be really easy to stay upset if I do it too often. Anyway, enough about me. I know a little girl that had better head back to bed. You don't want to sleep through your lessons when Miss Angie comes."

Ashton lowered her smooth and shiny head, but didn't speak.

"I thought you liked Miss Angie."

Ashton didn't look up. "I do. I just miss going to real school and playing with my friends."

Tears threatened again. Mara straightened her back, and with feigned enthusiasm pulled Ashton into her arms. She stood easily, Ashton's rapidly decreasing weight making her easy to lift. "C'mon, girlfriend. Time to get you in bed so you can get well and go back to real school and play with your friends."

Ashton glued her blue-eyed gaze to Mara's face as she tucked her beneath the covers. "Mommy?"

"Yes, honey?"

"I know."

Mara's pulse quickened. "Know what, pumpkin?"

"That I might die."

The softly-spoken words knocked Mara to her knees at the side of the bed, tears once more coursing down her face. She stroked Ashton's head and attempted a smile. "We all have to die sometime, sweetie. And besides that, they might find a don--"

"Mommy?"

"Yeah?"

Ashton's eyes took on a forcefulness always present when she had something important to say. "I know you don't believe in God, but would it be okay if I do?"

Bombarding thoughts struggled within, like a moth futilely flapping its wings against a window pane to get to the light inside. "I guess so. But I don't want you to do it because you're afraid of dying. Only believe it if you think God is real."

"I'm not afraid of dying, and I don't just think God is real. I know He is."

Mara sucked in a deep breath, rose to her feet, and tucked in the blanket that was already tucked in. "Oh, really? And how do you know?"

"Remember when I passed out at the Callahan's?"

"Yes." She picked up a few toys lying around Ashton's room and arranged them on the shelf.

"I saw Jesus."

Mara froze. Who was responsible for filling her daughter's head with this nonsense? Dani and Mama Beth? No. Ashton hadn't been around them since the news that she would die without a donor. A frown worried her brow, and she took a seat on the edge of Ashton's bed. "Like a dream? Dreams aren't real, you know."

"It wasn't like that. I knew I was about to faint, so I started praying. A man that looked like Jesus came toward me as I fell. He caught me and told me He was with me and that everything would be okay."

Her mouth fell open. She moved her lips to speak, then closed them again.

"So if you don't mind, I'm going to believe in Him. Good night." Without another word, Ashton flipped over on her side, her back to Mara.

In a daze, Mara half-stumbled to the hallway and closed the door. Her mind took off in a myriad of directions, but with no resolution. Fifteen minutes later, after she'd semi-gathered her emotions and wits, she tiptoed back into her daughter's room.

Sound asleep, Ashton wore an angelic smile, as though in some far-off land of perfect rest and peace.

Eighteen

"Dadburnit, Carter, I don't think you fully understand what this means!" Ernie's normally placid face flashed a livid anger supported by his irate tone. "You know the city police policy about waiting for backup. Yet once more you chose to do your own thing!" He stomped over to his desk and fell into the chair, his moustache a-twitch.

"C'mon, Ernie. I knew what to do. If I'd waited for you, the guy might've gotten away, and with that stash of cocaine in his car, we never would've seen him again." Carter's gaze wandered to the clock. He'd hoped to have time to stop by the real estate company to see Ashton. She and Mara had been back in town several days, but he just hadn't had time to drop in for a visit.

His boss shook his head forcefully, his beady eyes like steel. "No, you did it for the adrenaline rush. I know guys like you. You're easily bored, especially in a low-crime area like Miller's Creek. You're used to high action and this job is boring and routine. I've seen it in your eyes." Ernie rubbed at the wrinkles that inched up toward his bald head. "You unnecessarily put yourself in danger, a pretty selfish thing to do considering you have a teenaged daughter."

Carter's blood ran cold at the terse words. What would've happened to Chloe if the guy had shot and killed him?

"There's a city council meeting tonight at seven." Ernie's tone softened somewhat. "You might wanna be there."

Alarms rang in his head, as heart pounding, a thick goo coated his tongue. Carter glared at Ernie. "Why?"

"This was your second offense, Carter. I had to write it up and give it to them."

"Second offense?"

"Back in the spring you had that excessive force clai--"

"The guy was lying." An edge of panic and anger crept into his voice.

"Well, since you didn't wait for backup then either, you don't have any witnesses to prove it. Like it or not, this counts as your second strike. Your job's on the line." Ernie didn't blink or mince words.

A combination of fear and anger punched him in the gut. "As in I might lose it?" This couldn't be happening. Afraid of letting his anger get the best of him, Carter stormed from the police station, his fractured thoughts taking a toll on his ability to maintain control.

After checking to make sure Chloe was safely at home, he drove around the surrounding countryside until time for the meeting, trying to piece together all that had happened and how he should respond. Finally, his desperation turned to prayer. *Lord, whatever happens tonight I just want Your will to be done. Keep me calm and collected and very much aware of Your Presence with me.*

By time for the city council meeting, he'd brought his frustration under control and could better approach the time with humility rather than anger.

Wearily, Carter climbed the squeaky wood stairs and entered the conference room of City Hall. A combined odor of musty old building and his own sweat attacked his nostrils. What would he and Chloe do without this job? He had no choice but to do all he could to save his position. He sauntered to the long table in one corner of the open space where the council members had already congregated.

Steve Miller rose and stepped toward him, his boots clomping against the old wood floors. He shook Carter's hand. "Hey, Carter. Come on in."

In addition to Steve and Ernie, Gracie Tyler and Clay Barnes both smiled and spoke. But Otis Thacker, true to his reputation as town grump, merely grunted and scowled. Mara, the latest member appointed because someone had moved away, wouldn't meet his gaze at all.

Carter sighed and took a seat beside Ernie. Would things with her ever be right?

After the opening prayer, the council moved Carter's item to the top of their agenda. Steve presided, and he peered at Carter over the top of his reading glasses, his elbows at rest on the table, and his fingers steepled in front of him. "First let me say how grateful we are to have someone with your outstanding qualifications on our police force. Ernie has mentioned on more than one occasion what a big help you are to him." He paused, his eyes kind, but firm. "However, for the protection of the citizens of Miller's Creek, and for your protection as well, we have to insist that you follow proper police procedure.

That includes waiting for backup in a dangerous situation. Anything you want to say?"

Carter nodded, his nerves on edge at the gravity of the situation. "In the military, I was trained to act on the spur of the moment. It was part of my job and sometimes involved a split-second decision. In this case, I felt like my best option--and my best chance to protect Miller's Creek--was to put the guy in cuffs and arrest him before he saw what was coming. But in retrospect, I also see the wisdom of waiting for backup. I'm sorry, and I won't let it happen again." He made eye contact with each and every member of the council, and his gaze came to rest on Mara. "I hope you'll allow me to keep my job."

Mara rolled her lips between her teeth and lowered her head.

"Why don't you wait downstairs while we discuss this?" The words held a dark undertone in spite of the kind smile on Steve's face. "One of us will come get you when we're ready to announce our decision."

Carter swallowed against the nasty taste in his mouth, rose to his feet, and nodded. "Please keep in mind that I have a teenage daughter to support." No one answered. As he headed down the stairs, jumbled thoughts attacked. His job was probably history. Steve Miller held a great love for the town and didn't put up with a whole lot of nonsense when it came to Miller's Creek. Ernie was angry enough to influence the whole lot of them. Gracie, though soft-spoken and sweet, had developed quite the reputation as City Attorney for being hard on folks that crossed the line. Clay Barnes, the manager of Miller's Ranch and Steve's best friend, would most likely be swayed in whatever direction Steve went. And Otis? He twisted his lips to one side and released a sigh. Well, the fact that he already held a grudge concerning the events of the Holly Days Festival didn't bode well. And with Mara, who knew?

Several minutes later, Clay's cowboy boots thudded down the stairs. "We've reached a decision." He sent a kind-but-sad smile, then turned and headed back up the stairs.

Nerves throbbing, Carter inhaled deeply, then stepped up the stairs behind him. He glanced around the table as he took a seat. There was no deciphering the outcome in the poker faces of the committee, which only served to make his heart beat double time.

Steve, his lips clamped together in a thin line, looked him directly in the eye, and brought back memories of being called on the carpet by his CO. "All of us agree that what you did was not only wrong, but unnecessary. It's the decision of this council that you be placed on temporary suspension for three weeks."

His whole being screamed to object, but Carter ground his teeth together to keep angry words behind bars. At least his military days had taught him the wisdom of not speaking back to those in authority over him.

Steve continued. "After that you'll be on probation for two more months. If during that time Ernie has any issues with you following correct police procedure, you'll be terminated. Any questions?"

Only one thought crossed his mind. "I've already mentioned it, but I have a daughter to support."

Steve nodded. "Yes, you do. A fact you should've considered before you decided to take on this guy on your own."

The softly-spoken words sliced through him.

"The council has also decided it will continue your pay during suspension."

Relief released the air Carter held captive in his lungs. At least he'd still have money to put food on the table and to pay rent and utilities. His gaze once more landed on Mara, who still averted her gaze. Did she have money to meet her and Ashton's needs? An intense ache landed his chest at the thought of them possibly going hungry.

Carter sent a humble and grateful smile as he rose to his feet. "Thank you." Then with one more look Mara's way, Carter turned and headed for the stairs.

Once at the house, he stuck the key in the lock and then pulled mail from the mailbox. Even in the dim light, one envelope in particular caught his attention. The return address section said all he hoped for. Dallas Police Department. He ripped into the envelope and scanned the letter from the Dallas Police Chief offering him an interview. Finally things were turning his way.

A thrill of excitement pounded through his body. This couldn't have happened at a better time. But the thrill was quickly replaced by a sobering thought. He wasn't the only one who would be impacted by this news. It meant uprooting Chloe from her senior year in high school. And just as important, it would meant moving away from Mara and Ashton. How could he possibly choose?

He gnawed his bottom lip. Maybe the job would start after Chloe's graduation. Maybe he could completely close the door between himself and Mara and her very sick little girl. Maybe... Carter gave his head a shake. Enough of the 'maybes.' This kind of decision was only reached with prayer, and lots of it.

Just as he entered the house, a car pulled up to the curb and honked. Chloe careened around the corner of the hallway and almost bowled him over on her way out. "Bye, Dad. I'm headed over to Heather's to study for our Calculus mid-term. I'll be home by ten."

"Okay."

She flew down the sidewalk and disappeared into her friend's car.

Great. Just what he needed. A quiet house alone with his thoughts and a decision hanging over his head. Carter tossed the mail to a side table in the foyer, ambled to the kitchen, and opened the fridge. He stood there for a long minute trying to decide what he wanted to eat or if he was even hungry in light of all that had transpired.

The doorbell rang.

Carter frowned. Who could that be? Chloe had probably forgotten something, including her keys. He strode to the front door and yanked it open.

But instead of his daughter, Mara stood there, an apologetic look on her face.

Conflicting emotion ripped through his insides and sent his pulse racing. He stepped back and motioned her inside. "To what do I owe this nice surprise?"

"I can't stay long. Trish and Andy are keeping an eye on Ashton for me." She looked at him intently. "But I wanted to see how you were doing."

"Been better." That much was definitely true. How would she react to his other news? Maybe gauging her reaction was a way to help him reach a decision. He sent a quick prayer heavenward. "On a brighter note, I've been offered a new job."

Her eyebrows shot up her forehead, but she didn't speak.

"I--uh, you know I applied for a position with the Dallas Police force a while back. They're offering me an interview." Was it his imagination, or had her face paled at the news? "How's Ashton?"

A weary sorrow invaded her eyes. "That's another reason I stopped by." She paused, her gaze averted to the floor. "She's very weak right now, and I can tell she misses you and Chloe. If y'all can come over some time, I know she'd be glad to see you."

And what about you? He wanted to shout the words, but couldn't even give them voice. "No donor yet?"

She shook her head, then looked up at him. "Something else. Ashton claims to have seen Jesus."

A ribbon of hope unfurled within him. Was this the way God would bring her around? Is that what it would take for Him to get Mara's attention? "And?"

"She says that the day she fainted at the lake house, Jesus caught her and told her He was with her."

He shut his eyes with heartfelt praise, then opened them to Mara's frowning face.

"Well, I'd better be going." She took a step toward the door.

"Wait!"

Mara faced him, a curious light in her eyes.

Something inside compelled him into enemy territory, knowing full well it was a move she wouldn't appreciate. Carter stepped forward, his gaze locked on her beautiful eyes. "Would you come to church with us on Sunday?'

"I don't know." Her tone held uncertainty. "I'm not sure Ashton can handle it."

"We can leave if she starts feeling tired or sick."

She considered his words a moment, then nodded her assent.

Exquisite joy erupted in his heart and moved to his face. He put both hands on her shoulders. "Thank you, Mara." Dare he say all that was on his heart? But how would she know unless he expressed it? "I've missed you so much."

Tears sprang to her eyes, and a tender smile appeared. "I've missed you, too." She sent one last wavering smile, then opened the door and stepped out into the night.

Carter sauntered to the living room and fell to the couch, elbows on knees. *Oh, dear Jesus, thank You.* More words just wouldn't come, but of one thing he was certain. Even his wordless prayers reached God's ear. His earlier angst completely dissipated, replaced by the sweetest peace and joy. God was and would always be on His throne, so there was no need for worry.

Chloe arrived an hour later, flopped to the couch with her books in her lap, and studied him from a sideways glance. "You seem different. What's going on?"

He clicked off the TV and searched for words, but none came. How did a father explain to his teenage daughter that the woman he loved might at last be making a turnaround?

Chloe smiled knowingly, a smile that made her look more like a young woman than a teenager. "Does this have something to do with Mara?"

Carter nodded and chuckled, then rested one ankle on the opposite knee to face her. "She came over earlier and asked us to go see Ashton. I invited them to church. She accepted." Even still it seemed unbelievable.

A laugh bubbled from Chloe. "When I ran out earlier, I got the distinct impression something very bad had happened in your day. I prayed silently all the way to Heather's house that God would do something to make you happy. I'm starting to believe the way you do, Dad." Her last sentence was spoken softly, but with great resolve.

Carter laid a hand across his mouth. Two prayers answered on what had earlier seemed like one of the worst days of his life? He scooted closer, enveloped her in a bear hug, and rocked from side to side. "Oh, honey, that's the best news ever. Been praying you'd come around."

She pulled back, a contented smile on her face. "Why were you so down in the dumps earlier?"

He related to her the mishandled drug bust and the upcoming suspension and probation. "But I did get good news in the mail."

Questions filled her eyes. "News?"

"Yeah." He hesitated, fearful of breaking the sweet camaraderie between them. "Dallas Police have offered me an interview."

Chloe seemed to accept his words, but her smile had faded. "I know you'll pray about it, and God will lead you the right way." She paused, her expression thoughtful. "How do you feel about me seeing if I'm a bone marrow match for Ashton?"

The question caught him off guard, but the answer came immediately. "Makes me very proud of the young woman you're becoming. Takes a lot of maturity and unselfishness to think that way."

His daughter beamed. "I just feel like it's something I'm supposed to do." She leaned over and kissed his cheek, then stood and headed down the hall. "Love you, Dad. See you in the morning."

"Love you, too. Good night." Long after she left the room, Carter's thoughts lingered on the new job offer, Chloe's desire to donate marrow, and his gratitude that Mara and Ashton would once more be part of their lives. God's plan was unfolding right before him, and he'd been given the distinct privilege of having a front row seat.

Sunday morning arrived, a day more spring-like than the quickly approaching winter season. Mara marveled at how different this trip to church with Carter and Chloe felt compared to that first time just a few short weeks ago. So much had happened since then. Was time the difference, or was it something else?

Mara puzzled over the question throughout the service, first as Carter's deep voice boomed beside her as he held Ashton in his strong arms. Her daughter had climbed in his lap once they were seated and refused to let him go.

The action sent remorse shimmying through her bones. Had she been wrong to send Carter away? Had it worsened her daughter's already precarious position?

Seconds slipped into minutes, and before she knew it soft music signaling the invitation began to play. As Mara rose to her feet with the rest of the congregation, from her left Chloe squeezed by and made her way down the aisle.

She glanced nervously at Carter. His face beamed, and unchecked tears inched down his cheeks. Ashton leaned close and whispered something in his ear. He whispered back then set her feet on the floor.

Claws of panic raked at her heart, as her daughter, hospital mask firmly in place on her hairless head, traipsed down the aisle behind Chloe. Should she go after Ashton, or just discuss this with her later? Crippled by indecision, she gripped the pew in front of her, knuckles white.

A soft voice broke through the confusion, directing her from the fear that clutched her.

Finally, the moments of tension passed, and the four passed through the crowd to a sparkling day.

"I think this beautiful day calls for a picnic at the park." Carter, his face still aglow, looked her way as they descended the front steps of the church. "What do y'all think?"

Both girls immediately voiced their assent, leaving Mara with one less decision to make. She smiled and nodded. "It is a pretty day."

Later that day, after lunch was over, Carter leaned close while Chloe and Ashton headed toward the merry-go-round. "You have plans for Christmas?"

"How did I know you were about to ask that question?" She shook her head. "No, we don't have plans."

"Wanna try another go with the Callahan clan?"

Mara sighed, too overwhelmed by thoughts of the upcoming conversation with Ashton to object. "Sure. Why not?" A frown wriggled onto her face. Why was it that in this time of not knowing where to turn next, an invisible force seemed to plan her days and guide her steps?

Nineteen

Mara carried Ashton through the front door of the Callahan lake house mid-morning on Christmas Day, the aroma of lunch preparations already saturating the air to a more subdued and less noisy clan of Callahans than what she'd experienced on Thanksgiving.

Jo held the door, her compassionate eyes so much like Carter's. "Y'all come on in. Sorry you're having a rough day, Ashton."

Her lips pale and face ashen, Ashton managed a weak smile. "It's okay. I'm used to it."

Mara's mouth went bone dry. What horrible words to come from the mouth of a five-year old. But it was truth. Her daughter's normal life consisted of nausea, no hair, and enough medication to choke a horse. Mara laid Ashton on one end of the sectional sofa in the family room and helped her remove her coat.

Darcy, her round face smiling and cheerful, immediately took up residence near Ashton on the floor, and handed her one of the two Barbie dolls she held in her chubby little hands.

Carter nabbed a nearby snuggly blanket from the back of the sofa and tucked it around Ashton's legs. Next he pulled a stack of children's books from a nearby bookcase and plunked them down on the coffee table. "That ought to keep you two out of trouble for a while."

Ashton smiled. "Thank you." Already her eyelids grew heavy. A few minutes later, after all the hugs and greetings, she was sound asleep, despite Darcy playing nearby.

Chloe gently eased to the couch near Ashton's feet.

"You okay, Chlo?" Carter's face held a frown.

"Just not feeling real bueno. I'll be okay." The teenager's gaze landed on Ashton's sleeping figure, and moisture filled her eyes. Was Chloe making herself sick over concern for Ashton?

Mara made a mental note to talk to the teenager as the occasion rose. The last thing she wanted was for her bulimia to raise its ugly head because of stress over Ashton. She scanned the room, heavy with decoration for the holidays. Wreaths hung in each of the bank of windows that overlooked the lake, and the biggest Christmas tree she'd ever seen stood sentinel near the crackling wood fire in the massive stone fireplace. The chunky mantle supported the weight of several overloaded stockings, including ones for her and Ashton.

She lowered her head and released a sigh, suddenly weary of all the world had dealt her. Had she but one ounce of energy left after caring for a very sick child, she would've realized these people more than likely had gifts for them, and they had nothing to give in return.

A comforting hand landed on Mara's shoulder, and she raised her gaze to Carter's smiling face.

The look in his eyes was one of reassurance, immediately replaced by mischief. "You're in for a treat." His grin grew cheekier, and his eyes sported a twinkle.

"Oh, yeah? What's that?"

"It's time for the annual Callahan clan Christmas karaoke."

Mara waved both hands at waist level, palms facing the floor. "Not me. I'm tone deaf."

Carter stepped behind her, placed both hands on her shoulders, and gave a gentle nudge. "No matter. Everyone participates."

She planted both heels firmly in the thick Berber carpet. "Not me."

He pushed a little harder this time. "Okay, okay, but you can at least come listen."

Her fears laid to rest, Mara allowed him to steer her to a large open space filled with couches and game tables. She took a seat between Carter and Caleb. Within just a few minutes the two brothers joined Cade near the large television screen and sound system. Each one grabbed a microphone, and the music to *Frosty the Snowman* lilted into the air. The three brothers acted out the story while they sang, which made it more like a circus than karaoke. Mara couldn't help but laugh, in spite of the overwhelming sorrow that had dogged her steps since the Thanksgiving visit. By the time they finished their rousing rendition, tears of hysterical laughter inched down all their faces.

Next Jo and Cliff took center stage with a more serious performance of *Oh, Holy Night*. Their two voices blended as one, and their faces shone with conviction in the message of the song. The music ended to more moist eyes, but this time for a different reason.

Carter wiped his face, then stood and carried two small baskets to his mother. "Have to draw to see who goes next, since everyone else in the room is a big chicken."

Jo reached into one basket and unrolled the paper scrap she withdrew. "The next song is *Away in a Manger*."

She shuffled around in the second, and unrolled yet another piece of paper. "And the victim, I mean singer, is...Mara!"

Mara's nervous system sprang to full alert as cheers and applause erupted. "Uh, trust me, you really don't want to hear me sing. It's so bad." And after the previous two acts, it would be especially humiliating. But no matter how hard she tried to extricate herself from the performance, her protests only brought more applause and words of encouragement.

Carter sat the baskets on an end table and stretched out a hand toward her, his expression both challenging and encouraging. "C'mon, I'll help you." He latched onto her hand and pulled her to her feet.

Her breath caught in her throat, but an unexpected excitement also zinged within. She nodded her assent, moved with Carter to the front of the room, and accepted the microphone he handed her. Could she do this without making a fool of herself in front of his family? She pushed the negative thought from her mind, suddenly comforted by the knowledge that at least Carter was up here with her. He knew how mortified and uncomfortable she'd be if she had to do this on her own. Would this man ever stop being both a surprise and a true-blue friend for her?

The music began, a soft guitar strum. Mara's gaze alternated between the screen and Carter's face, hoping she'd at least be able to discern when to start singing. She needn't have worried, because Carter nodded when it was time to begin. His deep baritone joined her shaky, off-key voice. Never once did he glance at the words, singing them all by heart, his encouraging gaze focused on her.

"...the little Lord Jesus lay down His sweet head." The sweet words coiled around Mara's heart. Jesus was Lord, an Old Testament name given to God because He was so holy they feared to speak His name. Where had that tidbit of knowledge come from?

"...the little Lord Jesus asleep on the hay." Accustomed to the glory and splendor of heaven, Jesus had given it all up to come to earth, for no other reason than profound love. That kind of God she could get behind.

"Be near me, Lord Jesus, I ask Thee to stay..." Lord Jesus, I need Your help. Would the prayer of her heart be heard?

"...close by me forever, and love me I pray." Mara's gaze met Carter's. He sang the words with a special longing from somewhere deep inside him, and it leaked out his eyes. Is that how badly he wanted her to accept Christ? No longer able to maintain eye contact, she glanced away, surprised she still knew the words after all these years.

"Bless all the dear children in Thy tender care..." Mara's eyes landed on the doorway where Ashton now stood, her face alight with wonder to see her mother singing a song about Jesus. Her voice cracked in response.

"...and take us to heaven to live with Thee there." She squeaked out the last words. How, she had no clue. Instead her heart took up the cry of the last few words. Was that God's soon-to-be plan for Ashton? Tears spilled down her cheeks. *God, I have no right to even ask, but please don't take her away from me.*

The last note sounded, and Carter enveloped Mara in a hug. Applause mixed with sniffles sounded around the room.

Then Mara felt a tugging on her hand.

Ashton stood beside her, a huge grin on her face. "Group hug!" She hollered the words and followed it with a giggle as her arms wrapped around Mara's legs.

Carter laughed and swung Ashton up between them. "How about an Ashton sandwich instead?'

In a heartbeat, Chloe joined them. "Nope, group hug is right."

One by one, Carter's family came forward, until they were one big, tight-knit circle. How had this move to Miller's Creek joined her and Ashton with this boisterous and loving family?

A sacred hush fell as they stood there, all clinging to each other, and Cliff began to pray. "Oh, heavenly Father, thank You for Your presence among us. Thank You for being willing to come to this old earth and all its problems to take care of the sin problem once and for all. Thank You for loving us so much when we deserve it so little. Lord, we lift up Ashton to you, and pray for Your healing. Help her feel better and get well. Thank You for bringing her and Mara into our lives. In the all-powerful name of Jesus we pray. Amen."

They each stepped away from the circle wiping tears, but smiling and sharing individual hugs with one another. His eyes soft with emotion, Carter once more pulled Mara into his arms and planted a soft kiss on her head. "I love you, Mara."

Had she just imagined the whispered words, or had he actually stated his love for her? And what did she have to offer him in return? Yes, she enjoyed his company and needed his support and friendship during this awful time with Ashton's leukemia. And though her feelings for Carter had grown with each passing day, wouldn't it be a bit hypocritical for her to share those feelings, especially since she hadn't fully jumped on board with belief in God?

Her heart ripped open. If only she could see God like the baby Jesus mentioned in the song. Instead images of her father stomping across the stage and pounding on the pulpit--memories of him pronouncing God's judgment on her for her sins--rose to her mind. Was God looking down on her from a great distance, waiting to zap her for each infraction?

She disengaged from Carter's embrace, her cheeks covered with wet, sloppy tears. With her hands, she eradicated them, avoiding Carter's gaze at all cost. She wouldn't--no, she couldn't--return the words without not only accepting him and Chloe, but also his God. And that was just something she couldn't reconcile in her mind and heart at the moment.

Though more than aware of his questioning gaze on her, Mara turned toward the sound of Jo's voice near the doorway. "Let's open Christmas gifts in the family room."

Without a word or even a glance, Mara moved away from Carter and toward the family room. She took a seat between Chloe and Ashton, eager to put physical distance between her and Carter. She placed a palm over her aching heart and rubbed at its ache, aware of its tug toward the soft-eyed man who peered woefully at her from a nearby chair.

Darcy brought two gifts over, one for her and one for Ashton.

A wave of embarrassment swept over Mara. If only she had the money to bring gifts for all of them. If only there was some way to let them know how much she appreciated them including her and Ashton in their family celebration. How wonderful it had been to see that families like this existed in something other than a Currier and Ives lithograph or a Norman Rockwell painting. She tentatively pulled up one corner of the paper, until Chloe placed a hand on hers. Mara looked up at the girl who'd captured a piece of her heart.

Chloe leaned closer and whispered, "Not yet. Dad's family does things a little differently."

Mara smiled her appreciation, then raised her gaze to Cliff, who stood near the Christmas tree. "Who would like to read the Christmas story this year?"

No one volunteered.

Her heart pounded curiously. Maybe she could express her gratitude to the family this way. Her hand popped up without permission, and her voice sounded, clear and confident. "I will."

Cliff smiled warmly and headed toward where she sat, the large Bible already opened to the passage.

Mara took the Bible, and peered down at the pages, not as white and pristine as she'd imagined, but underlined and well-worn. Thankfully, her inner tremble didn't betray her, and she was able to read with a steady voice. She read how Mary and Joseph traveled to Bethlehem, even though Mary's time to deliver her baby was near, and how they couldn't find an empty room in which to stay. How amazing that Jesus had been born to peasant parents in a smelly old barn, the perfect picture of humility.

Then she read how angels appeared to shepherds in a heavenly chorus, proclaiming peace and goodwill to all men. Mara finished the passage and handed the Bible back to Cliff. In his eyes she glimpsed the peace and goodwill of which she'd just read. But more than that, she saw hope, a hope she desperately needed. But at what expense? At the cost of believing a fairy tale that would never be? The thoughts in her brain began their familiar game of chase and tag.

Following the tradition of the Callahan family, each person opened one present at a time, beginning with the youngest and moving to the oldest. Though the process took well over an hour, Mara couldn't remember a more enjoyable Christmas, made more special by observing each person's joy at receiving and giving gifts. A truly unforgettable experience.

As her turn approached, Mara reached for her last gift, one she'd purposefully avoided until now, since the dangling tag clearly revealed the words 'To Mara, from Carter.'

She swallowed and inhaled deeply as she lifted one edge of the red shiny paper, unsure of what to expect. A corner of something wooden and hand-carved came into view. The last bit of paper slipped away, leaving a beautifully-stained piece of oak in her hands, the message of the gift all-encapsulated by the carved word before her.

Believe.

Unexpected tears sprang to her eyes, and she peered in Carter's direction. Thankfully, his face was nothing but a blur. She just couldn't take anymore of those soft, compassionate eyes at the moment, not if she wanted to leave one small shard of her heart intact.

Then he spoke, taking that one last heart fragment captive. "Merry Christmas, Mara." His words were soft, but firm, and carried with them a deeper meaning not lost on her. Not the "Happy Holidays" from folks at the mall, instructed by their employers to not mention the name of Christ for fear of insulting patrons. Hadn't she at one time joined the ranks of those who demanded as much?

The simple words continued to dice her into small pieces and implied that only through Christ would she ever experience that merriness, that goodwill she'd read about. But was it true? And could she experience that promised joy and held-out hope in the midst of the most trying circumstances she'd ever encountered?

A few minutes later all of them piled around the long table near the back of the house that overlooked the glassy lake to enjoy the tasty spread of food. Though he sat near her at lunch, Carter must've intuited her conflicted feelings and kept any talk between them about surface matters. Great conversation and laughter dominated their holiday lunch. Even Ashton seemed more alert and perky. She laughed and actually ate without her usual nausea.

During lunch clean-up, feeling the need to momentarily escape, Mara stepped to the nearby powder room and opened the door.

Chloe huddled on the floor next to the toilet.

"Sorry, didn't know you were in here." Mara closed the door, but still clutched the knob as she considered her options.

An odd mixture of compassion and anger mounted with each second. Mara re-opened the door, stepped inside, and shut the door firmly behind her, her teeth locked together. She plopped to the tile floor beside Chloe, the room reeking of vomit stench. With fire in her belly, she met Chloe's woeful gaze. "How dare you do this. You promised me!"

"It's not what you think." Her weak tone supported the statement.

"Then by all means, fill me in."

Chloe shrugged. "There's a stomach virus going around school. I must've caught it."

She studied the teenager's face. No deceit or shame appeared in her eyes. Mara stood, wet a towel with cold tap water, and handed it to Chloe. "Sorry for morphing into the Wicked Witch from the West."

The teenager wiped her pale face and flushed the toilet. "I know it looks suspicious, but I haven't made myself throw up since that day we talked at the office."

Relief cascaded over Mara and relaxed her shoulders. One less kid to worry about was always a good thing. "Glad to hear it."

Chloe rose to her feet. "C'mon, let's go for a walk. There's something I wanted to talk to you about."

"Sure you feel up to it?"

She nodded, though somewhat unconvincingly. "At least for now. But we won't go far. Just in case. And I'll keep my distance."

A few minutes later, they both took a seat on the end of the boat dock in a sunny location. Mara folded up the collar of her heavy coat to ward off a sudden burst of icy wind that rippled the water.

Chloe faced her, her knees drawn to her chest. "Dad and I are checking into seeing if I'm a bone marrow match for Ashton. Is that okay?"

Tears pricked Mara's eyes. The pretty teenager should be thinking about college, what she wanted to do with her life, and what to wear to prom. But instead she thought about Ashton and how she could help. "Of course it's okay, but are you sure you're old enough?"

"You just have to be eighteen, and I'll be that in three days."

Mara leaned forward and hugged Chloe, virus germs and all. "You are so precious to me."

Chloe laughed as she pulled back. "I love you and Ashton like..."

"Like what?"

She ducked her head. "Like you're my mom and little sister." The words were so low Mara could barely hear them above the splashes of waves against the wooden dock.

Mara hugged her again, plans already forming in her head about a birthday party for Chloe. "I feel the same way about you, sweetheart."

"What about Dad?"

Mara straightened. Good question. "What about him?" She dead-panned the words and focused her efforts on keeping her face unreadable.

Chloe's gaze was clear-eyed and direct. "I've seen the way he looks at you, Mara. He's in love with you." Her lips turned down at the corners. "Don't break his heart. Don't break mine."

A thick knot of emotions landed in her throat, a knot she couldn't swallow or disregard. "That's not what I want, Chloe, but..."

"But what?" Her tone took on a petulant edge.

"I'm not sure my views about God will ever line up with his. That might be too big of a hurdle for us to overcome."

"It's not that hard, Mara. You're spending a lot more time and energy fighting the truth than it would take to believe." Chloe jumped to her feet and hurried from the dock, her knee-high boots a-clomp against the weathered-gray wood.

Mara drew her knees to her chest and faced the lake, welcoming the cold, brisk winds to hopefully whisk away the dark nothing that hovered over her heart. The warm rays of sunshine disappeared behind low gray clouds. She shivered and stood, then shoved her hands deep into the faux fur-lined pockets and traipsed down the sun-bleached boards toward the shore.

Carter stood in the grass at the other end, his hair tousled by the wind.

How long had he been there, watching her? As she approached, she sent a smile, hopefully one that offered no promises. "Hey, Carter."

"Hey. Wanna go for a walk?"

"As I recall, the last one we took here didn't turn out so well." Sarcasm dripped from her tone.

"All the more reason to take me up on my offer."

"I should probably check in on Ashton."

"Just did. She and Darcy are playing dress up and having a tea party. I was told in no uncertain terms that grown-ups weren't allowed." He paused. "I even offered to don a tiara and boa. Offer denied."

The forlorn edge to his voice elicited a laugh from Mara. And his fake sad demeanor only made her pity him less. "Oh, you are so pitiful. Yes, I'll take a walk, but only if you cut out the really bad drama."

His full-blossomed grin appeared. "Deal."

They meandered down the shoreline until they reached a forested area that ascended and blocked most of the biting winds. Carter broke the silence. "Sorry if I upset you earlier today, Mara, but I do care about you and Ashton as if you were my own."

How was she supposed to answer? "Your daughter and I actually just had this discussion."

"I know."

Her head whipped around.

"She came straight to me, probably because she was a little upset with you."

Mara lowered her gaze to the leaf-covered ground that crunched beneath their steps. "I didn't mean to upset her. I just wanted her to know where I stood."

"Which is?"

"I'm not in a place to reciprocate your feelings."

One shoulder jerked up and then down. "Then I'll keep waiting until you are."

Impossible situations. Since when had she become so talented at landing herself right in the big middle of them? "That's probably not a very wise move on your part."

"Why not?"

Hopefully her words wouldn't cut too deep, but better sooner than later. "Like I told Chloe, I'm not sure you and I will ever be on the same page when it comes to God."

Carter's eyes glinted with confidence, and his head moved from side to side. "I don't believe you. I saw the look in your eyes as you sang about Jesus. There's part of you that still believes, no matter how much you want to deny it." His words held heart-felt conviction.

Her pulse raced. Yes, her mind had filled with questions as she gave voice to the words about a sweet baby-God born in a barn. And she'd definitely remembered tidbits of religious indoctrination as a child. But she couldn't afford to let the sentiments of the season and her fractured heart draw her off course.

"Don't mean to pressure you in any way, and I certainly don't want to coerce something out of you that you don't feel."

That wasn't it, at all. She just couldn't express those feelings until they agreed about faith. It meant too much to Carter. She sent a tentative smile he didn't return. "Thanks for the breathing room."

His stride widened.

Mara followed suit to keep up with him.

"I haven't had a chance to ask." Carter turned his head her way. "How are you dealing with Ashton's decision to be saved and baptized?"

"We've talked about it." Mara answered as honestly as possible, knowing full well her answer wouldn't please him in the least. "I hope to convince her to wait until she's older and more capable of making an informed decision."

He came to an abrupt halt, his dark brows furrowed and knit together. "You're assuming she'll grow older. I'd be careful if I were you."

With the ominous words pounding in her brain and pressing against her heart, Carter pivoted and strode angrily toward the lake house.

Mara watched him until he disappeared from view. Was Carter's God more like the baby Jesus or the irate God of her father? Based on the scowl on Carter's face a minute earlier, it looked as though he sided with the latter.

And that was something she just couldn't tolerate.

Twenty

Though he missed his job, getting suspended with pay had been a huge blessing in disguise. Carter scrolled through his e-mail on his phone while he waited for Chloe to try on this last pile of clothes. Yeah, it still felt strange to not be confined to his desk at the Miller's Creek Police Department, but at least the time off allowed him to spend the school's Christmas break with his daughter. Their last-minute shopping spree hadn't been high on his want-to-do list of daddy-daughter time, but the sparkle in Chloe's eyes let him know it meant a lot to her.

She stepped from the ladies' dressing room area and pirouetted in front of him for at least the fifth time that morning, modeling yet another outfit for him to judge. He nodded his approval. "I like this one a lot better."

"Why?"

Couldn't she just try on clothes without commentary and questions? He scratched the back of his head. "Maybe 'cause there's more to it. If you're gonna pay those kind of prices with your Christmas money, you should get your money's worth."

She laughed and headed back to the dressing room for round six.

His phone ding-a-dinged, and he checked the screen. A text from Mara. "Whacha doing?"

Carter did his best to text back, not an easy feat for a person with thumbs the size of King Kong's. "Ugh. Shopping with C." He pictured her broad grin in response, which in turn brought a smile of his own.

A second later her reply sounded on his phone. "Ha-ha. You can do this. Hang in there. Don't be late for the party tonight."

Gratitude for Mara spilled from his entire being as he dropped the phone into his jacket pocket. He'd worried for months about what to do for Chloe's birthday--especially with it coming so close after Christmas--and all for no reason. Mara's idea for a surprise party for his daughter and her friends was the perfect solution. He tried to craft a decent reply that expressed his gratitude, but finally took the easy way out and thumbed a simple 'K.'

Once more Chloe appeared, this time in a pair of too-tight jeans with holes in the knees and a teeny t-shirt that left very little to the imagination.

Carter shook his head, his lips pressed together in a way intended to convey a strong message. "Over my dead body."

Chloe huffed and stomped back to the dressing room.

What was it Mara had said to him just the day before? Something about if you're not making a teenager mad at least half the time, you weren't doing your job. So far, he'd have to say he was right on target for the day.

Chloe traipsed from the dressing room a couple of minutes later, several clothes hangers in each hand. One pile she placed on a nearby rack, then brought the rest to where he sat.

Carter stood and scanned the hangers. All items he'd approved.

His daughter sent a saccharine smile. "No contraband clothing." An immediate apology appeared in her eyes. "I know I get grumpy sometimes when you tell me no."

His eyebrows arched upwards. Sometimes?

"But I appreciate you taking the time to at least let me try them on."

His mouth fell open in surprise, but he quickly coaxed his lips to form words. "You're welcome." The recent change in his daughter since her decision to follow Christ was nothing short of miraculous. "Ready for some lunch after we check out?"

"Definitely."

A half hour later, he and Chloe sat across from each other at their favorite catfish restaurant, the aroma of steaming catfish, fried okra, and hushpuppies setting off a growl in his stomach. Carter bit into a tender nugget of catfish and crunched it, the seasoned batter releasing a pop of tanginess into his mouth. Chloe also scarfed down a bite, obviously enjoying her food, too. Maybe this would be a good time to bring up her eating disorder. "Glad you're enjoying the food. Any, uh, more problems with the, uh, bulimia?"

Chloe stopped chewing and sent a withering look. "No."

No? That was it? "You know you can come to me at anytime. Right?"

A heavy sigh sounded from her side of the table. "I know, Dad. Really, you and Mara don't have to worry about me. I'm doing a lot better."

"Worrying about you is my job."

She turned her head halfway so that she peered at him sideways. "Oh really? Then why does Jesus say not to worry?"

Touché. He grinned and popped a hushpuppy in his mouth. "Point taken." He paused to gather his words. "Honestly, Chloe, I'm so proud of the young lady you're becoming. I feel very blessed."

Her happy smile was all the response he needed. Then her words belied the smile. "You really don't have to be so uptight about everything I do. And I'm fairly certain Mara feels the same."

"About you or her?"

"Her." She chewed the bite in her mouth and followed it with a swig of sweet tea. "You pressure her a lot. That might be why she put her house on the market."

The news slapped him across the face and brought an unsettled feeling to his chest and stomach. Mara was selling her house? "You think I'm too interfering?"

A snort sounded through her nose. "Not sure interfering is a strong enough word."

Carter considered her comment in silence as he finished off a bowl of beans. Hadn't Mara accused him of the same? He'd tried to rein himself in, but sometimes how he felt tumbled out in too-harsh words from some place deep inside. *Lord, help me not to run them further away from You. Set a guard over my lips.* He peered over at the half-woman, half-child before him. Where had the years gone? "Sorry for not being there for you when you were younger and for not always knowing the right thing to say." The words pounced from his mouth, pushed forward by regret. "Somehow you went from a tomboy in pigtails to a young woman who intimidates me."

A sweet smile appeared beneath her button nose. "Not my dad. He's not intimidated by anything." She sent a teasing grin. "Except beautiful women like me and Mara."

How did she know Mara intimidated him?

"It's not that hard to see, Dad. I know you like her. A lot. And I also know you want her to know God. I get that. I really do."

"But?"

"But you don't have to push so hard. God's got this." One shoulder notched upwards. "Mara's an intelligent woman. She'll come around in the long run."

Yeah, but at what cost? Intelligence didn't always manifest itself in wise decisions. "I have to do something, Chloe. I can't just let her head down the path away from God."

His daughter chuckled softly. "Yeah, it's definitely not in your nature to just stand there, Mr. Jump-To-The-Rescue. But be patient."

The words churned in Carter's mind throughout the rest of lunch and later as they waited to see Chloe's doctor. A nurse entered the waiting area from a nearby door and called Chloe's name, then lead them down the hall to an exam room.

Dr. Martinez, a short Hispanic woman with a ready smile, entered a few minutes after them. "Hi, Chloe." She patted his daughter on the back, then moved to shake his hand. "Good to see you again, Mr. Callahan." The woman took a seat on a stool near Chloe, her direct gaze focused on his daughter. "So you want to talk about the possibility of being a bone marrow donor?"

"Yes. I know a little girl who has leukemia." Her voice softened, and her eyes took on a moist sheen. "She'll die unless she finds a donor."

The doctor's face relaxed into a kind smile. "It's wonderful that you want to help, Chloe, but you might not be compatible."

"I know, but I have to try." Chloe's voice held conviction. "I turned eighteen yesterday. That means I'm old enough. Right?"

Dr. Martinez nodded. "Yes, but that's not the only factor we have to consider."

"What else?"

"Your health. I'll send the nurse in to take your vitals, and then we'll talk some more. Okay?"

Chloe nodded, but a dark cloud had descended on her face.

The doctor left, and a minute later a young nurse in multi-colored scrubs entered. "Hey, Chloe, I'm Melanie. Dr. Martinez wants me to get your height, weight, pulse rate, temp, and blood pressure."

Not long after the nurse finished up her work, Dr. Martinez returned, a file in hand. She scanned the information, and an immediate frown appeared as she gazed at Chloe over the top of her reading glasses. "Your weight has dropped since I saw you last. Have you been dieting?"

Carter could almost smell Chloe's fear.

Her face paled, and she inhaled sharply. "Actually I had a bit of a problem, but I'm doing better now."

The doctor looked over at Carter questioningly. "Eating disorder?"

He rubbed a hand across his face, suddenly feeling like a failure. "A friend of ours was the first to notice, since she had the same problem when she was Chloe's age. We've been monitoring Chloe closely."

"Good." Her direct gaze turned back to Chloe. "We'll take a blood sample while you're here, but until you regain that weight, I won't recommend you as a potential donor."

Chloe's mouth fell open in protest, but before she could speak, Dr. Martinez jumped in with a censorious click of her tongue. "Sorry, but it's my job to protect your health. Until I'm satisfied that you're eating correctly and maintaining your weight, I have no other choice." She stood and once more patted Chloe's shoulder. "You can do this, so don't give up."

His daughter nodded, but the down-turned slant of her mouth and lowered head proved how much the news upset her.

"Melanie will take you to the lab to draw blood. I'll forward the results to the doctor on file only when I'm convinced you're okay." She faced Carter. "You and Chloe might want to discuss the possibility of professional help."

Once back in the car, Chloe slouched in the seat with her arms wrapped around her waist.

Carter glanced at his watch. Still a couple of hours until the party. "Wanna do some more shopping?"

Her brown ringlets bounced from side to side, and her eyes filled with tears. She sniffled and flicked away the crocodile tears from beneath her eyes. "Can you take me to see Matt? I haven't made myself throw up in a long time, but sometimes I still want to. Maybe he can help me."

The words sliced through tender heart flesh. "Sure thing, sweetheart." He pulled up Matt's number on his phone.

"Hey, Carter. What's up?" Matt's always-friendly voice sounded.

"Hey. Would you possibly have any time this afternoon to speak with Chloe? We're in Morganville at the moment, but I can be there in a half hour."

"Sure can. See you in thirty."

A half hour later, Matt opened the door on the renovated two-story home he shared with his wife Gracie, the typical friendly expression on his face. "Hey, you two. Come on in." The door thudded shut behind them, and he motioned to a nearby sofa. "Y'all have a seat. What can I help you with?"

Chloe raked her bottom lip between her teeth then met Matt's gaze. "I've had problems with bulimia. I haven't thrown up in a long time, but sometimes the desire is still there." She hesitated and swallowed, her fingers flighty. "I want to be a bone marrow donor, but my doctor won't let me until I get my weight up where it needs to be."

Matt nodded reassuringly. "You feel comfortable talking in front of your dad, or you want him to get lost?"

Chloe giggled, instantly more relaxed. "Well, sometimes I want him to get lost, but..." She paused and cast a nervous glance his way. "I think it'll be good for him to know what I'm going through."

Carter's lungs barricaded air, refusing any sort of breath. He refrained from letting out a heavy breath. If Chloe could find the courage to go through this, he could too.

"Okay, then. First off, I just gotta say how impressed I am. It takes a lot of courage to admit you have a problem. That's the first step to getting better."

A sheepish grin appeared, along with pink-tinged cheeks.

Matt continued. "When did you first start having the desire to throw up?"

Chloe once more nibbled her lower lip, eyes averted and blinking rapidly. "When Mom dropped me off at Dad's house."

The blow hit hard, and Carter sucked in a deep breath. Coming to live with him was the cause of her bulimia?

"How'd that make you feel?"

She pressed her lips together momentarily as she gathered the courage to answer. "Like she didn't love me. I felt like there must be something wrong with me, you know?"

An ache spread across Carter's mid-section, as Matt's eyes took on compassion. "That's understandable." Matt leaned toward her and rested his elbows on his knees. "A lot of girls your age struggle with the same things. But I want you to realize that the incident had more to do with your mom than you."

Carter nodded, his gaze locked with Chloe's. "Your mom loves you, Chlo. She just couldn't take any more of being a single parent. That's my fault, not hers."

Chloe shook her head vehemently, her chin jutted out. "You were serving our country and providing for our family. She was just being selfish."

"Not so quick." Matt interrupted, his tone a bit on the sharp side. "It's easy to assign blame in things we struggle to understand."

Just like Mara blaming God for Ashton's condition.

"Your mom's the only one who can answer why it happened. And she may not completely understand it herself. But you gotta know it wasn't your fault. It just happened." Matt's words were firm, but kind. "When did you start making yourself throw up?"

"That first night."

"And what did you hope would happen as a result?"

Chloe considered the question. "Lots of things, I guess. I wanted to be skinnier, so people might like me more. It also helped me feel like I had some control."

Matt nodded. "And how often did it happen?"

A mixture of guilt and shame landed on her face. "Lots of times. Especially when I was stressed out."

"Can you give an example?"

"At first, the kids at school didn't accept me. I was used to having lots of friends in Morganville."

"You mentioned that you haven't thrown up in a long time. What brought about the change?"

She noisily inhaled through her nose and released it the same way. "Mara caught me, and I almost lost my job. She pretty much laid it on the line."

A sudden wave of appreciation for Mara washed over Carter. What would've happened to his daughter had she not noticed and intervened?

Matt remained silent for a long minute. "You're lucky you got help when you did, Chloe, even if it wasn't very pleasant. Mara must love you an awful lot. Some people wouldn't have bothered."

Chloe's eyes grew huge on her face, as though Matt had touched on something she hadn't considered.

"Had she not stepped in, you could've been in a very bad place and severely damaged your health." He paused to let the words sink in and leaned back against the leather arm chair. "Here are a few things I want you to do. First of all, keep the lines of communication open with your mom and dad. And it sounds like Mara is someone you want on your side. Don't be afraid to tell any of them that you're struggling. You can also call me any time. Okay?"

"I can do that."

Carter's heart pounded at the look of confidence on her face, a confidence brought on by her love for Ashton.

"Good girl." His friend smiled. "Next remember that feelings are just feelings. They're not necessarily reality. When you feel bad, tell someone. Don't stuff it inside."

"I've done that before, and a little while later I want to throw up."

"Stuffing your emotions never works. It just sets you up for an explosion down the road." Matt reached over and placed a hand on her arm. "You have a worthy goal to motivate you. You have supportive family members and friends. I know you can put this behind you."

A full smile descended on her pretty face. "Thank you. I already feel better."

As they walked down the sidewalk toward the Taurus a few minutes later, Carter draped an arm around his daughter's shoulders. "Proud of you, sweetheart. You're one brave cookie."

She laughed. "Only you would use a term like 'cookie' to someone who's trying to beat bulimia." Chloe put one arm around his waist as they neared the curb, her curly head against his chest. "I love you, Daddy."

Sudden emotion spilled out his eyes as he opened her car door. "Love you, too." He sauntered to the other side of the car using the back of his hands to dry his face. What an emotional roller coaster the day had been. Thankfully, the hard part was over and the fun was about to begin, made it even sweeter by the fact that Chloe had no clue.

Only when they bypassed their house and moved down another block did Chloe speak. "Why are we going to Mara's?"

"I told her we'd drop by later today. Hope that's okay."

"Of course. I always like to see her and Ashton."

He checked the dashboard clock as they pulled to the curb outside Mara's house. Perfect timing. And not a friend's car in sight. Carter frowned as they stepped past the 'For Sale' sign in the front yard and made a mental note to ask about it at first chance.

Mara answered the door with her gigantic grin in place and her hair pulled back into high ponytail. She hugged Chloe tightly. "There's the birthday girl. Happy Birthday!" She landed a kiss on Chloe's cheek and sent Carter a conspiratorial wink.

They entered the living area. "Surprise!" Chloe's friends--including Ashton-- popped out from behind doorways and furniture, and the place erupted with girlish screams and giggles.

Chloe's palms landed on her cheeks, and she spun around to smile at Mara. "I can't believe this!" She hurried over to her friends while Ashton cranked up the volume on the stereo.

A happy smile covered Mara's face in spite of the circles of fatigue beneath her eyes. She spatted his arm. "C'mon. Let's move to the kitchen where we can hear ourselves think." She yelled the words over the noisy din.

He followed her to the kitchen, all the while sending up a silent prayer. *Lord, help her not to get mad.*

Once in the kitchen, she faced him, her mouth open to speak.

Carter blurted out the question that dominated his thoughts. "Why are you selling your house?"

Her smile completely disappeared, replaced with a look of disappointment. She moved past him to the sink and began to fill plastic cups with ice. "Last time I checked, it's none of your business."

Carter stepped up beside her to help. "I'm not trying to be nosy. I just want to understand."

Mara released a heavy sigh that sagged both her head and shoulders. She spun around and leaned her weight against the counter, arms crossed. "Everyone's been so nice to help with my expenses while Ashton's been sick, but I can't continue to take advantage of their kindness. I can find us a much cheaper place to live."

A newfound appreciation for her landed in his heart, spurring on his resolve to help in whatever way he could. Especially in finding a donor for Ashton.

Twenty-One

How was it that life had once more turned upside down in the mere blink of an eye? The question on Mara's heart only partially captured her attention. In addition to trying to answer the question for which there was no answer, she also waited nervously in the oncologist's office. Upstairs in the children's hospital in downtown Dallas, Carter and Chloe sat by Ashton's bedside.

The question returned with an aching insistence to be answered. Was there something she'd done or hadn't done that had landed Ashton back in the hospital? One minute she'd been fine, climbing into bed with an incessant chatter of how much fun she'd had at Chloe's birthday party. Then in the middle of the night, she'd awakened Mara, screaming in pain.

And another question begged for an answer. What would she have done without Carter and Chloe? There was no way she could've driven to Dallas with Ashton clinging to her and crying out from the pain. Instead Carter drove through the wee hours of the morning, while Chloe did all she could to distract Ashton from focusing on the pain.

To Mara's left, the door opened and closed and Dr. Watts' shoes clipped against the sterile tile floor. She inhaled deeply and released it. What would she have to say? Was it news she could bear? She met Dr. Watts' gaze and immediately knew from her eyes that the news wasn't good. A tremor that rivaled any earthquake started in her feet and worked its way up to her heart and head. Only it didn't stop. It couldn't stop.

The woman's lips curved ever so slightly, but her eyes carried compassion. "I'm sorry to have to bring bad news, Mara, but it's my job." She hesitated briefly, as though she knew the words she spoke would shatter her world. "Despite all the people in Miller's Creek who have joined the donor list, none so far are a match. Ashton's numbers aren't good. Even with the chemo she's been on, her white blood cells are highly elevated. And as long as they're so high, I have no choice but to keep her hospitalized where we can monitor and treat her."

Mara wanted to feel something, for no other reason than to respond to the worst news she'd ever received. But instead, she felt nothing. It was as though her body had been shot full of Novocain, leaving an icy chill and numbness around her that nothing could penetrate.

The doctor moved to her side and laid a hand on her shoulder. "Are you okay?"

Okay? She'd just delivered the news that the beat of her heart had no hope, and she wanted to know if she was okay? But surprisingly, Mara found herself nodding yes. "Yeah. I just need to go upstairs to be with Ashton." If she could make her numb leg muscles work. How, she didn't know, but a strength from within forced her muscles into action and helped her stand. As though in a bad dream in which there was no escape, she moved out the door, down the hall, and into the elevator.

Before she knew it, she stood in front of Ashton's hospital room. How much time had elapsed? How long had she been standing here? Without warning, a dreadful thought entered her consciousness. How in the world could she deliver the news to Carter and Chloe, and especially to Ashton? The tremor started again, so much that she feared her knees would give way and spill her onto the floor. She backed up and leaned against the wall, her mind desperately searching for answers.

Pray. She needed to pray. Words spilled from her soul. *God, I know I have no reason to call on you right now, but I need your help. Give me words to say. Help me not to make the situation worse. Hold me up.* Then the words stopped, as though held behind some invisible dam, but still something inside continued to cry out a one-word prayer. *Help.*

With a calm and strength she didn't possess, Mara crossed the hall and pushed on the door.

Three pairs of expectant eyes latched onto her the minute she entered the room. Ignoring them all except one, Mara closed the distance between her and her little girl. Her eyes quickly took in Ashton's appearance. In one day's time her skin had gone gray, and her eyes held fragile fatigue beyond what Mara could comprehend. How could anyone endure all Ashton had been through in her short life?

"Hey, sweetie." Mara eased her weight onto the bed, dodging wires and tubes. She gently pulled Ashton into her arms, then rested her head against the bare-skin head of her little girl, and closed her eyes, not caring that the other two looked on. How many days? How much time did she have left? And what atrocities did that time hold?

Hours slipped away.

The next thing Mara knew she was startled awake by a dream. In the dream, Ashton was a healthy three-year old with an infectious giggle and rapidly-advancing vocabulary. And in the dream she had a Daddy. The one thing that plagued Mara in the dream--and had eventually awakened her--was a deep need to know the man her little girl called Daddy. Rather than a distinct image, all she could make out was a shadowy figure.

"Hey there, sleeping beauty." Carter leaned in close. "You both must've been exhausted."

Mara gently eased away from her sleeping daughter, once more dodging tubes and wires. "How long have I been asleep?"

Carter checked his watch. "Three to four hours."

"Where's Chloe?"

"Asleep on the floor."

Mara managed a weak smile. "And we left you on active duty."

He returned her smile. "That's my job."

A quick and tart comeback was her standard mode of operation, but this time she had nothing. Nothing but the all-too-familiar numbness that had descended during her talk with the oncologist.

"You missed lunch. Wanna grab a bite in the cafeteria?"

Mara shook her head. "Not hungry. But after I go to the bathroom, I do want to get something to drink." She swallowed against the mid-day nap breath that coated the inside of her mouth, but it stayed in place.

A few minutes later, the two arrived at the cafeteria. Carter quickly steered her toward a table for two near the window. "You sit here. I'll be back in a sec."

Mara nodded, and gazed out the window. People of various ages milled past. Didn't they know? Didn't they know that the rug of her life had been yanked from beneath her feet? And why did some of them dare to crack a smile or share a laugh with a loved one?

Carter interrupted her thoughts as he slid a tray with a burger in front of her.

"I told you I'm not hungry."

"That may be true, but you need to eat. You barely ate anything at the party last night because of taking care of everyone else. You didn't eat breakfast, and you missed lunch. It's time to eat." He lowered his head, his gaze steady through narrowed eyes lids. "Don't make me force the issue."

Mara sighed, and gazed at the burger. He was right. She did need to eat. Ashton needed her, and Chloe needed the example. She picked up the burger and took a bite, surprised at how good the food tasted.

Carter relaxed his stance and took the seat across from her. "Wanna talk about it?"

She finished chewing the bite she had in her mouth, then took a sip of Diet Coke to wash it down. "First you tell me to eat. Now you want me to talk. I can't do both without bad manners."

He shrugged. "I think you know me well enough by now to know that good manners matter very little."

Yeah. Come to think of it, she did know that about him. Not that he intentionally used bad manners. Just that they didn't mean much in the big scheme of things. And the big scheme of things had dealt her a fatal blow. She raised her gaze to his. "Ashton's white blood cells are off the charts. The doctor said she has to stay in the hospital until..."

Carter leaned forward and placed a hand on her arm. "It might not look good right now, Mara, but she's still with us. Don't give up on her, and whatever you do, don't forget God might have other plans. He deals in miracles."

A miracle. That's exactly what they needed. But had she messed up too much in God's eyes to warrant one?

Over the next few hours Ashton continued to sink lower, asleep much more than she was awake. Between the three of them, Mara, Carter, and Chloe managed to keep her waking moments pleasant, but once Ashton succumbed to sleep, life was shrouded by darkness. The room took on a deathly pallor in spite of Carter's insistence that they stay positive.

Late Wednesday afternoon, their second day back, Mara glided to Ashton's bed, leaned over her sleeping daughter, and gently laid a hand on her feverish forehead.

Chloe moved up to stand beside her. "Can I get you anything, Mara?"

She sent a gentle smile to the half-girl, half-woman that had captured part of her heart. "No thanks." Both Carter and Chloe had proved to be diligent warriors over the past couple of days, helping in whatever way they could.

Ashton stirred and her eyes flitted open.

Carter laid down the newspaper puzzle he'd been working on and moved up to the other side of the bed. "Hey, there's our munchkin."

A tired smile landed on Ashton's face. "I thought I was *your* munchkin." The words seemed to take so much effort.

Carter chuckled, his face a picture of tenderness, as he gripped Ashton's outreached hand. "Yeah, I thought so, too, but those two set me straight in a hurry." He nodded toward Mara and Chloe.

"Carter?"

"Yeah, sweetheart?"

"Would you read me another Bible story?"

A throbbing ache took up residence in Mara's chest. At one time she would've put her foot down and nixed that request in a hurry. But now it somehow brought comfort. "Which one do you want him to read?"

"David and Goliath." Ashton turned her big blue eyes Mara's way. "I saw the man again, Mommy."

"While you were sleeping?"

Ashton nodded.

Dreams could be disturbing at best and frightening at worst. Mara thought back to the dream about the younger Ashton, healthy and whole. "Does he make you afraid?"

"No. He makes me not afraid."

Mara looked up and caught Carter's gaze on her. His expression pleaded with her, 'don't blow this chance.'

Before she could open her mouth to speak, Ashton continued. "Because of Him, I'm not afraid...you know...of dying."

Mara's knees threatened to give way, but she latched onto the bed railing and gripped it with white knuckles.

Carter sent a supportive glance to Mara, then turned Ashton's focus his way. "You ready for that story?"

Ashton nodded, her once-bright eyes dulled by pain.

In his deep voice, Carter told the story of the shepherd boy-turned-victorious-warrior against a foe many times his size. The irony of the story wasn't lost. Ashton was a warrior, too. A very small and very tired warrior whose Goliath was a disease called leukemia. Could she rally and defeat the giant?

It wasn't long into the story before Ashton drifted back to sleep, but Carter continued. Why? For her benefit? Somehow the stories he'd told Ashton the past couple of days had seeped into her inner being, stirring up embers she thought long dead. And once the story ended, Mara met his gaze, a new intention in her heart. "Can I borrow that Bible for a minute?"

He handed it over immediately. "Sure."

"If you need me, I'll be in the chapel." As Mara left the room, she glanced back at the other three--a still and sleeping Ashton, Carter bending his knees to the cold tile floor and the side of the bed, and Chloe skirting the edge of the bed to join him. The scene brought fresh comfort as Mara made her way to the chapel. And in addition to the prayers she and Carter and Chloe had offered up, countless more prayers rose to storm heaven's door from the good people of Miller's Creek. But in light of how she'd denied God, had fought against Him, would it be enough?

After a couple of hours of pouring over the scriptures and praying the words before her back to God, Mara made her way back to the room. As she entered the room, Matt and Gracie Tyler both engulfed her in a big hug, one that brought tears she thought had dried up. She backed away, swiped tears, and sent them both a smile. "Thank you for coming."

"Our pleasure," said Gracie, her dark eyes soft and sympathetic.

"Sorry it's not under better circumstances." Matt smiled tenderly. "We were instructed to let you know that people are praying."

Mara nodded, assurance prodding her on. "I know they are. I feel it." How else could she explain her ability to function in circumstances like these? Over Matt's shoulder, she caught sight of Carter, who hung onto her comment as a nugget of gold in a sea of tin.

He moved up to join them. "Chloe's going back to Miller's Creek with Matt and Gracie. She starts school on Monday."

Chloe ducked beneath his left arm, her face awash with angst, tears pooling in her pleading eyes.

Mara moved forward and hugged the teenager. "Thank you for all your help."

"I don't want to leave her. I'm afraid..." Her words dried up, but not the tears. They started afresh as her face crumpled and her shoulders heaved with giant sobs.

It took every ounce of strength she had not to join in on Chloe's sob session, but instead Mara once more took the sweet teenager in her arms and did all she knew to do to comfort her. A half hour later, Matt, Gracie, and Chloe said their goodbyes and closed the door behind them.

With Chloe gone, Mara's crumbling facade shattered into a million pieces. She fell to the floor, Chloe's sobs now her own. In less than a heartbeat, strong arms encircled her, and her head came to rest on Carter's chest, his heart thudding in her ear.

"It's okay, Mara. Let it out. You need to cry."

So cry she did, and the tears lasted longer than she knew possible. Thankfully, Ashton slept through the whole ordeal. When at last her tears were spent, Mara pulled back and reached for a nearby box of tissues to swab her face and nose. "I'm so afraid God won't hear my prayers. That He'll punish me for rebelling against Him."

Carter reached a hand up to catch an escaping tear, his head moving from side to side. "God forgives us when we confess our wrongdoing, Mara. He's as near as my hand on your face."

"That's what I did in the chapel." Mara sniffed and wiped her leaky eyes. "It might sound weird, but verses I learned as a child flooded back into my mind. I couldn't look them up fast enough."

A weary smile crossed his face. "That's how God's Spirit works, Mara. He's here, and He loves you and Ashton even more than I do."

Her thoughts returned to one verse in particular that had been on instant replay in her brain. God is love. A loving God was not only what she wanted, but what she needed.

Carter had grown quiet, as though testing words inside before letting them slip from his lips. "In the end it all comes down to what you decide about Jesus. That decision is the one that every person faces, and the one that determines our eternity."

Mara nodded. "I know. But honestly, I get snagged on who Jesus is. So many people say he was just a good man, a teacher, or a prophet, and that there are many ways to heaven. How can I know for sure that he was God's Son?"

"Think about it this way. Remember the man Jesus healed by declaring that his sins were forgiven?"

She shook her head. One of the very stories she'd come across during her visit to the chapel.

"Well, no one in their right mind would enter a Jewish synagogue and claim to forgive sins."

"Exactly my point. What if he was just some crazy guy off the streets?"

Carter laughed at her choice of words and tenderly smoothed her hair away from her face. "Had He been a lunatic the people wouldn't have been drawn to Him the way they were. And the religious leaders whose power and authority were threatened would've dismissed him."

The words swam in her brain, an ever-shifting school of fish, until a shaft of light put them all in order. She lifted her gaze to Carter, her mouth agape. "He really is God's Son. That baby in a manger was sent from God to save the world."

Carter searched her face, his head a-nod. "Yes, Mara. He loves you no matter what you've done. In fact, He died on the cross to make a way for us to get to God."

The words wouldn't fly from her lips fast enough. She grabbed the fabric of Carter's sleeve. "I believe. What do I need to do now?"

The brightest and most tender smile she'd ever seen covered his face. "Tell Him."

Mara bowed her head, words flowing freely. "Jesus, I believe You are God's Son. I'm sorry I've had it messed up in my head for so long. Please help me follow You in a way that pleases God. And help Ashton to live." The last few words barely squeaked out before she gave way to more tears.

Carter rocked her back and forth and patted her back. When her tears subsided, he gently pulled her away and held her at arm's length. "Mara, there's something I need to say. But please don't take it the wrong way."

"Okay."

"Just because you've professed faith in Him doesn't mean Ashton will make it."

Good old Carter. He always managed to say even the tough things. The things she really didn't want to hear, but needed to hear. "I know. But if God and Jesus are real, then heaven is real." She stood, stepped to the bed, and peered down at her daughter whose precious face held suffering even in slumber. "Somehow knowing that if Ashton dies she'll be with God in a beautiful place is preferable to watching her suffer." Her eyes filled with more tears. "I pray that He'll heal her, but if He doesn't, I trust that she'll be with the One who loves her more than I ever can."

Out in the hall, a sudden ruckus arose. Carter and Mara both rushed to the door.

One nurse spied them and hurried over. "Sorry we disturbed you. But the year just passed. Happy New Year!" She sent a bright smile and stepped back to her crowd of co-workers.

It was a new year, a fact that had somehow escaped her in the routine of caring for a sick child. Old years always preceded new. Darkness always preceded dawn. God did new things all the time.

"Happy New Year, Mara." Carter wrapped a gentle arm around her waist, plopped a kiss on her forehead, and led her back into the hospital room.

Twenty-Two

Mara swallowed her disappointment as she peered out the hospital window at the wintry day outside. All of January and half of February had been brutal in so many ways, and now an ice storm had moved in overnight. The icy drizzle continued, coating trees and power lines with a thick coat of ice. Compared to the usual hustle and bustle of downtown Dallas, the place looked more like a ghost town. Very few cars made their way down the usually busy thoroughfare, and those that did, did so to their peril. Already there'd been more than one minor accident outside their temporary home.

The Black Abyss reared its ever-so-ugly head, it's ebony mouth gaping, a slippery slope that threatened to suck her in. How tempting to succumb to darkness, to allow herself to effortlessly slide down into the yawning abyss. To make matters worse, a sinister voice whispered in her ear, a sibilant suggestion that maybe God wasn't real after all.

Mara locked her shoulders into an upright position. But she couldn't allow herself either option, no matter how tempting. Not for the sake of her very sick little girl, who somehow clung to a mere thread of life to everyone's surprise. Not for the sake of her own soul, which clung to a fragile hope of more than eyes could see and heart imagine.

Her cell phone buzzed in her pocket. She retrieved it and cast a wary glance toward Ashton's bed. Still asleep. The norm these days.

"Hey, beautiful." Carter's deep voice sounded, sending her heart a-pound with fresh hope. How much she'd come to rely on his presence, his support, his comfort. How warm were the winter days when he and Chloe could join her and Ashton.

A tender smile flew to her lips. "Hey."

"How's the weather there?"

"Horrible. Everything's coated with ice, including the roads." His resulting heavy sigh sent her heart to pounding again, this time from fear.

"Afraid of that."

"I don't think you and Chloe should come this weekend." She pelted out the words in rapid-fire fashion. There. She'd said the words she didn't want to say, but the words that needed to be verbalized nonetheless.

"We really want to be there."

Tears sprang to her eyes, and her shoulders slumped. And she really wanted him here. Needed him here. But not at the risk of endangering their lives. A lump landed in her throat. Finally she managed an "I know." Such a poor substitute for what she really wanted to say.

"How's our girl?"

Mara faced Ashton's bed, which seemed to grow larger each day as her daughter shrank to Alice in Wonderland proportions. "Not good."

"And you?"

"About as well as can be expected." Boy, what a downer she must be to Carter when he'd given her so much, including his ever-present hope. Mara waited for his lecture of not giving up. But none came. "I'm okay." She infused her voice with an enthusiasm she didn't feel.

"Well, I gotta go. You hang in there. And let me know if the roads improve."

That was it? The room took on a blurry haze, like rain against window panes. "Will do. Bye."

The line went dead. The gaping black hole and its promise of blessed oblivion strutted back into view, and the hissing and persistent voice once more echoed in her thoughts.

Later that day, Mara sat next to Ashton's bed and tried to read the Bible Carter had given her on one of his trips to see her on his days off. For some reason, probably from lack of sleep, she just couldn't make her brain wrap around the words. Time after time, she re-read the same verse, her mind scrambling to understand. *Lord, help me.*

The door swung open. Carter's broad shoulders filled the doorway, his face lit with the familiar boyish grin.

In a heartbeat, Mara scooted across the room and landed in his arms.

He picked her up and swirled her around, her legs sailing through the air, then set her down with a smile that tingled her insides. Chloe stepped from behind him with a brief smile to Mara, but immediately moved to the bed.

"I thought I told you not to come." Mara garnered her best teacher voice to reprimand Carter and shook her finger. "Do you know how dangerous it is out there?" All morning reports had flashed across the television of accidents and stranded motorists across the northern and central portions of Texas.

He pulled her pointed finger toward the floor and winked. "You know me and danger."

Mara wanted to be stern, but couldn't. Instead she laughed, suddenly joyful. "Yeah, I know. You live for danger." She moved over to Chloe, wrapped her in a big hug, and swayed back and forth in semi-dance. "So good to see your sweet face."

Chloe pulled away, an inner light shining--no, make that beaming--from every pore of her being. "I have news."

"Let me guess. You and Bryce are back together?"

The smile faded, but only temporarily. "No, even better than that."

Footsteps sounded down the hallway and drew closer. Dr. Watts entered, her face also happy.

A sudden flame of hope ignited in Mara's heart. She glanced from one smiling face to the other. "Okay, spill it. What's going on?" A tremble sounded in her warbled words.

The doctor laughed as she closed the door behind her.

Mara's eyes glued to the doctor's face in hopeful expectation.

Carter's strong hands gripped Mara's upper arms from behind. "You might want to sit down." He steered her to a nearby chair.

A knot formed in her throat, and her heart thudded out an uneven rhythm. Was she getting her hopes up for nothing? She licked her dry lips as she took a seat. "Well, what is it?"

The doctor exchanged a smile with Carter and Chloe. "We have a donor."

Mara shrieked and jumped to her feet, tears instantly flooding her face. Then in the next moment, she clasped both hands over her mouth and looked at Ashton, who had slept through her mama's outburst. "I knew it. I just knew it." She whispered the words and glanced to the ceiling, one hand over her full heart. "Thank You, God."

"Hold on a sec, Mara." Carter stepped to her side, draped one hand around her back to clasp one shoulder, and clutched the other with his left hand then moved her to a sitting position again. He crouched beside the chair, holding her hand. "Let Dr. Watts finish."

The oncologist smiled. "Actually, I think Chloe should tell her."

Chloe knelt in front of Mara, her face angelic and radiant. "I'm a match, Mara." She glanced at Carter briefly. "Dad and Matt and Chance all helped me gain back the weight I'd lost. And I've been taking injections to increase my white blood cells."

The words weighted Mara's shoulders, and she shook her head. Could she allow it? "I can't let you do that, Chloe."

The teenager placed a hand on Mara's knee, her eyes pleading. "But I want to. I'll be okay." She rose and moved to the bedside, her face awash with concern. "She looks worse every time I see her." Now she faced Mara again, her eyes flooded with tears. "Mara, please."

Though the stabbing pain in her chest contradicted it, she nodded through an onslaught of tears. "Okay."

Dr. Watts sent a hopeful smile Mara's way. "I'll get the ball rolling on this end. Hopefully by next weekend if not before."

A cloud of light descended over Mara, both tender and strong, as the oncologist left the room. Had God at last answered their prayers? *Lord, please protect both Chloe and Ashton.*

Carter reached over and gently wiped tears from Mara's face. "It will all be okay. God is with us."

Oh, how she wanted to latch on to those words of hope and believe, but the realist part of her rushed to the forefront. What if this whole scenario ended not in one death, but two?

Carter clasped her hand and pulled Mara to her feet. "C'mon, you need to get out of this room for a few hours."

Mara started toward the door with him, then stopped to face Chloe.

Before the words could even escape her lips, Chloe smiled. "I'll call if she wakes up."

A surge of emotion swept over Mara, a wave of grace against a heat-dried desert. She pulled away from Carter's handhold and rushed to the one who could potentially restore Ashton's life. Both arms flew around the pretty teenager and held her fast, as words tumbled from Mara's lips. "Oh, Chloe, thank you so much. I can't express how much this means to both of us." Fresh tears fell, and she couldn't release her stranglehold on this sweet woman-child who'd become a daughter to her.

Finally it was Carter who separated them by once more putting a hand on each of Mara's shoulders and tugging her away. "Alright you two. Stop it before I start crying." Already his voice was thick with emotion.

Once down in the cafeteria, they sat across from each other, a steaming mug of hot chocolate before both of them. Carter rested his crossed arms on the table and peered across at her with dark eyes. "Why'd you lie to me?"

Mara's mouth gaped. "Lie to you?" About what?

"On the phone you told me you were okay." His face and tone held concern. "Not sleeping?"

She gave her head a shake, but forced her eyes to remain on his.

"And eating?"

Her head fell to her chest and took her shoulders with it. "I try, Carter, really I do. But my stomach is always upset."

He reached across the table. With gentle fingers, he coaxed her chin upward so that she met his gaze once more. Though his expression held gentleness, his jaw wore an authoritarian slant, indoctrinated into the fiber of his being from years of military service. "Did you ask the nurses or doctor for something to help you sleep and to soothe your stomach?"

She pressed her lips together and shook her head from side to side. The idea had crossed her mind when nurses and doctors weren't around, but when they arrived all her questions had been about Ashton. How foolish she'd been. Carter was right to scold her. Why hadn't she taken better care of herself for Ashton's sake? Large tears brimmed in her eyes and dripped down her cheeks.

Though blurry from her tears, Carter's mouth fell open, and his eyebrows furrowed. He yanked his chair near Mara's and took her in his arms. "Sorry for my pig-headedness. You're obviously exhausted."

She nodded as soft sobs continued to wrack her body. "I can't focus. I'm doing all I can not to slip into depression and despair."

His hand slid up and down her arm, and his lips made a shushing sound.

Finally she brought her tears under control, and she lifted knuckles to her face to whisk away tears. "Thank you for understanding."

Carter gave her one last shoulder rub and moved his chair back to the opposite side of the table, his face still darkened with concern and compassion. "Has Ashton been awake today?"

"Only long enough to eat a few bites, then she drowses off again."

He didn't respond verbally, but his face continued to darken.

Mara searched for words. They had to be said. "I know I've already said yes to Chloe, but I do have my concerns."

"Such as?"

"First of all, it could put Chloe in danger."

"Something we're both aware of. The risks are small."

"But they're still there." Mara snapped out the words, fire lighting in her belly. "I don't want either of you going into this without fully considering the risks."

A wry smile lifted one corner of his mouth. "She's her father's daughter, Mara. Her risk-taking is something she comes by naturally. I can't ask her to be any less than she is."

One by one, the words dripped comfort to Mara's heart. Carter was right, and God was with them all. After a long minute, she released a relieved sigh. "You risk-takers. What am I gonna do with the two of you?"

His eyes lit with amusement as he sipped from his cup. "Well, I have my ideas in that direction, too, but I'll save them for a later time."

The cryptic words set her heart a-pounding. For a later time or a better time? Then the sobering voice of reality sounded. That time might not come at all. She broke away from his gaze, lifted her cup, and took a sip of the creamy mixture, fighting against the negative thoughts. The hot chocolate, though delicious on her tongue, curdled in her stomach. *Strengthen my faith, Jesus.*

Back in the room a few minutes later, much to Carter's protests, the three played several rounds of Uno until Ashton woke up.

The minute she spoke, they all crowded around her bed. Mara planted a kiss on her daughter's bald head. "Hey, sweetheart. Look who drove through an ice storm just to see you."

With droopy eyelids, Ashton weakly turned her head toward Carter and Chloe, the fragile remains of her once blossoming smile on her lips. "Hi."

Chloe immediately turned her head away from the bed, her hands on her face. "Man, I have an eyelash in my eye." Her husky words belied the real reason for hiding her face.

Carter picked up Ashton's frail hand and cupped it in his big bear paws. "Guess what, squirt?"

Ashton didn't answer, but her weary eyes held questions.

"Chloe's gonna give you some of her bone marrow. Is that cool, or what?"

"She matches me?" Ashton's eyes brightened temporarily, then she frowned a frown that wrinkled her entire head. "How... dangerous?" It was all she could muster.

The teenager turned her head back with a forced smile. "Well, silly girl, do you think I really care?"

To Mara's surprise, Ashton managed a giggle and a bigger smile. With great effort, she struggled to move her head to face Mara. "Is it time for dinner?"

Greatly encouraged, Mara picked up the dangling switch with the red button and waved it in front of Ashton. "It is now."

Within a few minutes, a nurse wheeled in a meal for Ashton, complete with chicken nuggets, gravy, mashed potatoes, and red Jell-o, Ashton's personal favorite. Though she took a bite of everything, in the end it was only the Jell-o she consumed in its entirety before once more succumbing to sleep.

After that, the three moved to opposite corners, each absorbed in their own activities and thoughts. Mara looked up from her Bible around nine o'clock that night to see Carter, his head rolled back against the chair next to Ashton's bed, his eyes closed and his mouth open. A nasally snore sounded from his direction.

From her position at the foot of Ashton's bed, Chloe stood and clicked off the television. She peered first at Carter and then at Mara. "I'm going for a walk." She whispered the words and tiptoed toward the door.

"Okay, but stay inside." The words sent surprise. Since when had she started sounding like Chloe's mother?

Chloe smiled at her as she cracked open the door. "Yes, Mother." She followed the words with a bigger smile and a wink, instantly reminding Mara of Carter.

Once the door closed behind her, Mara laid down her Bible and tiptoed over to where Carter snoozed. She peered down at the ruggedly handsome face of the man she'd grown to love. Yes, she loved him. A love so fierce it sometimes stole her breath in its intensity. A love she'd battled with every ounce of her energy. A love she no longer wanted to force away.

Suddenly Carter's face crumpled into a total frown, making him almost unrecognizable. His head fidgeted one way and then the other, his breath coming in uneven spurts. A bead of sweat broke out on his upper lip. "No." Though still asleep, Carter's word held sheer terror.

Before she could stop herself, she reached out, grabbed Carter's thick shoulder, and shook. "Carter, wake up. You're dreaming."

He startled awake, ramrod straight, his eyes wild, his fists raised to chest level. When he finally realized his surroundings, he relaxed his posture. "Sorry."

Mara plopped to the floor beside the chair, her legs crossed like an Indian, and studied him.

His breathing slowed as he rubbed his eyes, more like a little boy than a grown man.

"That must've been some nightmare."

He nodded, but averted his gaze.

"Have those often?"

"Nah. Not too much."

Her eyes narrowed. "Now who's lying?"

A sheepish grin landed on his full lips, and his gaze held soft surrender. "Okay, okay. They happen more than I care for. Especially here lately."

"Wanna talk about it?"

He shook his head, once more hiding his eyes. "Nope. Just residual stuff--"

"--from your days in the service?"

Carter nodded abruptly, but said nothing further, his way of ending the conversation.

Well, too bad. Turnabout was fair play. "Must've been really hard."

An exasperated sigh fell from his mouth, and he raised a not-so-pleasant gaze to hers. "I really don't want to talk about it. Take the hint, will ya?"

"Nope." If he could be stubborn so could she. "Are you having the nightmares because of Ashton and Chloe?"

His stern gaze locked with hers for an uncomfortable minute. At last he relinquished control. "Matt thinks the situation might be stirring up old feelings."

"Fear?"

"Yeah."

The way he spoke the one-syllable word said volumes. Not just fear, but life-threatening and uncontrollable fear. Mara studied him a second more. Enough progress in the communication area for now. "How about a stroll down the halls?"

A wicked grin broke out on his face. "Actually I have another idea. I'm gonna leave for a second, but when I get back I'll take you up on that stroll."

A half hour later, Mara learned the reason for his wicked little smile when he led her to one darkened corner of the hospital cafeteria. A table had been draped with a red table-cloth. Atop it sat a vase with a dozen red roses, a flickering pillar candle, and a heart-shaped box of chocolate.

"Happy Valentine's Day, Mara." Carter pulled her into his arms, his lips soft on hers. A few seconds later he pulled away and sighed contentedly. "Once this is all over and behind us, there will be lots more where that came from."

She sent a bemused smile. "Oh, you think so, do you?"

He nodded, a goofy grin at rest on his unshaven face.

"What if I don't want to wait until later?" She leaned forward and kissed him with all the intensity she could muster.

The sound of Chloe clearing her throat broke the two apart. She stood arms crossed, one hip jutted out in typical teenager fashion, and a stern look on her face. "I've been looking all over the hospital for you two," she blurted out the words angrily, then relaxed her face into a full-blossomed grin. She turned on one foot and called back over her shoulder as she stepped away. "I'm going back to the room. And please, keep the public display of affection to a minimum."

The rest of the weekend flew by far too quickly. Ashton was awake only seconds at a time, and only long enough to take a few bites of food. When the time came for Carter and Chloe to leave, Mara walked with them as far as the sky bridge that connected to the parking garage across the street. Why was it that part of her heart lay sleeping on a deathbed, while the other part was about to drive away and leave her alone once more?

Carter retrieved his keys from his jeans pocket and handed them to Chloe. "Remember where we parked?"

She nodded.

"Go on without me. I'll be just a few steps behind."

Even though she mustered a brave smile, Chloe's eyes took on sadness as she embraced Mara. "See you soon. Love you."

Mara returned Chloe's hug. "Love you too. Even if I said thank you with every word I spoke to you for the rest of our lives, it wouldn't be enough."

Chloe pulled away, her tone wry. "Well, let's not do that, okay?"

A laugh bubbled out of Mara's chest at the mock consternation on the teenager's face. "Okay. If you insist."

She waved and stepped across the sky bridge.

Once she disappeared from view, Mara faced Carter. They exchanged a long glance with unspoken words.

"Come here, you." Carter pulled her into his arms with a brief kiss, but an all-encompassing hug.

How long they stood there locked in each others arms and hearts, Mara couldn't tell. Nor did she care.

Carter released her, a gentle smile splayed on his lips. He tucked a stray curl behind her ear. "I love you, lady." His words rushed like a torrent over her heart, embracing her both all at once and trickle by trickle.

"And I love you."

Unspoken words sounded between them until he finally leaned in, kissed her forehead, and sauntered off toward the parking garage, hands in his pockets.

Mara closed her eyes and relished both the sweet and sour of the moment, then made her way back to the room, forcing the sinister voice and its lies from her heart and mind. Hopefully the times for goodbyes would soon rest behind all of them.

Once in the room, she fell to her knees at Ashton's bedside, and poured out her heart to God. Prayers of thanksgiving for the love she shared with Carter and Chloe, but also a fervent plea that God would help her little girl hang on a few more days.

Twenty-Three

If the time off from work back in December and early January had taught him anything, it was that even the smallest of tasks--no matter how unexciting and boring--could be appreciated in the moment for what they were. Carter laced his fingers behind his head and leaned back in the office chair and gazed up at the suspended tile ceiling of the Miller's Creek Police Office. Yeah, it had been good to have the opportunity to spend the Christmas holidays with Chloe, Mara, and Ashton, but after Chloe went back to school, the few days left of his suspension had felt strangely out of whack, like he'd somehow lost his purpose in this world. Especially with Mara and Ashton still in Dallas.

He'd returned to his job, once something he wrestled to do because of tedium, with a newfound fervor to serve the fine folks of Miller's Creek. God had showed him that the privileges and responsibilities of his job weren't to be taken lightly.

Carter peered out the front door at the wintry weather, the freezing temps and icy drizzle still hanging on, coating not only everything outside, but also his heart. Would the roads be drivable by tomorrow? Everything was on schedule for him and Chloe to arrive in Dallas tomorrow night for the transplant on Friday. Ashton's fight for life made the situation even more precarious. *Oh, Lord, forgive me for being so hard-headed and unappreciative sometimes. Help Ashton hang on for one more day. And help us get there safely to get this bone marrow transplant over and done with. Please let it take with no problems for Ashton or Chloe. Give Mara an overwhelming sense of Your Presence. Amen.*

He leaned forward, one elbow on his desk, a hand across his mouth. Even now, when he remembered the time he'd shared with Mara, his heart grew giddy. How wonderful that his prayers for her to know God seemed to be answered. She'd spent much of their time together the past weekend pouring over God's Word, asking questions, latching onto it like one would a lifeguard ring, clinging to it as her rescue from stormy seas. But if Ashton didn't make it, would that all change?

The police scanner crackled to life beside him. "Accident on the highway near Miller's Creek High School."

Spine-tingling fear lit a flame within. School was just now letting out for the day. Without stopping to lock the door, he raced to the police car, careful not to slip on the ice, hit the lights and siren, and sped away as fast as he dared, his pulse whizzing like the tires on the pavement, only one word in his heart and mind. *Chloe.*

As Carter approached the railroad tracks, the crossing gate arms began their descent, and the familiar clang joined the throb in his temple. He floored the accelerator and pulled under the gates seconds before they reached their down position.

At the town square, he ignored the red traffic light and tore through the intersection despite the screeching brakes of a car he narrowly missed.

Less than a minute later, he reached the scene of the accident near Chloe's school. His car lurched forward as he threw the gearshift into park without coming to a complete stop and jumped from the vehicle, fire truck and ambulance sirens sounding in the distance. A shiny, new black Mustang lay in the middle of the road upside down. The car belonged to Heather Marks, Chloe's best friend. All-too-familiar screams sounded from within the car and left no doubt that his daughter was inside.

His blood turned to lava as he sprinted to the passenger side of the car, everything and everyone else a blur. Carter's nostrils flared at the tell-tale sign of gasoline, and his eyes honed in on the quickly-pooling liquid beneath the overturned car. As he rounded the corner of the car, Chloe's panicked and upside-down face came into view, her fingers splayed against the car window. Blood gushed from a wound on the left side of her forehead.

She broke into immediate cries and screams. "Dad! Get us out of here! I can't open the door."

Then another sound broke into his consciousness and sent ice through his veins. The motor was still running.

He yanked on the car door with all the force he could muster, and then pounded on the glass to hopefully get Chloe's attention. "Chloe! Stop screaming, and listen to me! Turn the ignition off!" His words didn't register with her as she continued to cry, scream, and pound on the window.

"Move back, Chloe!" Not waiting to see if she heard him, he went into automatic pilot. Where he found the adrenaline to do so, he didn't know, but he took a step back, balanced precariously on one foot on the icy road, and kicked with all his might, praying his martial arts training would pay off. The glass shattered, Chloe's screams more prevalent.

Carter squatted and reached into the car. Reaching past his daughter and a too-still Heather, he cut off the ignition, unbuckled Chloe's seatbelt, and dragged her from the wreckage. He didn't stop moving until he reached the police car, only then aware of Chloe's soft sobs as she clung to his neck while the car behind them burst into flames.

An hour later Carter slouched in the chair beside Chloe's bed in the hospital, his brain still struggling against the fog of shock. He ran both hands over his skull and down his neck. So this is what it felt like to face your child's death, to sit at her hospital bed and pray for her survival, things Mara knew all too well. All things she'd endured, mostly on her own.

He stood and adjusted the slipping cold pack on Chloe's forehead. "That's quite a goose-egg you've got on your noggin, kiddo." He tried to keep his tone light, anything to take away the lifeless chill in Chloe's normally-bright eyes. Yet another burden Mara had shouldered on her own. That of seeing her little girl slowly slip further and further away. "With those stitches and black eye it looks like you've been in hand-to-hand combat."

His daughter didn't speak, but continued to stare at the ceiling, as though part of her had gone some place very far away.

Chance entered the room behind Dr. Moore. He moved to the opposite side of the bed and smiled down at Chloe. "Need anything?"

Chloe gingerly moved her head from side to side, and winced in pain.

Dr. Moore stood at the end of the bed and addressed Chloe. "You're a very fortunate young lady. You have a mild to moderate concussion, but no skull fracture."

Carter leaned his head against the back of the chair and breathed a silent prayer of gratitude. Good news for all of them, including Mara and Ashton.

"However," the doctor continued, "there's some swelling of the brain, which is to be expected. We'll keep you tonight and see how you're doing tomorrow." He moved to where Chance stood, and leaned over the bed to peer into Chloe's eyes with a penlight.

"Is there a chance she can go home tomorrow?" Carter asked the question, not wanting to endanger Chloe in any way, but fearful of what this might mean for Ashton.

The doc pocketed his pen light and shook his head, lips planted in a firm, straight line. "Doubt it. Right now we just have to take things on a day-by-day basis. Sometimes a head trauma of this sort causes major swelling. If that happens, we'll have drill a hole to relieve the pressure. There's also a chance that any bleeding in the brain could worsen and require surgery. And she could develop seizures. All of those are worst-case scenarios, of course."

Carter licked dry lips. Of course.

As the two turned to leave, Chloe slowly rotated her head toward their retreating backs. "Chance?" Even the one word was slurred, more evidence of the concussion.

Chance turned and moved back to her. "Yeah?" He tucked the blanket around her shoulders.

Her dull eyes collected question marks. "Heather?"

Chance peered over at Carter with questions of his own.

Carter inhaled sharply. The moment he'd dreaded since Matt Tyler, one of the first volunteer firemen on the scene, had confirmed what he already suspected. He released a heavy sigh from a heavier heart and pushed himself to a standing position on still-wobbly legs. He stepped to the bed and laid a hand on Chloe's arm. "She didn't make it, Chlo."

Chloe's face crumpled as wails ripped from her mouth.

Carter quickly blinked away his own tears for Chloe's sake. He didn't dare try to lift her to a sitting position. Instead he did what he'd seen Mara do a hundred times and crawled into bed beside her, cradling her as gently as possible as he tried to bring comfort to her broken heart.

Later that night, with Chloe sleeping peacefully from the sedation, and after a visit from his mom and dad and Chloe's mother, Carter pulled out his cell phone to deliver the dreaded news.

Mara picked up on the first ring, excitement zinging in her tone. "Hi!"

Words eluded him. He raised his gaze to the ceiling, scrambling to retrieve the carefully-rehearsed speech that had scattered at the sound of her voice.

"Carter? Is everything okay?"

For the first time all day, tears came in earnest. "Chloe's been in a car accident."

At first no sounds came through the phone, followed by faint sobs. "Is she--is she--?" Her voice broke off, choked short.

"No, she's okay. They're keeping her in the hospital tonight to be safe. She has a concussion, but she remained conscious until they sedated her for the night."

Soft sobs slowly subsided, followed by a telling sigh. "So I guess this means you won't be coming tomorrow, huh?" The forced merriment combined with the tremble in her voice betrayed her fear.

"Doc says we have to take it one day at a time." He covered his phone with one hand, and released a slow breath through puffed out cheeks, praying for strength to ask the next question. For the ability to manage Mara's answer. "How's Ashton?"

Once more the phone grew quiet, this time deadly so. The soft sobs started again. "H-holding on by a thread."

His chest tightened, the ache intense. Judging by Mara's emotional state, she too, was dangling by a very thin thread. Tears once more pricked his eyes. *God, help us!*

Her broken voice sounded through the phone. "She's had a really rough day. One of those days that makes me question if she can make it through the night." Her sobs intensified.

How he longed to be with her, to take her in his arms and comfort her. "I'm so sorry, Mara." Then from somewhere deep inside, hope burst forth like a glorious sunrise in his soul. "But we cannot give up. Keep believing. Keep praying." His forcefulness echoed across the room.

"I am, Carter, but with each tick of the clock, it's like my words are attached to lead. Like they can't escape this jail cell. Like they're falling on deaf ears."

With a confidence only provided by the Sustainer of the universe, Carter did the only thing he knew to do. "Dear Father, this is one of those times that we don't understand. We don't know what Your plan is, but we trust You. You have a reason for everything that comes into our lives, and You use it for our good even when we don't understand. Lord, strengthen our faith, hold Mara up in Your unfathomable power, and breathe life and healing into Ashton and Chloe. We ask all this in the powerful name of Jesus. Amen."

Now the silence between them grew sacred and sweet, God's Presence tangible between them, though miles apart. A moment where Carter fathomed the fluttered hush of angel's wings.

Mara who broke the hush a few seconds later in a prayer-like whisper. "Thank you."

Whether she spoke the words to him or God, he didn't know. All that mattered now was that they both had that peace that surpassed all comprehension. "You gonna be all right?"

"Yeah." Her tone still held a sense of awe and wonder.

"That's my girl." Exultant joy in how far she'd come erupted in his heart. "I'll call as soon as I have any news, and remember that I love you." He imagined her tender smile.

"I love you, too."

Not more than fifteen minutes later, a knock sounded at the door. Carter stood, but before he reached the knob, the door opened. Familiar smiling faces greeted him *en masse.*

Matt reached in the door and pulled him out into the hallway where he was engulfed in multiple hugs from Mama Beth, Steve and Dani, Trish and Andy, Matt and Gracie, Chance and Dakota, and Coot. Conspicuously missing was Ernie. Carter stepped back after all the hugs. "Don't get me wrong, but it's a little scary when y'all all show up at once. What's going on?"

"Mara called as soon as she hung up speaking to you." The knowing look in Mama Beth's eyes let him know she was aware of the burgeoning relationship between him and Mara.

He chuckled a bit nervously and cast his gaze around at the other faces to gauge their expressions.

"And shame on you for not calling me before she did." Now Mama Beth's tone held censure, something the Miller's Creek matriarch used frequently on all her charges, young and old alike. Her expression softened, and her wise blue eyes twinkled. "I got on the horn and got as many of us as I could here for an impromptu prayer meeting."

Mama Beth was right to scold him. Why hadn't he thought to call and ask for prayer?

Matt slapped him gently on the back as the group gathered in a circle around him and joined hands. "We'll forgive you this time, bro, but don't let it happen again."

Soft laughter erupted from the rest of the crew, a typical response to Matt's wicked sense of humor.

They bowed their heads, and each one lifted up prayers for him, for Chloe's rapid improvement, for Mara to be strong in her newfound faith, and for miraculous healing for their tiniest angel. By the time they finished, tears coursed unashamedly down Carter's cheeks, but his unflappable peace remained firmly intact.

As Carter said his goodbye's to everyone, Ernie rounded the corner and approached with an indiscernible glint in his eyes, his felt cowboy hat in hand. He stood by patiently while the others hugged Carter and moved down the hallway.

Carter extended his right hand and used his left to clasp Ernie's shoulder. "Hey, Ernie. Thanks for coming."

"How's Chloe?"

"Doing well under the circumstances, but they're keeping her overnight."

Ernie shifted his weight from one foot to the other, his boots clicking against the tile floors. His fingers slid non-stop over the brim of his hat.

Something was eating at his boss. An uncanny feeling sent Carter's neck hairs to attention. Whatever words Ernie clamped behind his thick moustache wasn't good news. "Just say it, Ernie. No need to beat around the bush." Carter crossed his arms across his chest and leaned his weight against the wall.

His boss raised his gaze, his eyes and mouth set like cement. "Wish I had better news, especially under the circumstances."

In his chest, Carter's heart did a strange little flop and picked up speed. "Go on."

Ernie released an exasperated sigh. "If it were just me, I wouldn't be doing this now, but I work for the people of Miller's Creek."

Carter nodded, pretty sure he knew where this was headed. He opted not to speak.

"You almost ran into Otis Thacker with a police car on your way to the accident this afternoon."

Otis Thacker, of all people. Yeah, he would be one to raise a stink. As the town grouch, he probably saw it as his civic duty. "Sorry, but as you can imagine I wasn't thinking too clearly at the time."

"I know." Ernie's bald head nodded in understanding. "Unfortunately, that's not all."

Carter tucked his lips between his teeth, fearful of letting his anger get the best of him in the emotional backwash of this very trying day.

"Otis has filed a complaint, which means an investigation."

"Like I said--"

"I heard you the first time, Carter. Let me finish." He eyed Carter with the authority of a higher-up. "Another resident said you crossed the railroad tracks while the guard arms were going down, and teachers at the scene said you left the squad car running with gasoline spewing from the wreck. You didn't clear the area to make sure the high school kids and others nearby were safe."

Carter kept his mouth clamped shut in spite of growing resentment inside. Once Ernie quit spouting infractions, he inhaled a quick breath to still his ire. "Sorry. My child was in danger."

"I understand that, Carter, but you were on duty and risked not only your life, but the lives of many other citizens of Miller's Creek. If this were the first time, this could easily be overlooked."

Blood rushed from his head, and his mouth gaped open. This couldn't be going where Ernie seemed to be headed. Was his job in danger?

Ernie's shoulders raised perceptibly as he drew in a breath to finish speaking. "One of the parents at the high school has also filed a complaint and is threatening a civil suit. Says you endangered the life of her child."

"Mind telling me who?"

"Carla Clark."

"Brody Clark's mom?"

Ernie nodded.

"C'mon. You know that whole family is lawsuit happy." Carla was sure to step into Otis Thatcher's job as town grouch once he vacated the position. And Brody would line up behind his mother in the queue. "Besides, all those kids and their parents were old enough to move out of the way on their own."

"Well, I got an earful from her right before I came over here. Just wanted to give you a head's up about all that's going on."

Carter's mouth went sour as his mind raced through all Ernie had said. But almost instantaneously everything settled like a boat steadied by an anchor. His boss was a fair and good man, here to warn him, not scold him. "Thanks, Ernie. I know delivering that news was weighing heavy on you, but I appreciate you shooting straight with me."

Ernie's full moustache bobbed momentarily, the closest thing to emotion anyone ever got out of the stoic man. His boss placed a hand on Carter's shoulder, his eyes sincere. "Let me know if you need anything."

Carter nodded. "Will do."

"Y'all still travelling to Dallas tomorrow?"

"Don't know at this point, but if the doc gives the go ahead, we will. Depends on how Chloe's doing."

Ernie said his goodbyes and strode away just as Steve, Andy, Matt, and Chance appeared with a bucket of chicken and all the fixings from Granny's.

Carter's mouth watered at the smell. "Man, you guys didn't have to do this, but thank you."

"Our pleasure," said Andy with his laid-back grin as he eyed the others. "But we, uh, have ulterior motives."

Uh oh. Just what kind of hot water would this land him in with their wives? "Do tell." The words came out dry and sarcastic.

Matt laughed. "The women wanted us to take them to see the latest chick flick over in Morganville."

Carter grinned. "Ah, so I'm your excuse."

"You might say that." Steve drawled out the words and rubbed his chin, then leveled his gaze at Carter. "But I just got a really distinct impression that the situation needed intense prayer."

Peace descended once more. Carter smiled at his buddies, then opened the door to Chloe's room and ushered them inside. "I'm honored, and honestly, prayer was already on my agenda."

The next morning before sun-up, Carter arrived at the hospital, more than eager to see Chloe. Had she rested well? Would swelling or bleeding or seizures prevent her from helping Ashton? He entered the room to find her still asleep, so he positioned himself near the bed to watch his baby girl sleep, her pretty face framed by the curly ringlets she'd inherited from her mom.

Chloe stirred and slowly opened her eyes to take in her surroundings. Her gaze landed on him, and she smiled. Then just as suddenly, her smile morphed into a frown. "Did you spend the night in that chair?"

A chuckle sounded from his throat. She was obviously feeling better. "Nope. Just got here a few minutes ago."

Her frown grew larger. "Were you staring at me while I was asleep?"

He nodded, a grin spreading his cheeks tight.

"Dad, that's creepy."

Now his chuckle developed into a hearty laugh. Yep, definitely better.

Without warning, her mouth rounded, and her eyes widened. "I just remembered."

"Remembered what?"

"I had a dream, and I think it was the same kind of dream Ashton had. You know, the ones she has about--"

"Jesus?"

She nodded softly, and raised a hand to her head. "My bump's gone down."

Carter leaned in for a closer look. "Sure enough. Does it hurt?"

"Not really." Chloe pushed herself to a sitting position, threw back the bedding, and uncovered her legs.

Carter grabbed both shoulders, and gently forced her back toward the pillow. "Whoa there, missy. Just what do you think you're doing?"

"My dream. I have to do what Jesus told me to do."

Was all this because of the blow to her head? "Sorry, Chlo, but you can't get out of bed without a nurse or doctor."

Exasperation flooded her face, and she shot a teenager scowl that let him know exactly what she thought of him at the moment. "Then call one. We don't have any time to waste!"

Carter reached for the buzzer and pressed it, his thoughts swimming.

A nurse appeared and helped Chloe to the bathroom, though she had not one ounce of trouble maneuvering. Just a minute later, Chloe re-entered the room. "Where are my clothes?"

He scratched his head. "Uh, I took them home."

"Well, you'll just have to go get them."

Carter narrowed his eyes. "Okay, but we can't leave without the doctor's permission."

The nurse nodded in agreement. "Your dad's right, Chloe."

His daughter tilted her chin upward and crossed her arms. "Then call him and get him here as soon as possible."

Carter moved over to where his daughter stood and put an arm around her shoulder. "Honey, what else happened in your dream?"

Her face brightened. "Jesus said I was healed so I could heal. Dad, we've got to get to Ashton, like right now!"

Twenty-Four

Mara squinted against the shaft of sunlight that shone through the hospital window and took in the familiar sight of the same old ceiling tiles. Careful not to disturb Ashton, she slid her arm out from under her daughter's head and tried to massage away the pins and needles that pricked within from lying in one position too long.

In the bright rays of morning light, Ashton looked especially pale, like death had devoured several more ounces of her life during the awful night. After Carter's call, her daughter had awakened in the wee hours of the morning, screaming and holding her head.

"Mommy, it hurts! Make it stop!" Her almost unrecognizable features had scrunched in pain as she sobbed and held her head.

The words still sent knife-like hurt slicing through Mara as she bent over her daughter's still form. Still breathing, but her breaths were slow and labored. "Thank You for keeping her with us through another night, God." How many times had she repeated those words?

Mara gently nudged Ashton. While part of her hated to wake her after the long night, she just had to know that her daughter was okay.

Ashton didn't rouse.

Again, Mara shook, but with no results. Heart pounding, she raced to the opposite side of the bed and with shaky hands buzzed the nurse's station. Within seconds, footsteps sounded out in the hallways, and the door opened.

Chrissy, Ashton's favorite nurse, rushed into the room. "Is she okay?"

Mara's head swam, and a cold sweat broke out on her forehead. "I think so, but I can't wake her up." Her words sounded distant and warbled.

"I'll be right back." When Chrissy returned a minute later, two other nurses joined her. Chrissy moved to Mara, placed hands on her shoulder, and forced her attention. "Listen to me, Mara. I need you to go to the waiting room for now. I've called Dr. Watts. She'll be here soon."

Her heart hardened into a ball and rolled to her throat. Was this the end? A cold tremor sent an icy chill. In a daze, she stumbled to the waiting room and fell into a chair, elbows on knees, her face planted in her palms. *Oh, God, please.*

She wanted to pray more, but no words would come. Instead voices teased and mocked from inside her head. Why don't you just give up? You know prayers don't work anyway. If God really loved you, why would He put you and Ashton through this?

Mara emphatically gave her head a shake, attempting to dislodge the attack against her newfound faith. No! She wouldn't give in. Couldn't give in. Somehow she had to stand strong.

Then the familiar Black Abyss returned, grinning at her with gaping and toothless mouth, urging her to step closer, to peer into the depths, to allow herself the comfort of oblivion.

Mara squeezed her eyes shut. *God help me. Help Ashton.* If only Carter were here. He could help her through this. She patted her pockets for her phone, a sudden visual reminder coming to her thoughts of placing her cell phone on the table near the couch. She raised a teary gaze toward the ceiling of the dimly-lit waiting room. "I don't want to be alone."

I'm here.

The words were spoken so softly. Had she just imagined them?

I won't leave you alone, Mara. Be still. Believe and know. I AM.

A sudden warmth flooded in around her, as well as the slightest pressure on her arms and upper body, almost as though someone were there, embracing her and holding her close.

An unfathomable peace, like that she'd experienced yesterday when Carter had prayed through the phone, lifted the burden from her shoulders. Mara slumped back against the chair, and allowed the peaceful warmth to draw her even closer.

The elevator bell dinged down the hallway, rousing her from somewhere far away. The doors slid open, followed by the sounds of voices. One voice in particular caught her attention. That voice. No, it wasn't possible. It must be someone else. With energy she hadn't felt in weeks, she rose to her feet and rushed to the doorway. Her mouth flew open, and she rubbed her eyes to make sure she wasn't dreaming. "I don't believe it."

Chloe sat in a wheelchair pushed by Carter. He wheeled her up closer, and then stepped around to hug Mara tightly. "After a lot of praying with good friends last night, Chloe woke up this morning convinced that Jesus had told her to get here ASAP. The doc came and said he'd never seen anything like it."

Mara stared at Chloe, then fell in front of her and pushed back the curls that framed her sweet face, hungry just to gaze at her and marvel in the fact that she was alive. "I'm so glad you're okay."

Chloe smiled. "Me too. Now, take me to Ashton."

Tears flooded Mara's eyes. "We can't."

"We're not too late, are we?" Chloe's voice held panic.

"No, she's still breathing, but I couldn't get her to wake up. The nurse's are in there right now. Maybe the doctor, too." Had he slipped in without her knowledge as she'd rested in the safe strong arms of Jesus? Then realization dawned. It was still early morning. She raised a surprised gaze to Carter's unshaven face and weary eyes. "How'd you get here so quickly?"

The cheeky smile she'd grown to love appeared. "When Chance overheard Chloe tell the doctor that she had to get to Dallas right away, he arranged a flight via helicopter."

Down the hall, the door to Ashton's room opened, and Dr. Watts appeared. She stepped down the hall and came to a stop in front of Mara. "It's a good thing you tried to wake her when you did. I think we had time to get her going again. And miraculously enough, I think her vitals are strong enough for the transplant to take place." She smiled down at Chloe. "You're the one responsible for waking me up so early this morning, aren't you? I got a call from your doctor saying you were good to go. Are you ready for this?"

Chloe nodded, a confident grin so much like Carter's on her closed lips and courage radiating from her very core. "Yes, and I'm not afraid."

An unexpected laugh sounded from the doctor, and she peered up at Carter. "You've got yourself a go-getter, don't you?"

He shrugged, a moist sheen to his eyes. "What can I say? Guess she comes by it naturally."

The doctor motioned for a nurse to join them. "This is Chloe. She's the bone marrow donor for Ashton. Would you take her and start the prep work?"

As Chloe wheeled off down the hall with a casual wave over her shoulder, the doctor faced them with a bewildered shake to her head. "I've just gotta say, in all my years in this line of work, I've never seen such a close match between non-family members. It's almost like they're--"

"Sisters?" Carter spoke the word softly and smiled over at Mara.

Immediate tears formed in Mara's eyes and spilled over. "They *are* sisters in so many ways, but God is the one who made them a match."

Raw terror ripped through Carter, worse than anything he'd experienced in the military, as he took in Ashton's appearance. The horrors of war he'd been somewhat prepared for, and his training had kicked in to take up the slack. But nothing could've prepared him for seeing Ashton so close to death. How had her condition deteriorated so much in such a short time?

Tears pricked his eyes, and a cold shiver radiated from his core as he looked up at Mara. "I have to leave for a second, but I'll be back."

He moved to the hallway, collapsed against the wall, and slid down to a sitting position, his face buried in his hands, his breath in shallow spurts. *Oh, Lord, help her.*

The door opened beside him, and Mara joined him in the floor. She gave him a sideways hug. "You okay?"

He shook his head. "I don't know. All this time I felt confident, but when I saw her..."

"Yeah, she looks bad, and last night was the worst."

Carter faced Mara and took both her hands in his. "Why is it that you're holding it all together, and I'm the one with shaken faith? It's like the voices in my head won't shut up."

A half-smile curved her lips, and her eyes held understanding. "I've battled those same voices for weeks now."

He searched her face long and hard. The words she spoke were truth. "Looks like that battle made you stronger."

She nodded. "That and an overwhelming sense of His Presence with me."

"So you're not afraid?" *Lord, help me not to be afraid.*

She leaned her head back against the wall and stretched her long legs out in front of her. "The fear's still there. I don't want to lose my baby. But it's like whatever happens, I know God's still in control."

Awe and marvel trickled over him at the miraculous change in her. *Thank You, God.*

Mara rose to her feet and held out a hand. "C'mon. There's a little girl in there who needs us both."

Back in the room, Carter steeled himself with a deep breath, and moved to Ashton's bed. Now both her eyes were open, and a faint smile appeared on her face. "I knew you'd get here on time. Where's Chloe?"

Mara patted her arm. "They already have her in surgery to take the bone marrow. Just like Dr. Watts explained to you the other day."

She nodded weakly.

The door opened and two nurses stepped in, a cart in front of them. Chrissy smiled and moved up beside Mara. "Yay, my favorite girl is awake."

Ashton managed another smile.

"You remember when we talked earlier this week, and I told you about how we'd put a line into your chest?" Chrissy's face and tone held a calm, reassuring quality.

Ashton didn't speak, but nodded.

"Well, that's what we're about to do. Once Chloe's bone marrow is ready, we'll hook it up and let it go into your body through that line." She looked up at Mara. "You are both welcome to stay, but we will need you to move back."

Ashton endured the process like a practiced pro, and a few minutes later, Chrissy and the other nurse smiled their good-byes and wheeled the cart from the room.

Minutes dragged by as Carter awaited word about Chloe. Was she handling the procedure okay in light of her recent head trauma?

Finally, Dr. Watts entered the room, a smile on her face. First, she checked on Ashton, who slept peacefully, then turned her attention to Carter and Mara. "Chloe came through the procedure like a champ. She's just now coming out from under the anesthesia. More than likely her throat will hurt from the tube and she'll have mild pain at the site and probably a headache. Other than that she should be fine. I'd like to keep her overnight as a precaution."

Carter nodded his assent as his muscles uncoiled. Ashton and Chloe both were in wonderful hands. Not just the skilled hands of the medical staff, but also the hands of Almighty God.

The doctor sent an understanding smile. "You have nothing to worry about. Chloe's one tough teen-ager. You're very blessed." She headed to the door. "Oh, and if it's okay, I thought we'd put her in this room with Ashton. There seems to be a very special connection between them that I think will be good for both of them."

"That would be wonderful." Mara spoke the words he wanted to say.

But no words could escape his swollen throat and grateful heart.

Twenty-Five

The cold and icy winter melted into lush and glorious spring, and creek waters, higher than normal, gurgled and cranked out a merry tune that could be heard from Creekside Park all the way to the town square. Carter let out a cheerful whistle as he walked with Chloe toward Granny's Kitchen for their typical daddy-daughter Saturday morning breakfast outing. After that they'd head to Dallas to pick up Mara and Ashton for their trip home. Finally.

The usual crew of trucks crowded the street for an entire block, a big chunk of the local farmers extending their normal coffee klatch because fields were too wet to plow or plant.

Carter opened the glass door of Granny's Kitchen and stepped back to let Chloe enter. "Ladies first."

She grinned and rolled her eyes dramatically. "That's what you always say."

"That's 'cause I always mean it."

One of the Granny's had saved their little table for two in the back corner. When she spied them at the front of the cafe, she motioned them on back.

Within a few minutes, she'd taken their order and delivered a steaming cup of hot cocoa for Chloe and a cup of black coffee spiraling its heady aroma his way. He lifted the cup, inhaled deeply, and sipped the hot drink. That should help steel his nerves a bit. And why was he nervous, anyway? He was the guy who laughed at fear. Funny how he could take down a suspect with nothing but raw adrenaline running through his veins, but when it came to something that involved sharing emotions with his soon-to-be-graduated daughter, he morphed into one gigantic mass of nerves. He took one more sip, and then sat his cup down and peered across the table at Chloe.

He still marveled at how well everything had turned out in the bone marrow transplant. In spite of her head injury, Chloe had absolutely no complications from the procedure. And though it had taken a while for Ashton to spring back, every day she was a little more like the precocious little girl that had so easily taken his heart captive. Carter inhaled deep. "Uh, I've, er, been meaning to, uh, ask you about something."

Chloe frowned. "What are you stuttering for?"

He shrugged. "I don't know. Just let me get through this, okay?"

Now her eyebrows headed the opposite direction, but she said nothing.

"I've been thinking about, I mean, if it's okay with you and everything, but I think I might, you know..." Throughout his bumbling words, the smile on Chloe's face grew broader.

Finally her smiled bubbled into hearty laughter. "You have my permission and my blessing."

"For what?"

She gave him the 'why-are-dads-so incredibly-out-of-it?' look. "To ask Mara to marry you, of course. I knew this was coming."

"You did? How?"

An even louder laugh fell from her mouth, drawing stares from people at nearby tables. "You're so clueless."

"About what?"

"About the fact that Mr. G.I. Joe turns into the Stay-Puft Marshmallow Man whenever she's around."

Busted. And by a teenage girl. "That obvious, huh?"

"Oh, puh-lease." She gave her ringlets a shake.

"So you don't have any objections?"

"Why would I? Mara's wonderful. And she's tough enough to keep you in line, which is exactly what you need." Though Carter wanted to object, he couldn't. His daughter had hit the nail on its proverbial head.

At just that time, Matt and Andy Tyler, along with Andy's step-son, Bo, descended on the table next to theirs.

Carter stood and moved over to where Matt and Andy sat, and extended his hand. "What's up, guys?"

Andy released a weary sigh, took a sneak peak in Bo's direction, and lowered his voice to a conspiratorial whisper. "Me. Way too early for a Saturday morning." He cast one more surreptitious glance at Bo, who was already deep in conversation with Chloe. "But Bo was insistent that we eat out this morning. Now I know why."

Matt laughed softly. "Like you haven't done your fair share of he-ing and she-ing." He took a swig of his DP.

Carter frowned at Chloe from the other end of the table, but there was no catching her attention. Her eyes were locked on Bo. He addressed Andy. "How long has this been going on?"

"I think he's liked her for a while, but with him off at college, he doesn't get to see her that often."

A gamut of emotions coursed through Carter. First a sort of relief that Bo was several notches above the bad-boy types Chloe usually went for, and secondly, an immediate wariness that a college Freshman would be interested in a high school girl like his daughter. Surely with someone as good-looking as Bo, the college girls must be standing in line.

"Easy, Carter," teased Matt, a twinkle in his sand-colored eyes. "Your daddy-hood is showing."

Carter frowned. "Can't help it. If y'all will excuse me, I think I'd better play chaperone." He moved back to the table and took his seat.

Chloe shot a sarcastic "thanks, Dad" glare as Bo turned back to the conversation at his own table.

He just smiled good-naturedly. "Anyway, back to our previous conversation. I'd like for you to be in on the proposal. I need your help to make it sweet and romantic and memorable. You up for that?"

"Sure, Dad, whatever." Chloe's voice had taken on a trance-like quality which raised Carter's head from his just-arrived plate of biscuits and gravy.

Yep, like father like daughter. If Stay-Puft Marshmallow Man had a Marshmallow Daughter, Chloe definitely fit the description, especially if Little Bo--who wasn't so little anymore--was anywhere in the vicinity.

"Do you really think Ashton will be okay?" Mara directed the question to Carter at Creekside Park where a crowd had gathered on this warm and late spring day for a special baptism celebration. "I mean, I know it's a warm day and everything, but what if the water is too cold?"

Carter peered into her eyes, the very picture of strength and confidence. "Dr. Watts cleared her for this, Mara. She'll be fine. Chance is here, and I'll be standing on the shore with an extra warm blanket." With a soft smile, he latched onto her fingertips, raised her hand to his lips, and planted a soft kiss. "I know it's hard, especially with all you and Ashton have been through, but at some point you've got to let go of all this unnecessary worrying."

At one time his words would have set her to fuming, but if the past few months had taught her anything about Carter, it was that he loved and protected fiercely. His words were only spoken in light of who he was. She smiled back. "You're really getting on my nerves."

He pumped a fist with his other hand. "All right, mission accomplished."

She landed an elbow into the soft flesh of his side.

"Ow! Cut it out!" Carter laughed, a sound that bounced around on her insides, spreading splotches of warmth that erupted in a smile.

Oh, how she loved him. Did he even know how much? And when would he keep the promise he'd made while Ashton was in the hospital? She tugged her bottom lip between her teeth and peered down at the crystal clear water of Miller's Creek, where in a short time she would symbolically reveal her commitment to faith in Christ. Though it would hurt if Carter never proposed--or if their relationship one day ended--no one would ever be able to steal away the transformation that had taken place within her heart. And for that she would forever be in his debt. He and God had both pursued her relentlessly when it came to her faith, no greater proof of faithful love.

Carter bumped up against her. "Hey, you. You're not worried about being baptized yourself are you?"

"Not at all."

"Then why the long face?"

"I was born that way." Mara followed the words with a smile, bringing forth a soft chuckle from Carter. No way would she reveal that any long-faced expression was brought on by an odd sort of disappointment that he hadn't taken the next step in their relationship, despite the fact that several months had passed. No, the ball was definitely in his court, and she refused to do anything to manipulate the situation. God had a plan, and her prayer would continue to be for His will, no matter what happened between her and Carter.

Brother Mac, the pastor of Miller's Creek Community Church, stepped into the clear water, his long white robe floating behind him.

Mara gauged his reaction to the temp of the water. Good. No flinching or chattering teeth. A good sign for Ashton. She cast a glance to where Chloe and Ashton stood, both dressed in white robes that matched Brother Mac's and her own. Just seeing the two together, healthy and happy and whole, brought overwhelming gratitude to her heart.

"Brothers and sisters, is this not a glorious day the Lord has made?" The pastor held both hands outstretched at shoulder level, his face a-beam with an inner light.

Amens and other affirmative replies sounded through the crowd, which had quieted the moment he faced them.

"We're here to celebrate a symbolic act of something that has already taken place in the hearts of Mara, Chloe, and Ashton. In obedience to the Lord, they are following Him in believer's baptism today."

The congregation erupted with applause and cheers.

Mara smiled her thankfulness to these people, who'd become the family she'd always yearned for. Did they know how much she'd grown to love them through their constant friendship and faithfulness, even during the times when she'd doubted their sincerity? Tears sprang to her eyes as she turned her gaze back to Brother Mac.

He motioned her toward the water. "Normally, we start with the youngest and move to the oldest, but to guard against Ashton getting sick, we'll start with Mara."

More applause sounded and rumbled in her ears as she stepped into the surprisingly-warm water of Miller's Creek. She waded out to Brother Mac and crouched down as instructed previously. A melody of love, combined with countermelodies of peace and thankfulness, harmonized in her heart. *Oh God, thank You for pursuing me when I wanted nothing to do with You. Thank You for loving me so much.*

Tears of joy streamed down her cheeks, but she made no attempt to stop them.

Brother Mac put one hand on her shoulder and raised the other to the sky. "Mara because of your faith in the Lord Jesus Christ, as a sign of your obedience to Him, I baptize you, my sister, in the name of the Father, the Son, and the Holy Spirit. Buried with Him in baptism..."

She put her hands over her face, and leaned her weight against Brother Mac's strong hands, as he lowered her under the water. *Washed clean by the blood of the Lamb.*

Just as quickly, she was brought up out of the water to the glorious sunlight of the beautiful day.

"...raised to walk in newness of life."

Mara stood to her feet, the weight of her wet robe heavy and cumbersome, but her heart lighter than it had ever been. Yes, a new life that would never be taken away. *Thank You, Jesus.* She moved to the shore where Carter, Chloe, and Ashton waited with smiles.

As soon as she stepped on shore, Carter wrapped her in an over-sized towel. He pulled her toward him and engulfed her in a hug. "I love you, Mara, my sister in Christ."

Tears and emotion prevented her from answering. She simply smiled, praying he'd understand her lack of response.

Chloe entered the water next, the joy on her face unmistakable.

Mara and Carter exchanged tearful smiles as she came up out of the water.

Then Ashton, her golden hair once more evident and her sweet face serene and steadfast, moved out without hesitation and followed through with her own baptism. As she stepped ashore, Carter quickly gathered her in a soft blanket and lifted her into his arms.

The crowd applauded again, but this time without cheers.

Mara let her gaze travel around the faces of the people. Not one cheek was without the glisten of tears.

A few minutes later, after the applause had ended, Brother Mac spoke, his voice husky. "In celebration of this special day, Mama Beth and the Miller family have prepared a special meal for everyone. We'll meet in the fellowship hall in just a few minutes, but let me bless the food as we lift up a prayer of thanksgiving to God." He closed his eyes, his radiant face lifted skyward, his arms outstretched in worship. "Father God, our hearts are grateful and overflowing with joy..." His voice broke off. Finally he continued. "Thank you for the testimony of these who have put their trust in You. May they continue to live for You and share their belief in You with others. May we, as their church family, be committed to loving them and helping them. Bless this food we're about to eat. Thank You for the food and the ones who prepared it. In the precious name of Your Son, Jesus, we pray and give You all the honor and praise. Amen."

Several people made their way to Carter, Mara, and the two girls. Thankfully, they simply offered a few words and hugs, cognizant of their need to get Ashton into dry clothes.

Later, at the fellowship hall, one person after another offered their well wishes and congratulations. Somehow Mara continued to smile and say thank you, though eating the plate of delicious food in front of her grew increasingly difficult. And always at the front of her mind was Ashton and how she handled this first major outing after the transplant. Thankfully, Ashton seemed none the worse for wear, smiling and chatting with her friends as she devoured the plate of food in front of her.

But as the time wore on, a knee-sagging weariness weighted Mara down. Where had this come from? Probably her mind-numbing concern for her daughter. She turned to Carter, who finished his meal at her side. "I think

I'm gonna leave now and take Ashton home. I need a nap. Or something."

An instantaneous frown took up residence on his face, and he scanned the room. "Please stay just a few more minutes, Mara." Carter pushed back his metal chair so quickly it screeched against the tile floors. He stood and faced her with one finger raised. "I'll be right back, okay?" Carter strode around the long table and headed to where Chloe sat with Bo James.

A smile descended to Mara's lips as her gaze lit on Chloe and Bo. What a sweet couple they made.

With one hand on the table and one on her chair, Carter leaned down next to Chloe and whispered something in her ear. She nodded and stood, then followed Carter to the front of the fellowship hall.

Carter raised both hands and let out his infamous shrill whistle. "Hey, everyone, quiet down a sec."

Amidst continued conversation and humorous comments launched Carter's way by the likes of Coot and Matt, the group eventually quieted.

"Thank y'all so much for all you've done for us over the past few months." Carter faced the opening that led into the church kitchen. "And thanks to Mama Beth and Dani for this wonderful food." He applauded, his hands in front of his face. The rest of the room joined in. When the applause ended, he looked directly at her. "Mara, would you and Ashton join us up here at the front?"

More than a little discomfited, Mara stood and helped Ashton do the same. What was going on, and why hadn't he let her in on this ahead of time? Heart pounding curiously, she moved to the front of the room.

Carter held out a hand as she approached, so she put her hand in his. He smiled, one of such love and tenderness, that breathing was difficult. "I have a great idea." He spoke the words loud enough for everyone to hear.

Mara erupted into instant laughter. "Don't you always?"

His eyes twinkled, but lost none of their soft tenderness. "Yeah well, this is the best idea ever."

Okay, she could play along with whatever this was. "So what exactly is this brilliant idea of yours?"

Carter grinned broadly, his cheeks pulled back to his sideburns. "I thought you'd never ask." One hand travelled to his jacket pocket.

Now her lungs refused to work, and her heart pounded in her ears. Could this be happening? Was what she'd hoped for--no, what she'd prayed for--finally about to happen? She pulled both her lips between her teeth and pressed them together, eyes stinging with tears.

He tugged a large folded paper from his pocket.

Her excitement plummeted. No, it was a map. Her map, and not the little square jewelry box she'd anticipated. She ripped the paper from his grasp. "What're you doing with my map?"

The crowd laughed, and Carter joined in. He took the map back away from her and began to unfold it. "This isn't an ordinary map. It was the map you used to look for houses the first day I met you." He gave one corner to Chloe and he took the other, holding it up so everyone could see.

Okay, enough of the shenanigans. Where exactly was he going with all this? She skewed her lips to one side.

Knowing Carter, this whole scenario could end with humiliation. Should she bring it to a stop right then and there?

Carter pointed to a big X he'd added with red Magic Marker right in the middle of her map. "This intersection--this crossroads--is where you got lost." He smiled at her tenderly. "But somehow you were able to find your way." His voice softened, and the room grew even quieter. "Crossroads are like that, aren't they? They force us to choose. To make a decision."

Mara nodded and swallowed, the knot in her throat growing larger by the moment. Yes, coming to Miller's Creek had proved to be a place of decision for her, the one decision that mattered more than any other.

His eyes softened, and he tugged on her fingers. "Mara, I'm so grateful this crossroads for you was a meeting place for us. And now we're at another crossroads." He paused and breathed deep, his broad shoulders rising and settling again, but his gaze never left hers. "I never expected to fall in love with you the way I did."

Happy sighs came from all around the room.

Carter continued. "My love for you is like a journey." He pointed to the right side of the map. "It starts in the east at forever." He slid his index finger across the map to the opposite side. "And ends in the west. At never."

A smile she couldn't contain any longer broke out on her face as a tear escaped and made its way down one cheek.

Carter moved his finger back to the giant red cross in the middle of the map, to the crossroads and place of decision she'd come to know so well. He released the map and went down on one knee, holding onto her hand with one of his and once more reaching into the right pocket of his jacket, this time producing two jewelry boxes. He handed the bigger one to Chloe, who came and knelt in front of Ashton. He looked at both her and her daughter. "Mara and Ashton, would you marry me and Chloe?"

Mara turned and looked at Ashton. "What do you think, Ash? Should we let these two thrill-seekers into our lives?"

Ashton smiled and nodded with big bobs of her head. "Of course we should." She looked at the crowd and made a silly face, laughter quickly erupting from those who looked on. "It would be preposterous not to do so."

Laughter erupted from everyone present. Mara smiled at her daughter, whose penchant for using big words had even survived months of chemo and a bone marrow transplant.

Once they all quieted, Carter looked expectantly at Mara and cleared his throat. "My knee's getting tired, and you still haven't answered my question."

"Well, since it would be preposterous to say no, the answer is yes."

Loud cheers and applause sounded once more, and people rose to their feet in ovation. Carter placed an engagement ring on Mara's finger while Chloe fastened a golden heart chain around Ashton's neck, a matching one dangling from her neck.

As all of them turned to face the crowd, Mara's eyes fell on the map which now rested on the floor, the red cross highlighted as a vivid reminder of the One who made all things possible.

Twenty-Six

Carter rubbed the drowsiness from his eyes with both fists, then yawned and stretched. Jump-starting a new business while filling in for Ernie during his vacation had stolen away precious sleep. But he wasn't sorry. A satisfied smile landed on his lips in spite of overwhelming fatigue. Mara's suggestion that he start his own outdoorsmen business had been a God-send and answer to prayer.

Business had been better than expected. The women from the Metroplex that loved to shop in Miller's Creek during the summer now brought their husbands for fishing and rappelling trips. In the fall they'd be back for deer hunting, and the small cracks of time he had in between were scheduled with teaching gun safety and organizing other types of outdoor excursions.

He eyed the clock. Ernie would be back for official duty in just a few more minutes, which would finally allow him some much-needed sleep. Now if he and Mara could just eke out time for a wedding.

In addition to his business taking off, Mara's real estate company had grown so quickly she'd added another realtor to help with the load. Between work, attending the girls' activities, and getting ready to send Chloe to nursing school in the fall, there'd been very little time to even talk about wedding plans. And it weighed heavy, like an anchor that held him back when he wanted to move forward.

A car pulled up outside the front door of the Miller's Creek police station. Ernie.

His former boss wandered in, a huge grin on his face. "Hey, Carter. Ready for some relief?"

"You know it." He shook Ernie's hand and slapped him on the shoulder. "How was the beach?"

"Better than you can imagine."

Carter pushed against immediate feelings of envy. What he wouldn't give to be on his honeymoon with Mara at some tropical location. "Hope all those sunrays you caught don't disappear now that you're back on duty."

Ernie waved a hand and stepped behind the counter. "We've got a new guy who starts training tomorrow, so it should be okay."

Good. Knowing that he wasn't leaving everyone high and dry made him feel better. Carter stepped to the door. "Well, I'll see you around."

Carter stepped out into the hot August day, an immediate sweat breaking out on his forehead. Welcome to summertime in Texas. He adjusted his sunglasses against the white-hot sun and headed toward the Taurus.

Mara rested her weight against the hood and smiled at him as he approached.

He leaned in and kissed her. "Hey, gorgeous. To what do I owe this nice surprise?"

An enigmatic expression popped onto her face. "Well, to coin a phrase I've heard you use on more than one occasion, that's for me to know and you to find out." She tugged on his fingers. "Leave the Taurus. You're coming with me."

Carter groaned. "Honey, I appreciate this, but I'm bone tired. Can't we do this another time?" The look she returned told him all he needed to know. She wasn't about to budge. "Okay, okay."

She followed him to the passenger side of the Caddy. "First I need you to put this on." She held up a bandana.

"A do rag?"

"No, a blind fold."

He studied her through narrowed eyelids. "Okay, what's going on here?"

"Put it on, Callahan, or I will. And stop asking so many questions." Her tone and face allowed no argument.

With the blindfold obscuring his vision, he tried to keep track of where they were going, but by turn number ten, he was hopelessly lost. Finally the vehicle stopped moving, and Mara killed the ignition.

"Can I take off the blindfold?"

"Not yet you can't."

Her car door opened and then slammed shut. A second later his door opened and she tugged on his elbow to help him climb from the car. "Trust me?"

"Doesn't look like I have much choice."

For a while they walked across level ground, but then the smooth walking surface grew more uneven and climbed upward. Had he not had her beside him, talking him over the obstacles, he'd have been flat on his face in no time. Finally, out of breath from the climb and mind-numbing fatigue, they came to a stop.

"Okay, Carter, I need you to listen to me."

"All ears here." What was going on?

"When you asked me to marry you, you used my map to demonstrate the crossroads of decision, the perfect way to describe how our journey together started." Her voice cracked a bit, but she quickly regained control. "Words can't express how grateful I am to the Lord for bringing you to me at a crossroads in my life. A time when I didn't know which way to turn or even how to put one foot in front of the other."

His heart melted and sent a smile to his face. "Mara, I'm the one whose..."

"Hush, and let me finish, or I won't be able to get through this without breaking down."

"Yes, ma'am." A phrase he seemed to be using more and more often since he'd asked her to be his wife. An unexpected sound came from his right, and he turned his head toward the sound. Nothing.

Mara clasped both his hands in hers and forced his head back her direction. She released a heavy breath. "Anyway, it was you who reminded me how important little things were. Things like laughter and having fun. It was you who helped me climb to new heights." Her voice softened. "And taught me to take leaps of faith. Now it's time." She grew silent.

"Time for what?"

"I just helped you make a climb, and hopefully, you realized that it required teamwork and communication. Now it's time for a leap of faith. Take off your blindfold."

Carter reached up and tugged at the bandana. The sight before him stole his breath. He and Mara were surrounded by a whole slew of smiling people, friends who'd been through the thick and thin with them, friends that included his parents and the rest of the Callahan clan. And they all had somehow managed to squeeze onto the small bluff where he'd taken Mara rappelling last fall. "What is this?" He grinned at Mara, trying to understand.

Mara's broad grin erupted into raucous laughter, and her eyes shone. "We're gonna take the plunge."

Chloe stepped forward with his rappelling gear. "I know you think you're Superman, but you might wanna put this on."

Ashton handed Mara her own gear, which she quickly donned.

Carter laughed. As usual, she'd one-upped him. He took the harness from Chloe and stepped into it. "Where are the ropes?"

Matt stepped forward with one end of a rope in hand. "Already secured and ready to go, buddy."

A few seconds later, both of them tethered, Mara grabbed hold of his hand and led him to the edge of the bluff as Brother Mac stepped from the crowd.

"Y'all ready?"

Oh, so ready. Carter smiled over at his bride-to-be. How was it possible that she'd known exactly the kind of wedding he would've chosen? "Ready."

Brother Mac smiled and opened his Bible. "I just gotta say this is a first for me, but I couldn't be more delighted to be a part of a wedding ceremony than I am this one. We're here today to bring together this man and woman in holy matrimony. Since this isn't a traditional wedding ceremony Mara will say her vows first to give Carter time to think of what he wants to say."

She squeezed his hand. "Thank you for pursuing me for God's kingdom, for teaching me to trust again, for giving me wings. Thank you for loving me and my daughter."

Carter's gaze moved to Ashton who stood holding Chloe's hand, her smile big and bright, her body whole.

Tears surfaced, but he made no attempt to stop them. *Thank You, Lord.* He turned his attention back to Mara.

Her eyes also swam with tears, but she continued. "I promise to love you and our God with all that I am. I promise to help you climb upward in spite of obstacles in our path. I promise to take leaps of faith together with you and Chloe." Conviction sounded in every word.

He inhaled and released the breath, his heart soaring, for the first time in his life, words tumbling out with no hesitation or trouble. "Oh, Mara. Words can't begin to express how you've bolstered my own faith or how incredibly much I love you. Had it not been for you, I might never have grown so bold in my resolve to share Christ. Never would I have learned to force the issue of faith, or made myself read and study all those books Matt gave me." He made a face, which brought a round of laughter from the crowd. "I think I speak for Chloe as well as myself when I say that we promise to always love you and Ashton, and to love and protect you both with every fiber of our being."

Happy tears flowed, unchecked down Mara's cheeks, inching toward the toothy grin he'd grown to depend on.

Chloe stepped up to Mara, a man's wedding band gripped in her fingers. "Mara, for a long time you've been more than a friend to me. Thank you for seeing past the outside of me and for saving my life." She handed the ring to Mara, and then moved back to her previous position.

Now Ashton marched forward, a precocious look on her face and handed a ring to Carter. "Remember that day when you came to see me while I was taking chemo?"

Carter nodded. The day he'd fully realized how much both of them meant to his heart. The day Ashton's illness had become so real.

"I prayed that day that God would make you my daddy."

Mara gasped. "I knew you were up to something, you little imp." She and Ashton exchanged a smile. "Thank you for that prayer, Ash."

"You're most welcome." She pivoted and pranced back to Chloe amidst snickers from the onlookers.

A few minutes later, the rings now on their fingers and vows exchanged, Brother Mac once more stepped forward. "Ladies and gentlemen, may I present Mr. and Mrs. Carter Callahan. You may kiss your bride, and er...jump off a cliff."

The crowd laughed as Carter pulled Mara into his arms, lifted both her feet off the ground, and kissed her thoroughly to the applause and cheers of friends and family. As they headed down the face of the bluff, the sound of an approaching helicopter caught Carter's attention as it passed just a few feet over their heads and landed in the parking lot below.

"That's the next part of our adventure." Mara laughed out the words as she scooted closer to the bottom of the bluff.

"Honeymoon?"

"Not yet." She made landing and hurriedly removed her gear. "Hurry up, Callahan. Am I gonna be lugging you behind me for the rest of our lives?"

He laughed as his feet touched the ground. "Okay, bossy." He removed his gear as she headed toward the copter.

She stopped and yelled back at him. "C'mon. I'm tired of waiting."

Carter jogged across the lot to join her, and together they climbed in. As the helicopter lifted off, he intertwined his fingers with hers. "Now will you tell me what's going on?"

Raucous laughter erupted from her toothy grin. She leaned closer. "I already told you. We're gonna take the plunge." She pulled a folded brochure from her right hip pocket and handed it over.

Carter opened it, and his jaw gaped. Across the front of the brochure were sprawled the words, Central Texas SkyDive. The image was an airplane and parachutists. Obviously, she meant a different kind of plunge, and one he thought she'd never go for. A chuckle burst forth, and he pulled her close, inhaling the scent of her hair. Life with Mara would be nothing short of an all-out, hair-on-fire, breathless adventure of gigantic leaps of faith.

THE END

About Cathy

A native Texas gal, Cathy currently resides in a mall town much like Miller's Creek with her husband of almost forty years. When she's not writing you'll find her digging in the dirt, rummaging through thrift stores, spending time with her family, or up to her elbows in yet another home improvement project. In addition to the Miller's Creek novels, Cathy has also written novellas, Bible studies and devotional books.

Visit Cathy at CathyBryantBooks.wordpress.com.

Dear reader friends and fellow believers,

My prayer for each of us is that God's Spirit would strengthen and embolden us to share our faith, especially with those whose faith has faltered. I pray that He will make us aware of those divine appointments in our lives and give us clarity of mind and speech.

Life is hard, sometimes so difficult it causes us to question all we believe about God. This, of course, is the enemy's plan. As time grows short for Satan, his attacks will become more pronounced. Already many have defected from the faith--some because our culture negates God's existence and His care and concern for people--some because the difficulty of life's circumstances has blinded them to the reality of God's love.

That's why it is imperative to be prepared! Those that once professed faith in Christ know all the 'Sunday School answers.' They have tough questions, and questions we must be ready to answer if we are to direct them back to the arms of our Father.

In the end, as is the case with Carter and Mara in the story, the best thing we can do to win back these defectors from the faith is to pray for them and love them unconditionally. Let's be always ready to give a defense for the hope that is in us as fellow watchmen for God's Kingdom.

Defending the faith,
Cathy

BOOK CLUB DISCUSSION QUESTIONS

1. Do you personally know someone who once professed faith in Christ, but who has allowed life's difficulties to move them away from God? Have you tried speaking with them about your faith? What objections do they have against God and Christianity? Did they have questions you couldn't answer?

2. Carter tries to make excuses for why someone else should be the one to speak with Mara about belief in God, mainly because he felt inadequate. Have you made similar excuses? Why is it important for you to share your faith with those the Lord has placed in your life, rather than expecting others to do it instead?

3. Do you know any single parents, troubled teens, ex-soldiers, or terminally-ill children who could use your help? What are some ways in which you could minister to single parents, troubled teens, ex-soldiers, or terminally-ill children in your community?

4. Mara and Chloe have both struggled with bulimia in their lives. Name other ways in which the characters and us wear masks and resort to unhealthy coping mechanisms. What are the necessary steps to overcome these masks and unhealthy coping mechanisms?

5. Do you believe God places certain people in our lives for a reason? Why or why not? How is this shown in the course of the story of Crossroads?

6. What is the significance of the title in this story? What are crossroads? Why are they important?

7. When Carter confronts Mara with issues of faith, she often responds with anger and antagonism. Is this a typical response from prodigals? Why or why not? What is the best way to answer the anger and antagonism?

8. Do you think that it's possible for our relationship with our earthly father to skew our opinions and perceptions of God? If so, what can be done to overcome these misperceptions?

9. As an ex-military man, Carter often makes parallels between leading Mara back to the faith and the rigors of battle. Do you think this is an accurate metaphor? Why or why not?

10. What do you think would be the particular struggles of being a single parent of a terminally-ill child? Of an ex-military man trying to adjust to civilian life?

11. What does Mara do correctly in confronting Chloe about her bulimia? Incorrectly?

12. What do you think of the difference between Mara's professional persona and her 'real' persona?

13. God often uses difficulties to draw us out of ourselves and draw us back to Himself. Can you think of some

instances this has happened in your life? In the lives of friends and family?

Sneak Peek at *STILL I WILL FOLLOW* Chapter One

"I don't really care what you do." Daddy spat out the razored words without even looking Bella's direction, the oxygen tube creating a "V" beneath his chin.

Rather than responding from the familiar place of continuous hurt, Bella ducked her head and hurried to the front door. Stepping outside was like being born into a new reality. Out here mockingbirds sang, and the fresh-smelling late February air held a warmth that signaled advancing spring. Wet with dew, the grass sparkled as sunlight filtered through the branches of still-bare trees. Wisps of fog curled across the dirt road in front of the house she shared with her emotionally-distant father. The one who still blamed her for his only son's death.

Bella filled her lungs with air and then released a satisfied sigh that curled the corners of her mouth heavenward. The perfect day for a jog. Hopefully it would be enough to whisk away the pain in her heart.

She fell into an easy rhythm, her feet crunching against the gravel driveway and then the white dusty road. It didn't really matter where she went, as long as it took her away from here.

Freedom, freedom, freedom.

The word pounded through her heart with each strike of her feet against the dirt. That same word--freedom--had vibrated through every fiber of her being since last year. She'd followed God's leading back to Miller's Creek, the one place to which she'd sworn to never return. But beyond all of it, the desire and quest of her heart was to break free from chains.

One question still haunted her. How could chains be broken when so many held so much against her?

Lord, help me get through to Daddy before it's too late. Help us build a relationship we've never really had. And show me how to convince people I'm not the same person they remember.

Bella swallowed against her cotton-coated mouth, released a cleansing breath, and gulped in another big one. Her lungs and legs burned more intensely with each step. She jogged a few steps further on her usual Saturday morning run, then slowed to a walk at the city limits sign, hands akimbo.

Yes, she should probably head back home where a mile-long list of teacher and daughter to-dos awaited. But something propelled her forward. Was it the dread of returning to a place where she wasn't wanted? Or was it the beautiful morning that begged her to linger?

Finally her breathing slowed to normal. She resumed her jog and headed for the quaint downtown area of Miller's Creek, a place that never failed to captivate her.

In no time at all she reached the two- and three-story historic buildings and picturesque town square of Main Street. The tantalizing aroma of Granny's Kitchen lassoed her nose. Yeah, one of Granny's gigantic homemade cinnamon rolls or fried pies was just what she needed before heading back to the house.

Bella rounded the corner, her thoughts entirely on her cinnamon roll goal, and ran smack dab into something as unyielding as a brick wall. The force of the impact propelled her backwards. She crashed to the ground, her backside against the unforgiving concrete sidewalk. Immediate pain shot electric sparks through her spine. Rather than trying to stand, she opted to lie back and close her eyes, her right wrist against her forehead, until the pain subsided.

"Bella?"

No. It couldn't be. That voice. The one person she'd been able to successfully avoid since her return to Miller's Creek last fall. She cracked open one eye, peered up from beneath her arm, and then immediately squeezed her eyes shut. Yep. It was him all right.

"Here. Let me help you up."

Both eyes popped open to see a strong, calloused hand stretched out toward her. Not a chance. Her palms hit the pavement, and she scooted to a sitting position, lightning-like pain shooting down both legs. She brought knees to her chest and rested her arms there. "I'm fine." Well, fine, except she still couldn't bring herself to make eye contact. A woozy feeling swam in her head and swirled into her stomach. She blinked, trying to focus her eyes on the blurry blue-jeaned legs and cowboy boots in front of her.

"You sure? Look a little pale to me."

Without proper warning, the boots and jeans shifted to a squatting position, revealing a white t-shirt, tattered green John Deere cap, and an all-too-familiar face. Now the world came into focus. Of all times. Really. "Hi, Clay."

He grinned that cheeky grin of his and raised one hand in front of his face to make a peace sign. "How many fingers am I holding up?"

His two fingers morphed into multiples as her eyes honed in on his face. Time had been cruelly kind to him. Though frown lines and the dimples in his cheeks had deepened--though his brown hair had taken on shades of gray around the temples--he still looked good enough to resurrect old memories.

Clay's smile disappeared, and the peace sign returned to the outstretched hand. "You look awful."

How like him to make that kind of comment when her thoughts of him had run the opposite direction. The dull ache throbbed to full throttle in her tail bone and further fogged her brain. *Enough already!* The only way to end this unwanted exchange with her nemesis was to get outta here. And fast. She latched on to his proffered hand and let him pull her to a standing position. Ugh. Let the Texas-tornado spinning commence. To keep from falling again, she gripped his arm with both hands.

"Still up to your old tricks?" His throaty words held an unveiled accusation.

Bella's gaze fluttered to his. "What do you mean?"

"You know. Still trying to trap any man around?"

Cold liquid steel coated her heart. Though still dizzy from pain, she released her grip and took a wobbly step backward, her head turned to one side in response to his verbal attack. Now what was she supposed to do? She scanned the opposite side of the street.

One solitary figure leaned against a street post, his eyes honed in on them.

A warning signal sounded in her brain. A face she didn't recognize. And why was he just standing there staring at them? She shook the thought away. That wasn't her problem. Her problem stood directly in front of her. To make matters worse, there was no way she could make it back home in this condition. No way she could ask her tormentor for help. Absolutely no escape.

Clanging bells sounded, and the glass-paneled door to Granny's Kitchen opened, raising her gaze. Steve and Dani Miller exited and stepped up behind Clay.

"Hi Bella." Dani's contagious grin split her small face, then she immediately sobered, her big blue eyes revealing concern. "Are you okay?" She took a step forward and placed a gentle hand on Bella's arm.

"I took a spill on my jog. I think I might have broken my tail bone. Could I impose on you to take me to the hospital to get it checked?"

"No imposition at all. Of course I will. Can you walk?"

Bella managed a shaky laugh. "I'm not sure."

Before she realized what was happening, Clay stepped forward and swooped her into his arms, then faced Dani and Steve. "Where are y'all parked?"

It was impossible not to notice the unspoken communication that took place between Clay and Steve, best friends since grade school. Steve's lips flat-lined. He jerked a thumb over one shoulder and then took off walking in that direction. "This way."

Bella's heart did flip-flops all the way to the Miller's Suburban, her thoughts snagged in a gnarly mess. How had she managed in such a short amount of time to not only run into Clay, but end up like a sack of taters in his arms?

To his credit, once they reached the vehicle, Clay set her down gently in the leather back seat and searched her face through frown-hooded eyes. At long last he backed away, his face bathed in blatant distrust.

* * *

"Your tail bone is fractured." To emphasize his point Dr. Clint Nichols--a recent addition to Miller's Creek hospital--pointed to the X-rays.

Sure enough, a tell-tale line crisscrossed her last vertebrae. Which meant there was nothing she could do except deal with the pain.

Bella focused her eyes on the handsome doctor's face. "I injured it before when I was in high school. During a volleyball game." Only it hadn't hurt quite this bad back then. "I guess this means a donut cushion and ice packs?" And lots of pain relievers.

"Oh yeah. How's the pain?"

"Um...somewhere between unbearable and excruciating?"

He laughed out loud, not in an 'I'm-glad-you're-hurt' kind of way, but as though genuinely amused by her lame attempt to be funny. "Want me to prescribe something a little stronger than over-the-counter meds?"

Bella shook her head from side to side. No way could she take something stronger and still function at school on Monday. Might as well just tough it out. "No thanks."

Admiration spilled from his dark eyes as he helped her to a standing position. "You're one gutsy lady."

Not exactly the truth. Still it meant a lot to have someone see her in a different light. Especially after her run-in with Clay, who clearly still saw her in shades of scarlet.

"You new here in town?" A soft glint of curiosity rested in his eyes.

"Yes and no. I lived here most of my childhood. Now I'm back, teaching music at the school."

"Really?" He stopped fiddling with his charts. "What kind of music?"

"Elementary music and choir. Everything except band."

Dr. Nichols moved to the door and patiently waited while she took small shuffling steps to join him. "So were you in choir when you lived here before?"

She nodded.

"You look really familiar. Were you in Area Choir by any chance?"

"Yeah, my Junior and Senior years." At least until she'd messed up so badly.

"And what year was that?"

"I graduated in '93."

"Ah, I'm a '96. Graduated from Morganville High." He grew silent, but his direct gaze still focused on her with unabashed interest. "Here, let me help you down to the waiting room." He offered his elbow.

Bella hooked her arm in his as they traversed the sanitary-smelling hallway. As double metal swinging doors clunked behind them, Dani and Steve both rose to their feet.

Dani grinned. "Well, Dr. Nichols, is she gonna make it?"

The doctor turned his head to make eye contact with Bella. "No doubt. Something tells me this one doesn't give up easily." A smile lit his face, and he sent a conspiratorial wink.

A furious pounding thudded against Bella's rib cage, but she quickly squelched it by looking away.

A laugh sounded from Dani, but Steve's features remained stony. The petite blonde stepped forward and replaced the doctor's elbow with her own. "We'll take it from here, Doc."

Dr. Nichols took one step backward, a smile curling his lips, his eyes still focused on Bella. "Good to know she's in capable hands. Bella, why don't you schedule an appointment for next Friday? Just so we can make sure you're healing okay."

She nodded. "Will do."

"See y'all around." The doctor smiled at each of them in turn, then focused one last time on Bella. He waved a hand, pivoted, and strode back through the double swinging doors, his dark curly head still visible through the small squares of glass.

Dani gave a gentle nudge and sing-songed her comment. "I smell romance brewing."

An odd mixture of fear and hope spiraled from Bella's heart to her mouth, a tinny taste now prevalent there. She released a half laugh and shook her head for added emphasis. "No. No, you don't. Besides, he's a few years younger than I am."

Steve, who had remained completely silent up to this point, strode toward the sliding glass doors that led outside, his stony-expression words trailing behind him. "Never stopped you before."

The words knifed into Bella's heart. But even as she considered his statement, she also realized why it had been made. Steve Miller was the kind of guy who deeply loved his friends, his town, and its citizens. Any affront to them--intentional or not--was also an affront to him.

* * *

Though the sun had moved to high-noon position and grown warm on this Saturday in February, Clay spurred Rusty through the brushy undergrowth of scrub oak to the pile of wire and t-posts he'd left there for work on the fences of Miller's ranch. Today he needed both hard physical labor and solitude to erase the heart-stabbing pain he'd felt since settling Bella into the back seat of the Miller's Suburban and watching them drive away with a chunk of his heart.

He inhaled through his nose, the scent of cedar instantly bringing comfort. He'd known for some time she was back in town and working at the school. Of all places. Since when had she earned a teaching degree? And were the kids of Miller's Creek truly safe in her hands?

Questions continued to assault his brain as he dismounted and yanked on the soft cowhide gloves. He moved to the fence. stretched out the wire, and secured it to the metal t-posts which had replaced the old cedar posts. But no matter how hard he tried, he could not put Bella--or her shameful past--out of his mind. Still just as gorgeous as ever, and just as able to re-open the wound in his heart. And that wounded heart of his had hurled hurtful words her way. Words he never intended to speak, but that somehow brought a wicked satisfaction in seeing her flinch with pain.

The sun bore down on him, continuing to rob the day of its coolness. A rivulet of sweat dripped into his eyes, stinging.

The undergrowth rustled behind him. "Thought I might find you here." Steve Miller, his best friend and boss, sat atop his horse Biscuit. Though somewhat shaded by the brim of his cowboy hat, his eyes held understanding and compassion.

"Hey." Clay turned back to his work and finished securing the strand of barbed wire, then headed to the cool shade of a nearby live oak for relief from the sun and a swig of water.

Steve climbed from the spotted gelding and joined him in the shade. They both took a seat on the ground and rested their backs against the gnarly bark of the tree. "You okay?"

Clay swirled the cool water to wash away his cotton mouth, then rested his elbows on his knees, and lowered his head. "Yeah. At least, I..." No. Who was he kidding? He wasn't okay. He tugged off his yellow leather gloves and slapped them against the ground. "Why can't I get over her? It's been twenty years, but seeing her this morning brought it all back like it was yesterday."

Steve didn't respond. Typical of his friend to just let him vent.

“Is Bella okay?” Clay couldn’t resist asking the question that had been on his heart all day.

“Broken tail bone, but that didn’t stop her from making a connection with Clint Nichols, who, as you well know, is younger than she is." His words held underlying condemnation.

The ache in his chest intensified. So she *was* still the same old Bella. "I don't wanna care for her, but I do."

"She doesn't deserve it."

Clay released pent-up air from his lungs. No one deserved any good in this earthly life. That much he knew for sure. It was only by the grace of God that any of them enjoyed anything good. *God, help me remember that truth. Especially when it comes to Bella.* Even as the prayer rose from his heart, he knew it was easier prayed than done. "Maybe she's changed." Or maybe not.

"Maybe." Steve's one-word answer echoed his thoughts. His best bud peered out toward the sun-drenched ranch land that had been in his family for generations.

"How did she get a job at the school anyway? Dani's president of the school board, right?"

Steve nodded, but didn't answer.

"Why would they hire someone with her history to teach our kids?"

"Believe it or not, I asked Dani that same question."

"And?"

His friend's mouth tightened. "She said Bella came with a great set of credentials and high praise from references."

A curt laugh fell from Clay's lips. "Must have the wrong person." Even as he spoke the words, a shard of regret pierced his heart. Time and difficulty--no, make that the Lord--had a way of changing even the most hardened hearts. Why not Bella's? "What about you? How are you doing?"

Steve's face turned steely. "Been better."

"You and Dani still at odds over the baby issue?"

"Yeah." His friend didn't volunteer any more information, so Clay opted to let the matter drop. He picked up his gloves and wiggled his fingers into them, then stood. "Guess I'd better get back to work."

Steve grunted and rose to his feet. "It's Saturday, Clay. Why are you working on your day off?"

A rabbit they'd chased more than once. "Might as well be doing something productive."

One corner of his friend's mouth turned up wryly. "And just what do you do for fun?"

Fun? Since when had anything in his life been fun? He shook his head and straightened his grimy green John Deere cap, pulling the brim low. "This is fun." He sauntered back to the fence.

A disbelieving snort sounded through Steve's nose. He obviously wasn't gonna let the matter rest. "Then why aren't you working on your own place?"

Clay picked up the roll of barbed wire, cautious of the sharp metal thorns, and unrolled it to the next post. "My fences are done."

Steve laughed. "Of course they are. And you wanted something difficult and solitary to work on to get your mind off Bella. How's that working for ya?"

He chose not to respond. Steve knew him too well.

His friend let loose a soft chuckle and shook his head from side to side. "Some day I'm gonna figure out a way to teach you the benefits of freedom."

Like Steve was one to talk about freedom. Wasn't he letting his fear of the future keep him from having more kids? "I am free."

"No, you're not. You're enslaved to hard work. You think it'll help you forget, but all it does is help you remember." Steve sauntered to Biscuit and swung his tall frame atop the horse. "You also need a woman. Just not her."

Not true. He didn't need anyone. Not anymore. Not since Bella had broken his heart. Clay turned back to his work.

Steve's voice drawled behind him, "See ya around." As the sound of Biscuit's hooves grew gradually fainter, Clay resumed his work with increased fervor, determined to prove his friend wrong. But only seconds later, the unvarnished truth hit him between the eyes.

He was indeed enslaved, not only to his work but to his past in the form of the beautiful Bella. But how in the world was he supposed to free himself from the rusty chains that had held him captive far too long?

Then another thought punched him in the gut. If he'd been blind to those particular chains, what other things had him imprisoned?